The Author

JOHN RICHARDSON was born in 1796 in Queenston, Ontario. At the age of fifteen he enlisted as a gentleman volunteer with the 41st Regiment of the British Army. During the War of 1812, he was imprisoned for a year in the United States. His later military service took him to England and, for two years, to the West Indies.

The first Canadian-born novelist to achieve international recognition, Richardson began his fiction-writing career with novels about the British and French societies of his time. In his third and most successful novel, *Wacousta* (1832), he turned to the North American frontier for his setting and to its recent history for its historical framework. He followed the same practice in *The Canadian Brothers*, the sequel to *Wacousta*.

In 1838 Richardson returned from England to Canada, now promoted to the rank of major. He tried to earn his livelihood by writing fiction and by setting up a series of weekly newspapers. He was appointed superintendent of police on the Welland Canal in 1845, but was relieved of these duties the following year. In 1849 he moved to the United States and settled in New York City, where he continued to write fiction.

John Richardson died in New York City in 1852.

THE NEW CANADIAN LIBRARY

General Editor: David Staines

ADVISORY BOARD
Alice Munro
W.H. New
Guy Vanderhaeghe

John Richardson

WACOUSTA;
OR, THE PROPHECY

A Tale of the Canadas

With an Afterword by James Reaney

"Vengeance is still alive; from her dark covert,
With all her snakes erect upon her crest,
She stalks in view, and fires me with her charms."
The Revenge

M&S

This edition is an unabridged reprint of the first edition of *Wacousta*, published in London, England, by T. Cadell, Strand; and W. Blackwood, Edinburgh, in 1832.

Complete edition 1991

Canadian Cataloguing in Publication Data

Richardson, John, 1796–1852
Wacousta, or The prophecy

(New Canadian library)
Unabridged.
Includes bibliographical references.
ISBN 0-7710-9877-4

1. Pontiac's Conspiracy, 1763-1765 – Fiction.
I. Title. II. Title: The prophecy. III. Series.

PS8435.I33W3 1991   813'.3   C91-094386-9
PR9199.2.R5W3 1991

The publishers acknowledge the assistance of the Canada Council and the Ontario Arts Council for their publishing program.

Typesetting by Pickwick
Printed and bound in Canada

McClelland & Stewart Inc.
The Canadian Publishers
481 University Avenue
Toronto, Ontario
M5G 2E9

2 3 4 5   01 00 99 98 97

TO
HIS MAJESTY'S 41ST REGIMENT,
WHO BEAR ON THEIR COLOURS
THE "DETROIT,"
CONNECTED WITH WHICH ARE
THE PRINCIPAL INCIDENTS OF HIS TALE,

THESE VOLUMES ARE INSCRIBED
BY
A ONCE SHARER IN THEIR SERVICE,
THE AUTHOR

London, Dec. 1832.

Contents

WACOUSTA

Volume I

One

Introductory

A S W E A R E about to introduce our readers to scenes with which the European is little familiarised, some few cursory remarks, illustrative of the general features of the country into which we have shifted our labours, may not be deemed misplaced at the opening of this volume.

Without entering into minute geographical detail, it may be necessary merely to point out the outline of such portions of the vast continent of America as still acknowledge allegiance to the English crown, in order that the reader, understanding the localities, may enter with deeper interest into the incidents of a tale connected with a ground hitherto untouched by the wand of the modern novelist.

All who have ever taken the trouble to inform themselves of the features of a country so little interesting to the majority of Englishmen in their individual character must be aware, – and for the information of those who are not, we state, – that that portion of the northern continent of America which is known as the United States is divided from the Canadas by a continuous chain of lakes and rivers, commencing at the ocean into which they empty themselves, and extending in a north-western direction to the remotest parts of these wild regions, which have never yet been pressed by other footsteps than those of the native hunters of the soil. First we have the magnificent St. Lawrence, fed from the lesser and tributary streams, rolling her sweet and silver waters into the foggy seas of the Newfoundland. – But perhaps it will better tend to impress our readers with a panoramic picture of the country in which our scene of action is more immediately laid, by commencing at those extreme and remotest points of our Canadian possessions to which their attention will be especially directed in the course of our narrative.

The most distant of the north-western settlements of America is Michillimackinac, a name given by the Indians, and preserved by the Americans, who possess the fort even to this hour. It is situated at the head of the Lakes Michigan and Huron, and adjacent to the Island of St. Joseph's, where, since the existence of the United States as an independent republic, an English garrison has been maintained, with a view of keeping the original fortress in check. From the lakes above mentioned we descend into the River Sinclair, which, in turn, disembogues itself into the lake of the same name. This again renders tribute to the Détroit, a broad majestic river, not less than a mile in breadth at its source, and progressively widening towards its mouth until it is finally lost in the beautiful Lake Erie, computed at about one hundred and sixty miles in circumference. From the embouchure of this latter lake commences the Chippawa, better known in Europe from the celebrity of its stupendous falls of Niagara, which form an impassable barrier to the seaman, and, for a short space, sever the otherwise uninterrupted chain connecting the remote fortresses we have described with the Atlantic. At a distance of a few miles from the falls, the Chippawa finally empties itself into the Ontario, the most splendid of the gorgeous American lakes, on the bright bosom of which, during the late wars, frigates, seventy-fours, and even a ship of one hundred and twelve guns, manned by a crew of one thousand men, reflected the proud pennants of England! At the opposite extremity of this magnificent and sea-like lake, which is upwards of two hundred miles in circumference, the far-famed St. Lawrence takes her source; and after passing through a vast tract of country, whose elevated banks bear every trace of fertility and cultivation, connects itself with the Lake Champlain, celebrated, as well as Erie, for a signal defeat of our flotilla during the late contest with the Americans. Pushing her bold waters through this somewhat inferior lake, the St. Lawrence pursues her course seaward with impetuosity, until arrested near La Chine by rock-studded shallows, which produce those strong currents and eddies, the dangers of which are so beautifully expressed in the Canadian Boat Song, – a composition that has rendered the "rapids" almost as familiar to the imagination of the European as the falls of Niagara themselves. Beyond La Chine the St. Lawrence gradually unfolds herself into greater majesty and expanse, and rolling past the busy commercial town of Montreal, is once more increased in volume by the insignificant lake of St. Peter's, nearly opposite to the settlement of Three Rivers, midway between Montreal and Quebec. From thence she pursues her course unfed, except by a few inferior streams, and gradually widens as she rolls past the capital of the Canadas, whose tall and precipitous battlements, bristled with cannon, and frowning defiance from the clouds in which they appear half imbedded, might be taken by the imaginative enthusiast for the strong tower of the Spirit of those stupendous scenes. From this point the St. Lawrence increases in expanse, until, at length, after traversing a country where the traces of civilisation become gradually less and less visible, she finally merges in the gulf, from the centre of which the shores on either hand are often invisible to the naked eye; and in this manner is it imperceptibly lost in that misty ocean, so dangerous to mariners from its deceptive and almost perpetual fogs.

In following the links of this extensive chain of lakes and rivers, it must be borne in recollection, that, proceeding seaward from Michillimackinac and its contiguous district, all that tract of country which lies to the right constitutes what is now known as the United States of America, and all on the left the two provinces of Upper and Lower Canada, tributary to the English government, subject to the English laws, and garrisoned by English troops. The several forts and harbours established along the left bank of the St. Lawrence, and throughout that portion of our possessions which is known as Lower Canada, are necessarily, from the improved condition and more numerous population of that province, on a larger scale and of better appointment; but in Upper Canada, where the traces of civilisation are less evident throughout, and become gradually more faint as we advance westward, the fortresses and harbours bear the same proportion in strength and extent to the scantiness of the population they are erected to protect. Even at the present day, along that line of remote country we have selected for the theatre of our labours, the garrisons are both few in number and weak in strength, and evidence of cultivation is seldom to be found at any distance in the interior; so that all beyond a certain extent of clearing, continued along the banks of the lakes and rivers, is thick, impervious, rayless forest, the limits of which have never yet been explored, perhaps, by the natives themselves.

Such being the general features of the country even at the present day, it will readily be comprehended how much more wild and desolate was the character they exhibited as far back as the middle of the last century, about which period our story commences. At that epoch, it will be borne in mind, what we have described as being the United States were then the British colonies of America dependent on the mother-country; while the Canadas, on the contrary, were, or had very recently been, under the dominion of France, from whom they had been wrested after a long struggle, greatly advanced in favour of England by the glorious battle fought on the plains of Abraham, near Quebec, and celebrated for the defeat of Montcalm and the death of Wolfe.

The several attempts made to repossess themselves of the strong hold of Quebec having, in every instance, been met by discomfiture and disappointment, the French, in despair, relinquished the contest, and, by treaty, ceded their claims to the Canadas, – an event that was hastened by the capitulation of the garrison of Montreal, commanded by the Marquis de Vaudreuil, to the victorious arms of General Amherst. Still, though conquered as a people, many of the leading men in the country, actuated by that jealousy for which they were remarkable, contrived to oppose obstacles to the quiet possession of a conquest by those whom they seemed to look upon as their hereditary enemies; and in furtherance of this object, paid agents, men of artful and intriguing character, were dispersed among the numerous tribes of savages, with a view of exciting them to acts of hostility against their conquerors. The long and uninterrupted possession, by the French, of those countries immediately bordering on the hunting grounds and haunts of the natives, with whom they carried on an extensive traffic in furs, had established a communionship of interest between themselves and those savage and warlike people, which failed not to turn to account the vindictive views of the former. The whole of the province of Upper Canada at that time possessed but a scanty population, protected in its most flourishing and defensive points by stockade forts; the chief object of which was to secure the garrisons, consisting each of a few companies, from any sudden surprise on the part of the natives, who, although apparently inclining to acknowledge the change of neighbours, and professing amity, were, it was well known, too much in the interest of their old friends the French, and even the French Canadians themselves, not to be regarded with the most cautious distrust.

These stockade forts were never, at any one period, nearer to each other than from one hundred and fifty to two hundred miles, so that, in the event of surprise or alarm, there was little prospect of obtaining assistance from without. Each garrison, therefore, was almost wholly dependent on its own resources; and, when surrounded unexpectedly by numerous bands of hostile Indians, had no other alternative than to hold out to the death. Capitulation was out of the question; for, although the wile and artifice of the natives might induce them to promise mercy, the moment their enemies were in their power promises and treaties were alike broken, and indiscriminate massacre ensued. Communication by water was, except during a period of profound peace, almost impracticable; for, although of late years the lakes of Canada have been covered with vessels of war, many of them, as we have already remarked, of vast magnitude, and been the theatres of conflicts that would not have disgraced the salt waters of ocean itself, at the period to which our story refers the flag of England was seen to wave only on the solitary mast of some ill-armed and ill-manned gunboat, employed rather for the purpose of conveying despatches from fort to fort, than with any serious view to acts either of aggression or defence.

In proportion as the colonies of America, now the United States, pushed their course of civilisation westward, in the same degree did the numerous tribes of Indians, who had hitherto dwelt more seaward, retire upon those of their own countrymen, who, buried in vast and impenetrable forests, had seldom yet seen the face of the European stranger; so that, in the end, all the more central parts of those stupendous wilds became doubly peopled. Hitherto, however, that civilisation had not been carried beyond the state of New York; and all those countries which have, since the American revolution, been added to the Union under the names of Kentucky, Ohio, Missouri, Michigan, &c., were, at the period embraced by our story, inhospitable and unproductive woods, subject only to the dominion of the native, and as yet unshorn by the axe of the cultivator. A few portions only of the opposite shores of Michigan were occupied by emigrants from the Canadas, who, finding no one to oppose or molest them, selected the most fertile spots along the banks of the river; and of the existence of these infant settlements, the English colonists, who had never ventured so far, were not even aware until after the conquest of Canada by the mother-country. This particular district was the centre around which the numerous warriors, who had been driven westward by the colonists, had finally assembled; and rude villages and encampments rose far and near for a circuit of many miles around this infant settlement and fort of the Canadians, to both of which they had given the name of Détroit, after the river on whose elevated banks they stood. Proceeding westward from this point, and along the tract of country that diverged from the banks of the Lakes Huron, Sinclair, and Michigan, all traces of that partial civilisation were again lost in impervious wilds, tenanted only by the fiercest of the Indian tribes, whose homes were principally along the banks of that greatest of American waters, the Lake Superior, and in the country surrounding the isolated fort of Michillimackinac, the last and most remote of the European fortresses in Canada.

When at a later period the Canadas were ceded to us by France, those parts of the opposite frontier which we have just described became also tributary to the English crown, and were, by the peculiar difficulties that existed to communication with the more central and populous districts, rendered especially favourable to the exercise of hostile intrigue by the numerous active French emissaries every where dispersed among the Indian tribes. During the first few years of the conquest, the inhabitants of Canada, who were all either European French, or immediate descendants of that nation, were, as might naturally be expected, more than restive under their new governors, and many of the most impatient spirits of the country sought every opportunity of sowing the seeds of distrust and jealousy in the hearts of the natives. By these people it was artfully suggested to the Indians, that their new oppressors were of the race of those who had driven them from the sea, and were progressively advancing on their territories until scarce a hunting ground or a village would be left to them. They described them, moreover, as being the hereditary enemies of their great father, the King of France, with whose governors they had buried the hatchet for ever, and smoked the calumet of perpetual peace. Fired by these wily suggestions, the high and jealous spirit of the Indian chiefs took the alarm, and they beheld with impatience the "Red Coat," or "Saganaw*," usurping, as they deemed it, those possessions which had so recently acknowledged the supremacy of the pale flag of their ancient ally. The cause of the Indians, and that of the Canadians, became, in some degree, identified as one, and each felt it was the interest, and it may be said the natural instinct, of both, to hold communionship of purpose, and to indulge the same jealousies and fears. Such was the state of things in 1763, the period at which our story commences, – an epoch fruitful in designs of hostility and treachery on the part of the Indians, who, too crafty and too politic to manifest their feelings by overt acts declaratory of the hatred carefully instilled into their breasts, sought every opportunity to compass the destruction of the English, wherever they were most vulnerable to the effects of stratagem. Several inferior forts situated on the Ohio had already fallen into their hands, when they summoned all their address and cunning to accomplish the fall of the two important though remote posts of Détroit and Michillimackinac. For a length of time they were baffled by the activity and vigilance of the respective governors of these forts, who had had too much fatal experience in the fate of their companions not to be perpetually on the alert against their guile; but when they had at length, in some degree, succeeded in lulling the suspicions of the English, they determined on a scheme, suggested by a leading chief, a man of more than ordinary character, which promised fair to rid them altogether of a race they so cordially detested. We will not, however, mar the interest of our tale, by anticipating, at this early stage, either

---

* This word thus pronounced by themselves, in reference to the English soldiery, is, in all probability, derived from the original English settlers in Saganaw Bay.

the nature or the success of a stratagem which forms the essential groundwork of our story.

While giving, for the information of the many, what, we trust, will not be considered a too compendious outline of the Canadas, and the events connected with them, we are led to remark, that, powerful as was the feeling of hostility cherished by the French Canadians towards the English when the yoke of early conquest yet hung heavily on them, this feeling eventually died away under the mild influence of a government that preserved to them the exercise of all their customary privileges, and abolished all invidious distinctions between the descendants of France and those of the mother-country. So universally, too, has this system of conciliation been pursued, we believe we may with safety aver, of all the numerous colonies that have succumbed to the genius and power of England, there are none whose inhabitants entertain stronger feelings of attachment and loyalty to her than those of Canada; and whatever may be the transient differences, – differences growing entirely out of circumstances and interests of a local character, and in no way tending to impeach the acknowledged fidelity of the mass of French Canadians, – whatever, we repeat, may be the ephemeral differences that occasionally spring up between the governors of those provinces and individual members of the Houses of Assembly, they must, in no way, be construed into a general feeling of disaffection towards the English crown.

In proportion also as the Canadians have felt and acknowledged the beneficent effects arising from a change of rulers, so have the Indian tribes been gradually weaned from their first fierce principle of hostility, until they have subsequently become as much distinguished by their attachment to, as they were three quarters of a century ago remarkable for their untameable aversion for, every thing that bore the English name, or assumed the English character. Indeed, the hatred which they bore to the original colonists has been continued to their descendants, the subjects of the United States; and the same spirit of union subsisted between the natives and British troops, and people of Canada, during the late American war, that at an earlier period of the history of that country prevailed so powerfully to the disadvantage of England.

And now we have explained a course of events which were in some measure necessary to the full understanding of the country by the majority of our readers, we shall, in furtherance of the same object, proceed to sketch a few of the most prominent scenes more immediately before us.

The fort of Détroit, as it was originally constructed by the French, stands in the middle of a common, or description of small prairie, bounded by woods, which, though now partially thinned in their outskirts, were at that period untouched by the hand of civilisation. Erected at a distance of about half a mile from the banks of the river, which at that particular point are high and precipitous, it stood then just far enough from the woods that swept round it in a semicircular form to be secure from the rifle of the Indian; while from its batteries it commanded a range of country on every hand, which no enemy unsupported by cannon could traverse with impunity. Immediately in the rear, and on the skirt of the wood, the French had constructed a sort of bomb-proof, possibly intended to serve as a cover to the workmen originally employed in clearing the woods, but long since suffered to fall into decay. Without the fortification rose a strong and triple line of pickets, each of about two feet and a half in circumference, and so fitted into each other as to leave no other interstices than those which were perforated for the discharge of musketry. They were formed of the hardest and most knotted pines that could be procured; the sharp points of which were seasoned by fire until they acquired nearly the durability and consistency of iron. Beyond these firmly imbedded pickets was a ditch, encircling the fort, of about twenty feet in width, and of proportionate depth, the only communication over which to and from the garrison was by means of a drawbridge, protected by a strong chevaux-de-frise. The only gate with which the fortress was provided faced the river; on the more immediate banks of which, and to the left of the fort, rose the yet infant and straggling village that bore the name of both. Numerous farm-houses, however, almost joining each other, contributed to form a continuity of many miles along the borders of the river, both on the right and on the left; while the opposite shores of Canada, distinctly seen in the distance, presented, as far as the eye could reach, the same enlivening character of fertility. The banks, covered with verdure on either shore, were more or less undulating at intervals; but in general they were high without being abrupt, and picturesque without being bold, presenting, in their partial cultivation, a striking contrast to the dark, tall, and frowning forests bounding every point of the perspective.

At a distance of about five miles on the left of the town the course of the river was interrupted by a small and thickly wooded island, along whose sandy beach occasionally rose the low cabin or wigwam which the birch canoe, carefully upturned and left to dry upon the sands, attested to be the temporary habitation of the wandering Indian. That branch of the river which swept by the shores of Canada was (as at this day) the only navigable one for vessels of burden, while that on the opposite coast abounded in shallows and bars, affording passage merely to the light barks of the natives, which seemed literally to skim the very surface of its waves. Midway, between that point of the continent which immediately faced the eastern extremity of the island we have just named and the town of Détroit, flowed a small tributary river, the approaches to which, on either hand, were over a slightly sloping ground, the view of which could be entirely commanded from the fort. The depth of this river, now nearly dried up, at that period varied from three to ten or twelve feet; and over this, at a distance of about twenty yards from the Détroit, into which it emptied itself, rose, communicating with the high road, a bridge, which will more than once be noticed in the course of our tale. Even to the present hour it retains the name given to it during these disastrous times; and there are few modern Canadians, or even Americans, who traverse the "Bloody Bridge," especially at the still hours of advanced night, without recalling to memory the tragic events of those days, (handed down as they have been by their fathers, who were eyewitnesses of the transaction,) and peopling the surrounding gloom with the shades of those whose life-blood erst crimsoned the once pure waters of that now nearly exhausted stream; and whose mangled and headless corses were slowly borne by its tranquil current into the bosom of the parent river, where all traces of them finally disappeared.

These are the minuter features of the scene we have brought more immediately under the province of our pen. What Détroit was in 1763 it nearly is at the present day, with this differendce, however, that many of those points which were then in a great degree isolated and rude are now redolent with the beneficent effects of improved cultivation; and in the immediate vicinity of that memorable bridge, where formerly stood merely the occasional encampment of the Indian warrior, are now to be seen flourishing farms and crops, and other marks of agricultural industry. Of the fort of Détroit itself we will give the following brief history: – It was, as we have already stated, erected by the French while in the occupancy of the country by which it is more immediately environed; subsequently, and at the final cession of the Canadas, it was delivered over to England, with whom it remained until the acknowledgement of the independence of the colonists by the mother-country, when it hoisted the colours of the republic; the British garrison marching out, and crossing over into Canada, followed by such of the loyalists as still retained their attachment to the English crown. At the commencement of the late war with America it was the first and more immediate theatre of conflict, and was remarkable, as well as Michillimackinac, for being one of the first posts of the Americans that fell into our hands.

The gallant daring, and promptness of decision, for which the lamented general, Sir Isaac Brock, was so eminently distinguished, achieved the conquest almost as soon as the American declaration of war had been made known in Canada; and on this occasion we ourselves had the good fortune to be selected as part of the guard of honour, whose duty it was to lower the flag of America, and substitute that of England in its place. On the approach, however, of an overwhelming army of the enemy in the autumn of the ensuing year it was abandoned by our troops, after having been dismantled and reduced, in its more combustible parts, to ashes. The Americans, who have erected new fortifications on the site of the old, still retain possession of a post to which they attach considerable importance, from the circumstance of its being a key to the more western portions of the Union.

Two

I T W A S D U R I N G the midnight watch, late in September, 1763, that the English garrison of Détroit, in North America, was thrown into the utmost consternation by the sudden and mysterious introduction of a stranger within its walls. The circumstance at this moment was particularly remarkable; for the period was so fearful and pregnant with events of danger, the fort being assailed on every side by a powerful and vindictive foe, that a caution and vigilance of no common kind were unceasingly exercised by the prudent governor for the safety of those committed to his charge. A long series of hostilities had been pursued by the North-American Indians against the subjects of England, within the few years that had succeeded to the final subjection of the Canadas to her victorious arms; and many and sanguinary were the conflicts in which the devoted soldiery were made to succumb to the cunning and numbers of their savage enemies. In those lone regions, both officers and men, in their respective ranks, were, by a communionship of suffering, isolation, and peculiarity of duty, drawn towards each other with feelings of almost fraternal affection; and the fates of those who fell were lamented with sincerity of soul, and avenged, when opportunity offered, with a determination prompted equally by indignation and despair. This sentiment of union, existing even between men and officers of different corps, was, with occasional exceptions, of course doubly strengthened among those who fought under the same colours, and acknowledged the same head; and, as it often happened in Canada, during this interesting period, that a single regiment was distributed into two or three fortresses, each so far removed from the other that communication could with the utmost facility be cut off, the anxiety and uncertainty of these detachments became proportioned to the danger with which they knew themselves to be more immediately beset. The garrison of Détroit, at the date above named, consisted of a third of the —— regiment, the remainder of which occupied the forts of Michillimackinac and Niagara, and to each division of this regiment was attached an officer's command of artillery. It is true that no immediate overt act of hostility had for some time been perpetrated by the Indians, who were assembled in force around the former garrison; but the experienced officer to whom the command had been intrusted was too sensible of the craftiness of the surrounding hordes to be deceived, by any outward semblance of amity, into neglect of those measures of precaution which were so indispensable to the surety of his trust.

In this he pursued a line of policy happily adapted to the delicate nature of his position. Unwilling to excite the anger or wound the pride of the chiefs, by any outward manifestation of distrust, he affected to confide in the sincerity of their professions, and, by inducing his officers to mix occasionally in their councils, and his men in the amusements of the inferior warriors, contrived to impress the conviction that he reposed altogether on their faith. But, although these acts were in some degree coerced by the necessity of the times, and a perfect knowledge of all the misery that must accrue to them in the event of their provoking the Indians into acts of open hostility, the prudent governor took such precautions as were deemed efficient to defeat any treacherous attempt at violation of the tacit treaty on the part of the natives. The officers never ventured out, unless escorted by a portion of their men, who, although appearing to be dispersed among the warriors, still kept sufficiently together to be enabled, in a moment of emergency, to afford succour not only to each other but to their superiors. On these occasions, as a further security against surprise, the troops left within were instructed to be in readiness, at a moment's warning, to render assistance, if necessary, to their companions, who seldom, on any occasion, ventured out of reach of the cannon of the fort, the gate of which was hermetically closed, while numerous supernumerary sentinels were posted along the ramparts, with a view to give the alarm if any thing extraordinary was observed to occur without.

Painful and harassing as were the precautions it was found necessary to adopt on these occasions, and little desirous as were the garrison to mingle with the natives on such terms, still the plan was pursued by the Governor from the policy already named: nay, it was absolutely essential to the future interests of England that the Indians should be won over by acts of confidence and kindness; and so little disposition had hitherto been manifested by the English to conciliate, that every thing was to be apprehended from the untameable rancour with which these people were but too well disposed to repay a neglect at once galling to their pride and injurious to their interests.

Such, for a term of many months, had been the trying and painful duty that had devolved on the governor of Détroit; when, in the summer of 1763, the whole of the western tribes of Indians, as if actuated by one common impulse, suddenly threw off the mask, and commenced a series of the most savage trespasses upon the English settlers in the vicinity of the several garrisons, who were cut off in detail, without mercy, and without reference to either age or sex. On the first alarm the weak bodies of troops, as a last measure of security, shut themselves up in their respective forts, where they were as incapable of rendering assistance to others as of receiving it themselves. In this emergency the prudence and forethought of the governor of Détroit were eminently conspicuous; for, having long foreseen the possibility of such a crisis, he had caused a plentiful supply of all that was necessary to the subsistence and defence of the garrison to be provided at an earlier period, so that, if foiled in their attempts at stratagem, there was little chance that the Indians would speedily reduce them by famine. To guard against the former, a vigilant watch was constantly kept by the garrison both day and night, while the sentinels, doubled in number, were constantly on the alert. Strict attention, moreover, was paid to such parts of the ramparts as were considered most assailable by a cunning and midnight enemy; and, in order to prevent any imprudence on the part of the garrison, all egress or ingress was prohibited that had not the immediate sanction of the chief. With this view the keys of the gate were given in trust to the officer of the guard; to whom, however, it was interdicted to use them unless by direct and positive order of the Governor. In addition to this precaution, the sentinels on duty at the gate had strict private instructions not to suffer any one to pass either in or out unless conducted by the governor in person; and this restriction extended even to the officer of the guard.

Such being the cautious discipline established in the fort, the appearance of a stranger within its wall at the still hour of midnight could not fail to be regarded as an extraordinary event, and to excite an apprehension which could scarcely have been surpassed had a numerous and armed band of savages suddenly appeared among them. The first intimation of this fact was given by the violent ringing of an alarm bell; a rope communicating with which was suspended in the Governor's apartments, for the purpose of arousing the slumbering soldiers in any case of pressing emergency. Soon afterwards the Governor himself was seen to issue from his rooms into the open area of the parade, clad in his dressing-gown, and bearing a lamp in one hand and a naked sword in the other. His countenance was pale; and his features, violently agitated, betrayed a source of alarm which those who were familiar with his usual haughtiness of manner were ill able to comprehend.

"Which way did he go? – why stand ye here? – follow – pursue him quickly – let him not escape, on your lives!"

These sentences, hurried and impatiently uttered, were addressed to the two sentinels who, stationed in front of his apartments, had, on the first sound of alarm from the portentous bell, lowered their muskets to the charge, and now stood immovable in that position.

"Who does your honour mane?" replied one of the men, startled, yet bringing his arms to the recover, in salutation of his chief.

"Why, the man – the stranger – the fellow who has just passed you."

"Not a living soul has passed us since our watch commenced, your honour," observed the second sentinel; "and we have now been here upwards of an hour."

"Impossible, sirs: ye have been asleep on your posts, or ye must have seen him. He passed this way, and could not have escaped your observation had ye been attentive to your duty."

"Well, sure, and your honour knows bist," rejoined the first sentinel; "but so hilp me St. Patrick, as I have sirved man and boy in your honour's rigimint this twilve years, not even the fitch of a man has passed me this blissed night. And here's my comrade, Jack Halford, who will take his Bible oath to the same, with all due difirince to your honour."

The pithy reply to this eloquent attempt at exculpation was a brief "Silence, sirrah, walk about!"

The men brought their muskets once more, and in silence, to the shoulder, and, in obedience to the command of their chief, resumed the limited walk allotted to them; crossing each other at regular intervals in the semicircular course that enfiladed, as it were, the only entrance to the Governor's apartments.

Meanwhile every thing was bustle and commotion among the garrison, who, roused from sleep by the appalling sound of the alarm bell at that late hour, were hastily arming. Throughout the obscurity might be seen the flitting forms of men, whose already fully accoutred persons proclaimed them to be of the guard; while in the lofty barracks, numerous lights flashing to and fro, and moving with rapidity, attested the alacrity with which the troops off duty were equipping themselves for some service of more than ordinary interest. So noiseless, too, was this preparation, as far as speech was concerned, that the occasional opening and shutting of pans, and ringing of ramrods to ascertain the efficiency of the muskets, might be heard distinctly in the stillness of the night at a distance of many furlongs.

He, however, who had touched the secret spring of all this picturesque movement, whatever might be his gratification and approval of the promptitude with which the summons to arms had been answered by his brave troops, was far from being wholly satisfied with the scene he had conjured up. Recovered from the first and irrepressible agitation which had driven him to sound the tocsin of alarm, he felt how derogatory to his military dignity and proverbial coolness of character it might be considered, to have awakened a whole garrison from their slumbers, when a few files of the guard would have answered his purpose equally well. Besides, so much time had been suffered to elapse, that the stranger might have escaped; and if so, how many might be disposed to ridicule his alarm, and consider it as emanating from an imagination disturbed by sleep, rather than caused by the actual presence of one endowed like themselves with the faculties of speech and motion. For a moment he hesitated whether he should not countermand the summons to arms which had been so precipitately given; but when he recollected the harrowing threat that had been breathed in his ear by his midnight visiter, – when he reflected, moreover, that even now it was probable he was lurking within the precincts of the fort with a view to the destruction of all that it contained, – when, in short, he thought of the imminent danger that must attend them should he be suffered to escape, – he felt the necessity of precaution, and determined on his measures, even at the risk of manifesting a prudence which might be construed unfavourably. On re-entering his apartments, he found his orderly, who, roused by the midnight tumult, stood waiting to receive the commands of his chief.

"Desire Major Blackwater to come to me immediately."

The mandate was quickly obeyed. In a few seconds a short, thick-set, and elderly officer made his appearance in a grey military undress frock.

"Blackwater, we have traitors within the fort. Let diligent search be made in every part of the barracks for a stranger, an enemy, who has managed to procure admittance among us: let every nook and cranny, every empty cask, be examined forthwith; and cause a number of additional sentinels to be stationed along the ramparts, in order to intercept his escape."

"Good Heaven, is it possible?" said the Major, wiping the perspiration from his brows, though the night was unusually chilly for the season of the year: – "how could he contrive to enter a place so vigilantly guarded?"

"Ask me not *how*, Blackwater," returned the Governor seriously; "let it suffice that he has been in this very room, and that ten minutes since he stood where you now stand."

The Major looked aghast. – "God bless me, how singular! How could the savage contrive to obtain admission? or was he in reality an Indian?"

"No more questions, *Major* Blackwater. Hasten to distribute the men, and let diligent search be made every where; and recollect, neither officer nor man courts his pillow until dawn."

The "Major" emphatically prefixed to his name was a sufficient hint to the stout officer that the doubts thus familiarly expressed were here to cease, and that he was now addressed in the language of authority by his superior, who expected a direct and prompt compliance with his orders. He therefore slightly touched his hat in salutation, and withdrew to make the dispositions that had been enjoined by his Colonel.

On regaining the parade, he caused the men, already forming into companies and answering to the roll-call of their respective non-commissioned officers, to be wheeled into square, and then in a low but distinct voice stated the cause of alarm; and, having communicated the orders of the Governor, finished by recommending to each the exercise of the most scrutinising vigilance; as on the discovery of the individual in question, and the means by which he had contrived to procure admission, the safety of the whole garrison, it was evident, must depend.

The soldiers now dispersed in small parties throughout the interior of the fort, while a select body were conducted to the ramparts by the officers themselves, and distributed between the sentinels already posted there, in such numbers, and at such distances, that it appeared impossible any thing wearing the human form could pass them unperceived, even in the obscurity that reigned around.

When this duty was accomplished, the officers proceeded to the posts of the several sentinels who had been planted since the last relief, to ascertain if any or either of them had observed aught to justify the belief that an enemy had succeeded in scaling the works. To all their enquiries, however, they received a negative reply, accompanied by a declaration, more or less positive with each, that such had been their vigilance during the watch, had any person come within their beat, detection must have been inevitable. The first question was put to the sentinel stationed at the gate of the fort, at which point the whole of the officers of the garrison were, with one or two exceptions, now assembled. The man at first evinced a good deal of confusion; but this might arise from the singular fact of the alarm that had been given, and the equally singular circumstance of his being thus closely interrogated by the collective body of his officers: he, however, persisted in declaring that he had been in no wise inattentive to his duty, and that no cause for alarm or suspicion had occurred near his post. The officers then, in order to save time, separated into two parties, pursuing opposite circuits, and arranging to meet at that point of the ramparts which was immediately in the rear, and overlooking the centre of the semicircular sweep of wild forest we have described as circumventing the fort.

"Well, Blessington, I know not what you think of this sort of work," observed Sir Everard Valletort, a young lieutenant of the —— regiment, recently arrived from England, and one of the party who now traversed the rampart to the right; "but confound me if I would not rather be a barber's apprentice in London, upon nothing, and find myself, than continue a life of this kind much longer. It positively quite knocks me up; for what with early risings, and watchings (I had almost added prayings), I am but the shadow of my former self."

"Hist, Valletort, hist! speak lower," said Captain Blessington, the senior officer present, "or our search must be in vain. Poor fellow!" he pursued, laughing low and good humouredly at the picture of miseries thus solemnly enumerated by his subaltern; – "how much, in truth, are you to be pitied, who have so recently basked in all the sunshine of enjoyment at home. For our parts, we have lived so long amid these savage scenes, that we have almost forgotten what luxury, or even comfort, means. Doubt not, my friend, that in time you will, like us, be reconciled to the change."

"Confound me for an idiot, then, if I give myself time," replied Sir Everard affectedly. "It was only five minutes before that cursed alarm bell was sounded in my ears, that I had made up my mind fully to resign or exchange the instant I could do so with credit to myself; and, I am sure, to be called out of a warm bed at this unseasonable hour offers little inducement for me to change my opinion."

"Resign or exchange with credit to yourself!" sullenly observed a stout tall officer of about fifty, whose spleen might well be accounted for in his rank of "Ensign"

Delme. "Methinks there can be little credit in exchanging or resigning, when one's companions are left behind, and in a post of danger."

"By Jasus, and ye may say that with your own pritty mouth," remarked another veteran, who answered to the name of Lieutenant Murphy; "for it isn't now, while we are surrounded and bediviled by the savages, that any man of the —— rigimint should be after talking of bating a retrate."

"I scarcely understand you, gentlemen," warmly and quickly retorted Sir Everard, who, with all his dandyism and effeminacy of manner, was of a high and resolute spirit. "Do either of you fancy that I want courage to face a positive danger, because I may not happen to have any particular vulgar predilection for early rising?"

"Nonsense, Valletort, nonsense," interrupted, in accents of almost feminine sweetness, his friend Lieutenant Charles de Haldimar, the youngest son of the Governor: "Murphy is an eternal echo of the opinions of those who look forward to promotion; and as for Delme – do you not see the drift of his observation? Should you retire, as you have threatened, of course another lieutenant will be appointed in your stead; but, should you chance to lose your scalp during the struggle with the savages, the step goes in the regiment, and he, being the senior ensign, obtains promotion in consequence."

"Ah!" observed Captain Blessington, "this is indeed the greatest curse attached to the profession of a soldier. Even among those who most esteem, and are drawn towards each other as well by fellowship in pleasure as companionship in danger, this vile and debasing principle – this insatiable desire for personal advancement – is certain to intrude itself; since we feel that over the mangled bodies of our dearest friends and companions, we can alone hope to attain preferment and distinction."

A moment or two of silence ensued, in the course of which each individual appeared to be bringing home to his own heart the application of the remark just uttered;

and which, however they might seek to disguise the truth from themselves, was too forcible to find contradiction from the secret monitor within. And yet of those assembled there was not one, perhaps, who would not, in the hour of glory and of danger, have generously interposed his own frame between that of his companion and the steel or bullet of an enemy. Such are the contradictory elements which compose a soldier's life.

This conversation, interrupted only by occasional questioning of the sentinels whom they passed in their circuit, was carried on in an audible whisper, which the close approximation of the parties to each other, and the profound stillness of the night, enabled them to hear with distinctness.

"Nay, nay, De Haldimar," at length observed Sir Everard, in reply to the observation of his friend, "do not imagine I intend to gratify Mr. Delme by any such exhibition as that of a scalpless head; but, if such be his hope, I trust that the hour which sees my love-locks dangling at the top of an Indian pole may also let daylight into his own carcass from a rifle bullet or a tomahawk."

"And yit, Captin, it sames to me," observed Lieutenant Murphy, in allusion to the remark of Blessington rather than in reply to the last speaker, – "it sames to me, I say, that promotion in ony way is all fair and honourable in times of hardship like thase; and though we may drop a tare over our suparior when the luck of war, in the shape of a tommyhawk, knocks him over, still there can be no rason why we shouldn't stip into his shoes the viry nixt instant; and it's that, we all know, that we fight for. And the divil a bitter chance any man of us all has of promotion thin yoursilf, Captin: for it'll be mighty strange if our fat Major doesn't git riddlid like a cullinder through and through with the bullits from the Ingians' rifles before we have quite done with this business, and thin you will have the rigimintal majority, Captin; and it may be that one Liftinint Murphy, who is now the sanior of his rank, may come in for the vacant captincy."

"And Delme for the lieutenancy," said Charles de Haldimar significantly. "Well, Murphy, I am happy to find that you, at least, have hit on another than Sir Everard Valletort: one, in fact, who will render the promotion more general than it would otherwise have been. Seriously, I should be sorry if any thing happened to our worthy Major, who, with all his bustling and grotesque manner, is as good an officer and as brave a soldier as any his Majesty's army in Canada can boast. For my part, I say, perish all promotion for ever, if it is only to be obtained over the dead bodies of those with whom I have lived so long and shared so many dangers!"

"Nobly uttered, Charles," said Captain Blessington: "the sentiment is, indeed, one well worthy of our present position; and God knows we are few enough in number already, without looking forward to each other's death as a means of our own more immediate personal advancement. With you, therefore, I repeat, perish all my hopes of promotion, if it is only to be obtained over the corses of my companions! And let those who are most sanguine in their expectations beware lest they prove the first to be cut off, and that even before they have yet enjoyed the advantages of the promotion they so eagerly covet."

This observation, uttered without acrimony, had yet enough of delicate reproach in it to satisfy Lieutenant Murphy that the speaker was far from approving the expression of such selfish anticipations at a moment like the present, when danger, in its most mysterious guise, lurked around, and threatened the safety of all most dear to them.

The conversation now dropped, and the party pursued their course in silence. They had just passed the last sentinel posted in their line of circuit, and were within a few yards of the immediate rear of the fortress, when a sharp "Hist!" and sudden halt of their leader, Captain Blessington, threw them all into an attitude of the most profound attention.

"Did you hear?" he asked in a subdued whisper, after a

few seconds of silence, in which he had vainly sought to
catch a repetition of the sound.

"Assuredly," he pursued, finding that no one answered,
"I distinctly heard a human groan."

"Where? – in what direction?" asked Sir Everard and
De Haldimar in the same breath.

"Immediately opposite to us on the common. But see,
here are the remainder of the party stationary, and listening also."

They now stole gently forward a few paces, and were
soon at the side of their companions, all of whom were
straining their necks and bending their heads in the attitude of men listening attentively.

"Have you heard any thing, Erskine?" asked Captain
Blessington in the same low whisper, and addressing the
officer who led the opposite party.

"Not a sound ourselves, but here is Sir Everard's black
servant, Sambo, who has just riveted our attention, by
declaring that *he* distinctly heard a groan towards the
skirt of the common."

"He is right," hastily rejoined Blessington; "I heard it
also."

Again a death-like silence ensued, during which the
eyes of the party were strained eagerly in the direction of
the common. The night was clear and starry, yet the dark
shadow of the broad belt of forest threw all that part of the
waste which came within its immediate range into impenetrable obscurity.

"Do you see any thing?" whispered Valletort to his
friend, who stood next him: "look – look!" and he pointed
with his finger.

"Nothing," returned De Haldimar, after an anxious
gaze of a minute, "but that dilapidated old bomb-proof."

"See you not something dark, and slightly moving immediately in a line with the left angle of the bomb-
proof?"

De Haldimar looked again. – "I do begin to fancy I see
something," he replied; "but so confusedly and indis-

tinctly, that I know not whether it be not merely an illusion of my imagination. Perhaps it is a stray Indian dog devouring the carcass of the wolf you shot yesterday."

"Be it dog or devil, here is for a trial of his vulnerability. – Sambo, quick, my rifle."

The young negro handed to his master one of those long heavy rifles, which the Indians usually make choice of for killing the buffalo, elk, and other animals whose wildness renders them difficult of approach. He then, unbidden, and as if tutored to the task, placed himself in a stiff upright position in front of his master, with every nerve and muscle braced to the most inflexible steadiness. The young officer next threw the rifle on the right shoulder of the boy for a rest, and prepared to take his aim on the object that had first attracted his attention.

"Make haste, massa, – him go directly, – Sambo see him get up."

All was breathless attention among the group of officers; and when the sharp ticking sound produced by the cocking of the rifle of their companion fell on their ears, they bent their gaze upon the point towards which the murderous weapon was levelled with the most aching and intense interest.

"Quick, quick, massa, – him quite up," again whispered the boy.

The words had scarcely passed his lips, when the crack of the rifle, followed by a bright blaze of light, sounded throughout the stillness of the night with exciting sharpness. For an instant all was hushed; but scarcely had the distant woods ceased to reverberate the spirit-stirring echoes, when the anxious group of officers were surprised and startled by a sudden flash, the report of a second rifle from the common, and the whizzing of a bullet past their ears. This was instantly succeeded by a fierce, wild, and prolonged cry, expressive at once of triumph and revenge. It was that peculiar cry which an Indian utters when the reeking scalp has been wrested from his murdered victim.

"Missed him, as I am a sinner," exclaimed Sir Everard,

springing to his feet, and knocking the butt of his rifle on the ground with a movement of impatience. "Sambo, you young scoundrel, it was all your fault, – you moved your shoulder as I pulled the trigger. Thank Heaven, however, the aim of the Indian appears to have been no better, although the sharp whistling of his ball proves his piece to have been well levelled for a random shot."

"His aim has been too true," faintly pronounced the voice of one somewhat in the rear of his companions. "The ball of the villain has found a lodgment in my breast. God bless ye all, my boys; may your fates be more lucky than mine!" While he yet spoke, Lieutenant Murphy sank into the arms of Blessington and De Haldimar, who had flown to him at the first intimation of his wound, and was in the next instant a corpse.

Three

"TO YOUR companies, gentlemen, to your companies on the instant. There is treason in the fort, and we had need of all our diligence and caution. Captain de Haldimar is missing, and the gate has been found unlocked. Quick, gentlemen, quick; even now the savages may be around us, though unseen."

"Captain de Haldimar missing ! – the gate unlocked!" exclaimed a number of voices. "Impossible! – surely we are not betrayed by our own men."

"The sentinel has been relieved, and is now in irons," resumed the communicator of this startling piece of intelligence. It was the adjutant of the regiment.

"Away, gentlemen, to your posts immediately," said Captain Blessington, who, aided by De Haldimar, hastened to deposit the stiffening body of the unfortunate Murphy, which they still supported, upon the rampart. Then addressing the adjutant, "Mr. Lawson, let a couple of files be sent immediately to remove the body of their officer."

"That shot which I heard from the common, as I approached, was not fired at random, then, I find," observed the adjutant, as they all now hastily descended to join their men. – "Who has fallen?"

"Murphy, one of the grenadiers," was the reply of one near him.

"Poor fellow! our work commences badly," resumed

Mr. Lawson: "Murphy killed, and Captain de Haldimar missing. We had few officers enough to spare before, and their loss will be severely felt; I greatly fear, too, these casualties may have a tendency to discourage the men."

"Nothing more easy than to supply their place, by promoting some of our oldest sergeants," observed Ensign Delme, who, as well as the ill-fated Murphy, had risen from the ranks. "If they behave themselves well, the King will confirm their appointments."

"But my poor brother, what of him, Lawson? what have you learnt connected with his disappearance?" asked Charles de Haldimar with deep emotion.

"Nothing satisfactory, I am sorry to say," returned the adjutant; "in fact, the whole affair is a mystery which no one can unravel; even at this moment the sentinel, Frank Halloway, who is strongly suspected of being privy to his disappearance, is undergoing a private examination by your father the governor."

"Frank Halloway!" repeated the youth with a start of astonishment; "surely Halloway could never prove a traitor, – and especially to my brother, whose life he once saved at the peril of his own."

The officers had now gained the parade, when the "Fall in, gentlemen, fall in," quickly pronounced by Major Blackwater, prevented all further questioning on the part of the younger De Haldimar.

The scene, though circumscribed in limit, was picturesque in effect, and might have been happily illustrated by the pencil of the painter. The immediate area of the parade was filled with armed men, distributed into three divisions, and forming, with their respective ranks facing outwards, as many sides of a hollow square, the mode of defence invariably adopted by the Governor in all cases of sudden alarm. The vacant space, which communicated with the powder magazine, was left open to the movements of three three-pounders, which were to support each face in the event of its being broken by numbers. Close to these, and within the square, stood the number of gunners necessary to the duty of the field-pieces, each of which was commanded by a bombardier. At the foot of the ramparts, outside the square, and immediately opposite to their several embrasures, were stationed the gunners required for the batteries, under a non-commissioned officer also, and the whole under the direction of a superior officer of that arm, who now walked to and fro, conversing in a low voice with Major Blackwater. One gunner at each of these divisions of the artillery held in his hand a blazing torch, reflecting with picturesque yet gloomy effect the bright bayonets and equipment of the soldiers, and the anxious countenances of the women and invalids, who, bending eagerly through the windows of the surrounding barracks, appeared to await the issue of these preparations with an anxiety increased by the very consciousness of having no other parts than those of spectators to play in the scene that was momentarily expected.

In a few minutes from the falling in of the officers with their respective companies, the clank of irons was heard in the direction of the guard-room, and several forms were seen slowly advancing into the area already occupied as we have described. This party was preceded by the Adjutant Lawson, who, advancing towards Major Blackwater, communicated a message, that was followed by the command of the latter officer for the three divisions to face inwards. The officer of artillery also gave the word to his men to form lines of single files immediately in the rear of their respective guns, leaving space enough for the entrance of the approaching party, which consisted of half a dozen files of the guard, under a non-commissioned officer, and one whose manacled limbs, rather than his unaccoutred uniform, attested him to be not merely a prisoner, but a prisoner confined for some serious and flagrant offence.

This party now advanced through the vacant quarter of the square, and took their stations immediately in the centre. Here the countenances of each, and particularly that of the prisoner, who was, if we may so term it, the centre of that centre, were thrown into strong relief by the bright glare of the torches as they were occasionally waved in air, to disencumber them of their dross, so that the features of the prisoner stood revealed to those around as plainly as if it had been noonday. Not a sound, not a murmur, escaped from the ranks: but, though the etiquette and strict laws of military discipline chained all speech, the workings of the inward mind remained unchecked; and as they recognised in the prisoner Frank Halloway, one of the bravest and boldest in the field, and, as all had hitherto imagined, one of the most devoted to his duty, an irrepressible thrill of amazement and dismay crept throughout the frames, and for a moment blanched the cheeks of those especially who belonged to the same company. On being summoned from their fruitless search after the stranger, to fall in without delay, it had been whispered among the men that treason had crept into the fort, and a traitor, partly detected in his crime, had been arrested and thrown into irons; but the idea of Frank Halloway being that traitor was the last that could have entered into their thoughts, and yet they now beheld him covered with every mark of ignominy, and about to answer his high offence, in all human probability, with his life.

With the officers the reputation of Halloway for courage and fidelity stood no less high; but, while they secretly lamented the circumstance of his defalcation, they could not disguise from themselves the almost certainty of his guilt, for each, as he now gazed upon the prisoner, recollected the confusion and hesitation of manner he had evinced when questioned by them preparatory to their ascending to the ramparts.

Once more the suspense of the moment was interrupted by the entrance of other forms into the area. They were those of the Adjutant, followed by a drummer, bearing his instrument, and the Governor's orderly, charged with pens, ink, paper, and a book which, from its peculiar form and colour, every one present knew to be a copy of the Articles of War. A variety of contending emotions passed through the breasts of many, as they witnessed the silent progress of these preparations, rendered painfully interesting by the peculiarity of their position, and the wildness of the hour at which they thus found themselves assembled together. The prisoner himself was unmoved: he stood proud, calm, and fearless amid the guard, of whom he had so recently formed one; and though his countenance was pale, as much, perhaps, from a sense of the ignominious character in which he appeared as from more private considerations, still there was nothing to denote either the abjectness of fear or the consciousness of merited disgrace. Once or twice a low sobbing, that proceeded at intervals from one of the barrack windows, caught his ear, and he turned his glance in that direction with a restless anxiety, which he exerted himself in the instant afterwards to repress; but this was the only mark of emotion he betrayed.

The above dispositions having been hastily made, the adjutant and his assistants once more retired. After the lapse of a minute, a tall martial-looking man, habited in a blue military frock, and of handsome, though stern, haughty, and inflexible features, entered the area. He was followed by Major Blackwater, the captain of artillery, and Adjutant Lawson.

"Are the garrison all present, Mr. Lawson? are the officers all present?"

"All except those of the guard, sir," replied the Adjutant, touching his hat with a submission that was scrupulously exacted on all occasions of duty by his superior.

The Governor passed his hand for a moment over his brows. It seemed to those around him as if the mention of that guard had called up recollections which gave him pain; and it might be so, for his eldest son, Captain Frederick de Haldimar, had commanded the guard. Whither he had disappeared, or in what manner, no one knew.

"Are the artillery all present, Captain Wentworth?" again demanded the Governor, after a moment of silence, and in his wonted firm authoritative voice.

"All present, sir," rejoined the officer, following the example of the Adjutant, and saluting his chief.

"Then let a drum-head court-martial be assembled immediately, Mr. Lawson, and without reference to the roster let the senior officers be selected."

The Adjutant went round to the respective divisions, and in a low voice warned Captain Blessington, and the four senior subalterns, for that duty. One by one the officers, as they were severally called upon, left their places in the square, and sheathing their swords, stepped into that part of the area appointed as their temporary court. They were now all assembled, and Captain Blessington, the senior of his rank in the garrison, was preparing to administer the customary oaths, when the prisoner Halloway advanced a pace or two in front of his escort, and removing his cap, in a clear, firm, but respectful voice, thus addressed the Governor: –

"Colonel de Haldimar, that I am no traitor, as I have already told you, the Almighty God, before whom I swore allegiance to his Majesty, can bear me witness. Appearances, I own, are against me; but, so far from being a traitor, I would have shed my last drop of blood in defence of the garrison and your family. – Colonel de Haldimar," he pursued, after a momentary pause, in which he seemed to be struggling to subdue the emotion which rose, despite of himself, to his throat, "I repeat, I am no traitor, and I scorn the imputation – but here is my best answer to the charge. This wound (and he unbuttoned his jacket, opened his shirt, and disclosed a deep scar upon his white chest,) this wound I received in defence of my captain's life at Quebec. Had I not loved him, I should not so have exposed myself, neither but for that should I now stand in the situation of shame and danger, in which my comrades behold me."

Every heart was touched by this appeal – this bold and

manly appeal to the consideration of the Governor. The officers, especially, who were fully conversant with the general merit of Halloway, were deeply affected, and Charles de Haldimar – the young, the generous, the feeling Charles de Haldimar, – even shed tears.

"What mean you, prisoner?" interrogated the Governor, after a short pause, during which he appeared to be weighing and deducing inferences from the expressions just uttered. "What mean you, by stating, but for *that* (alluding to your regard for Captain de Haldimar) you would not now be in this situation of shame and danger?"

The prisoner hesitated a moment; and then rejoined, but in a tone that had less of firmness in it than before, – "Colonel de Haldimar, I am not at liberty to state my meaning; for, though a private soldier, I respect my word, and have pledged myself to secrecy."

"You respect your word, and have pledged yourself to secrecy! What mean you, man, by this rhodomontade? To whom can you have pledged yourself, and for what, unless it be to some secret enemy without the walls? Gentlemen, proceed to your duty: it is evident that the man is a traitor, even from his own admission. – On my life," he pursued, more hurriedly, and speaking in an under tone, as if to himself, "the fellow has been bribed by, and is connected with ——." The name escaped not his lips; for, aware of the emotion he was betraying, he suddenly checked himself, and assumed his wonted stern and authoritative bearing.

Once more the prisoner addressed the Governor in the same clear firm voice in which he had opened his appeal.

"Colonel de Haldimar, I have no connection with any living soul without the fort; and again I repeat, I am no traitor, but a true and loyal British soldier, as my services in this war, and my comrades, can well attest. Still, I seek not to shun that death which I have braved a dozen times at least in the —— regiment. All that I ask is, that I may not be tried – that I may not have the shame of hearing sentence pronounced against me *yet*; but if nothing should

occur before eight o'clock to vindicate my character from
this disgrace, I will offer up no further prayer for mercy. In
the name of that life, therefore, which I once preserved to
Captain de Haldimar, at the price of my own blood, I
entreat a respite from trial until then."

"In the name of God and all his angels, let mercy reach
your soul, and grant his prayer!"

Every ear was startled – every heart touched by the
plaintive, melancholy, silver tones of the voice that faintly
pronounced the last appeal, and all recognised it for that
of the young, interesting, and attached wife of the prisoner. Again the latter turned his gaze towards the window whence the sounds proceeded, and by the glare of the
torches a tear was distinctly seen by many coursing down
his manly cheek. The weakness was momentary. In the
next instant he closed his shirt and coat, and resuming his
cap, stepped back once more amid his guard, where he
remained stationary, with the air of one who, having nothing further to hope, has resolved to endure the worst that
can happen with resignation and fortitude.

After the lapse of a few moments, again devoted to
much apparent deep thought and conjecture, the Governor once more, and rather hurriedly, resumed, –

"In the event, prisoner, of this delay in your trial being
granted, will you pledge yourself to disclose the secret to
which you have alluded? Recollect, there is nothing but
that which can save your memory from being consigned
to infamy for ever; for who, among your comrades, will
believe the idle denial of your treachery, when there is the
most direct proof against you? If your secret die with you,
moreover, every honest man will consider it as having
been one so infamous and injurious to your character, that
you were ashamed to reveal it."

These suggestions of the Colonel were not without their
effect; for, in the sudden swelling of the prisoner's chest, as
allusion was made to the disgrace that would attach to his
memory, there was evidence of a high and generous spirit,

to whom obloquy was far more hateful than even death itself.

"I do promise," he at length replied, stepping forward, and uncovering himself as before, – "if no one appear to justify my conduct at the hour I have named, a full disclosure of all I know touching this affair shall be made. And may God, of his infinite mercy, grant, for Captain de Haldimar's sake, as well as mine, I may not then be wholly deserted!"

There was something so peculiarly solemn and impressive in the manner in which the unhappy man now expressed himself, that a feeling of the utmost awe crept into the bosoms of the surrounding throng; and more than one veteran of the grenadiers, the company to which Halloway belonged, was heard to relieve his chest of the long pent-up sigh that struggled for release.

"Enough, prisoner," rejoined the Governor; "on this condition do I grant your request; but recollect, – your disclosure ensures no hope of pardon, unless, indeed, you have the fullest proof to offer in your defence. Do you perfectly understand me?"

"I do," replied the soldier firmly; and again he placed his cap on his head, and retired a step or two back among the guard.

"Mr. Lawson, let the prisoner be removed, and conducted to one of the private cells. Who is the subaltern of the guard?"

"Ensign Fortescue," was the answer.

"Then let Ensign Fortescue keep the key of the cell himself. Tell him, moreover, I shall hold him individually responsible for his charge."

Once more the prisoner was marched out of the area; and, as the clanking sound of his chains became gradually fainter in the distance, the same voice that had before interrupted the proceedings, pronounced a "God be praised! – God be praised!" with such melody of sorrow in its intonations that no one could listen to it unmoved. Both

officers and men were more or less affected, and all hoped
– they scarcely knew why or what – but all hoped something favourable would occur to save the life of the brave
and unhappy Frank Halloway.

Of the first interruption by the wife of the prisoner the
Governor had taken no notice; but on this repetition of the
expression of her feelings he briefly summoned, in the
absence of the Adjutant, the sergeant-major of the regiment to his side.

"Sergeant-major Bletson, I desire that, in future, on all
occasions of this kind, the women of the regiment may be
kept out of the way. Look to it, sir!"

The sergeant-major, who had stood erect as his own
halbert, which he held before him in a saluting position,
during this brief admonition of his colonel, acknowledged,
by a certain air of deferential respect and dropping of the
eyes, unaccompanied by speech of any kind, that he felt
the reproof, and would, in future, take care to avoid all
similar cause for complaint. He then stalked stiffly away,
and resumed, in a few hasty strides, his position in rear of
the troops.

"Hard-hearted man!" pursued the same voice: "if my
prayers of gratitude to Heaven give offence, may the hour
never come when my lips shall pronounce their bitterest
curse upon your severity!"

There was something so painfully wild – so solemnly
prophetic – in these sounds of sorrow as they fell faintly
upon the ear, and especially under the extraordinary circumstances of the night, that they might have been taken
for the warnings of some supernatural agency. During
their utterance, not even the breathing of human life was
to be heard in the ranks. In the next instant, however,
Sergeant-major Bletson was seen repairing, with long and
hasty strides, to the barrack whence the voice proceeded,
and the interruption was heard no more.

Meanwhile the officers, who had been summoned from
the ranks for the purpose of forming the court-martial,
still lingered in the centre of the square, apparently wait-

ing for the order of their superior, before they should resume their respective stations. As the quick and comprehensive glance of Colonel de Haldimar now embraced the group, he at once became sensible of the absence of one of the seniors, all of whom he had desired should be selected for the court-martial.

"Mr. Lawson," he remarked, somewhat sternly, as the Adjutant now returned from delivering over his prisoner to Ensign Fortescue, "I thought I understood from your report the officers were all present!"

"I believe, sir, my report will be found perfectly correct," returned the Adjutant, in a tone which, without being disrespectful, marked his offended sense of the implication.

"And Lieutenant Murphy – "

"Is here, sir," said the Adjutant, pointing to a couple of files of the guard, who were bearing a heavy burden, and following into the square. "Lieutenant Murphy," he pursued, "has been shot on the ramparts; and I have, as directed by Captain Blessington, caused the body to be brought here, that I may receive your orders respecting the interment." As he spoke, he removed a long military grey cloak, which completely enshrouded the corpse, and disclosed, by the light of the still brightly flaming torches of the gunners, the features of the unfortunate Murphy.

"How did he meet his death?" enquired the governor; without, however, manifesting the slightest surprise, or appearing at all moved at the discovery.

"By a rifle shot fired from the common, near the old bomb proof," observed Captain Blessington, as the adjutant looked to him for the particular explanation he could not render himself.

"Ah! this reminds me," pursued the austere commandant, – "there was a shot fired also from the ramparts. By whom, and at what?"

"By me, sir," said Lieutenant Valletort, coming forward from the ranks, "and at what I conceived to be an Indian, lurking as a spy upon the common."

"Then, Lieutenant Sir Everard Valletort, no repetition of these firings, if you please; and let it be borne in mind by all, that although, from the peculiar nature of the service in which we are engaged, I so far depart from the established regulations of the army as to permit my officers to arm themselves with rifles, they are to be used only as occasion may require in the hour of conflict, and not for the purpose of throwing a whole garrison into alarm by trials of skill and dexterity upon shadows at this unseasonable hour."

"I was not aware, sir," returned Sir Everard proudly, and secretly galled at being thus addressed before the men, "it could be deemed a military crime to destroy an enemy at whatever hour he might present himself, and especially on such an occasion as the present. As for my firing at a shadow, those who heard the yell that followed the second shot, can determine that it came from no shadow, but from a fierce and vindictive enemy. The cry denoted even something more than the ordinary defiance of an Indian: it seemed to express a fiendish sentiment of personal triumph and revenge."

The governor started involuntarily. "Do you imagine, Sir Everard Valletort, the aim of your rifle was true – that you hit him?"

This question was asked so hurriedly, and in a tone so different from that in which he had hitherto spoken, that the officers around simultaneously raised their eyes to those of their colonel with an expression of undissembled surprise. He observed it, and instantly resumed his habitual sternness of look and manner.

"I rather fear not, sir," replied Sir Everard, who had principally remarked the emotion; "but may I hope (and this was said with emphasis), in the evident disappointment you experience at my want of success, my offence may be overlooked?"

The governor fixed his penetrating eyes on the speaker, as if he would have read his inmost mind; and then calmly, and even impressively, observed, –

"Sir Everard Valletort, I do overlook the offence, and hope you may as easily forgive yourself. It were well, however, that your indiscretion, which can only find its excuse in your being so young an officer, had not been altogether without some good result. Had you killed or disabled the – the savage, there might have been a decent palliative offered; but what must be your feelings, sir, when you reflect, the death of yon officer," and he pointed to the corpse of the unhappy Murphy, "is, in a great degree, attributable to yourself? Had you not provoked the anger of the savage, and given a direction to his aim by the impotent and wanton discharge of your own rifle, this accident would never have happened."

This severe reproving of an officer, who had acted from the most praiseworthy of motives, and who could not possibly have anticipated the unfortunate catastrophe that had occurred, was considered especially harsh and unkind by every one present; and a low and almost inaudible murmur passed through the company to which Sir Everard was attached. For a minute or two that officer also appeared deeply pained, not more from the reproof itself than from the new light in which the observation of his chief had taught him to view, for the first time, the causes that had led to the fall of Murphy. Finding, however, that the governor had no further remark to address to him, he once more returned to his station in the ranks.

"Mr. Lawson," resumed the commandant, turning to the adjutant, "let this victim be carried to the spot on which he fell, and there interred. I know no better grave for a soldier than beneath the sod that has been moistened with his blood. Recollect," he continued, as the adjutant once more led the party out of the area, – "no firing, Mr. Lawson. The duty must be silently performed, and without the risk of provoking a forest of arrows, or a shower of bullets from the savages. Major Blackwater," he pursued, as soon as the corpse had been removed, "let the men pile their arms even as they now stand, and remain ready to fall in at a minute's notice. Should any thing extraordinary happen before the morning, you will, of course, apprise me." He then strode out of the area with the same haughty and measured step that had characterised his entrance.

"Our colonel does not appear to be in one of his most amiable moods to-night," observed Captain Blessington, as the officers, after having disposed of their respective companies, now proceeded along the ramparts to assist at the last funeral offices of their unhappy associate. "He was disposed to be severe, and must have put you, in some measure, out of conceit with your favourite rifle, Valletort."

"True," rejoined the Baronet, who had already rallied from the momentary depression of his spirits, "he hit me devilish hard, I confess, and was disposed to display more of the commanding officer than quite suits my ideas of the service. His words were as caustic as his looks; and could both have pierced me to the quick, there was no inclination on his part wanting. By my soul I could . . . . but I forgive him. He is the father of my friend: and for that reason will I chew the cud of my mortification, nor suffer, if possible, a sense of his unkindness to rankle at my heart. At all events, Blessington, my mind is made up, and resign or exchange I certainly shall the instant I can find a decent loop-hole to creep out of."

Sir Everard fancied the ear of his captain was alone listening to these expressions of his feeling, or in all probability he would not have uttered them. As he concluded the last sentence, however, he felt his arm gently grasped by one who walked a pace or two silently in their rear. He turned, and recognised Charles de Haldimar.

"I am sure, Valletort, you will believe how much pained I have been at the severity of my father; but, indeed, there was nothing personally offensive intended. Blessington can tell you as well as myself it is his manner altogether. Nay, that although he is the first in seniority after Blackwater, the governor treats him with the same distance and hauteur he would use towards the youngest ensign in the service. Such are the effects of his long military habits, and his ideas of the absolutism of command. Am I not right, Blessington?"

"Quite right, Charles. Sir Everard may satisfy himself his is no solitary instance of the stern severity of your father. Still, I confess, notwithstanding the rigidity of manner which he seems, on all occasions, to think so indispensable to the maintenance of authority in a commanding officer, I never knew him so inclined to find fault as he is to-night."

"Perhaps," observed Valletort, good humouredly, "his conscience is rather restless; and he is willing to get rid of it and his spleen together. I would wager my rifle against the worthless scalp of the rascal I fired at to-night, that this same stranger, whose asserted appearance has called us from our comfortable beds, is but the creation of his disturbed dreams. Indeed, how is it possible any thing formed of flesh and blood could have escaped us with the vigilant watch that has been kept on the ramparts? The old gentleman certainly had that illusion strongly impressed on my mind when he so sapiently spoke of my firing at a shadow."

"But the gate," interrupted Charles de Haldimar, with something of mild reproach in his tones, – "you forget, Valletort, the gate was found unlocked, and that my brother is missing. *He*, at least, was flesh and blood, as you say, and yet he has disappeared. What more probable, therefore, than that this stranger is at once the cause and the agent of his abduction?"

"Impossible, Charles," observed Captain Blessington; "Frederick was in the midst of the guard. How, therefore, could he be conveyed away without the alarm being given? Numbers only could have succeeded in so desperate an enterprise; and yet there is no evidence, or even suspicion, of more than one individual having been here."

"It is a singular affair altogether," returned Sir Everard, musingly. "Of two things, however, I am satisfied. The first is, that the stranger, whoever he may be, and if he really has been here, is no Indian; the second, that he is personally known to the governor, who has been, or I mistake much, more alarmed at his individual presence than if Ponteac and his whole band had suddenly broken in upon us. Did you remark his emotion, when I dwelt on the peculiar character of personal triumph and revenge which the cry of the lurking villain outside seemed to express? and did you notice the eagerness with which he enquired if I thought I had hit him? Depend upon it, there is more in all this than is dreamt of in our philosophy."

"And it was your undisguised perception of that emotion," remarked Captain Blessington, "that drew down his severity upon your own head. It was, however, too palpable not to be noticed by all; and I dare say conjecture is as busily and as vaguely at work among our companions as it is with us. The clue to the mystery, in a great degree, now dwells with Frank Halloway; and to him we must look for its elucidation. His disclosure will be one, I apprehend, full of ignominy to himself, but of the highest interest and importance to us all. And yet I know not how to believe the man the traitor he appears."

"Did you remark that last harrowing exclamation of his wife?" observed Charles de Haldimar, in a tone of unspeakable melancholy. "How fearfully prophetic it sounded in my ears. I know not how it is," he pursued, "but I wish I had not heard those sounds; for since that moment I have had a sad strange presentiment of evil at my heart. Heaven grant my poor brother may make his appearance, as I still trust he will, at the hour Halloway seems to expect, for if not, the latter most assuredly dies. I know my father well; and, if convicted by a court martial, no human power can alter the destiny that awaits Frank Halloway."

"Rally, my dear Charles, rally," said Sir Everard, affecting a confidence he did not feel himself; "indulge not in these idle and superstitious fancies. I pity Halloway from my soul, and feel the deepest interest in his pretty and unhappy wife; but that is no reason why one should attach importance to the incoherent expressions wrung from her in the agony of grief."

"It is kind of you, Valletort, to endeavour to cheer my spirits, when, if the truth were confessed, you acknowledge the influence of the same feelings. I thank you for the attempt, but time alone can show how far I shall have reason, or otherwise, to lament the occurrences of this night."

They had now reached that part of the ramparts whence the shot from Sir Everard's rifle had been fired. Several men were occupied in digging a grave in the precise spot on which the unfortunate Murphy had stood when he received his death-wound; and into this, when completed, the body, enshrouded in the cloak already alluded to, was deposited by his companions.

Four

WHILE THE adjutant was yet reading, in a low and solemn voice, the service for the dead, a fierce and distant yell, as if from a legion of devils, burst suddenly from the forest, and brought the hands of the startled officers instinctively to their swords. This appalling cry lasted, without interruption, for many minutes, and was then as abruptly checked as it had been unexpectedly delivered. A considerable pause succeeded, and then again it rose with even more startling vehemence than before. By one unaccustomed to those devilish sounds, no distinction could have been made in the two several yells that had been thus savagely pealed forth; but those to whom practice and long experience in the warlike habits and customs of the Indians had rendered their shouts familiar, at once divined, or fancied they divined, the cause. The first was, to their conception, a yell expressive at once of vengeance and disappointment in pursuit, – perhaps of some prisoner who had escaped from their toils; the second, of triumph and success, – in all probability, indicative of the recapture of that prisoner. For many minutes afterwards the officers continued to listen, with the most aching attention, for a repetition of the cry, or even fainter sounds, that might denote either a nearer approach to the fort, or the final departure of the Indians. After the second yell, however, the woods, in the heart of which it appeared to have been uttered, were buried in as profound a silence as if they had never yet echoed back the voice of man; and all at length became satisfied that the Indians, having accomplished some particular purpose, had retired once more to their distant encampments for the night. Captain Erskine was the first who broke the almost breathless silence that prevailed among themselves.

"On my life De Haldimar is a prisoner with the Indians. He has been attempting his escape, – has been detected, – followed, and again fallen into their hands. I know their infernal yells but too well. The last expressed their savage joy at the capture of a prisoner; and there is no one of us missing but De Haldimar."

"Not a doubt of it," said Captain Blessington; "the cry was certainly what you describe it, and Heaven only knows what will be the fate of our poor friend."

No other officer spoke, for all were oppressed by the weight of their own feelings, and sought rather to give indulgence to speculation in secret, than to share their impressions with their companions. Charles de Haldimar stood a little in the rear, leaning his head upon his hand against the box of the sentry, (who was silently, though anxiously, pacing his walk,) and in an attitude expressive of the deepest dejection and sorrow.

"I suppose I must finish Lawson's work, although I am but a poor hand at this sort of thing," resumed Captain Erskine, taking up the prayer book the adjutant had, in hastening on the first alarm to get the men under arms, carelessly thrown on the grave of the now unconscious Murphy.

He then commenced the service at the point where Mr. Lawson had so abruptly broken off, and went through the remainder of the prayers. A very few minutes sufficed for the performance of this solemn duty, which was effected by the faint dim light of the at length dawning day, and the men in attendance proceeded to fill up the grave of their officer.

Gradually the mists, that had fallen during the latter hours of the night, began to ascend from the common, and disperse themselves in air, conveying the appearance of a rolling sheet of vapour retiring back upon itself, and disclosing objects in succession, until the eye could embrace all that came within its extent of vision. As the officers yet lingered near the rude grave of their companion, watching with abstracted air the languid and almost mechanical action of their jaded men, as they emptied shovel after shovel of the damp earth over the body of its new tenant, they were suddenly startled by an expression of exultation from Sir Everard Valletort.

"By Jupiter, I have pinked him," he exclaimed triumphantly. "I knew my rifle could not err; and as for my sight, I have carried away too many prizes in target-shooting to have been deceived in that. How delighted the old governor will be, Charles, to hear this. No more lecturing, I am sure, for the next six months at least;" and the young officer rubbed his hands together, at the success of his shot, with as much satisfaction and unconcern for the future, as if he had been in his own native England, in the midst of a prize-ring.

Roused by the observation of his friend, De Haldimar quitted his position near the sentry box, and advanced to the outer edge of the rampart. To him, as to his companions, the outline of the old bomb proof was now distinctly visible, but it was sometime before they could discover, in the direction in which Valletort pointed, a dark speck upon the common; and this so indistinctly, they could scarcely distinguish it with the naked eye.

"Your sight is quite equal to your aim, Sir Everard," remarked Lieutenant Johnstone, one of Erskine's subalterns, "and both are decidedly superior to mine; yet I used to be thought a good rifleman too, and have credit for an eye no less keen than that of an Indian. You have the advantage of me, however; for I honestly admit I never could have picked off yon fellow in the dark as you have done."

As the dawn increased, the dark shadow of a human form, stretched at its length upon the ground, became perceptible; and the officers, with one unanimous voice, bore loud testimony to the skill and dexterity of him who had, under such extreme disadvantages, accomplished the death of their skulking enemy.

"Bravo, Valletort," said Charles de Haldimar, recovering his spirits, as much from the idea, now occurring to him, that this might indeed be the stranger whose appearance had so greatly disturbed his father, as from the gratification he felt in the praises bestowed on his friend. "Bravo, my dear fellow;" then approaching, and in a half whisper, "when next I write to Clara, I shall request her, with my cousin's assistance, to prepare a chaplet of bays, wherewith I shall myself crown you as their proxy. But what is the matter now, Valletort? Why stand you there gazing upon the common, as if the victim of your murderous aim was rising from his bloody couch, to reproach you with his death? Tell me, shall I write to Clara for the prize, or will you receive it from her own hands?"

"Bid her rather pour her curses on my head; and to those, De Haldimar, add your own," exclaimed Sir Everard, at length raising himself from the statue-like position he had assumed. "Almighty God," he pursued, in the same tone of deep agony, "what have I done? Where, where shall I hide myself?"

As he spoke he turned away from his companions, and covering his eyes with his hand, with quick and unequal steps, even like those of a drunken man, walked, or rather ran, along the rampart, as if fearful of being overtaken.

The whole group of officers, and Charles de Haldimar in particular, were struck with dismay at the language and action of Sir Everard; and for a moment they fancied that fatigue, and watching, and excitement, had partially affected his brain. But when, after the lapse of a minute or two, they again looked out upon the common, the secret of his agitation was too faithfully and too painfully explained.

What had at first the dusky and dingy hue of a half-naked Indian, was now perceived, by the bright beams of light just gathering in the east, to be the gay and striking uniform of a British officer. Doubt as to who that officer was there could be none, for the white sword-belt suspended over the right shoulder, and thrown into strong relief by the field of scarlet on which it reposed, denoted the wearer of this distinguishing badge of duty to be one of the guard.

To comprehend effectually the feelings of the officers, it would be necessary that one should have been not merely a soldier, but a soldier under the same circumstances. Surrounded on every hand by a fierce and cruel enemy – prepared at every moment to witness scenes of barbarity and bloodshed in their most appalling shapes – isolated from all society beyond the gates of their own fortress, and by consequence reposing on and regarding each other as vital links in the chain of their wild and adventurous existence, – it can easily be understood with what sincere and unaffected grief they lamented the sudden cutting off even of those who least assimilated in spirit and character with themselves. Such, in a great degree, had been the case in the instance of the officer over whose grave they were now met to render the last offices of companionship, if not of friendship. Indeed Murphy – a rude, vulgar, and illiterate, though brave Irishman – having risen from the ranks, the coarseness of which he had never been able to shake off, was little calculated, either by habits or education, to awaken feelings, except of the most ordinary description, in his favour; and he and Ensign Delme were the only exceptions to those disinterested and tacit friendships that had grown up out of circumstances in common among the majority. If, therefore, they could regret the loss of such a companion as Murphy, how deep and heartfelt must have been the sorrow they experienced when they beheld the brave, generous, manly, amiable, and highly-talented Frederick de Haldimar – the pride of the garrison, and the idol of his family – lying extended, a cold, senseless corpse, slain by the hand of the bosom friend of his own brother! – Notwithstanding the stern severity and

distance of the governor, whom few circumstances, however critical or exciting, could surprise into relaxation of
his habitual stateliness, it would have been difficult to
name two young men more universally liked and esteemed by their brother officers than were the De Haldi-
mars – the first for the qualities already named – the
second, for those retiring, mild, winning manners, and
gentle affections, added to extreme and almost feminine
beauty of countenance for which he was remarkable.
Alas, what a gloomy picture was now exhibited to the
minds of all! – Frederick de Haldimar a corpse, and slain
by the hand of Sir Everard Valletort! What but disunion
could follow this melancholy catastrophe? and how could
Charles de Haldimar, even if his bland nature should survive the shock, ever bear to look again upon the man who
had, however innocently or unintentionally, deprived him
of a brother whom he adored?

These were the impressions that passed through the
minds of the compassionating officers, as they directed
their glance alternately from the common to the pale and
marble-like features of the younger De Haldimar, who,
with parted lips and stupid gaze, continued to fix his eyes
upon the inanimate form of his ill-fated brother, as if the
very faculty of life itself had been for a period suspended.
At length, however, while his companions watched in silence the mining workings of that grief which they feared
to interrupt by ill-timed observations, even of condolence,
the death-like hue, which had hitherto suffused the usually blooming cheek of the young officer, was succeeded
by a flush of the deepest dye, while his eyes, swollen by
the tide of blood now rushing violently to his face, appeared to be bursting from their sockets. The shock was
more than his delicate frame, exhausted as it was by
watching and fatigue, could bear. He tottered, reeled,
pressed his hand upon his head, and before any one could
render him assistance, fell senseless on the ramparts.

During the interval between Sir Everard Valletort's exclamation, and the fall of Charles de Haldimar, the men

employed at the grave had performed their duty, and were gazing with mingled astonishment and concern, both on the body of their murdered officer, and on the dumb scene acting around them. Two of these were now despatched for a litter, with which they speedily re-appeared. On this Charles de Haldimar, already delirious with the fever of intense excitement, was carefully placed, and, followed by Captain Blessington and Lieutenant Johnstone, borne to his apartment in the small range of buildings constituting the officers' barracks. Captain Erskine undertook the disagreeable office of communicating these distressing events to the governor; and the remainder of the officers once more hastened to join or linger near their respective companies, in readiness for the order which it was expected would be given to despatch a numerous party of the garrison to secure the body of Captain de Haldimar.

Five

THE SUN was just rising above the horizon, in all that peculiar softness of splendour which characterises the early days of autumn in America, as Captain Erskine led his company across the drawbridge that communicated with the fort. It was the first time it had been lowered since the investment of the garrison by the Indians; and as the dull and rusty chains performed their service with a harsh and grating sound, it seemed as if an earnest were given of melancholy boding. Although the distance to be traversed was small, the risk the party incurred was great; for it was probable the savages, ever on the alert, would not suffer them to effect their object unmolested. It was perhaps singular, and certainly contradictory, that an officer of the acknowledged prudence and forethought ascribed to the governor – qualities which in a great degree neutralised his excessive severity in the eyes of his troops – should have hazarded the chance of having his garrison enfeebled by the destruction of a part, if not of the whole, of the company appointed to this dangerous duty; but with all his severity, Colonel de Haldimar was not without strong affection for his children. The feeling of the father, therefore, in a great degree triumphed over the prudence of the commander; and to shield the corpse of his son from the indignities which he well knew would be inflicted on it by Indian barbarity, he had been induced to accede to the earnest prayer of Cap-

tain Erskine, that he might be permitted to lead out his
company for the purpose of securing the body. Every
means were, however, taken to cover the advance, and
ensure the retreat of the detachment. The remainder of
the troops were distributed along the rear of the ramparts,
with instructions to lie flat on their faces until summoned
by their officers from that position; which was to be done
only in the event of close pursuit from the savages. Artillerymen were also stationed at the several guns that
flanked the rear of the fort, and necessarily commanded
both the common and the outskirt of the forest, with
orders to fire with grape-shot at a given signal. Captain
Erskine's instructions were, moreover, if attacked, to retreat back under the guns of the fort slowly and in good
order, and without turning his back upon the enemy.

Thus confident of support, the party, after traversing the
drawbridge with fixed bayonets, inclined to the right, and
following the winding of the ditch by which it was surrounded, made the semi-circuit of the rampart until they
gained the immediate centre of the rear, and in a direct
line with the bomb-proof. Here their mode of advance
was altered, to guard more effectually against the enemy
with whom they might possibly have to contend. The front
and rear ranks of the company, consisting in all of ninety
men, were so placed as to leave space in the event of
attack, of a portion of each wheeling inwards so as to
present in an instant three equal faces of a square. As the
rear was sufficiently covered by the cannon of the fort to
defeat any attempt to turn their flanks, the manoeuvre
was one that enabled them to present a fuller front in
whatever other quarter they might be attacked; and had
this additional advantage, that in the advance by single
files a narrower front was given to the aim of the Indians,
who, unless they fired in an oblique direction, could only,
of necessity, bring down two men (the leading files) at a
time.

In this order, and anxiously overlooked by their comrades, whose eyes alone peered from above the surface of

the rampart on which they lay prostrate, the detachment crossed the common; one rank headed by Captain Erskine, the other by Lieutenant Johnstone. They had now approached within a few yards of the unfortunate victim, when Captain Erskine commanded a halt of his party; and two files were detached from the rear of each rank, to place the body on a litter with which they had provided themselves. He and Johnstone also moved in the same direction in advance of the men, prepared to render assistance if required. The corpse lay on its face, and in no way despoiled of any of its glittering habiliments, a circumstance that too well confirmed the fact of De Haldimar's death having been accomplished by the ball from Sir Everard Valletort's rifle. It appeared, however, the ill-fated officer had struggled much in the agonies of death; for the left leg was drawn up into an unnatural state of contraction, and the right hand, closely compressed, grasped a quantity of grass and soil, which had evidently been torn up in a paroxysm of suffering and despair.

The men placed the litter at the side of the body, which they now proceeded to raise. As they were in the act of depositing it on this temporary bier, the plumed hat fell from the head, and disclosed, to the astonishment of all, the scalpless crown completely saturated in its own clotted blood and oozing brains.

An exclamation of horror and disgust escaped at the same moment from the lips of the two officers, and the men started back from their charge as if a basilisk had suddenly appeared before them. Captain Erskine pursued: –

"What the devil is the meaning of all this, Johnstone?"

"What, indeed!" rejoined his lieutenant, with a shrug of the shoulders, that was intended to express his inability to form any opinion on the subject.

"Unless it should prove," continued Erskine, "as I sincerely trust it may, that poor Valletort is not, after all, the murderer of his friend. It must be so. De Haldimar has been slain by the same Indian who killed Murphy. – Do you recollect his scalp cry? He was in the act of despoiling

his victim of this trophy of success, when Sir Everard
fired. Examine the body well, Mitchell, and discover
where the wound lies."

The old soldier to whom this order was addressed now
prepared, with the assistance of his comrades, to turn the
body upon its back, when suddenly the air was rent with
terrific yells, that seemed to be uttered in their very ears,
and in the next instant more than a hundred dark and
hideous savages sprang simultaneously to their feet within
the bomb-proof, while every tree along the skirt of the
forest gave back the towering form of a warrior. Each of
these, in addition to his rifle, was armed with all those
destructive implements of warfare which render the Indians of America so formidable and so terrible an enemy.

"Stand to your arms, men," shouted Captain Erskine,
recovering from his first and unavoidable, though but momentary, surprise. "First and fourth sections, on your right
and left backwards wheel: – Quick, men, within the
square, for your lives." As he spoke, he and Lieutenant
Johnstone sprang hastily back, and in time to obtain admittance within the troops, who had rapidly executed the
manoeuvre commanded. Not so with Mitchell and his
companions. On the first alarm they had quitted the body
of the mutilated officer, and flown to secure their arms,
but even while in the act of stooping to take them up, they
had been grappled by a powerful and vindictive foe; and
the first thing they beheld on regaining their upright position, was a dusky Indian at the side, and a gleaming tomahawk flashing rapidly round the head of each.

"Fire not, on your lives," exclaimed Captain Erskine
hastily, as he saw several of the men in front levelling, in
the excitement of the moment, their muskets at the threatening savages. "Prepare for attack," he pursued; and in
the next instant each man dropped on his right knee, and
a barrier of bristling bayonets seemed to rise from the
very bowels of the earth. Attracted by the novelty of the
sight, the bold and daring warriors, although still retaining
their firm grasp of the unhappy soldiers, were for a mo-

ment diverted from their bloody purpose, and temporarily suspended the quick and rotatory motion of their weapons. Captain Erskine took advantage of this pause to seize the halbert of one of his sergeants, to the extreme point of which he hastily attached a white pocket handkerchief, that was loosely thrust into the breast of his uniform; this he waved on high three several times, and then relinquishing the halbert, dropped also on his knee within the square.

"The dog of a Saganaw asks for mercy," said a voice from within the bomb-proof, and speaking in the dialect of the Ottawas. "His pale flag bespeaks the quailing of his heart, and his attitude denotes the timidity of the hind. His warriors are like himself, and even now upon their knees they call upon their Manitou to preserve them from the vengeance of the red-skins. But mercy is not for dogs like these. Now is the time to make our tomahawks warm in their blood; and every head that we count shall be a scalp upon our war poles."

As he ceased, one universal and portentous yell burst from the fiend-like band; and again the weapons of death were fiercely brandished around the heads of the stupified soldiers who had fallen into their power.

"What can they be about?" anxiously exclaimed Captain Erskine, in the midst of this deafening clamour, to his subaltern. – "Quiet, man; damn you, quiet, or I'll cut you down," he pursued, addressing one of his soldiers, whose impatience caused him to bring his musket half up to the shoulder. And again he turned his head in the direction of the fort: – "Thank God, here it comes at last, – I feared my signal had not been noticed."

While he yet spoke, the loud roaring of a cannon from the ramparts was heard, and a shower of grape-shot passed over the heads of the detachment, and was seen tearing up the earth around the bomb-proof, and scattering fragments of stone and wood into the air. The men simultaneously and unbidden gave three cheers.

In an instant the scene was changed. As if moved by

some mechanical impulse, the fierce band that lined the bomb-proof sank below the surface, and were no longer visible, while the warriors in the forest again sought shelter behind the trees. The captured soldiers were also liberated without injury, so sudden and startling had been the terror produced in the savages by the lightning flash that announced its heavy messengers of destruction. Discharge after discharge succeeded without intermission; but the guns had been levelled so high, to prevent injury to their own men, they had little other effect than to keep the Indians from the attack. The rush of bullets through the close forest, and the crashing of trees and branches as they fell with startling force upon each other, were, with the peals of artillery, the only noises now to be heard; for not a yell, not a word was uttered by the Indians after the first discharge; and but for the certainty that existed in every mind, it might have been supposed the whole of them had retired.

"Now is your time," cried Captain Erskine; "bring in the litter to the rear, and stoop as much as possible to avoid the shot."

The poor half-strangled fellows, however, instead of obeying the order of their captain, looked round in every direction for the enemy by whom they had been so rudely handled, and who had glided from them almost as imperceptibly and swiftly as they had first approached. It seemed as if they apprehended that any attempt to remove the body would be visited by those fierce devils with the same appalling and ferocious threatenings.

"Why stand ye there, ye dolts," continued their captain, "looking around as if ye were bewitched? Bring the litter in to the rear. - Mitchell, you old fool, are you grown a coward in your age? Are you not ashamed to set such an example to your comrades?"

The doubt thus implied of the courage of his men, who, in fact, were merely stupified with the scene they had gone through, had, as Captain Erskine expected, the desired effect. They now bent themselves to the litter, on which they had previously deposited their muskets, and with a self-possession that contrasted singularly with their recent air of wild astonishment, bore it to the rear at the risk of being cut in two at every moment by the fire from the fort.

One fierce yell, instinctively proffered by several of the lurking band in the forest, marked their disappointment and rage at the escape of their victims; but all attempt at uncovering themselves, so as to be enabled to fire, was prevented by the additional showers of grape which that yell immediately brought upon them.

The position in which Captain Erskine now found himself was highly critical. Before him, and on either flank, was a multitude of savages, who only awaited the cessation of the fire from the fort to commence their fierce and impetuous attack. That that fire could not long be sustained was evident, since ammunition could ill be spared for the present inefficient purpose, where supplies of all kinds were so difficult to be obtained; and, if he should attempt a retreat, the upright position of his men exposed them to the risk of being swept away by the ponderous metal, that already fanned their cheeks with the air it so rapidly divided. Suddenly, however, the fire from the batteries was discontinued, and this he knew to be a signal for himself. He gave an order in a low voice, and the detachment quitted their recumbent and defensive position, still remaining formed in square. At the same instant, a gun flashed from the fort; but not as before was heard the rushing sound of the destructive shot crushing the trees in its resistless course. The Indians took courage at this circumstance, for they deemed the bullets of their enemies were expended; and that they were merely discharging their powder to keep up the apprehension originally produced. Again they showed themselves, like so many demons, from behind their lurking places; and yells and shouts of the most terrific and threatening character once more rent the air, and echoed through the woods. Their cries of anticipated triumph were, however, but of short duration. Presently, a hissing noise was heard in the air; and close to the bomb-proof, and at the very skirt of the forest, they beheld a huge globe of iron fall perpendicularly to the earth, to the outer part of which was attached what they supposed to be a reed, that spat forth innumerable sparks of fire, without however, seeming to threaten the slightest injury. Attracted by the novel sight, a dozen warriors sprang to the spot, and fastened their gaze upon it with all the childish wonder and curiosity of men in a savage state. One, more eager and restless than his fellows, stooped over it to feel with his hand of what it was composed. At that moment it burst, and limbs, and head, and entrails, were seen flying in the air, with the fragments of the shell, and prostrate and struggling forms lay writhing on every hand in the last, fierce agonies of death.

A yell of despair and a shout of triumph burst at the same moment from the adverse parties. Taking advantage of the terror produced, by this catastrophe, in the savages, Captain Erskine caused the men bearing the corpse to retreat, with all possible expedition, under the ramparts of the fort. He waited until they got nearly half way, and then threw forward the wheeling section, that had covered this movement, once more into single file, in which order he commenced his retreat. Step by step, and almost imperceptibly, the men paced backwards, ready, at a moment's notice, to reform the square. Partly recovered from the terror and surprise produced by the bursting of the shell, the Indians were quick in perceiving this movement: filled with rage at having been so long baulked of their aim, they threw themselves once more impetuously from their cover; and, with stimulating yells, at length opened their fire. Several of Captain Erskine's men were wounded by this discharge; when, again, and furiously the cannon opened from the fort. It was then that the superiority of the artillery was made manifest. Both right and left of the retreating files the ponderous shot flew heavily past, carrying death and terror to the Indians; while not a man of those who intervened was scathed or touched in its progress. The warriors in the forest were once more compelled to shelter themselves behind the trees; but in the bomb-proof, where they were more secure, they were also more bold. From this a galling fire, mingled with the most hideous yells, was now kept up; and the detachment, in their slow retreat, suffered considerably. Several men had been killed; and, about twenty, including Lieutenant Johnstone, wounded, when again, one of those murderous globes fell, hissing in the very centre of the bomb-proof. In an instant, the Indian fire was discontinued; and their dark and pliant forms were seen hurrying with almost incredible rapidity over the dilapidated walls, and flying into the very heart of the forest, so that when the shell exploded, a few seconds afterwards, not a warrior was to be seen. From this moment the attack was not renewed, and Captain Erskine made good his retreat without further molestation.

"Well, old buffers!" exclaimed one of the leading files, as the detachment, preceded by its dead and wounded, now moved along the moat in the direction of the drawbridge, "how did you like the grip of them black savages? – I say, Mitchell, old Nick will scarcely know the face of you, it's so much altered by fright. – Did you see," turning to the man in his rear, "how harum-scarum he looked, when the captain called out to him to come off?"

"Hold your clapper, you spooney, and be damned to you!" exclaimed the angry veteran. – "Had the Ingian fastened his paw upon your ugly neck as he did upon mine, all the pitiful life your mother ever put into you would have been spirited away from very fear; so you needn't brag."

"Sure, and if any of ye had a grain of spunk, ye would have fired, and freed a fellow from the clutch of them hell thieves," muttered another of the men at the litter. "All the time, the devil had me by the throat, swinging his tommy-hawk about my head, I saw ye dancing up and down in the heavens, instead of being on your marrow bones on the common."

"And didn't I want to do it?" rejoined the first speaker.

"Ask Tom Winkler here, if the captain didn't swear he'd cut the soul out of my body if I even offered so much as to touch the trigger of my musket."

"Faith, and lucky he did," replied his covering man (for the ranks had again joined), "since but for that, there wouldn't be at this moment so much as a hair of the scalp of one of you left."

"And how so, Mr. Wiseacre?" rejoined his comrade.

"How so! Because the first shot that we fired would have set the devils upon them in right earnest – and then their top-knots wouldn't have been worth a brass farthing. They would have been scalped before they could say Jack Robinson."

"It was a hell of a risk," resumed another of the litter men, "to give four men a chance of having their skull pieces cracked open like so many egg-shells, and all to get possession of a dead officer."

"And sure, you beast," remarked a different voice in a tone of anger, "the dead body of the brave captain was worth a dozen such rotten carcasses with all the life in them. What matter would it be if ye had all been scalped?" Then with a significant half glance to the rear, which was brought up by their commander, on whose arm leaned the slightly wounded Johnstone, "Take care the captain doesn't hear ye prating after that fashion, Will Burford."

"By Jasus," said a good-humoured, quaint looking Irishman, who had been fixing his eyes on the litter during this pithy and characteristic colloquy; "it sames to me, my boys, that ye have caught the wrong cow by the horns, and that all your pains has been for nothing at all, at all. By the holy pope, ye are all wrong; it's like bringing salt butter to Cork, or coals to your Newcastle, as ye call it. Who the divil ever heard of the officer wearing ammunition shoes?"

The men all turned their gaze on that part of the vestment of the corpse to which their attention had been directed by this remark, when it was at once perceived, although it had hitherto escaped the observation even of the officers, that, not only the shoes were those usually worn by the soldiers, and termed ammunition or store shoes, but also, the trowsers were of the description of coarse grey, peculiar to that class.

"By the piper that played before Moses, and ye're right, Dick Doherty," exclaimed another Irishman; "sure, and it isn't the officer at all! Just look at the great black fist of him too, and never call me Phil Shehan, if it ever was made for the handling of an officer's spit."

"Well said, Shehan," observed the man who had so warmly reproved Will Burford, and who had formerly been servant to De Haldimar; "the captain's hand is as white and as soft as my cross-belt, or, what's saying a great deal more, as Miss Clara's herself, heaven bless her sweet countenance! and Lieutenant Valletort's nigger's couldn't well be much blacker nor this."

"What a set of hignoramuses ye must be," grunted old Mitchell, "not to see that the captain's hand is only covered with dirt; and as for the ammunition shoes and trowsers, why you know our officers wear any thing since we have been cooped up in this here fort."

"Yes, by the holy poker," (and here we must beg to refer the reader to the soldier's vocabulary for any terms that may be, in the course of this dialogue, incomprehensible to him or her,) – "Yes, by the holy poker, off duty, if they like it," returned Phil Shehan; "but it isn't even the colonel's own born son that dare to do so while officer of the guard."

"Ye are right, comrade," said Burford; "there would soon be hell and tommy to pay if he did."

At this point of their conversation, one of the leading men at the litter, in turning to look at its subject, stumbled over the root of a stump that lay in his way, and fell violently forward. The sudden action destroyed the equilibrium of the corpse, which rolled off its temporary bier upon the earth, and disclosed, for the first time, a face begrimmed with masses of clotted blood, which had streamed forth from the scalped brain during the night.

"It's the divil himself," said Phil Shehan, making the

sign of the cross, half in jest, half in earnest: "for it isn't the captin at all, and who but the divil could have managed to clap on his rigimintals?"

"No, it's an Ingian," remarked Will Burford, sagaciously; "it's an Ingian that has killed the captain, and dressed himself in his clothes. I thought he smelt strong, when I helped to pick him up."

"And that's the reason why the bloody heathens wouldn't let us carry him off," said another of the litter men. "I thought they wouldn't ha' made such a rout about the officer, when they had his scalp already in their pouchbelts."

"What a set of prating fools ye are," interrupted the leading sergeant; "who ever saw an Ingian with light hair? and sure this hair in the neck is that of a Christian."

At that moment Captain Erskine, attracted by the sudden halt produced by the falling of the body, came quickly up to the front.

"What is the meaning of all this, Cassidy?" he sternly demanded of the sergeant; "why is this halt without my orders, and how comes the body here?"

"Carter stumbled against a root, sir, and the body rolled over upon the ground."

"And was the body to roll back again?" angrily rejoined his captain. – "What mean ye, fellows, by standing there; quick, replace it upon the litter, and mind this does not occur again."

"They say, sir," said the sergeant, respectfully, as the men proceeded to their duty, "that it is not Captain de Haldimar after all, but an Ingian."

"Not Captain de Haldimar! are ye all mad? and have the Indians, in reality, turned your brains with fear?"

What, however, was his own surprise, and that of Lieutenant Johnstone, when, on a closer examination of the corpse, which the men had now placed with its face uppermost, they discovered the bewildering fact that it was not, indeed, Captain de Haldimar who lay before them, but a stranger, dressed in the uniform of that officer.

There was no time to solve, or even to dwell on the

singular mystery; for the Indians, though now retired, might be expected to rally and renew the attack. Once more, therefore, the detachment moved forward; the officers dropping as before to the rear, to watch any movements of the enemy should he re-appear. Nothing, however, occurred to interrupt their march; and in a few minutes the heavy clanking sound of the chains of the drawbridge, as it was again raised by its strong pullies, and the dull creaking sound of the rusty bolts and locks that secured the ponderous gate, announced the detachment was once more safely within the fort.

While the wounded men were being conveyed to the hospital, a group, comprising almost all the officers of the garrison, hastened to meet Captain Erskine and Lieutenant Johnstone. Congratulations on the escape of the one, and compliments, rather than condolences, on the accident of the other, which the arm *en écharpe* denoted to be slight, were hastily and warmly proffered. These felicitations were the genuine ebullitions of the hearts of men who really felt a pride, unmixed with jealousy, in the conduct of their fellows; and so cool and excellent had been the manner in which Captain Erskine had accomplished his object, that it had claimed the undivided admiration of all who had been spectators of the affair, and had, with the aid of their telescopes, been enabled to follow the minutest movements of the detachment.

"By heaven!" he at length replied, his chest swelling with gratified pride at the warm and generous approval of his companions, "this more than repays me for every risk. Yet, to be sincere, the credit is not mine, but Wentworth's. But for you, my dear fellow," grasping and shaking the hand of that officer, "we should have rendered but a Flemish account of ourselves. How beautifully those guns covered our retreat! and the first mortar that sent the howling devils flying in air like so many Will-o'the-wisps, who placed that, Wentworth?"

"I did," replied the officer, with a quickness that denoted a natural feeling of exultation; "but Bombardier Kitson's was the most effective. It was his shell that drove the

Indians finally out of the bomb-proof, and left the coast clear for your retreat."

"Then Kitson, and his gunners also, merit our best thanks," pursued Captain Erskine, whose spirits, now that his detachment was in safety, were more than usually exhilarated by the exciting events of the last hour; "and what will be more acceptable, perhaps, they shall each have a glass of my best old Jamaica before they sleep, – and such stuff is not to be met with every day in this wilderness of a country. But, confound my stupid head! where are Charles de Haldimar and Sir Everard Valletort?"

"Poor Charles is in a high fever, and confined to his bed," remarked Captain Blessington, who now came up adding his congratulations in a low tone, that marked the despondency of his heart; "and Sir Everard I have just left on the rampart with the company, looking, as he well may, the very image of despair."

"Run to them, Sumners, my dear boy," said Erskine, hastily addressing himself to a young ensign who stood near him; "run quickly, and relieve them of their error. Say it is not De Haldimar who has been killed, therefore they need not make themselves any longer uneasy on that score."

The officers gave a start of surprise. Sumners, however, hastened to acquit himself of the pleasing task assigned him, without waiting to hear the explanation of the singular declaration.

"Not De Haldimar!" eagerly and anxiously exclaimed Captain Blessington; "who then have you brought to us in his uniform, which I clearly distinguished from the rampart as you passed? Surely you would not tamper with us at such a moment, Erskine?"

"Who it is, I know not more than Adam," rejoined the other; "unless, indeed, it be the devil himself. All I *do* know, is, it is not our friend De Haldimar; although, as you observe, he most certainly wears his uniform. But you shall see and judge for yourselves, gentlemen. Sergeant Cassidy," he enquired of that individual, who now came to ask if the detachment was to be dismissed, "where have you placed the litter?"

"Under the piazza of the guard-room, Sir," answered the sergeant.

These words had scarcely been uttered, when a general and hasty movement of the officers, anxious to satisfy themselves by personal observation it was not indeed De Haldimar who had fallen, took place in the direction alluded to, and in the next moment they were at the side of the litter.

A blanket had been thrown upon the corpse to conceal the loathsome disfigurement of the face, over which masses of thick coagulated blood were laid in patches and streaks, that set all recognition at defiance. The formation of the head alone, which was round and short, denoted it to be *not* De Haldimar's. Not a feature was left undefiled; and even the eyes were so covered, it was impossible to say whether their lids were closed or open. More than one officer's cheek paled with the sickness that rose to his heart as he gazed on the hideous spectacle; yet, as the curiosity of all was strongly excited to know who the murdered man really was who had been so unaccountably inducted in the uniform of their lost companion, they were resolved to satisfy themselves without further delay. A basin of warm water and a sponge were procured from the guard-room of Ensign Fortescue, who now joined them, and with these Captain Blessington proceeded to remove the disguise.

In the course of this lavation, it was discovered the extraordinary flow of blood and brains had been produced by the infliction of a deep wound on the back of the head, by the sharp and ponderous tomahawk of an Indian. It was the only blow that had been given; and the circumstance of the deceased having been found lying on his face, accounted for the quantity of gore, that, trickling downwards, had so completely disguised every feature. As the coat of thick encrusted matter gave way beneath the frequent application of the moistening sponge, the pallid hue of the countenance denoted the murdered man to be a white. All doubt, however, was soon at an end. The ammunition shoes, the grey trowsers, the coarse linen, and the stiff leathern stock encircling the neck, attested the sufferer to be a soldier of the garrison; but it was not until the face had been completely denuded of its unsightly covering, and every feature fully exposed, that that soldier was at length recognised to be Harry Donellan, the trusty and attached servant of Captain de Haldimar.

While yet the officers stood apart, gazing at the corpse, and forming a variety of conjectures, as vague as they were unsatisfactory, in regard to their new mystery, Sir Everard Valletort, pale and breathless with the speed he had used, suddenly appeared among them.

"God of heaven! can it be true – and is it really not De Haldimar whom I have shot?" wildly asked the agitated young man. "Who is this, Erskine?" he continued, glancing at the litter. "Explain, for pity's sake, and quickly."

"Compose yourself, my dear Valletort," replied the officer addressed. "You see this is not De Haldimar, but his servant Donellan. Neither has the latter met his death from your rifle; there is no mark of a bullet about him. It was an Indian tomahawk that did his business; and I will stake my head against a hickory nut the blow came from the same rascal at whom you fired, and who gave back the shot and the scalp halloo."

This opinion was unanimously expressed by the remainder of the officers. Sir Everard was almost as much overpowered by his joy, as he had previously been overwhelmed by his despair, and he grasped and shook the hand of Captain Erskine, who had thus been the means of relieving his conscience, with an energy of gratitude and feeling that almost drew tears from the eyes of that blunt but gallant officer.

"Thank God, thank God!" he fervently exclaimed: "I have not then even the death of poor Donellan to answer for;" and hastening from the guard-room, he pursued his course hurriedly and delightedly to the barrack-room of his friend.

Six

THE HOUR fixed for the trial of the prisoner Halloway
had now arrived, and the officers composing the court
were all met in the mess-room of the garrison, surrounding a long table covered with green cloth, over which were
distributed pens, ink, and paper for taking minutes of the
evidence, and such notes of the proceedings as the several
members might deem necessary in the course of the trial.
Captain Blessington presided; and next him, on either
hand, were the first in seniority, the two junior occupying
the lowest places. The demeanour of the several officers,
serious and befitting the duty they were met to perform,
was rendered more especially solemn from the presence
of the governor, who sat a little to the right of the president, and without the circle, remained covered, and with
his arms folded across his chest. At a signal given by the
president to the orderly in waiting, that individual disappeared from the room, and soon afterwards Frank Halloway, strongly ironed, as on the preceding night, was
ushered in by several files of the guard, under Ensign
Fortescue himself.

The prisoner having been stationed a few paces on the
left of the president, that officer stood up to administer the
customary oath. His example was followed by the rest of
the court, who now rose, and extending each his right
hand upon the prayer book, repeated, after the president,
the form of words prescribed by military law. They then,

after successively touching the sacred volume with their lips, once more resumed their seats at the table.

The prosecutor was the Adjutant Lawson, who now handed over to the president a paper, from which the latter officer read, in a clear and distinct voice, the following charges, viz. –

"1st. For having on the night of the —th September 1763, while on duty at the gate of the Fortress of Détroit, either admitted a stranger into the garrison himself, or suffered him to obtain admission, without giving the alarm, or using the means necessary to ensure his apprehension, such conduct being treasonable, and in breach of the articles of war.

"2d. For having been accessary to the abduction of Captain Frederick de Haldimar and private Harry Donellan, the disappearance of whom from the garrison can only be attributed to a secret understanding existing between the prisoner and the enemy without the walls, such conduct being treasonable, and in breach of the articles of war."

"Private Frank Halloway," continued Captain Blessington, after having perused these two short but important charges, "you have heard what has been preferred against you; what say you, therefore? Are you guilty, or not guilty?"

"Not guilty," firmly and somewhat exultingly replied the prisoner, laying his hand at the same time on his swelling heart.

"Stay, sir," sternly observed the governor, addressing the president; "you have not read *all* the charges."

Captain Blessington took up the paper from the table, on which he had carelessly thrown it, after reading the accusations above detailed, and perceived, for the first time, that a portion had been doubled back. His eye now glanced over a third charge, which had previously escaped his attention.

"Prisoner," he pursued, after the lapse of a minute,

"there is a third charge against you, viz. for having, on the night of the —th Sept. 1763, suffered Captain de Haldimar to unclose the gate of the fortress, and, accompanied by his servant, private Harry Donellan, to pass your post without the sanction of the governor, such conduct being in direct violation of a standing order of the garrison, and punishable with death."

The prisoner started. "What!" he exclaimed, his cheek paling for the first time with momentary apprehension; "is this voluntary confession of my own to be turned into a charge that threatens my life? Colonel de Haldimar, is the explanation which I gave you only this very hour, and in private, to be made the public instrument of my condemnation? Am I to die because I had not firmness to resist the prayer of my captain and of your son, Colonel de Haldimar?"

The president looked towards the governor, but a significant motion of the head was the only reply; he proceeded, -

"Prisoner Halloway, what plea you to this charge? Guilty, or not guilty?"

"I see plainly," said Halloway, after the pause of a minute, during which he appeared to be summoning all his energies to his aid; "I see plainly that it is useless to strive against my fate. Captain de Haldimar is not here, and I must die. Still I shall not have the disgrace of dying as a traitor, though I own I have violated the orders of the garrison."

"Prisoner," interrupted Captain Blessington, "whatever you may have to urge, you had better reserve for your defence. Meanwhile, what answer do you make to the last charge preferred? - Are you guilty, or not guilty?"

"Guilty," said Halloway, in a tone of mingled pride and sorrow, "guilty of having listened to the earnest prayer of my captain, and suffered him, in violation of my orders, to pass my post. Of the other charges I am innocent."

The court listened with the most profound attention and

interest to the words of the prisoner, and they glanced at
each other in a manner that marked their sense of the
truth they attached to his declaration.

"Halloway, prisoner," resumed Captain Blessington,
mildly, yet impressively; "recollect the severe penalty
which the third charge, no less than the others, entails,
and recall your admission. Be advised by me," he pursued,
observing his hesitation. "Withdraw your plea, then, and
substitute that of not guilty to the whole."

"Captain Blessington," returned the prisoner with deep
emotion, "I feel all the kindness of your motive; and if any
thing can console me in my present situation, it is the
circumstance of having presiding at my trial an officer so
universally beloved by the whole corps. Still," and again
his voice acquired its wonted firmness, and his cheek
glowed with honest pride, "still, I say, I scorn to retract my
words. Of the two first charges I am as innocent as the
babe unborn. To the last I plead guilty; and vain would it
be to say otherwise, since the gate was found open while I
was on duty, and I know the penalty attached to the disobedience of orders."

After some further but ineffectual remonstrance on the
part of the president, the pleas of the prisoner were recorded, and the examination commenced. Governor de
Haldimar was the first witness.

That officer, having been sworn, stated, that on the
preceding night he had been intruded upon in his apartment by a stranger, who could have obtained admission
only through the gate of the fortress, by which also he
must have made good his escape. That it was evident the
prisoner had been in correspondence with their enemies;
since, on proceeding to examine the gate it had been
found unlocked, while the confusion manifested by him
on being accused, satisfied all who were present of the
enormity of his guilt. Search had been made every where
for the keys, but without success.

The second charge was supported by presumptive evidence alone; for although the governor swore to the disap-

pearance of his son, and the murder of his servant, and dwelt emphatically on the fact of their having been forcibly carried off with the connivance of the prisoner, still there was no other proof of this, than the deductions drawn from the circumstances already detailed. To meet this difficulty, however, the third charge had been framed.

In proof of this the governor stated, that the prisoner, on being interrogated by him immediately subsequent to his being relieved from his post, had evinced such confusion and hesitation, as to leave no doubt whatever of his guilt; that, influenced by the half promise of communication, which the court had heard as well as himself, he had suffered the trial of the prisoner to be delayed until the present hour, strongly hoping he might then be induced to reveal the share he had borne in these unworthy and treasonable practices; that, with a view to obtain this disclosure, so essential to the safety of the garrison, he had, conjointly with Major Blackwater, visited the cell of the prisoner, to whom he related the fact of the murder of Donellan, in the disguise of his master's uniform, conjuring him, at the same time, if he regarded his own life, and the safety of those who were most dear to him, to give a clue to the solution of this mysterious circumstance, and disclose the nature and extent of his connection with the enemy without; that the prisoner however resolutely denied, as before, the guilt imputed to him, but having had time to concoct a plausible story, stated, (doubtless with a view to shield himself from the severe punishment he well knew to be attached to his offence,) that Captain de Haldimar himself had removed the keys from the guard-room, opened the gate of the fortress, and accompanied by his servant, dressed in a coloured coat, had sallied forth upon the common. And this, emphatically pursued the governor, the prisoner admits he permitted, although well aware that, by an order of long standing for the security of the garrison, such a flagrant dereliction of his duty subjected him to the punishment of death.

Major Blackwater was the next witness examined. His

testimony went to prove the fact of the gate having been found open, and the confusion manifested by the prisoner. It also substantiated that part of the governor's evidence on the third charge, which related to the confession recently made by Halloway, on which that charge had been framed.

The sergeant of the guard, and the governor's orderly having severally corroborated the first portions of Major Blackwater's evidence, the examination on the part of the prosecution terminated; when the president called on the prisoner Halloway for his defence. The latter, in a clear, firm, and collected tone, and in terms that surprised his auditory, thus addressed the Court: –

"Mr. President, and gentlemen, – Although standing before you in the capacity of a private soldier, and, oh! bitter and humiliating reflection, in that most wretched and disgraceful of all situations, a suspected traitor, I am not indeed what I seem to be. It is not for me here to enter into the history of my past life; neither will I tarnish the hitherto unsullied reputation of my family by disclosing my true name. Suffice it to observe, I am a gentleman by birth; and although, of late years, I have known all the hardships and privations attendant on my fallen fortunes, I was once used to bask in the luxuries of affluence, and to look upon those who now preside in judgment over me as my equals. A marriage of affection, – a marriage with one who had nothing but her own virtues and her own beauty to recommend her, drew upon me the displeasure of my family, and the little I possessed, independently of the pleasure of my relations, was soon dissipated. My proud soul scorned all thought of supplication to those who had originally spurned my wife from their presence; and yet my heart bled for the privations of her who, alike respectable in family, was, both from sex and the natural delicacy of her frame, so far less constituted to bear up against the frowns of adversity than myself. Our extremity had now become great, – too great for human endurance; when, through the medium of the public prints, I became ac-

quainted with the glorious action that had been fought in
this country by the army under General Wolfe. A new
light burst suddenly upon my mind, and visions of after
prosperity constantly presented themselves to my view.
The field of honour was open before me, and there was a
probability I might, by good conduct, so far merit the
approbation of my superiors, as to obtain, in course of
time, that rank among themselves to which by birth and
education I was so justly entitled to aspire. Without waiting to consult my Ellen, whose opposition I feared to
encounter until opposition would be fruitless, I hastened
to Lieutenant Walgrave, the recruiting officer of the regiment, – tendered my services, – was accepted and approved, – received the bounty money, – and became
definitively a soldier, under the assumed name of Frank
Halloway.

"It would be tedious and impertinent, gentlemen," resumed the prisoner, after a short pause, "to dwell on the
humiliations of spirit to which both my wife and myself
were subjected at our first introduction to our new associates, who, although invariably kind to us, were, never-
theless, ill suited, both by education and habit, to awaken
any thing like congeniality of feeling or similarity of pursuit. Still we endeavoured, as much as possible, to lessen
the distance that existed between us; and from the first
moment of our joining the regiment, determined to adopt
the phraseology and manners of those with whom an adverse destiny had so singularly connected us. In this we
succeeded; for no one, up to the present moment, has
imagined either my wife or myself to be other than the
simple and unpretending Frank and Ellen Halloway.

"On joining the regiment in this country," pursued the
prisoner, after another pause, marked by much emotion,
"I had the good fortune to be appointed to the grenadier
company. Gentlemen, you all know the amiable qualities
of Captain de Haldimar. But although, unlike yourselves, I
have learnt to admire that officer only at a distance, my
devotion to his interests has been proportioned to the

kindness with which I have ever been treated by him; and may I not add, after this avowal of my former condition, my most fervent desire has all along been to seize the first favourable opportunity of performing some action that would eventually elevate me to a position in which I might, without blushing for the absence of the ennobling qualities of birth and condition, avow myself his friend, and solicit that distinction from my equal which was partially extended to me by my superior? The opportunity I sought was not long wanting. At the memorable affair with the French general, Levi, at Quebec, in which our regiment bore so conspicuous a part, I had the good fortune to save the life of my captain. A band of Indians, as you all, gentlemen, must recollect, had approached our right flank unperceived, and while busily engaged with the French in front, we were compelled to divide our fire between them and our new and fierce assailants. The leader of that band was a French officer, who seemed particularly to direct his attempts against the life of Captain de Haldimar. He was a man of powerful proportions and gigantic stature —— "

"Hold!" said the governor, starting suddenly from the seat in which he had listened with evident impatience to this long outline of the prisoner's history. "Gentlemen," addressing the court, "that is the very stranger who was in my apartment last night, – the being with whom the prisoner is evidently in treacherous correspondence, and all this absurd tale is but a blind to deceive your judgment, and mitigate his own punishment. Who is there to prove the man he has just described was the same who aimed at Captain de Haldimar's life at Quebec?"

A flush of deep indignation overspread the features of the prisoner, whose high spirit, now he had avowed his true origin, could ill brook the affront thus put upon his veracity.

"Colonel de Haldimar!" he proudly replied, while his chains clanked with the energy and force with which he drew up his person into an attitude of striking dignity; "for once I sink the private soldier, and address you in the character of the gentleman and your equal. I have a soul, Sir, notwithstanding my fallen fortunes, as keenly alive to honour as your own; and not even to save my wretched life, would I be guilty of the baseness you now attribute to me. You have asked," he pursued, in a more solemn tone, "what proof I have to show this individual to be the same who attempted the life of Captain de Haldimar. To Captain de Haldimar himself, should Providence have spared his days, I shall leave the melancholy task of bearing witness to all I here advance, when I shall be no more. Nay, Sir," and his look partook at once of mingled scorn and despondency, "well do I know the fate that awaits me; for in these proceedings – in that third charge – I plainly read my death-warrant. But what, save my poor and wretched wife, have I to regret? Colonel de Haldimar," he continued, with a vehemence meant to check the growing weakness which the thought of his unfortunate companion called up to his heart, "I saved the life of your son, even by your own admission, no matter whose arm that threatened his existence; and in every other action in which I have been engaged, honourable mention has ever been made of my conduct. Now, Sir, I ask what has been my reward? So far from attending to the repeated recommendations of my captain for promotion, even in a subordinate rank, have you once deemed it necessary to acknowledge my services by even a recognition of them in any way whatever?"

"Mr. President, Captain Blessington," interrupted the governor, haughtily, "are we met here to listen to such language from a private soldier? You will do well, Sir, to exercise your prerogative, and stay such impertinent matter, which can have no reference whatever to the defence of the prisoner."

"Prisoner," resumed the president, who, as well as the other members of the court, had listened with the most profound and absorbing interest to the singular disclosure of him whom they still only knew as Frank Halloway, "this language cannot be permitted; you must confine yourself to your defence."

"Pardon me, gentlemen," returned Halloway, in his usual firm but respectful tone of voice; "pardon me, if, standing on the brink of the grave as I do, I have so far forgotten the rules of military discipline as to sink for a moment the soldier in the gentleman; but to be taxed with an unworthy fabrication, and to be treated with contumely when avowing the secret of my condition, was more than human pride and human feeling could tolerate."

"Confine yourself, prisoner, to your defence," again remarked Captain Blessington, perceiving the restlessness with which the governor listened to these bold and additional observations of Halloway.

Again the governor interposed: – "What possible connexion can there be between this man's life, and the crime with which he stands charged? Captain Blessington, this is trifling with the court, who are assembled to try the prisoner for his treason, and not to waste their time in listening to a history utterly foreign to the subject."

"The history of my past life – Colonel de Haldimar," proudly returned the prisoner, "although tedious and uninteresting to you, is of the utmost importance to myself; for on that do I ground the most essential part of my defence. There is nothing but circumstantial evidence against me on the two first charges; and as those alone can reflect dishonour on my memory, it is for the wisdom of this court to determine whether that evidence is to be credited in opposition to the solemn declaration of him, who, in admitting one charge, equally affecting his life with the others, repudiates as foul those only which would attaint his honour. Gentlemen," he pursued, addressing the court, "it is for you to determine whether my defence is to be continued or not; yet, whatever be my fate, I would fain remove all injurious impression from the minds of my judges; and this can only be done by a simple detail of circumstances, which may, by the unprejudiced, be as simply believed."

Here the prisoner paused: when, after some low and earnest conversation among the members of the court, two or three slips of written paper were passed to the President. He glanced his eye hurriedly over them, and then directed Halloway to proceed with his defence.

"I have stated," pursued the interesting soldier, "that the officer who led the band of Indians was a man of gigantic stature, and of apparently great strength. My attention was particularly directed to him from this circumstance, and as I was on the extreme flank of the grenadiers, and close to Captain de Haldimar, had every opportunity of observing his movements principally pointed at that officer. He first discharged a carbine, the ball of which killed a man of the company at his (Captain de Haldimar's) side; and then, with evident rage at having been defeated in his aim, he took a pistol from his belt, and advancing with rapid strides to within a few paces of his intended victim, presented it in the most deliberate manner. At that moment, gentlemen, (and it was but the work of a moment,) a thousand confused and almost inexplicable feelings rose to my heart. The occasion I had long sought was at length within my reach; but even the personal considerations, which had hitherto influenced my mind, were sunk in the anxious desire I entertained to preserve the life of an officer so universally beloved, and so every way worthy of the sacrifice. While yet the pistol remained levelled, I sprang before Captain de Haldimar, received the ball in my breast, and had just strength sufficient to fire my musket at this formidable enemy when I sank senseless to the earth.

"It will not be difficult for you, gentlemen, who have feeling minds, to understand the pleasurable pride with which, on being conveyed to Captain de Haldimar's own apartments in Quebec, I found myself almost overwhelmed by the touching marks of gratitude showered on me by his amiable relatives. Miss Clara de Haldimar, in particular, like a ministering angel, visited my couch of suffering at almost every hour, and always provided with some little delicacy, suitable to my condition, of which I had long since tutored myself to forget even the use. But what principally afforded me pleasure, was to remark the consolations which she tendered to my poor drooping Ellen, who, already more than half subdued by the melancholy change in our condition in life, frequently spent hours together in silent grief at the side of my couch, and watching every change in my countenance with all the intense anxiety of one who feels the last stay on earth is about to be severed for ever. Ah! how I then longed to disclose to this kind and compassionating being the true position of her on whom she lavished her attention, and to make her known, not as the inferior honored by her notice, but as the equal alike worthy of her friendship and deserving of her esteem; but the wide, wide barrier that divided the wife of the private soldier from the daughter and sister of the commissioned officer sealed my lips, and our true condition continued unrevealed.

"Gentlemen," resumed Halloway, after a short pause, "if I dwell on these circumstances, it is with a view to show how vile are the charges preferred against me. Is it likely, with all the incentives to good conduct I have named, I should have proved a traitor to my country? And, even if so, what to gain, I would ask; and by what means was a correspondence with the enemy to be maintained by one in my humble station? As for the second charge, how infamous, how injurious is it to my reputation, how unworthy to be entertained! From the moment of my recovery from that severe wound, every mark of favour that could be bestowed on persons in our situation had been extended to my wife and myself, by the family of Colonel de Haldimar; and my captain, knowing me merely as the simple and low born Frank Halloway, although still the preserver of his life, has been unceasing in his exertions to obtain such promotion as he thought my conduct generally, independently of my devotedness to his person, might claim. How these applications were met, gentlemen, I have already stated; but notwithstanding Colonel de

Haldimar has never deemed me worthy of the promotion solicited, that circumstance could in no way weaken my regard and attachment for him who had so often demanded it. How then, in the name of heaven, can a charge so improbable, so extravagant, as that of having been instrumental in the abduction of Captain de Haldimar, be entertained? and who is there among you, gentlemen, who will for one moment believe I could harbour a thought so absurd as that of lending myself to the destruction of one for whom I once cheerfully offered up the sacrifice of my blood? And now," pursued the prisoner, after another short pause, "I come to the third charge, – that charge which most affects my life, but impugns neither my honour nor my fidelity. That God, before whom I know I shall shortly appear, can attest the sincerity of my statement, and before him do I now solemnly declare what I am about to relate is true.

"Soon after the commencement of my watch last night, I heard a voice distinctly on the outside of the rampart, near my post, calling in a low and subdued tone on the name of Captain de Haldimar. The accents, hastily and anxiously uttered, were apparently those of a female. For a moment I continued irresolute how to act, and hesitated whether or not I should alarm the garrison; but, at length, presuming it was some young female of the village with whom my captain was acquainted, it occurred to me the most prudent course would be to apprize that officer himself. While I yet hesitated whether to leave my post for a moment for the purpose, a man crossed the parade a few yards in my front; it was Captain de Haldimar's servant, Donellan, then in the act of carrying some things from his master's apartment to the guard-room. I called to him, to say the sentinel at the gate wished to see the captain of the guard immediately. In the course of a few minutes he came up to my post, when I told him what I had heard. At that moment, the voice again repeated his name, when he abruptly left me and turned to the left of the gate, evidently on his way to the rampart. Soon afterwards I heard

Captain de Haldimar immediately above me, sharply calling out, 'Hist, hist!' as if the person on the outside, despairing of success, was in the act of retreating. A moment or two of silence succeeded, when a low conversation ensued between the parties. The distance was so great I could only distinguish inarticulate sounds; yet it seemed to me as if they spoke not in English, but in the language of the Ottawa Indians, a tongue with which, as you are well aware, gentlemen, Captain de Haldimar is familiar. This had continued about ten minutes, when I again heard footsteps hastily descending the rampart, and moving in the direction of the guard-house. Soon afterwards Captain de Haldimar re-appeared at my post, accompanied by his servant Donellan; the former had the keys of the gate in his hand, and he told me that he must pass to the skirt of the forest on some business of the last importance to the safety of the garrison.

"At first I peremptorily refused, stating the severe penalty attached to the infringement of an order, the observation of which had so especially been insisted upon by the governor, whose permission, however, I ventured respectfully to urge might, without difficulty, be obtained, if the business was really of the importance he described it. Captain de Haldimar, however, declared he well knew the governor would not accord that permission, unless he was positively acquainted with the nature and extent of the danger to be apprehended; and of these, he said, he was not himself sufficiently aware. All argument of this nature proving ineffectual, he attempted to enforce his authority, not only in his capacity of officer of the guard, but also as my captain, ordering me, on pain of confinement, not to interfere with or attempt to impede his departure. This, however, produced no better result; for I knew that, in this instance, I was amenable to the order of the governor alone, and I again firmly refused to violate my duty.

"Finding himself thwarted in his attempt to enforce my obedience, Captain de Haldimar, who seemed much agitated and annoyed by what he termed my obstinacy, now descended to entreaty; and in the name of that life which I had preserved to him, and of that deep gratitude which he had ever since borne to me, conjured me not to prevent his departure. 'Halloway,' he urged, 'your life, my life, my father's life, – the life of my sister Clara perhaps, who nursed you in illness, and who has ever treated your wife with attention and kindness, – all these depend upon your compliance with my request. Hear me,' he pursued, following up the impression which he clearly perceived he had produced in me by this singular and touching language: 'I promise to be back within the hour; there is no danger attending my departure, and here will I be before you are relieved from your post; no one can know I have been absent, and your secret will remain with Donellan and myself. Do you think,' he concluded, 'I would encourage a soldier of my regiment to disobey a standing order of the garrison, unless there was some very extraordinary reason for my so doing? But there is no time to be lost in parley. Halloway! I entreat you to offer no further opposition to my departure. I pledge myself to be back before you are relieved.'

"Gentlemen," impressively continued the prisoner, after a pause, during which each member of the court seemed to breathe for the first time, so deeply had the attention of all been riveted by the latter part of this singular declaration, "how, under these circumstances, could I be expected to act? Assured by Captain de Haldimar, in the most solemn manner, that the existence of those most dear to his heart hung on my compliance with his request, how could I refuse to him, whose life I had saved, and whose character I so much esteemed, a boon so earnestly, nay, so imploringly solicited? I acceded to his prayer, intimating, at the same time, if he returned not before another sentinel should relieve me, the discovery of my breach of duty must be made, and my punishment inevitable. His last words, however, were to assure me he should return at the hour he had named, and when I closed the gate upon him it was under the firm impression his absence would only prove of the temporary nature he had stated. – Gentlemen," abruptly concluded Halloway, "I have nothing further to add; if I have failed in my duty as a soldier, I have, at least, fulfilled that of a man; and although the violation of the first entail upon me the punishment of death, the motives which impelled me to that violation will not, I trust, be utterly lost sight of by those by whom my punishment is to be awarded."

The candid, fearless, and manly tone in which Halloway had delivered this long and singular statement, however little the governor appeared to be affected by it, evidently made a deep impression on the court, who had listened with undiverted attention to the close. Some conversation again ensued, in a low tone, among several members, when two slips of written paper were passed up, as before, to the president. These elicited the following interrogatories: –

"You have stated, prisoner, that Captain de Haldimar left the fort accompanied by his servant Donellan. How were they respectively dressed?"

"Captain de Haldimar in his uniform; Donellan, as far as I could observe, in his regimental clothing also, with this difference, that he wore his servant's round glazed hat and his grey great coat.".

"How then do you account for the extraordinary circumstance of Donellan having been found murdered in his master's clothes? Was any allusion made to a change of dress before they left the fort?"

"Not the slightest," returned the prisoner; "nor can I in any way account for this mysterious fact. When they quitted the garrison, each wore the dress I have described."

"In what manner did Captain de Haldimar and Donellan effect their passage across the ditch?" continued the president, after glancing at the second slip of paper. "The draw-bridge was evidently not lowered, and there were no other means at hand to enable him to effect his object with promptitude. How do you explain this, prisoner?"

When this question was put, the whole body of officers, and the governor especially, turned their eyes simultaneously on Halloway, for on his hesitation or promptness in replying seemed to attach much of the credit they were disposed to accord his statement. Halloway observed it, and coloured. His reply, however, was free, unfaltering, and unstudied.

"A rope with which Donellan had provided himself, was secured to one of the iron hooks that support the pullies immediately above the gate. With this they swung themselves in succession to the opposite bank."

The members of the court looked at each other, apparently glad that an answer so confirmatory of the truth of the prisoner's statement, had been thus readily given.

"Were they to have returned in the same manner?" pursued the president, framing his interrogatory from the contents of another slip of paper, which, at the suggestion of the governor, had been passed to him by the prosecutor, Mr. Lawson.

"They were," firmly replied the prisoner. "At least I presumed they were, for, I believe in the hurry of Captain de Haldimar's departure, he never once made any direct allusion to the manner of his return; nor did it occur to me until this moment how they were to regain possession of the rope, without assistance from within."

"Of course," observed Colonel de Haldimar, addressing the president, "the rope still remains. Mr. Lawson, examine the gate, and report accordingly."

The adjutant hastened to acquit himself of this laconic order, and soon afterwards returned, stating not only that there was no rope, but that the hook alluded to had disappeared altogether.

For a moment the cheek of the prisoner paled; but it was evidently less from any fear connected with his individual existence, than from the shame he felt at having been detected in a supposed falsehood. He however speedily recovered his self-possession, and exhibited the same character of unconcern by which his general bearing throughout the trial had been distinguished.

On this announcement of the adjutant, the governor

betrayed a movement of impatience, that was meant to convey his utter disbelief of the whole of the prisoner's statement, and his look seemed to express to the court it should also arrive, and without hesitation, at the same conclusion. Even all authoritative as he was, however, he felt that military etiquette and strict discipline prevented his interfering further in this advanced state of the proceedings.

"Prisoner," again remarked Captain Blessington, "your statement in regard to the means employed by Captain de Haldimar in effecting his departure, is, you must admit, unsupported by appearances. How happens it the rope is no longer where you say it was placed? No one could have removed it but yourself. Have you done so? and if so, can you produce it, or say where it is to be found?"

"Captain Blessington," replied Halloway, proudly, yet respectfully, "I have already invoked that great Being, before whose tribunal I am so shortly to appear, in testimony of the truth of my assertion; and again, in his presence, do I repeat, every word I have uttered is true. I did not remove the rope, neither do I know what is become of it. I admit its disappearance is extraordinary, but a moment's reflection must satisfy the court I would not have devised a tale, the falsehood of which could at once have been detected on an examination such as that which has just been instituted. When Mr. Lawson left this room just now, I fully expected he would have found the rope lying as it had been left. What has become of it, I repeat, I know not; but in the manner I have stated did Captain de Haldimar and Donellan cross the ditch. I have nothing further to add," he concluded once more, drawing up his fine tall person, the native elegance of which could not be wholly disguised even in the dress of a private soldier; "nothing further to disclose. Yet do I repel with scorn the injurious insinuation against my fidelity, suggested in these doubts. I am prepared to meet my death as best may become a soldier, and, let me add, as best may become a proud and well born gentleman; but humanity and common justice should at least be accorded to my memory. I am an unfortunate man, but no traitor."

The members were visibly impressed by the last sentences of the prisoner. No further question however was asked, and he was again removed by the escort, who had been wondering spectators of the scene, to the cell he had so recently occupied. The room was then cleared of the witnesses and strangers, the latter comprising nearly the whole of the officers off duty, when the court proceeded to deliberate on the evidence, and pass sentence on the accused.

Seven

ALTHOUGH the young and sensitive De Haldimar had found physical relief in the summary means resorted to by the surgeon, the moral wound at his heart not only remained unsoothed, but was rendered more acutely painful by the wretched reflections, which, now that he had full leisure to review the past, and anticipate the future in all the gloom attached to both, so violently assailed him. From the moment when his brother's strange and mysterious disappearance had been communicated by the adjutant in the manner we have already seen, his spirits had been deeply and fearfully depressed. Still he had every reason to expect, from the well-known character of Halloway, the strong hope expressed by the latter might be realised; and that, at the hour appointed for trial, his brother would be present to explain the cause of his mysterious absence, justify the conduct of his subordinate, and exonerate him from the treachery with which he now stood charged. Yet, powerful as this hope was, it was unavoidably qualified by dispiriting doubt; for a nature affectionate and bland, as that of Charles de Haldimar, could not but harbour distrust, while a shadow of uncertainty, in regard to the fate of a brother so tenderly loved, remained. He had forced himself to believe as much as possible what he wished, and the effort had, to a certain extent succeeded; but there had been something so solemn and so impressive in the scene that had passed when the prisoner was first brought up for trial, something so fearfully prophetic in the wild language of his unhappy wife, he had found it impossible to resist the influence of the almost superstitious awe they had awakened in his heart.

What the feelings of the young officer were subsequently, when in the person of the murdered man on the common, the victim of Sir Everard Valletort's aim, he recognised that brother, whose disappearance had occasioned him so much inquietude, we shall not attempt to describe: their nature is best shown in the effect they produced – the almost overwhelming agony of body and mind, which had borne him, like a stricken plant, unresisting to the earth. But now that, in the calm and solitude of his chamber, he had leisure to review the fearful events conspiring to produce this extremity, his anguish of spirit was even deeper than when the first rude shock of conviction had flashed upon his understanding. A tide of suffering, that overpowered, without rendering him sensible of its positive and abstract character, had, in the first instance, oppressed his faculties, and obscured his perception; but now, slow, sure, stinging, and gradually succeeding each other, came every bitter thought and reflection of which that tide was composed; and the generous heart of Charles de Haldimar was a prey to feelings that would have wrung the soul, and wounded the sensibilities of one far less gentle and susceptible than himself.

Between Sir Everard Valletort and Charles de Haldimar, who, it has already been remarked, were lieutenants in Captain Blessington's company, a sentiment of friendship had been suffered to spring up almost from the moment of Sir Everard's joining. The young men were nearly of the same age; and although the one was all gentleness, the other all spirit and vivacity, not a shade of disunion had at any period intervened to interrupt the almost brotherly attachment subsisting between them, and each felt the disposition of the other was the one most assimilated to his own. In fact, Sir Everard was far from being the ephemeral character he was often willing to appear. Under a semblance of affectation, and much assumed levity of manner, never, however, personally offensive, he concealed a brave, generous, warm, and manly heart, and talents becoming the rank he held in society, such as would not have reflected discredit on one numbering twice his years. He had entered the army, as most young men of rank usually did at that period, rather for the *agrémens* it held forth, than with any serious view to advancement in it as a profession. Still he entertained the praiseworthy desire of being something more than what is, among military men, emphatically termed a feather-bed soldier; and, contrary to the wishes of his fashionable mother, who would have preferred seeing him exhibit his uniform in the drawing-rooms of London, had purchased the step into his present corps from a cavalry regiment at home. Not that we mean, however, to assert he was not a feather-bed soldier in its more literal sense: no man that ever glittered in gold and scarlet was fonder of a feather-bed than the young baronet; and, in fact, his own observations, recorded in the early part of this volume, sufficiently prove his predilection for an indulgence which, we take it, in no way impugned his character as a soldier. Sir Everard would have fought twenty battles in the course of the month, if necessary, and yet not complained of the fatigue or severity of his service, provided only he had been suffered to press his downy couch to what is termed a decent hour in the day. But he had an innate and, perhaps, it may be, an instinctive horror of drills and early rising; a pastime in which the martinets and disciplinarians of the last century were very much given to indulge. He frequently upheld an opinion that must have been little less than treason in the eyes of a commander so strict as Colonel de Haldimar, that an officer who rose at eight, with all his faculties refreshed and invigorated, might evince as much of the true bearing of the soldier in the field, as he who, having quitted his couch at dawn, naturally felt the necessity of repose at a moment when activity and exertion were most required.

We need scarcely state, Sir Everard's theories on this important subject were seldom reduced to practice; for, even long before the Indians had broken out into open acts of hostility, when such precautions were rendered indispensable, Colonel de Haldimar had never suffered either officer or man to linger on his pillow after the first faint dawn had appeared. This was a system to which Sir Everard could never reconcile himself. He had quitted England with a view to active service abroad, it is true, but he had never taken "active service" in its present literal sense, and, as he frequently declared to his companions, he preferred giving an Indian warrior a chance for his scalp any hour after breakfast, to rising at daybreak, when, from very stupefaction, he seldom knew whether he stood on his head or his heels. "If the men must be drilled," he urged, "with a view to their health and discipline, why not place them under the direction of the adjutant or the officer of the day, whoever he might chance to be, and not unnecessarily disturb a body of gentlemen from their comfortable slumbers at that unconscionable hour?" Poor Sir Everard! this was the only grievance of which he complained, and he complained bitterly. Scarcely a morning passed without his inveighing loudly against the barbarity of such a custom; threatening at the same time, amid the laughter of his companions, to quit the service in disgust at what he called so ungentlemanly and gothic a habit. All he waited for, he protested, was to have an opportunity of bearing away the spoils of some Indian chief, that, on his return to England, he might afford his lady mother an opportunity of judging with her own eyes of the sort of enemy he had relinquished the comforts of home to contend against, and exhibiting to her very dear friends the barbarous proofs of the prowess of her son. Though these observations were usually made half in jest half in earnest, there was no reason to doubt the young and lively baronet was, in truth, heartily tired of a service which seemed to offer nothing but privations and annoyances, unmixed with even the chances of obtaining those trophies to which he alluded; and, but for two motives, there is every probability he would have seriously availed himself of the earliest opportunity of retiring. The first of these was his growing friendship for the amiable and gentle Charles de Haldimar; the second the secret, and scarcely to himself acknowledged, interest which had been created in his heart for his sister Clara; whom he only knew from the glowing descriptions of his friend, and the strong resemblance she was said to bear to him by the other officers.

Clara de Haldimar was the constant theme of her younger brother's praise. Her image was ever uppermost in his thoughts – her name ever hovering on his lips; and when alone with his friend Valletort, it was his delight to dwell on the worth and accomplishments of his amiable and beloved sister. Then, indeed, would his usually calm blue eye sparkle with the animation of his subject, while his colouring cheek marked all the warmth and sincerity with which he bore attestation to her gentleness and her goodness. The heart of Charles de Haldimar, soldier as he was, was pure, generous, and unsophisticated as that of the sister whom he so constantly eulogized; and, while listening to his eloquent praises, Sir Everard learnt to feel an interest in a being whom all had declared to be the counterpart of her brother, as well in personal attraction as in singleness of nature. With all his affected levity, and notwithstanding his early initiation into fashionable life – that matter-of-fact life which strikes at the existence of our earlier and dearer illusions – there was a dash of romance in the character of the young baronet which tended much to increase the pleasure he always took in the warm descriptions of his friend. The very circumstance of her being personally unknown to him, was, with Sir Everard, an additional motive for interest in Miss de Haldimar.

Imagination and mystery generally work their way together; and as there was a shade of mystery attached to Sir Everard's very ignorance of the person of one whom he admired and esteemed from report alone, imagination was not slow to improve the opportunity, and to endow the object with characteristics, which perhaps a more intimate knowledge of the party might have led him to qualify. In this manner, in early youth, are the silken and willing fetters of the generous and the enthusiastic forged. We invest some object, whose praises, whispered secretly in the ear, have glided imperceptibly to the heart, with all the attributes supplied by our own vivid and readily according imaginations; and so accustomed do we become to linger on the picture, we adore the semblance with an ardour which the original often fails to excite. When, however, the high standard of our fancy's fair creation is attained, we worship as something sacred that which was to our hearts a source of pure and absorbing interest, hallowed by the very secresy in which such interest was indulged. Even where it fails, so unwilling are we to lose sight of the illusion to which our thoughts have fondly clung, so loth to destroy the identity of the semblance with its original, that we throw a veil over that reason which is then so little in unison with our wishes, and forgive much in consideration of the very mystery which first gave a direction to our interest, and subsequently chained our preference. How is it to be lamented, that illusions so dear, and images so fanciful, should find their level with time; or that intercourse with the world, which should be the means rather of promoting than marring human happiness, should leave on the heart so little vestige of those impressions which characterize the fervency of youth; and which, dispassionately considered, constitute the only true felicity of riper life! It is then that man, in all the vigour and capacity of his intellectual nature, feels the sentiment of love upon him in all its ennobling force. It is then that his impetuous feelings, untinged by the romance which imposes its check upon the more youthful, like the wild flow of the mighty torrent, seeks a channel wherein they may empty themselves; and were he to follow the guidance of those feelings, of which in that riper life he seems ashamed as of a weakness unworthy his sex, in the warm and glowing bosom of Nature's divinity – *woman* – would he pour forth the swollen tide of his affection; and acknowledge, in the fulness of his expanding heart, the vast bounty of Providence, who had bestowed on him so invaluable – so unspeakably invaluable, a blessing. – But no; in the pursuit of ambition, in the acquisition of wealth, in the thirst after power, and the craving after distinction, nay, nineteen times out of twenty, in the most frivolous occupations, the most unsatisfactory amusements, do the great mass of the maturer man sink those feelings; divested of which, we become mere plodders on the earth, mere creatures of materialism: nor is it until after age and infirmity have overtaken them, they look back with regret to that real and substantial, but unenjoyed happiness, which the occupied heart and the soul's communion alone can bestow. Then indeed, when too late, are they ready to acknowledge the futility of those pursuits, the inadequacy of those mere ephemeral pleasures, to which in the full meridian of their manhood they sacrificed, as a thing unworthy of their dignity, the mysterious charm of woman's influence and woman's beauty.

We do not mean to say Clara de Haldimar would have fallen short of the high estimate formed of her worth by the friend of her brother; neither is it to be understood, Sir Everard suffered this fair vision of his fancy to lead him into the wild and labyrinthian paths of boyish romance; but certain it is, the floating illusions, conjured up by his imagination, exercised a mysterious influence over his heart, that hourly acquired a deeper and less equivocal character. It might have been curiosity in the first instance, or that mere repose of the fancy upon an object of its own creation, which was natural to a young man placed like himself for the moment out of the pale of all female society. It has been remarked, and justly, there is nothing so dangerous to the peace of the human heart as solitude. It is in solitude, our thoughts, taking their colouring from our feelings, invest themselves with the power of multiplying ideal beauty, until we become in a measure tenants of a world of our own creation, from which we never descend, without loathing and disgust, into the dull and matter-of-fact routine of actual existence. Hence the misery of the imaginative man! – hence his little sympathy with the mass, who, tame and soulless, look upon life and the things of life, not through the refining medium of ideality, but through the grossly magnifying optics of mere sense and materialism.

But, though we could, and perhaps may, at some future period, write volumes on this subject, we return for the present from a digression into which we have been insensibly led by the temporary excitement of our own feelings.

Whatever were the impressions of the young baronet, and however he might have been inclined to suffer the fair image of the gentle Clara, such as he was perhaps wont to paint it, to exercise its spell upon his fancy, certain it is, he never expressed to her brother more than that esteem and interest which it was but natural he should accord to the sister of his friend. Neither had Charles de Haldimar, even amid all his warmth of commendation, ever made the slightest allusion to his sister, that could be construed into a desire she should awaken any unusual or extraordinary sentiment of preference. Much and fervently as he desired such an event, there was an innate sense of decorum, and it may be secret pride, that caused him to abstain from any observation having the remotest tendency to compromise the spotless delicacy of his adored sister; and such he would have considered any expression of his own hopes and wishes, where no declaration of preference had been previously made. There was another motive for this reserve on the part of the younger officer. The baronet was an only child, and would, on attaining his majority, of which he wanted only a few months, become the possessor of a large fortune. His sister Clara, on the contrary, had little beyond her own fair fame and the beauty transmitted to her by the mother she had lost. Colonel de Haldimar was a younger son, and had made his way through life with his sword, and an unblemished reputation alone, – advantages he had shared with his children, for the two eldest of whom his interest and long services had procured commissions in his own regiment.

But even while Charles de Haldimar abstained from all expression of his hopes, he had fully made up his mind that Sir Everard and his sister were so formed for each other, it was next to an impossibility they could meet without loving. In one of his letters to the latter, he had alluded to his friend in terms of so high and earnest panegyric, that Clara had acknowledged, in reply, she was prepared to find in the young baronet one whom she should regard with partiality, if it were only on account of the friendship subsisting between him and her brother. This admission, however, was communicated in confidence, and the young officer had religiously preserved his sister's secret.

These and fifty other recollections now crowded on the mind of the sufferer, only to render the intensity of his anguish more complete; among the bitterest of which was the certainty that the mysterious events of the past night had raised up an insuperable barrier to this union; for how could Clara de Haldimar become the wife of him whose hands were, however innocently, stained with the life-blood of her brother! To dwell on this, and the loss of that brother, was little short of madness, and yet De Haldimar could think of nothing else; nor for a period could the loud booming of the cannon from the ramparts, every report of which shook his chamber to its very foundations, call off his attention from a subject which, while it pained, engrossed every faculty and absorbed every thought. At length, towards the close, he called faintly to the old and faithful soldier, who, at the foot of the bed, stood watching every change of his master's countenance, to know the cause of the cannonade. On being informed the batteries in the rear were covering the retreat of Captain Erskine, who, in his attempt to obtain the body, had been surprised by the Indians, a new direction was temporarily given to his thoughts, and he now manifested the utmost impatience to know the result.

In a few minutes Morrison, who, in defiance of the surgeon's strict order not on any account to quit the room, had flown to obtain some intelligence which he trusted might remove the anxiety of his suffering master, again made his appearance, stating the corpse was already secured, and close under the guns of the fort, beneath which the detachment, though hotly assailed from the forest, were also fast retreating.

"And is it really my brother, Morrison? Are you quite certain that it is Captain de Haldimar?" asked the young officer, in the eager accents of one who, with the fullest conviction on his mind, yet grasps at the faintest shadow of a consoling doubt. "Tell me that it is *not* my brother, and half of what I possess in the world shall be yours."

The old soldier brushed a tear from his eye. "God bless you, Mr. de Haldimar, I would give half my grey hairs to be able to do so; but it is, indeed, too truly the captain who has been killed. I saw the very wings of his regimentals as he lay on his face on the litter."

Charles de Haldimar groaned aloud. "Oh God! oh God! would I had never lived to see this day." Then springing suddenly up in his bed. – "Morrison, where are my clothes? I insist on seeing my slaughtered brother myself."

"Good Heaven, sir, consider," said the old man approaching the bed, and attempting to replace the covering which had been spurned to its very foot, – "consider you are in a burning fever, and the slightest cold may kill you altogether. The doctor's orders are, you were on no account to get up."

The effort made by the unfortunate youth was momentary. Faint from the blood he had lost, and giddy from the excitement of his feelings, he sank back exhausted on his pillow, and wept like a child.

Old Morrison shed tears also; for his heart bled for the

sufferings of one whom he had nursed and played with even in early infancy, and whom, although his master, he regarded with the affection he would have borne to his own child. As he had justly observed, he would have willingly given half his remaining years to be able to remove the source of the sorrow which so deeply oppressed him.

When this violent paroxysm had somewhat subsided, De Haldimar became more composed; but his was rather that composure which grows out of the apathy produced by overwhelming grief, than the result of any relief afforded to his suffering heart by the tears he had shed. He had continued some time in this faint and apparently tranquil state, when confused sounds in the barrack-yard, followed by the raising of the heavy drawbridge, announced the return of the detachment. Again he started up in his bed and demanded his clothes, declaring his intention to go out and receive the corpse of his murdered brother. All opposition on the part of the faithful Morrison was now likely to prove fruitless, when suddenly the door opened and an officer burst hurriedly into the room.

"Courage! courage! my dear De Haldimar; I am the bearer of good news. Your brother is not the person who has been slain."

Again De Haldimar sank back upon his pillow, overcome by a variety of conflicting emotions. A moment afterwards, and he exclaimed reproachfully, yet almost gasping with the eagerness of his manner, –

"For God's sake, Sumners – in the name of common humanity, do not trifle with my feelings. If you would seek to lull me with false hopes, you are wrong. I am prepared to hear and bear the worst at present; but to be undeceived again would break my heart."

"I swear to you by every thing I have been taught to revere as sacred," solemnly returned Ensign Sumners, deeply touched by the affliction he witnessed, "what I state is strictly true. Captain Erskine himself sent me to tell you."

"What, is he only wounded then?" and a glow of

mingled hope and satisfaction was visible even through the flush of previous excitement on the cheek of the sufferer. "Quick, Morrison, give me my clothes. – Where is my brother, Sumners?" and again he raised up his debilitated frame with the intention of quitting his couch.

"De Haldimar, my dear De Haldimar, compose yourself, and listen to me. Your brother is still missing, and we are as much in the dark about his fate as ever. All that is certain is, we have no positive knowledge of his death; but surely that is a thousand times preferable to the horrid apprehensions under which we have all hitherto laboured."

"What mean you, Sumners? or am I so bewildered by my sufferings as not to comprehend you clearly? – Nay, nay, forgive me; but I am almost heart-broken at this loss, and scarcely know what I say. But what is it you mean? I saw my unhappy brother lying on the common with my own eyes. Poor Valletort himself – " here a rush of bitter recollections flashed on the memory of the young man, and the tears coursed each other rapidly down his cheek. His emotion lasted for a few moments, and he pursued, – "Poor Valletort himself saw him, for he was nearly as much overwhelmed with affliction as I was; and even Morrison beheld him also, not ten minutes since, under the very walls of the fort; nay, distinguished the wings of his uniform: and yet you would persuade me my brother, instead of being brought in a corpse, is still missing and alive. This is little better than trifling with my wretchedness, Sumners," and again he sank back exhausted on his pillow.

"I can easily forgive your doubts, De Haldimar," returned the sympathizing Sumners, taking the hand of his companion, and pressing it gently in his own; "for, in truth, there is a great deal of mystery attached to the whole affair. I have not seen the body myself; but I distinctly heard Captain Erskine state it certainly was not your brother, and he requested me to apprise both Sir Everard Valletort and yourself of the fact."

"Who is the murdered man, then? and how comes he to be clad in the uniform of one of our officers? Pshaw! it is too absurd to be credited. Erskine is mistaken – he must be mistaken – it can be no other than my poor brother Frederick. Sumners, I am sick, faint, with this cruel uncertainty: go, my dear fellow, at once, and examine the body; then return to me, and satisfy my doubts, if possible."

"Most willingly, if you desire it," returned Sumners, moving towards the door; "but believe me, De Haldimar, you may make your mind tranquil on the subject – Erskine spoke with certainty."

"Have you seen Valletort?" asked De Haldimar, while an involuntary shudder pervaded his frame.

"I have. He flew on the instant to make further enquiries; and was in the act of going to examine the body of the murdered man when I came here. – But here he is himself, and his countenance is the harbinger of any thing but a denial of my intelligence."

"Oh, Charles, what a weight of misery has been removed from my heart!" exclaimed that officer, now rushing to the bedside of his friend, and seizing his extended hand, – "Your brother, let us hope, still lives."

"Almighty God, I thank thee!" fervently ejaculated De Haldimar; and then, overcome with joy, surprise, and gratitude, he again sank back upon his pillow, sobbing and weeping violently.

Sumners had, with delicate tact, retired the moment Sir Everard made his appearance; for he, as well as the whole body of officers, was aware of the close friendship that subsisted between the young men, and he felt, at such a moment, the presence of a third person must be a sort of violation of the sacredness of their interview.

For some minutes the young baronet stood watching in silence, and with his friend's hand closely clasped in his own, the course of those tears which seemed to afford so much relief to the overcharged heart of the sufferer. At length they passed gradually away; and a smile, expressive of the altered state of his feelings, for the first time animated the flushed but handsome features of the younger De Haldimar.

We shall not attempt to paint all that passed between the friends during the first interesting moments of an interview which neither had expected to enjoy again, or the delight and satisfaction with which they congratulated themselves on the futility of those fears, which, if realised, must have embittered every future moment of their lives with the most harrowing recollections. Sir Everard, particularly, felt, and was not slow to express, his joy on this occasion; for, as he gazed upon the countenance of his friend, he was more than ever inclined to confess an interest in the sister he was said so much to resemble.

With that facility with which in youth the generous and susceptible are prone to exchange their tears for smiles, as some powerful motive for the reaction may prompt, the invalid had already, and for the moment, lost sight of the painful past in the pleasurable present, so that his actual excitement was strongly in contrast with the melancholy he had so recently exhibited. Never had Charles de Haldimar appeared so eminently handsome; and yet his beauty resembled that of a frail and delicate woman, rather than that of one called to the manly and arduous profession of a soldier. It was that delicate and Medor-like beauty which might have won the heart and fascinated the sense of a second Angelica. The light brown hair flowing in thick and natural waves over a high white forehead; the rich bloom of the transparent and downy cheek; the large, blue, long, dark-lashed eye, in which a shade of languor harmonised with the soft but animated expression of the whole countenance, – the dimpled mouth, – the small, clear, and even teeth, – all these now characterised Charles de Haldimar; and if to these we add a voice rich, full, and melodious, and a smile sweet and fascinating, we shall be at no loss to account for the readiness with which Sir Everard suffered his imagination to draw on the brother for those attributes he ascribed to the sister.

It was while this impression was strong upon his fancy,

he took occasion to remark, in reply to an observation of De Haldimar's, alluding to the despair with which his sister would have been seized, had she known one brother had fallen by the hand of the friend of the other.

"The grief of my own heart, Charles, on this occasion, would have been little inferior to her own. The truth is, my feelings during the last three hours have let me into a secret, of the existence of which I was, in a great degree, ignorant until then: I scarcely know how to express myself, for the communication is so truly absurd and romantic you will not credit it." He paused, hesitated, and then, as if determined to anticipate the ridicule he seemed to feel would be attached to his confession, with a forced half laugh pursued: "The fact is, Charles, I have been so much used to listen to your warm and eloquent praises of your sister, I have absolutely, I will not say fallen in love with (that would be going too far), but conceived so strong an interest in her, that my most ardent desire would be to find favour in her eyes. What say you, my friend? are you inclined to forward my suit; and if so, is there any chance for me, think you, with herself?"

The breast of Charles de Haldimar, who had listened with deep and increasing attention to this avowal, swelled high with pleasurable excitement, and raising himself up in his bed with one hand, while he grasped one of Sir Everard's with the other, he exclaimed with a transport of affection too forcible to be controlled, –

"Oh, Valletort, Valletort! this is, indeed, all that was wanting to complete my happiness. My sister Clara I adore with all the affection of my nature; I love her better than my own life, which is wrapped up in hers. She is an angel in disposition, – all that is dear, tender, and affectionate, – all that is gentle and lovely in woman; one whose welfare is dearer far to me than my own, and without whose presence I could not live. Valletort, that prize, – that treasure, that dearer half of myself, is yours, – yours for ever. I have long wished you should love each other, and I felt, when you met, you would. If I have hitherto forborne from expressing this fondest wish of my heart, it has been from delicacy – from a natural fear of compromising the purity of my adored Clara. Now, however, you have confessed yourself interested, by a description that falls far short of the true merit of that dear girl, I can no longer disguise my gratification and delight. Valletort," he concluded, impressively, "there is no other man on earth to whom I would say so much; but you were formed for each other, and you will, you must, be the husband of my sister."

If the youthful and affectionate De Haldimar was happy, Sir Everard was no less so; for already, with the enthusiasm of a young man of twenty, he painted to himself the entire fruition of those dreams of happiness that had so long been familiarised to his imagination. One doubt alone crossed his mind.

"But if your sister should have decided differently, Charles," he at length remarked, as he gently quitted the embrace of his friend: "who knows if her heart may not already throb for another; and even if not, it is possible she may judge me far less flatteringly than you do."

"Valletort, your fears are groundless. Having admitted thus far, I will even go farther, and add, you have been the subject of one of my letters to Clara, who, in her turn, 'confesses a strong interest in one of whom she has heard so much.' She writes playfully, of course, but it is quite evident to me she is prepared to like you."

"Indeed! But, Charles, liking is many degrees removed you know from loving; besides, I understand there are two or three handsome and accomplished fellows among the garrison of Michillimackinac, and your sister's visit to her cousin may not have been paid altogether with impunity."

"Think not thus meanly of Clara's understanding, Valletort. There must be something more than mere beauty and accomplishment to fix the heart of my sister. The dark eyed and elegant Baynton, and the musical and sonnetteering Middleton, to whom you, doubtless, allude, are very excellent fellows in their way; but handsome and accomplished as they are, they are not exactly the men to please Clara de Haldimar."

"But, my dear Charles, you forget also any little merit of my own is doubly enhanced in your eyes, by the sincerity of the friendship subsisting between us; your sister may think very differently."

"Psha, Valletort! these difficulties are all of your own creation," returned his friend, impatiently; "I know the heart of Clara is disengaged. What would you more?"

"Enough, De Haldimar; I will no longer doubt my own prospects. If she but approve me, my whole life shall be devoted to the happiness of your sister."

A single knock was now heard at the door of the apartment; it was opened, and a sergeant appeared at the entrance.

"The company are under arms for punishment parade, Lieutenant Valletort," said the man, touching his cap.

In an instant, the visionary prospects of the young men gave place to the stern realities connected with that announcement of punishment. The treason of Halloway, – the absence of Frederick de Haldimar, – the dangers by which they were beset, – and the little present probability of a re-union with those who were most dear to them, – all these recollections now flashed across their minds with the rapidity of thought; and the conversation that had so recently passed between them seemed to leave no other impression than what is produced from some visionary speculation of the moment.

Eight

A S THE BELLS of the fort tolled the tenth hour of morning, the groups of dispersed soldiery, warned by the rolling of the assembly drum, once more fell into their respective ranks in the order described in the opening of this volume. Soon afterwards the prisoner Halloway was re-conducted into the square by a strong escort, who took their stations as before in the immediate centre, where the former stood principally conspicuous to the observation of his comrades. His countenance was paler, and had less, perhaps, of the indifference he had previously manifested; but to supply this there was a certain subdued air of calm dignity, and a composure that sprang, doubtless, from the consciousness of the new character in which he now appeared before his superiors. Colonel de Haldimar almost immediately followed, and with him were the principal staff of the garrison, all of whom, with the exception of the sick and wounded and their attendants, were present to a man. The former took from the hands of the adjutant, Lawson, a large packet, consisting of several sheets of folded paper closely written upon. These were the proceedings of the court martial.

After enumerating the several charges, and detailing the evidence of the witnesses examined, the governor came at length to the finding and sentence of the court, which were as follows: –

"The court having duly considered the evidence adduced

against the prisoner private Frank Halloway, together with what he has urged in his defence, are of opinion, –

"That with regard to the first charge, it is not proved.

"That with regard to the second charge, it is not proved.

"That with regard to the third charge, even by his own voluntary confession, the prisoner is guilty.

"The court having found the prisoner private Frank Halloway guilty of the third charge preferred against him, which is in direct violation of a standing order of the garrison, entailing capital punishment, do hereby sentence him, the said prisoner, private Frank Halloway, to be shot to death at such time and place as the officer commanding may deem fit to appoint."

Although the utmost order pervaded the ranks, every breath had been suspended, every ear stretched during the reading of the sentence; and now that it came arrayed in terror and in blood, every glance was turned in pity on its unhappy victim. But Halloway heard it with the ears of one who has made up his mind to suffer; and the faint half smile that played upon his lip spoke more in scorn than in sorrow. Colonel de Haldimar pursued: –

"The court having found it imperatively incumbent on them to award the punishment of death to the prisoner, private Frank Halloway, at the same time gladly avail themselves of their privilege by strongly recommending him to mercy. The court cannot, in justice to the character of the prisoner, refrain from expressing their unanimous conviction, that notwithstanding the mysterious circumstances which have led to his confinement and trial, he is entirely innocent of the treachery ascribed to him. The court have founded this conviction on the excellent character, both on duty and in the field, hitherto borne by the prisoner, – his well-known attachment to the officer with whose abduction he stands charged, – and the manly, open, and (as the court are satisfied) correct history given of his former life. It is, moreover, the impression of the court, that, as stated by the prisoner, his guilt on the third charge has been the result only of his attachment for Cap-

tain de Haldimar. And for this, and the reasons above
assigned, do they strongly recommend the prisoner to
mercy.
　　(Signed)　　　　　　　"NOEL BLESSINGTON,
　　　　　　　　　　　　　　Captain and President.

"Sentence approved and confirmed.
　　　　　　　　　"CHARLES DE HALDIMAR,
　　　　　　　　　　Colonel Commandant."

While these concluding remarks of the court were
being read, the prisoner manifested the deepest emotion.
If a smile of scorn had previously played upon his lip, it
was because he fancied the court, before whom he had
sought to vindicate his fame, had judged him with a severity not inferior to his colonel's; but now that, in the presence of his companions, he heard the flattering attestation
of his services, coupled even as it was with the sentence
that condemned him to die, tears of gratitude and pleasure rose despite of himself to his eyes; and it required all
his self-command to enable him to abstain from giving
expression to his feelings towards those who had so generously interpreted the motives of his dereliction from duty.
But when the melancholy and startling fact of the approval and confirmation of the sentence met his ear, without the slightest allusion to that mercy which had been so
urgently recommended, he again overcame his weakness,
and exhibited his wonted air of calm and unconcern.

"Let the prisoner be removed, Mr. Lawson," ordered
the governor, whose stern and somewhat dissatisfied expression of countenance was the only comment on the
recommendation for mercy.

The order was promptly executed. Once more Halloway
left the square, and was re-conducted to the cell he had
occupied since the preceding night.

"Major Blackwater," pursued the governor, "let a detachment consisting of one half the garrison be got in
readiness to leave the fort within the hour. Captain Wentworth, three pieces of field artillery will be required. Let

them be got ready also." He then retired from the area with the forbidding dignity and stately haughtiness of manner that was habitual to him; while the officers, who had just received his commands, prepared to fulfil the respective duties assigned them.

Since the first alarm of the garrison no opportunity had hitherto been afforded the officers to snatch the slightest refreshment. Advantage was now taken of the short interval allowed by the governor, and they all repaired to the mess-room, where their breakfast had long since been provided.

"Well, Blessington," remarked Captain Erskine, as he filled his plate for the third time from a large haunch of smoke-dried venison, for which his recent skirmish with the Indians had given him an unusual relish, "so it appears your recommendation of poor Halloway to mercy is little likely to be attended to. Did you remark how displeased the colonel looked as he bungled through it? One might almost be tempted to think he had an interest in the man's death, so determined does he appear to carry his point."

Although several of his companions, perhaps, felt and thought the same, still there was no one who would have ventured to avow his real sentiments in so unqualified a manner. Indeed such an observation proceeding from the lips of any other officer would have excited the utmost surprise; but Captain Erskine, a brave, bold, frank, and somewhat thoughtless soldier, was one of those beings who are privileged to say any thing. His opinions were usually expressed without ceremony; and his speech was not the most circumspect *now*, as since his return to the fort he had swallowed, fasting, two or three glasses of a favourite spirit, which, without intoxicating, had greatly excited him.

"I remarked enough," said Captain Blessington, who sat leaning his head on one hand, while with the other he occasionally, and almost mechanically, raised a cup filled with a liquid of a pale blood colour to his lips, – "quite enough to make me regret from my very soul I should have been his principal judge. Poor Halloway, I pity him much; for, on my honour, I believe him to be the gentleman he represents himself."

"A finer fellow does not live," remarked the last remaining officer of the grenadiers. "But surely Colonel de Haldimar cannot mean to carry the sentence into effect. The recommendation of a court, couched in such terms as these, ought alone to have some weight with him."

"It is quite clear, from the fact of his having been remanded to his cell, the execution of the poor fellow will be deferred at least," observed one of Captain Erskine's subalterns. "If the governor had intended he should suffer immediately, he would have had him shot the moment after his sentence was read. But what is the meaning and object of this new sortie? and whither are we now going? Do you know, Captain Erskine, our company is again ordered for this duty?"

"Know it, Leslie! of course I do; and for that reason am I paying my court to the more substantial part of the breakfast. Come, Blessington, my dear fellow, you have quite lost your appetite, and we may have sharp work before we get back. Follow my example: throw that nasty blood-thickening sassafras away, and lay a foundation from this venison. None sweeter is to be found in the forests of America. A few slices of that, and then a glass each of my best Jamaica, and we shall have strength to go through the expedition, if its object be the capture of the bold Ponteac himself."

"I presume the object is rather to seek for Captain de Haldimar," said Lieutenant Boyce, the officer of grenadiers; "but in that case why not send out his own company?"

"Because the Colonel prefers trusting to cooler heads and more experienced arms," good-humouredly observed Captain Erskine. "Blessington is our senior, and his men are all old stagers. My lads, too, have had their mettle up already this morning, and there is nothing like that to prepare men for a dash of enterprise. It is with them as with blood horses, the more you put them on their speed the less anxious are they to quit the course. Well, Johnstone, my brave Scot, ready for another skirmish?" he asked, as that officer now entered to satisfy the cravings of an appetite little inferior to that of his captain.

"With 'Nunquam non paratus' for my motto," gaily returned the young man, "it were odd, indeed, if a mere scratch like this should prevent me from establishing my claim to it by following wherever my gallant captain leads."

"Most courteously spoken, and little in the spirit of a man yet smarting under the infliction of a rifle wound, it must be confessed," remarked Lieutenant Leslie. "But, Johnstone, you should bear in mind a too close adherence to that motto has been, in some degree, fatal to your family."

"No reflections, Leslie, if you please," returned his brother subaltern, slightly reddening. "If the head of our family was unfortunate enough to be considered a traitor to England, he was not so, at least, to Scotland; and Scotland was the land of his birth. But let his political errors be forgotten. Though the winged spur no longer adorn the booted heel of an Earl of Annandale, the time may not be far distant when some liberal and popular monarch of England shall restore a title forfeited neither through cowardice nor dishonour, but from an erroneous sense of duty."

"That is to say," muttered Ensign Delme, looking round for approval as he spoke, "that our present king is neither liberal nor popular. Well, Mr. Johnstone, were such an observation to reach the ears of Colonel de Haldimar you would stand a very fair chance of being brought to a court martial."

"That is to say nothing of the kind, sir," somewhat fiercely retorted the young Scot; "but any thing I do say you are at liberty to repeat to Colonel de Haldimar, or whom you will. I cannot understand, Leslie, why you should have made any allusion to the misfortunes of my family at this particular moment, and in this public manner. I trust it was not with a view to offend me;" and he fixed his large black eyes upon his brother subaltern, as if he would have read every thought of his mind.

"Upon my honour, Johnstone, I meant nothing of the kind," frankly returned Leslie. "I merely meant to hint that as you had had your share of service this morning, you might, at least, have suffered me to borrow your spurs, while you reposed for the present on your laurels."

"There are my gay and gallant Scots," exclaimed Captain Erskine, as he swallowed off a glass of the old Jamaica which lay before him, and with which he usually neutralised the acidities of a meat breakfast. "Settled like gentlemen and lads of spirit as ye are," he pursued, as the young men cordially shook each other's hand across the table. "What an enviable command is mine, to have a company of brave fellows who would face the devil himself were it necessary; and two hot and impatient subs., who are ready to cut each other's throat for the pleasure of accompanying me against a set of savages that are little better than so many devils. Come, Johnstone, you know the Colonel allows us but one sub. at a time, in consequence of our scarcity of officers, therefore it is but fair Leslie should have his turn. It will not be long, I dare say, before we shall have another brush with the rascals."

"In my opinion," observed Captain Blessington, who had been a silent and thoughtful witness of what was passing around him, "neither Leslie nor Johnstone would evince so much anxiety, were they aware of the true nature of the duty for which our companies have been ordered. Depend upon it, it is no search after Captain de Haldimar in which we are about to be engaged; for much as the colonel loves his son, he would on no account compromise the safety of the garrison, by sending a party into the forest, where poor De Haldimar, if alive, is at all likely to be found."

"Faith you are right, Blessington; the governor is not one to run these sorts of risks on every occasion. My chief surprise, indeed, is, that he suffered me to venture even upon the common; but if we are not designed for some hostile expedition, why leave the fort at all?"

"The question will need no answer, if Halloway be found to accompany us."

"Psha! why should Halloway be taken out for the purpose? If he be shot at all, he will be shot on the ramparts, in the presence of, and as an example to, the whole garrison. Still, on reflection, I cannot but think it impossible the sentence should be carried into full effect, after the strong, nay, the almost unprecedented recommendation to mercy recorded on the face of the proceedings."

Captain Blessington shook his head despondingly. "What think you, Erskine, of the policy of making an example, which may be witnessed by the enemy as well as the garrison? It is evident, from his demeanour throughout, nothing will convince the colonel that Halloway is not a traitor, and he may think it advisable to strike terror in the minds of the savages, by an execution which will have the effect of showing the treason of the soldier to have been discovered."

In this opinion many of the officers now concurred; and as the fate of the unfortunate Halloway began to assume a character of almost certainty, even the spirit of the gallant Erskine, the least subdued by the recent distressing events, was overclouded; and all sank, as if by one consent, into silent communion with their thoughts, as they almost mechanically completed the meal, at which habit rather than appetite still continued them. Before any of them had yet risen from the table, a loud and piercing scream met their ears from without; and so quick and universal was the movement it produced, that its echo had scarcely yet died away in distance, when the whole of the breakfast party had issued from the room, and were already spectators of the cause.

The barracks of the officers, consisting of a range of low buildings, occupied the two contiguous sides of a square, and in the front of these ran a narrow and covered piazza, somewhat similar to those attached to the guard-houses in England, which description of building the barracks themselves most resembled. On the other two faces of the square stood several block-houses, a style of structure which, from their adaptation to purposes of defence as well as of accommodation, were every where at that period in use in America, and are even now continued along the more exposed parts of the frontier. These, capable of containing each a company of men, were, as their name implies, formed of huge masses of roughly-shapen timber, fitted into each other at the extremities by rude incisions from the axe, and filled in with smaller wedges of wood. The upper part of these block-houses projected on every side several feet beyond the ground floor, and over the whole was a sheathing of planks, which, as well as those covering the barracks of the officers, were painted of a brick-red colour. Unlike the latter, they rose considerably above the surface of the ramparts; and, in addition to the small window to be seen on each side of each story of the block-house, were numerous smaller square holes, perforated for the discharge of musketry. Between both these barracks and the ramparts there was just space sufficient to admit of the passage of artillery of a heavy calibre; and at each of the four angles, composing the lines of the fort, was an opening of several feet in extent, not only to afford the gunners room to work their batteries, but to enable them to reach their posts with greater expedition in the event of any sudden emergency. On the right, on entering the fort over the drawbridge, were the block-houses of the men; and immediately in front, and on the left, the barracks of the officers, terminated at the outer extremity by the guard-house, and at the inner by the quarters of the commanding officer.

As the officers now issued from the mess-room nearly opposite to the gate, they observed, at that part of the barracks which ran at right angles with it, and immediately in front of the apartment of the younger De Haldimar, whence he had apparently just issued, the governor, struggling, though gently, to disengage himself from a female, who, with disordered hair and dress, lay almost prostrate upon the piazza, and clasping his booted leg with an energy evidently borrowed from the most rooted despair. The quick eye of the haughty man had already rested on the group of officers drawn by the scream of the supplicant. Numbers, too, of the men, attracted by the same cause, were collected in front of their respective block-houses, and looking from the windows of the rooms in which they were also breakfasting, preparatory to the expedition. Vexed and irritated beyond measure, at being thus made a conspicuous object of observation to his inferiors, the unbending governor made a violent and successful effort to disengage his leg; and then, without uttering a word, or otherwise noticing the unhappy being who lay extended at his feet, he stalked across the parade to his apartments at the opposite angle, without appearing to manifest the slightest consciousness of the scene that had awakened such universal attention.

Several of the officers, among whom was Captain Blessington, now hastened to the assistance of the female, whom all had recognised, from the first, to be the interesting and unhappy wife of Halloway. Many of the comrades of the latter, who had been pained and pitying spectators of the scene, also advanced for the same purpose; but, on perceiving their object anticipated by their superiors, they withdrew to the block-houses, whence they had issued. Never was grief more forcibly depicted, than in the whole appearance of this unfortunate woman; never did anguish assume a character more fitted to touch the soul, or to command respect. Her long fair hair, that had hitherto been hid under the coarse mob-cap, usually worn by the wives of the soldiers, was now divested of all fastening, and lay shadowing a white and polished bosom, which, in her violent struggles to detain the governor, had burst from its rude but modest confinement, and was now displayed in all the dazzling delicacy of youth and sex. If the officers gazed for a moment with excited look upon charms that had long been strangers to their sight, and of an order they had little deemed to find in Ellen Halloway, it was but the involuntary tribute rendered by nature unto beauty. The depth and sacredness of that sorrow, which had left the wretched woman unconscious of her exposure, in the instant afterwards imposed a check upon admiration, which each felt to be a violation of the first principles of human delicacy, and the feeling was repressed almost in the moment that gave it birth.

They were immediately in front of the room occupied by Charles de Haldimar, in the piazza of which were a few old chairs, on which the officers were in the habit of throwing themselves during the heat of the day. On one of these Captain Blessington, assisted by the officer of grenadiers, now seated the suffering and sobbing wife of Halloway. His first care was to repair the disorder of her dress; and never was the same office performed by man with greater delicacy, or absence of levity by those who witnessed it. This was the first moment of her consciousness. The inviolability of modesty for a moment rose paramount even to the desolation of her heart, and putting rudely aside the hand that reposed unavoidably upon her person, the poor woman started from her seat, and looked wildly about her, as if endeavouring to identify those by whom she was surrounded. But when she observed the pitying gaze of the officers fixed upon her, in earnestness and commiseration, and heard the benevolent accents of the ever kind Blessington exhorting her to composure, her weeping became more violent, and her sobs more convulsive. Captain Blessington threw an arm round her waist to prevent her from falling; and then motioning to two or three women of the company to which her husband was attached, who stood at a little distance, in front of one of the block-houses, prepared to deliver her over to their charge.

"No, no, not yet!" burst at length from the lips of the agonised woman, as she shrank from the rude but well-intentioned touch of the sympathising assistants, who had promptly answered the signal; then, as if obeying some new direction of her feelings, some new impulse of her grief, she liberated herself from the slight grasp of Captain Blessington, turned suddenly round, and before any one could anticipate the movement, entered an opening on the piazza, raised the latch of a door situated at its extremity, and was, in the next instant, in the apartment of the younger De Haldimar.

The scene that met the eyes of the officers, who now followed close after her, was one well calculated to make an impression on the hearts even of the most insensible. In the despair and recklessness of her extreme sorrow, the young wife of Halloway had already thrown herself upon her knees at the bedside of the sick officer; and, with her hands upraised and firmly clasped together, was now supplicating him in tones, contrasting singularly in their gentleness with the depth of the sorrow that had rendered her thus regardless of appearances, and insensible to observation.

"Oh, Mr. de Haldimar!" she implored, "in the name of God and of our blessed Saviour, if you would save me from madness, intercede for my unhappy husband, and preserve him from the horrid fate that awaits him. You are too good, too gentle, too amiable, to reject the prayer of a heart-broken woman. Moreover, Mr. de Haldimar," she proceeded, with deeper energy, while she caught and pressed, between her own white and bloodless hands, one nearly as delicate that lay extended near her, "consider all my dear but unfortunate husband has done for your family. Think of the blood he once spilt in the defence of your brother's life; that brother, through whom alone, oh God! he is now condemned to die. Call to mind the days and nights of anguish I passed near his couch of suffering, when yet writhing beneath the wound aimed at the life of Captain de Haldimar. Almighty Providence!" she pursued, in the same impassioned yet plaintive voice, "why is not Miss Clara here to plead the cause of the innocent, and to touch the stubborn heart of her merciless father? She would, indeed, move heaven and earth to save the life of him to whom she so often vowed eternal gratitude and acknowledgment. Ah, she little dreams of his danger now; or, if prayer and intercession could avail, my husband should yet live, and this terrible struggle at my heart would be no more."

Overcome by her emotion, the unfortunate woman suffered her aching head to droop upon the edge of the bed, and her sobbing became so painfully violent, that all who heard her expected, at every moment, some fatal termination to her immoderate grief. Charles de Haldimar was little less affected; and his sorrow was the more bitter, as he had just proved the utter inefficacy of any thing in the shape of appeal to his inflexible father.

"Mrs. Halloway, my dear Mrs. Halloway, compose yourself," said Captain Blessington, now approaching, and endeavouring to raise her gently from the floor, on which she still knelt, while her hands even more firmly grasped that of De Haldimar. "You are ill, very ill, and the consequences of this dreadful excitement may be fatal. Be advised by me, and retire. I have desired my room to be prepared for you, and Sergeant Wilmot's wife shall remain with you as long as you may require it."

"No, no, no!" she again exclaimed with energy; "what care I for my own wretched life – my beloved and unhappy husband is to die. Oh God! to die without guilt – to be cut off in his youth – to be shot as a traitor – and that simply for obeying the wishes of the officer whom he loved! – the son of the man who now spurns all supplication from his presence. It is inhuman – it is unjust – and Heaven will punish the hard-hearted man who murders him – yes, murders him! for such a punishment for such an offence is nothing less than murder." Again she wept bitterly, and as Captain Blessington still essayed to soothe and raise her: – "No, no! I will not leave this spot," she continued; "I will not quit the side of Mr. de Haldimar, until he pledges himself to intercede for my poor husband. It is his duty to save the life of him who saved his brother's life; and God and human justice are with my appeal. Oh, tell me, then, Mr. de Haldimar, – if you would save my wretched heart from breaking, – tell me you will intercede for, and obtain the pardon of, my husband!"

As she concluded this last sentence in passionate appeal, she had risen from her knees; and, conscious only of the importance of the boon solicited, now threw herself upon the breast of the highly pained and agitated young officer. Her long and beautiful hair fell floating over his face, and mingled with his own, while her arms were wildly clasped around him, in all the energy of frantic and hopeless adjuration.

"Almighty God!" exclaimed the agitated young man, as he made a feeble and fruitless effort to raise the form of the unhappy woman; "what shall I say to impart comfort to this suffering being? Oh, Mrs. Halloway," he pursued, "I would willingly give all I possess in this world to be the means of saving your unfortunate husband, – and as much for his own sake as for yours would I do this; but, alas! I have not the power. Do not think I speak without conviction. My father has just been with me, and I have pleaded the cause of your husband with an earnestness I should scarcely have used had my own life been at stake. But all my entreaties have been in vain. He is obstinate in the belief my brother's strange absence, and Donellan's death, are attributable only to the treason of Halloway. Still there is a hope. A detachment is to leave the fort within the hour, and Halloway is to accompany them. It may be, my father intends this measure only with a view to terrify him into a confession of guilt; and that he deems it politic to make him undergo all the fearful preliminaries without carrying the sentence itself into effect."

The unfortunate woman said no more. When she raised her heaving chest from that of the young officer, her eyes, though red and shrunk to half their usual size with weeping, were tearless; but on her countenance there was an expression of wild woe, infinitely more distressing to behold, in consequence of the almost unnatural check so suddenly imposed upon her feelings. She tottered, rather than walked, through the group of officers, who gave way on either hand to let her pass; and rejecting all assistance from the women who had followed into the room, and who now, in obedience to another signal from Captain Blessington, hastened to her support, finally gained the door, and quitted the apartment.

Nine

THE SUN was high in the meridian, as the second detachment, commanded by Colonel de Haldimar in person, issued from the fort of Détroit. It was that soft and hazy season, peculiar to the bland and beautiful autumns of Canada, when the golden light of Heaven seems as if transmitted through a veil of tissue, and all of animate and inanimate nature, expanding and fructifying beneath its fostering influence, breathes the most delicious languor and voluptuous repose. It was one of those still, calm, warm, and genial days, which in those regions come under the vulgar designation of the Indian summer; a season that is ever hailed by the Canadian with a satisfaction proportioned to the extreme sultriness of the summer, and the equally oppressive rigour of the winter, by which it is immediately preceded and followed. It is then that Nature, who seems from the creation to have bestowed all of grandeur and sublimity on the stupendous Americas, looks gladly and complacently on her work; and, staying the course of parching suns and desolating frosts, loves to luxuriate for a period in the broad and teeming bosom of her gigantic offspring. It is then that the forest-leaves, alike free from the influence of the howling hurricane of summer, and the paralysing and unfathomable snows of winter, cleave, tame and stirless in their varying tints, to the parent branch; while the broad rivers and majestic lakes exhibit a surface resembling rather the incrustation of the polished mirror than the resistless, viewless particles of which the golden element is composed. It is then that, casting its satisfied glance across those magnificent rivers, the eye beholds, as if reflected from a mirror (so similar in production and appearance are the contiguous shores), both the fertility of cultivated and the rudeness of uncultivated nature, that every where surround and diversify the view. The tall and sloping banks, covered with verdure to the very sands, that unite with the waters lying motionless at their base; the continuous chain of neat farm-houses (we speak principally of Détroit and its opposite shores); the luxuriant and bending orchards, teeming with fruits of every kind and of every colour; the ripe and yellow corn vying in hue with the soft atmosphere, which reflects and gives full effect to its abundance and its richness, – these, with the intervening waters unruffled, save by the lazy skiff, or the light bark canoe urged with the rapidity of thought along its surface by the slight and elegantly ornamented paddle of the Indian; or by the sudden leaping of the large salmon, the unwieldy sturgeon, the bearded cat-fish, or the delicately flavoured maskinongé, and fifty other tenants of their bosom; – all these contribute to form the foreground of a picture bounded in perspective by no less interesting, though perhaps ruder marks of the magnificence of that great architect – Nature, on which the eye never lingers without calm; while feelings, at once voluptuous and tender, creep insensibly over the heart, and raise the mind in adoration to the one great and sole Cause by which the stupendous whole has been produced.

Such a day as that we have just described was the —— of September, 1763, when the chief portion of the English garrison of Détroit issued forth from the fortifications in which they had so long been cooped up, and in the presumed execution of a duty undeniably the most trying and painful that ever fell to the lot of soldier to perform. The heavy dull movement of the guns, as they traversed the drawbridge resembled in that confined atmosphere the rumbling of low and distant thunder; and as they shook the rude and hollow sounding planks, over which they were slowly dragged, called up to every heart the sad recollection of the service for which they had been required. Even the tramp of the men, as they moved heavily and measuredly across the yielding bridge, seemed to wear the character of the reluctance with which they proceeded on so hateful a duty; and more than one individual, as he momentarily turned his eye upon the ramparts, where many of his comrades were grouped together watching the departure of the detachment, testified by the significant and mournful movement of his head how much he envied their exemption from the task.

The direct military road runs in a straight line from the fort to the banks of the Détroit, and the eastern extremity of the town. Here it is intersected by the highway running parallel with the river, and branching off at right angles on either hand; the right, leading in the direction of the more populous States; the left, through the town, and thence towards the more remote and western parts, where European influence has yet been but partially extended. The only difference between its present and former character is, that what is now a flourishing commercial town was then a mere village; while the adjacent country, at present teeming with every mark of vegetation, bore no other evidence of fertility than what was afforded by a few scattered farm-houses, many of which skirted various parts of the forest. Along this road the detachment now wended its slow and solemn course, and with a mournful pageantry of preparation that gave fearful earnest of the tragedy expected to be enacted.

In front, and dragged by the hands of the gunners, moved two of the three three-pounders, that had been ordered for the duty. Behind these came Captain Blessington's company, and in their rear, the prisoner Halloway, divested of his uniform, and clad in a white cotton jacket, and cap of the same material. Six rank and file of the grenadiers followed, under the command of a corporal, and behind these again, came eight men of the same company; four of whom bore on their shoulders a coffin, covered with a coarse black pall that had perhaps already assisted at fifty interments; while the other four carried, in addition to their own, the muskets of their burdened comrades. After these, marched a solitary drummer-boy; whose tall bear-skin cap attested him to be of the grenadiers also, while his muffled instrument marked the duty for which he had been selected. Like his comrades, none of whom exhibited their scarlet uniforms, he wore the collar of his great coat closely buttoned beneath his chin, which was only partially visible above the stiff leathern stock that encircled his neck. Although his features were half buried in his huge cap and the high collar of his coat, there was an air of delicacy about his person that seemed to render him unsuited to such an office; and more than once was Captain Erskine, who followed immediately behind him at the head of his company, compelled to call sharply to the urchin, threatening him with a week's drill unless he mended his feeble and unequal pace, and kept from under the feet of his men. The remaining gun brought up the rear of the detachment, who marched with fixed bayonets and two balls in each musket; the whole presenting a front of sections, that completely filled up the road along which they passed. Colonel de Haldimar, Captain Wentworth, and the Adjutant Lawson followed in the extreme rear.

An event so singular as that of the appearance of the English without their fort, beset as they were by a host of fierce and dangerous enemies, was not likely to pass unnoticed by a single individual in the little village of Détroit. We have already observed, that most of the colonist settlers had been cruelly massacred at the very onset of hostilities. Not so, however, with the Canadians, who, from their anterior relations with the natives, and the mutual and tacit good understanding that subsisted between both parties, were suffered to continue in quiet and unmolested possession of their homes, where they preserved an avowed neutrality, never otherwise infringed than by the assistance secretly and occasionally rendered to the English troops, whose gold they were glad to receive in exchange for the necessaries of life.

Every dwelling of the infant town had commenced giving up its tenants, from the moment when the head of the detachment was seen traversing the drawbridge; so that, by the time it reached the highway, and took its direction to the left, the whole population of Détroit were already assembled in groups, and giving expression to their several conjectures, with a vivacity of language and energy of gesticulation that would not have disgraced the parent land itself. As the troops drew nearer, however, they all sank at once into a silence, as much the result of certain unacknowledged and undefined fears, as of the respect the English had ever been accustomed to exact. The men removed their short dingy clay pipes from their mouths with one hand, and uncovered themselves with the other, while the women made their hasty reverence with the air of people who seek to propitiate by an act of civility; even the very children scraped and bowed, as if they feared the omission might be fatal to them, and, clinging to the hands and dress of their parents, looked up occasionally to their countenances to discover whether the apprehensions of their own fluttering and timid hearts were likely to be realised. Still there was sufficient of curiosity with all to render them attentive spectators of the passing troop. Hitherto, it had been imagined, the object of the English was an attack on the encampments of their enemies; but when the gaze of each adult inhabitant fell on the unaccoutred form of the lone soldier, who, calm though pale, now moved among his comrades in the ignominious garb of death, they could no longer doubt its true destination.

The aged made the sign of the cross, and mumbled over a short prayer for the repose of his soul, while the more youthful indulged in half-breathed ejaculations of pity and concern that so fine and interesting a man should be doomed to so dreadful a fate.

At the farther extremity of the town, and at a bend in the road, which branched off more immediately towards the river, stood a small public house, whose creaking sign bore three ill executed fleurs-de-lis, apologetic emblems of the arms of France. The building itself was little more than a rude log hut, along the front of which ran a plank, supported by two stumps of trees, and serving as a temporary accommodation both for the traveller and the inmate. On this bench three persons, apparently attracted by the beauty of the day and the mildness of the autumnal sun, were now seated, two of whom were leisurely puffing their pipes, while the third, a female, was employed in carding wool, a quantity of which lay in a basket at her feet, while she warbled, in a low tone, one of the simple airs of her native land. The elder of the two men, whose age might be about fifty, offered nothing particularly remarkable in his appearance: he was dressed in one of those thick coats made of the common white blanket, which, even to this day, are so generally worn by the Canadians, while his hair, cut square upon the forehead, and tied into a club of nearly a foot long, fell onto the cape, or hood, attached to it: his face was ruddy and shining as that of any rival Boniface among the race of the hereditary enemies of his forefathers; and his thick short neck, and round fat person, attested he was no more an enemy to the good things of this world than themselves, while he was as little oppressed by its cares: his nether garments were of a coarse blue homespun, and his feet were protected by that rudest of all rude coverings, the Canadian shoe-pack. This was composed of a single piece of stiff brown leather, curved and puckered round the sides and front, where it was met by a tongue of softer material, which helped to confine it in that position, and to form the shoe. A bandana handkerchief fell from his neck upon his chest; the covering of which was so imperfectly drawn, as to disclose a quantity of long, coarse, black, and grisly hair.

His companion was habited in a still more extraordinary manner. His lower limbs were cased, up to the mid-thigh, in leathern leggings, the seam of which was on the outside, leaving a margin, or border, of about an inch wide, which had been slit into innumerable small fringes, giving them an air of elegance and lightness: a garter of leather, curiously wrought, with the stained quills of the porcupine, encircled each leg, immediately under the knee, where it was tied in a bow, and then suffered to hang pendant half way down the limb; to the fringes of the leggings, moreover, were attached numerous dark-coloured horny substances, emitting, as they rattled against each other, at the slightest movement of the wearer, a tinkling sound, resembling that produced by a number of small thin delicate brass bells; these were the tender hoofs of the wild deer, dried, scraped, and otherwise prepared for this ornamental purpose. Upon his large feet he wore mocassins, made of the same pliant material with his leggings, and differing in shape from the foot-gear of his companion in this particular only, that they had no tongue introduced into the front: they were puckered together by a strong sinew of the deer, until they met along the instep in a seam concealed by the same ornamental quill-work that decorated the garters: a sort of flap, fringed like the leggings, was folded back from the ankle, upon the sides of the foot, and the whole was confined by a strong though neat leathern thong, made of smoked deer-skin also, which, after passing once or twice under the foot, was then tightly drawn several times round the ankle, where it was finally secured. Two strips of leather, about an inch and a half in width, attached to the outer side of each legging, were made fast at their opposite extremities to a strong girdle, encircling the loins, and supporting a piece of coarse blue cloth, which, after passing completely under the body, fell in short flaps both before and behind. The remainder of the dress consisted of a cotton shirt, figured and sprigged on a dark ground, that fell uncon-fined over the person; a close deer-skin hunting-coat, fringed also at its edges; and a coarse common felt hat, in the string of which (for there was no band) were twisted a number of variegated feathers, furnished by the most beautiful and rare of the American autumnal birds. Outside this hunting-coat, and across the right shoulder, was flung an ornamental belt, to which were appended, on the left side, and in a line with the elbow, a shot-pouch, made of the untanned hide of some wild animal, and a flask for powder, formed of the horn of the buffalo; on which, highly polished for this purpose, were inscribed, with singular accuracy of proportion, a variety of figures, both of men, and birds, and beasts, and fishes; two or three small horn measures for powder, and a long thin wire, intended to serve as a pricker for the rifle that reclined against the outside of the hut, were also attached to this belt by strips of deer-skin of about six inches in length. Into another broad leathern belt, that confined the hunting coat, was thrust a tomahawk, the glittering head of which was uppermost, and unsheathed; while at the opposite side, and half supporting the powder-horn, the huge handle of a knife, whose blade was buried in a strong leathern sheath, was distinctly visible.

The form and face of this individual were in perfect keeping with the style of his costume, and the formidable character of his equipment. His stature was considerably beyond that of the ordinary race of men, and his athletic and muscular limbs united the extremes of strength and activity in a singular degree. His features, marked and prominent, wore a cast of habitual thought, strangely tinctured with ferocity; and the general expression of his otherwise not unhandsome countenance was repellent and disdainful. At the first glance he might have been taken for one of the swarthy natives of the soil; but though time and constant exposure to scorching suns had given to his complexion a dusky hue, still there were wanting the quick, black, penetrating eye; the high cheek-bone; the straight, coarse, shining, black hair; the small bony hand and foot; and the placidly proud and serious air, by which the former is distinguished. His own eye was of a deep bluish gray; his hair short, dark, and wavy; his hands large and muscular; and so far from exhibiting any of the self-command of the Indian, the constant play of his features betrayed each passing thought with the same rapidity with which it was conceived. But if any doubt could have existed in the mind of him who beheld this strangely accoutred figure, it would have been instantly dispelled by a glance at his lower limbs. We have already stated the upper part of his leggings terminated about mid-thigh; from this to the hip, that portion of the limb was completely bare, and disclosed, at each movement of the garment that was suffered to fall loosely over it, not the swarthy and copper-coloured flesh of the Indian, but the pale though sun-burnt skin of one of a more temperate clime. His age might be about forty-five.

At the moment when the English detachment approached the bend in the road, these two individuals were conversing earnestly together, pausing only to puff at intervals thick and wreathing volumes of smoke from their pipes, which were filled with a mixture of tobacco and odoriferous herbs. Presently, however, sounds that appeared familiar to his ear arrested the attention of the wildly accoutred being we have last described. It was the heavy roll of the artillery carriages already advancing along the road, and somewhat in the rear of the hut. To dash his pipe to the ground, seize and cock and raise his rifle to his shoulder, and throw himself forward in the eager attitude of one waiting until the object of his aim should appear in sight, was but the work of a moment. Startled by the suddenness of the action, his male companion moved a few paces also from his seat, to discover the cause of this singular movement. The female, on the contrary, stirred not, but ceasing for a moment the occupation in which she had been engaged, fixed her dark and brilliant eyes upon the tall and picturesque form of the rifleman, whose active and athletic limbs, thrown into powerful relief by the distention of each nerve and muscle, appeared to engross her whole admiration and interest, without any reference to the cause that had produced this abrupt and hostile change in his movements. It was evident that, unlike the other inhabitants of the town, this group had been taken by surprise, and were utterly unprepared to expect any thing in the shape of interruption.

For upwards of a minute, during which the march of the men became audible even to the ears of the female, the formidable warrior, for such his garb denoted him to be, continued motionless in the attitude he had at first assumed - his right cheek reposing on the ornamented stock of his rifle, and his quick and steady eye fixed in one undeviating line with the sight near the breech, and that which surmounted the extreme end of the deadly weapon. No sooner, however, had the head of the advancing column come within sight, than the trigger was pulled, and the small and ragged bullet sped hissing from the grooved and delicate barrel. A triumphant cry was next pealed from the lips of the warrior, - a cry produced by the quickly repeated application and removal of one hand to and from the mouth, while the other suffered the butt end of the now harmless weapon to fall loosely upon the earth. He then slowly and deliberately withdrew within the cover of the hut.

This daring action, which had been viewed by the leading troops with astonishment not unmingled with alarm, occasioned a temporary confusion in the ranks, for all believed they had fallen into an ambuscade of the Indians. A halt was instantly commanded by Captain Blessington, in order to give time to the governor to come up from the rear, while he proceeded with one of the leading sections to reconnoitre the front of the hut. To his infinite surprise, however, he found neither enemy, nor evidence that an enemy had been there. The only individuals visible were the Canadian already alluded to, and the dark-eyed female. Both were seated on the bench; - the one smoking his pipe with a well assumed appearance of unconcern - the other carding her wool, but with a hand that by a close observer might be seen to tremble in its office, and a cheek that was paler considerably than at the moment when we first placed her before the imagination of the reader. Both, however, started with unaffected surprise on seeing Captain Blessington and his little force turn the corner of the house from the main road; and certain looks of recognition passed between all parties, that proved them to be no strangers to each other.

"Ah, monsieur," said the Canadian, in a mingled dialect, neither French nor English, but partaking in some degree of the idiom of both, while he attempted an ease and freedom of manner that was too miserably affected to pass current with the mild but observant officer whom he addressed, "how much surprise I am, and glad to see you. It is a long times since you came out of de fort. I hope de gouverneur and de officir be all very well. I was tinking to go to-day to see if you want any ting. I have got some nice rum of the Jamaïque for Capitaine Erskine. Will you please to try some?" While speaking, the voluble host of the Fleur de lis had risen from his seat, laid aside his pipe, and now stood with his hands thrust into the pockets of his blanket coat.

"It is, indeed, a long time since we have been here, master François," somewhat sarcastically and drily replied Captain Blessington; "and you have not visited us quite so often latterly yourself, though well aware we were in want of fresh provisions. I give you all due credit, however, for your intention of coming to-day, but you see we have anticipated you. Still this is not the point. Where is the Indian who fired at us just now? and how is it we find you leagued with our enemies?"

"What, sir, is it you say?" asked the Canadian, holding up his hands with feigned astonishment. "Me league myself with de savage. Upon my honour I did not see nobody fire, or I should tell you. I love de English too well to do dem harms."

"Come, come, François, no nonsense. If I cannot make you confess, there is one not far from me who will. You know Colonel de Haldimar too well to imagine he will be trifled with in this manner: if he detects you in a falsehood, he will certainly cause you to be hanged up at the first tree. Take my advice, therefore, and say where you have secreted this Indian; and recollect, if we fall into an ambuscade, your life will be forfeited at the first shot we hear fired."

At this moment the governor, followed by his adjutant, came rapidly up to the spot. Captain Blessington communicated the ill success of his queries, when the former cast on the terrified Canadian one of those severe and searching looks which he so well knew how to assume.

"Where is the rascal who fired at us, sirrah? tell me instantly, or you have not five minutes to live."

The heart of mine host of the Fleur de lis quailed within him at this formidable threat; and the usually ruddy hue of his countenance had now given place to an ashy paleness. Still, as he had positively denied all knowledge of the matter on which he was questioned, he appeared to feel his safety lay in adhering to his original statement. Again, therefore, he assured the governor, on his honour (laying his hand upon his heart as he spoke), that what he had already stated was the fact.

"Your honour – you pitiful trading scoundrel – how dare you talk to me of your honour? Come, sir, confess at once where you have secreted this fellow, or prepare to die."

"If I may be so bold, your Honour," said one of Captain Blessington's men, "the Frenchman lies. When the Ingian fired among us, this fellow was peeping under his shoulder and watching us also. If I had not seen him too often at the fort to be mistaken in his person, I should have known him, at all events, by his blanket coat and red handkerchief."

This blunt statement of the soldier, confirmed as it was the instant afterwards by one of his comrades, was damning proof against the Canadian, even if the fact of the rifle being discharged from the front of the hut had not already satisfied all parties of the falsehood of his assertion.

"Come forward, a couple of files, and seize this villain," resumed the governor with his wonted sternness of manner. "Mr. Lawson, see if his hut does not afford a rope strong enough to hang the traitor from one of his own apple trees."

Both parties proceeded at the same moment to execute the two distinct orders of their chief. The Canadian was now firmly secured in the grasp of the two men who had given evidence against him, when, seeing all the horror of the summary and dreadful fate that awaited him, he confessed the individual who had fired had been sitting with him the instant previously, but that he knew no more of him than of any other savage occasionally calling at the Fleur de lis. He added, that on discharging the rifle he had bounded across the palings of the orchard, and fled in the direction of the forest. He denied, on interrogation, all knowledge or belief of an enemy waiting in ambush; stating, moreover, even the individual in question had not been aware of the sortie of the detachment until apprised of their near approach by the heavy sound of the gun-carriages.

"Here are undeniable proofs of the man's villany, sir," said the adjutant, returning from the hut and exhibiting objects of new and fearful interest to the governor. "This hat and rope I found secreted in one of the bed-rooms of the auberge. The first is evidently Donellan's; and from the hook attached to the latter, I apprehend it to be the same stated to have been used by Captain de Haldimar in crossing the ditch."

The governor took the hat and rope from the hands of his subordinate, examined them attentively, and after a few moments of deep musing, during which his countenance underwent several rapid though scarcely perceptible changes, turned suddenly and eagerly to the soldier who had first convicted the Canadian in his falsehood, and demanded if he had seen enough of the man who had fired to be able to give even a general description of his person.

"Why yes, your Honour, I think I can; for the fellow stood long enough after firing his piece, for a painter to have taken him off from head to foot. He was a taller and larger man by far than our biggest grenadier, and that is poor Harry Donellan, as your Honour knows. But as for his dress, though I could see it all, I scarcely can tell how to describe it. All I know is, he was covered with smoked deer-skin, in some such fashion as the great chief Ponteac, only, instead of having his head bare and shaved, he wore a strange outlandish sort of a hat, covered over with wild birds' feathers in front."

"Enough," interrupted the governor, motioning the man to silence; then, in an under-tone to himself – "By Heaven, the very same." A shade of disappointment, not unmingled with suppressed alarm, passed rapidly across his brow; it was but momentary. "Captain Blessington," he ordered quickly and impatiently, "search the hut and grounds for this lurking Indian, who is, no doubt, secreted in the neighbourhood. Quick, quick, sir; there is no time to be lost." Then in an angry and intimidating tone to the Canadian, who had already dropped on his knees, supplicating mercy, and vociferating his innocence in the same breath, – "So, you infernal scoundrel, this is the manner in which you have repaid our confidence. Where is my son, sir? or have you already murdered him, as you did his servant? Tell me, you villain, what have you to say to these proofs of your treachery? But stay, I shall take another and fitter opportunity to question you. Mr. Lawson, secure this traitor properly, and let him be conveyed to the centre of the detachment."

The mandate was promptly obeyed; and in despite of his own unceasing prayers and protestations of innocence, and the tears and entreaties of his dark-eyed daughter Babette, who had thrown herself on her knees at his side, the stout arms of mine host of the Fleur de lis were soon firmly secured behind his back with the strong rope that had been found under such suspicious circumstances in his possession. Before he was marched off, however, two of the men who had been sent in pursuit, returned from the orchard, stating that further search was now fruitless.

They had penetrated through a small thicket at the extremity of the grounds, and had distinctly seen a man answering the description given by their comrades, in full flight towards the forest skirting the heights in front.

The governor was evidently far from being satisfied with the result of a search too late instituted to leave even a prospect of success. "Where are the Indians principally encamped, sirrah?" he sternly demanded of his captive; "answer me truly, or I will carry off this wench as well, and if a single hair of a man of mine be even singed by a shot from a skulking enemy, you may expect to see her bayoneted before your eyes."

"Ah, my God! Monsieur le Gouverneur," exclaimed the affrighted aubergiste, "as I am an honest man, I shall tell de truth, but spare my child. They are all in de forest, and half a mile from de little river dat runs between dis and de Pork Island."

"Hog Island, I suppose you mean."

"Yes sir, de Hog Island is de one I means."

"Conduct him to the centre, and let him be confronted with the prisoner," directed the governor, addressing his adjutant; "Captain Blessington, your men may resume their stations in the ranks."

The order was obeyed; and notwithstanding the tears and supplications of the now highly excited Babette, who flung herself upon his neck, and was only removed by force, the terrified Canadian was borne off from his premises by the troops.

Ten

WHILE THIS scene was enacting in front of the Fleur de lis, one of a far more touching and painful nature was passing in the very heart of the detachment itself. At the moment when the halt was ordered by Captain Blessington, a rumour ran through the ranks that they had reached the spot destined for the execution of their ill-fated comrade. Those only in the immediate front were aware of the true cause; but although the report of the rifle had been distinctly heard by all, it had been attributed by those in the rear to the accidental discharge of one of their own muskets. A low murmur, expressive of the opinion generally entertained, passed gradually from rear to front, until it at length reached the ears of the delicate drummer boy who marched behind the coffin. His face was still buried in the collar of his coat; and what was left uncovered of his features by the cap, was in some degree hidden by the forward drooping of his head upon his chest. Hitherto he had moved almost mechanically along, tottering and embarrassing himself at every step under the cumbrous drum that was suspended from a belt round his neck over the left thigh; but now there was a certain indescribable drawing up of the frame, and tension of the whole person, denoting a concentration of all the moral and physical energies, – a sudden working up, as it were, of the intellectual and corporeal being to some determined and momentous purpose.

At the first halt of the detachment, the weary supporters of the coffin had deposited their rude and sombre burden upon the earth, preparatory to its being resumed by those appointed to relieve them. The dull sound emitted by the hollow fabric, as it touched the ground, caught the ear of him for whom it was destined, and he turned to gaze upon the sad and lonely tenement so shortly to become his final resting place. There was an air of calm composure and dignified sorrow upon his brow, that infused respect into the hearts of all who beheld him; and even the men selected to do the duty of executioners sought to evade his glance, as his steady eye wandered from right to left of the fatal rank. His attention, however, was principally directed towards the coffin, which lay before him; on this he gazed fixedly for upwards of a minute. He then turned his eyes in the direction of the fort, shuddered, heaved a profound sigh, and looking up to heaven with the apparent fervour that became his situation, seemed to pray for a moment or two inwardly and devoutly. The thick and almost suffocating breathing of one immediately beyond the coffin, was now distinctly heard by all. Halloway started from his attitude of devotion, gazed earnestly on the form whence it proceeded, and then wildly extending his arms, suffered a smile of satisfaction to illumine his pale features. All eyes were now turned upon the drummer boy, who, evidently labouring under convulsive excitement of feeling, suddenly dashed his cap and instrument to the earth, and flew as fast as his tottering and uncertain steps would admit across the coffin, and into the arms extended to receive him.

"My Ellen! oh, my own devoted, but too unhappy Ellen!" passionately exclaimed the soldier, as he clasped the slight and agitated form of his disguised wife to his throbbing heart. "This, this, indeed, is joy even in death. I thought I could have died more happily without you, but nature tugs powerfully at my heart; and to see you once more, to feel you once more *here*" (and he pressed her wildly to his chest) "is indeed a bliss that robs my approaching fate of half its terror."

"Oh Reginald! my dearly beloved Reginald! my murdered husband!" shrieked the unhappy woman; "your Ellen will not survive you. Her heart is already broken, though she cannot weep; but the same grave shall contain us both. Reginald, do you believe me? I swear it; the same grave shall contain us both."

Exhausted with the fatigue and excitement she had undergone, the faithful and affectionate creature now lay, without sense or motion, in the arms of her wretched husband. Halloway bore her, unopposed, a pace or two in advance, and deposited her unconscious form on the fatal coffin.

No language of ours can render justice to the trying character of the scene. All who witnessed it were painfully affected, and over the bronzed cheek of many a veteran coursed a tear, that, like that of Sterne's recording angel, might have blotted out a catalogue of sins. Although each was prepared to expect a reprimand from the governor, for suffering the prisoner to quit his station in the ranks, humanity and nature pleaded too powerfully in his behalf, and neither officer nor man attempted to interfere, unless with a view to render assistance. Captain Erskine, in particular, was deeply pained, and would have given any thing to recall the harsh language he had used towards the supposed idle and inattentive drummer boy. Taking from a pocket in his uniform a small flask of brandy, which he had provided against casualties, the compassionating officer slightly raised the head of the pale and unconscious woman with one hand, while with the other he introduced a few drops between her parted lips. Halloway knelt at the opposite side of the coffin; one hand searching, but in vain, the suspended pulse of his inanimate wife; the other, unbuttoning the breast of the drum-boy's jacket, which, with every other part of the equipment, she wore beneath the loose great coat so effectually accomplishing her disguise.

Such was the position of the chief actors in this truly distressing drama, at the moment when Colonel de Haldimar came up with his new prisoner, to mark what effect would be produced on Halloway by his unexpected appearance. His own surprise and disappointment may be easily conceived, when, in the form of the recumbent being who seemed to engross universal attention, he recognised, by the fair and streaming hair, and half exposed bosom, the unfortunate being whom, only two hours previously, he had spurned from his feet in the costume of her own sex, and reduced, by the violence of her grief, to almost infantine debility. Question succeeded question to those around, but without eliciting any clue to the means by which this mysterious disguise had been effected. No one had been aware, until the truth was so singularly and suddenly revealed, the supposed drummer was any other than one of the lads attached to the grenadiers; and as for the other facts, they spoke too plainly to the comprehension of the governor to need explanation. Once more, however, the detachment was called to order. Halloway struck his hand violently upon his brow, kissed the wan lips of his still unconscious wife, breathing, as he did so, a half murmured hope she might indeed be the corpse she appeared. He then raised himself from the earth with a light and elastic yet firm movement, and resumed the place he had previously occupied, where, to his surprise, he beheld a second victim bound, and, apparently, devoted to the same death. When the eyes of the two unhappy men met, the governor closely watched the expression of the countenance of each; but although the Canadian started on beholding the soldier, it might be merely because he saw the latter arrayed in the garb of death, and followed by the most unequivocal demonstrations of a doom to which he himself was, in all probability, devoted. As for Halloway, his look betrayed neither consciousness nor recognition; and though too proud to express complaint or to give vent to the feelings of his heart, his whole soul appeared to be absorbed in the unhappy partner of his luckless destiny. Presently he saw her borne, and in the same state of insensibility, in the arms of Captain Erskine and Lieutenant Leslie, towards the hut of his fellow prisoner, and he heard the former officer enjoin the weeping girl, Babette, to whose charge they delivered her over, to pay every attention to her her situation might require. The detachment then proceeded.

The narrow but deep and rapid river alluded to by the Canadian, as running midway between the town and Hog Island, derived its source far within the forest, and formed the bed of one of those wild, dark, and thickly wooded ravines so common in America. As it neared the Détroit, however, the abruptness of its banks was so considerably lessened, as to render the approach to it on the town side over an almost imperceptible slope. Within a few yards of its mouth, as we have already observed in our introductory chapter, a rude but strong wooden bridge, over which lay the high road, had been constructed by the French; and from the centre of this, all the circuit of intermediate clearing, even to the very skirt of the forest, was distinctly commanded by the naked eye. To the right, on approaching it from the town, lay the adjacent shores of Canada, washed by the broad waters of the Détroit, on which it was thrown into strong relief, and which, at the distance of about a mile in front, was seen to diverge into two distinct channels, pursuing each a separate course, until they again met at the western extremity of Hog Island. On the left, and in the front, rose a succession of slightly undulating hills, which, at a distance of little more than half a mile, terminated in an elevation considerably above the immediate level of the Détroit side of the ravine. That, again, was crowned with thick and overhanging forest, taking its circular sweep, as we have elsewhere shown, around the fort. The intermediate ground was studded over with rude stumps of trees, and bore, in various directions, distinct proofs of the spoliation wrought among the infant possessions of the murdered English settlers. The view to the rear was less open; the town being partially hidden by the fruit-laden orchards that lined the intervening high road, and hung principally on its left. This was not the case with the fort. Between these orchards and the distant forest lay a line of open country, fully commanded by its cannon, even to the ravine we have described, and in a sweep that embraced every thing from the bridge itself to the forest, in which all traces of its source was lost.

When the detachment had arrived within twenty yards of the bridge, they were made to file off to the left, until the last gun had come up. They were then fronted; the rear section of Captain Erskine's company resting on the road, and the left flank, covered by the two first guns pointed obliquely, both in front and rear, to guard against surprise, in the event of any of the Indians stealing round to the cover of the orchards. The route by which they had approached this spot was upwards of two miles in extent; but, as they now filed off into the open ground, the leading sections observed, in a direct line over the cleared country, and at the distance of little more than three quarters of a mile, the dark ramparts of the fortress that contained their comrades, and could even distinguish the uniforms of the officers and men drawn up in line along the works, where they were evidently assembled to witness the execution of the sentence on Halloway.

Such a sight as that of the English so far from their fort, was not likely to escape the notice of the Indians. Their encampment, as the Canadian had truly stated, lay within the forest, and beyond the elevated ground already alluded to; and to have crossed the ravine, or ventured out of reach of the cannon of the fort, would have been to have sealed the destruction of the detachment. But the officer to whom their security was entrusted, although he had his own particular views for venturing thus far, knew also at what point to stop; and such was the confidence of his men in his skill and prudence, they would have fearlessly followed wherever he might have chosen to lead. Still, even amid all the solemnity of preparation attendant on the duty they were out to perform, there was a natural and secret apprehensiveness about each, that caused him to cast his eyes frequently and fixedly on that part of the forest which was known to afford cover to their merciless foes. At times they fancied they beheld the dark and flitting forms of men gliding from tree to tree along the skirt of the wood; but when they gazed again, nothing of the kind was to be seen, and the illusion was at once ascribed to the heavy state of the atmosphere, and the action of their own precautionary instincts.

Meanwhile the solemn tragedy of death was preparing in mournful silence. On the centre of the bridge, and visible to those even within the fort, was placed the coffin of Halloway, and at twelve paces in front were drawn up the six rank and file on whom had devolved, by lot, the cruel duty of the day. With calm and fearless eye the prisoner surveyed the preparations for his approaching end; and whatever might be the inward workings of his mind, there was not among the assembled soldiery one individual whose countenance betrayed so little of sorrow and emotion as his own. With a firm step, when summoned, he moved towards the fatal coffin, dashing his cap to the earth as he advanced, and baring his chest with the characteristic contempt of death of the soldier. When he had reached the centre of the bridge, he turned facing his comrades, and knelt upon the coffin. Captain Blessington, who, permitted by the governor, had followed him with a sad heart and heavy step, now drew a Prayer-book from his pocket, and read from it in a low voice. He then closed the volume, listened to something the prisoner earnestly communicated to him, received a small packet which he drew from the bosom of his shirt, shook him long and cordially by the hand, and then hastily resumed his post at the head of the detachment.

The principal inhabitants of the village, led by curiosity, had followed at a distance to witness the execution of the condemned soldier; and above the heads of the line, and crowning the slope, were collected groups of both sexes and of all ages, that gave a still more imposing character to the scene. Every eye was now turned upon the firing party, who only awaited the signal to execute their melancholy office, when suddenly, in the direction of the forest, and upon the extreme height, there burst the tremendous and deafening yells of upwards of a thousand savages. For an instant Halloway was forgotten in the instinctive sense of individual danger, and all gazed eagerly to ascertain the movements of their enemy. Presently a man, naked to the waist, his body and face besmeared with streaks of black and red paint, and his whole attitude expressing despair and horror, was seen flying down the height with a rapidity proportioned to the extreme peril in which he stood. At about fifty paces in his rear followed a dozen bounding, screaming Indians, armed with uplifted toma-hawks, whose anxiety in pursuit lent them a speed that even surpassed the efforts of flight itself. It was evident the object of the pursued was to reach the detachment, that of the pursuers to prevent him. The struggle was maintained for a few moments with equality, but in the end the latter were triumphant, and at each step the distance that sepa-rated them became less. At the first alarm, the detach-ment, with the exception of the firing party, who still occupied their ground, had been thrown into square, and, with a gun planted in each angle, awaited the attack mo-mentarily expected. But although the heights were now alive with the dusky forms of naked warriors, who, from the skirt of the forest, watched the exertions of their fel-lows, the pursuit of the wretched fugitive was confined to these alone. Foremost of the latter, and distinguished by his violent exertions and fiendish cries, was the tall and wildly attired warrior of the Fleur de lis. At every bound he took he increased the space that divided him from his companions, and lessened that which kept him from his panting and nearly exhausted victim. Already were they descending the nearest of the undulating hills, and both now became conspicuous objects to all around; but princi-pally the pursuer, whose gigantic frame and extraordinary speed riveted every eye, even while the interest of all was excited for the wretched fugitive alone.

At that moment Halloway, who had been gazing on the

scene with an astonishment little inferior to that of his comrades, sprang suddenly to his feet upon the coffin, and waving his hand in the direction of the pursuing enemy, shouted aloud in a voice of mingled joy and triumph, –

"Ha! Almighty God, I thank thee! Here, here comes one who alone has the power to snatch me from my impending doom."

"By Heaven, the traitor confesses, and presumes to triumph in his guilt," exclaimed the voice of one, who, while closely attending to every movement of the Indians, was also vigilantly watching the effect likely to be produced on the prisoner by this unexpected interruption. "Corporal, do your duty."

"Stay, stay – one moment stay!" implored Halloway with uplifted hands.

"Do your duty, sir," fiercely repeated the governor.

"Oh stop – for God's sake, stop! Another moment and he will be here, and I —— "

He said no more – a dozen bullets penetrated his body – one passed directly through his heart. He leaped several feet in the air, and then fell heavily, a lifeless bleeding corpse, across the coffin.

Meanwhile the pursuit of the fugitive was continued, but by the warrior of the Fleur de lis alone. Aware of their inefficiency to keep pace with this singular being, his companions had relinquished the chace, and now stood resting on the brow of the hill where the wretched Halloway had first recognised his supposed deliverer, watching eagerly, though within musket shot of the detachment, the result of a race on which so much apparently depended. Neither party, however, attempted to interfere with the other, for all eyes were now turned on the flying man and his pursuer with an interest that denoted the extraordinary efforts of the one to evade and the other to attain the accomplishment of his object. Although the exertions of the former had been stupendous, such was the eagerness and determination of the latter, that at each step he gained perceptibly on his victim. The immediate course taken was in a direct line for the ravine, which it evidently was the object of the fugitive to clear at its nearest point. Already had he approached within a few paces of its brink, and every eye was fastened on the point where it was expected the doubtful leap would be taken, when suddenly, as if despairing to accomplish it at a bound, he turned to the left, and winding along its bank, renewed his efforts in the direction of the bridge. This movement occasioned a change in the position of the parties which was favourable to the pursued. Hitherto they had been so immediately on a line with each other, it was impossible for the detachment to bring a musket to bear upon the warrior, without endangering him whose life they were anxious to preserve. For a moment or two his body was fairly exposed, and a dozen muskets were discharged at intervals from the square, but all without success. Recovering his lost ground, he soon brought the pursued again in a line between himself and the detachment, edging rapidly nearer to him as he advanced, and uttering terrific yells, that were echoed back from his companions on the brow of the hill. It was evident, however, his object was the recapture, not the destruction, of the flying man, for more than once did he brandish his menacing tomahawk in rapid sweeps around his head, as if preparing to dart it, and as often did he check the movement. The scene at each succeeding moment became more critical and intensely interesting. The strength of the pursued was now nearly exhausted, while that of his formidable enemy seemed to suffer no diminution. Leap after leap he took with fearful superiority, sideling as he advanced. Already had he closed upon his victim, while with a springing effort a large and bony hand was extended to secure his shoulder in his grasp. The effort was fatal to him; for in reaching too far he lost his balance, and fell heavily upon the sward. A shout of exultation burst from the English troops, and numerous voices now encouraged the pursued to renew his exertions. The advice was not lost; and although only a few seconds had elapsed between the fall and recovery of his pursuer, the wretched fugitive had already greatly increased the distance that separated them. A cry of savage rage and disappointment burst from the lips of the gigantic warrior; and concentrating all his remaining strength and speed into one final effort, he bounded and leapt like a deer of the forest whence he came. The opportunity for recapture, however, had been lost in his fall, for already the pursued was within a few feet of the high road, and on the point of turning the extremity of the bridge. One only resource was now left: the warrior suddenly checked himself in his course, and remained stationary; then raising and dropping his glittering weapon several times in a balancing position, he waited until the pursued had gained the highest point of the open bridge. At that moment the glittering steel, aimed with singular accuracy and precision, ran whistling through the air, and with such velocity of movement as to be almost invisible to the eyes of those who attempted to follow it in its threatening course. All expected to see it enter into the brain against which it had been directed; but the fugitive had marked the movement in time to save himself by stooping low to the earth, while the weapon, passing over him, entered with a deadly and crashing sound into the brain of the weltering corpse. This danger passed, he sprang once more to his feet, nor paused again in his flight, until, faint and exhausted, he sank without motion under the very bayonets of the firing party.

A new direction was now given to the interest of the assembled and distinct crowds that had witnessed these startling incidents. Scarcely had the wretched man gained the protection of the soldiery, when a shriek divided the air, so wild, so piercing, and so unearthly, that even the warrior of the Fleur de lis seemed to lose sight of his victim, in the harrowing interest produced by that dreadful scream. All turned their eyes for a moment in the quarter whence it proceeded; when presently, from behind the groups of Canadians crowning the slope, was seen flying, with the rapidity of thought, one who resembled rather a spectre than a being of earth; – it was the wife of Halloway. Her long fair hair was wild and streaming – her feet, and legs, and arms were naked – and one solitary and scanty garment displayed rather than concealed the symmetry of her delicate person. She flew to the fatal bridge, threw herself on the body of her bleeding husband, and imprinting her warm kisses on his bloody lips, for a moment or two presented the image of one whose reason has fled for ever. Suddenly she started from the earth; her face, her hands, and her garment so saturated with the blood of her husband, that a feeling of horror crept throughout the veins of all who beheld her. She stood upon the coffin, and across the corpse – raised her eyes and hands imploringly to Heaven – and then, in accents wilder even than her words, uttered an imprecation that sounded like the prophetic warning of some unholy spirit.

"Inhuman murderer!" she exclaimed, in tones that almost paralysed the ears on which it fell, "if there be a God of justice and of truth, he will avenge this devilish deed. Yes, Colonel de Haldimar, a prophetic voice whispers to my soul, that even as I have seen perish before my eyes all I loved on earth, without mercy and without hope, so even shall you witness the destruction of your accursed race. Here – here – here," and she pointed downwards, with singular energy of action, to the corpse of her husband, "here shall their blood flow till every vestige of his own is washed away; and oh, if there be spared one branch of thy detested family, may it only be that they may be reserved for some death too horrible to be conceived!"

Overcome by the frantic energy with which she had uttered these appalling words, she sank backwards, and fell, uttering another shriek, into the arms of the warrior of the Fleur de lis.

"Hear you this, Colonel de Haldimar?" shouted the latter in a fierce and powerful voice, and in the purest English accent; "hear you the curse and prophecy of this heart-broken woman? You have slain her husband, but she has found another. Ay, she shall be my bride, if only for her detestation of yourself. When next you see us here," he thundered, "tremble for your race. Ha, ha, ha! no doubt this is another victim of your cold and calculating guile; but it shall be the last. By Heaven, my very heart leaps upward in anticipation of thy coming hour. Woman, thy hatred to this man has made me love thee; yes, thou shalt be my bride, and with my plans of vengeance will I woo thee. By this kiss I swear it."

As he spoke, he bent his face over that of the pale and inanimate woman, and pressed his lips to hers, yet red and moist with blood spots from the wounds of her husband. Then wresting, with a violent effort, his reeking toma-hawk from the cranched brain of the unfortunate soldier, and before any one could recover sufficiently from the effect of the scene altogether to think even of interfering, he bore off his prize in triumph, and fled, with nearly the same expedition he had previously manifested, in the direction of the forest.

WACOUSTA

Volume II

One

I T WAS ON the evening of that day, so fertile in melancholy incident, to which our first volume has been devoted, that the drawbridge of Détroit was, for the third time since the investment of the garrison, lowered; not, as previously, with a disregard of the intimation that might be given to those without by the sullen and echoing rattle of its ponderous chains, but with a caution attesting how much secrecy of purpose was sought to be preserved. There was, however, no array of armed men within the walls, that denoted an expedition of a hostile character. Overcome with the harassing duties of the day, the chief portion of the troops had retired to rest, and a few groups of the guard alone were to be seen walking up and down in front of their post, apparently with a view to check the influence of midnight drowsiness, but, in reality, to witness the result of certain preparations going on by torchlight in the centre of the barrack square.

In the midst of an anxious group of officers, comprising nearly all of that rank within the fort, stood two individuals, attired in a costume having nothing in common with the gay and martial habiliments of the former. They were tall, handsome young men, whose native elegance of carriage was but imperfectly hidden under an equipment evidently adopted for, and otherwise fully answering, the purpose of disguise. A blue cotton shell jacket, closely fitting to the person, trowsers of the same material, a pair

of strong deer-skin mocassins, and a coloured handkerchief tied loosely round the collar of a checked shirt, the
whole surmounted by one of those rough blanket coats,
elsewhere described, formed the principal portion of their
garb. Each, moreover, wore a false *queue* of about nine
inches in length, the effect of which was completely to
change the character of the countenance, and lend to the
features a Canadian-like expression. A red worsted cap,
resembling a *bonnet de nuit*, was thrown carelessly over
the side of the head, which could, at any moment, when
deeper disguise should be deemed necessary, command
the additional protection of the rude hood that fell back
upon the shoulders from the collar of the coat to which it
was attached. They were both well armed. Into a broad
belt, that encircled the jacket of each, were thrust a brace
of pistols and a strong dagger; the whole so disposed,
however, as to be invisible when the outer garment was
closed: this, again, was confined by a rude sash of worsted
of different colours, not unlike, in texture and quality,
what is worn by our sergeants at the present day. They
were otherwise armed, however, and in a less secret
manner. Across the right shoulder of each was thrown a
belt of worsted also, to which were attached a rude
powder horn and shot pouch, with a few straggling bullets,
placed there as if rather by accident than design. Each
held carelessly in his left hand, and with its butt resting on
the earth, a long gun; completing an appearance, the attainment of which had, in all probability, been sedulously
sought, – that of a Canadian duck-hunter.

A metamorphosis so ludicrously operated in the usually
elegant costume of two young English officers, – for such
they were, – might have been expected to afford scope to
the pleasantry of their companions, and to call forth those
sallies which the intimacy of friendship and the freema-
sonry of the profession would have fully justified. But the
events that had occurred in such rapid succession, since
the preceding midnight, were still painfully impressed on
the recollection of all, and some there were who looked as

if they never would smile again; neither laugh nor jeering, therefore, escaped the lips of one of the surrounding group. Every countenance wore a cast of thought, – a character of abstraction, ill suited to the indulgence of levity; and the little conversation that passed between them was in a low and serious tone. It was evident some powerful and absorbing dread existed in the mind of each, inducing him rather to indulge in communion with his own thoughts and impressions, than to communicate them to others. Even the governor himself had, for a moment, put off the dignity and distance of his usually unapproachable nature, to assume an air of unfeigned concern, and it might be dejection, contrasting strongly with his habitual haughtiness. Hitherto he had been walking to and fro, a little apart from the group, and with a hurriedness and indecision of movement that betrayed to all the extreme agitation of his mind. For once, however, he appeared to be insensible to observation, or, if not insensible, indifferent to whatever comments might be formed or expressed by those who witnessed his undissembled emotion. He was at length interrupted by the adjutant, who communicated something in a low voice.

"Let him be brought up, Mr. Lawson," was the reply. Then advancing into the heart of the group, and addressing the two adventurers, he enquired, in a tone that startled from its singular mildness, "if they were provided with every thing they required."

An affirmative reply was given, when the governor, taking the taller of the young men aside, conversed with him earnestly, and in a tone of affection strangely blended with despondency. The interview, however, was short, for Mr. Lawson now made his appearance, conducting an individual who has already been introduced to our readers. It was the Canadian of the Fleur de lis. The adjutant placed a small wooden crucifix in the hands of the governor.

"François," said the latter, impressively, "you know the terms on which I have consented to spare your life. Swear, then, by this cross; that you will be faithful to your trust;

164 of John Richardson

that neither treachery nor evasion shall be practised; and that you will, to the utmost of your power, aid in conveying these gentlemen to their destination. Kneel and swear it."

"I do swear it!" fervently repeated the aubergiste, kneeling and imprinting his lips with becoming reverence on the symbol of martyrdom. "I swear to do dat I shall engage, and may de bon Dieu have mercy to my soul as I shall fulfil my oat."

"Amen," pronounced the governor, "and may Heaven deal by you even as you deal by us. Bear in mind, moreover, that as your treachery will be punished, so also shall your fidelity be rewarded. But the night wears apace, and ye have much to do." Then turning to the young officers who were to be his companions, – "God bless you both; may your enterprise be successful! I fear," offering his hand to the younger, "I have spoken harshly to you, but at a moment like the present you will no longer cherish a recollection of the unpleasant past."

The only answer was a cordial return of his own pressure. The Canadian in his turn now announced the necessity for instant departure, when the young men, following his example, threw their long guns carelessly over the left shoulder. Low, rapid, and fervent adieus were uttered on both sides; and although the hands of the separating parties met only in a short and hurried grasp, there was an expression in the touch of each that spoke to their several hearts long after the separation had actually taken place.

"Stay one moment!" exclaimed a voice, as the little party now moved towards the gateway; "ye are both gallantly enough provided without, but have forgotten there is something quite as necessary to sustain the inward man. Duck shooting, you know, is wet work. The last lips that were moistened from this," he proceeded, as the younger of the disguised men threw the strap of the proffered canteen over his shoulder, "were those of poor Ellen Halloway."

The mention of that name, so heedlessly pronounced by

the brave but inconsiderate Erskine, produced a startling effect on the taller of the departing officers. He struck his brow violently with his hand, uttered a faint groan, and bending his head upon his chest, stood in an attitude expressive of the deep suffering of his mind. The governor, too, appeared agitated; and sounds like those of suppressed sobs came from one who lingered at the side of him who had accepted the offer of the canteen. The remainder of the officers preserved a deep and mournful silence.

"It is times dat we should start," again observed the Canadian, "or we shall be taken by de daylight before we can clear de river."

This intimation once more aroused the slumbering energies of the taller officer. Again he drew up his commanding figure, extended his hand to the governor in silence, and turning abruptly round, hastened to follow close in the footsteps of his conductor.

"You will not forget all I have said to you," whispered the voice of one who had reserved his parting for the last, and who now held the hand of the younger adventurer closely clasped in his own. "Think, oh, think how much depends on the event of your dangerous enterprise."

"When you behold me again," was the reply, "it will be with smiles on my lip and gladness in my heart; for if we fail, there is that within me, which whispers I shall never see you more. But keep up your spirits, and hope for the best. We embark under cheerless auspices, it is true; but let us trust to Providence for success in so good a cause, – God bless you!"

In the next minute he had joined his companions; who, with light and noiseless tread, were already pursuing their way along the military road that led to the eastern extremity of the town. Soon afterwards, the heavy chains of the drawbridge were heard grating on the ear, in despite of the evident caution used in restoring it to its wonted position, and all again was still.

It had at first been suggested their course should be held

in an angular direction across the cleared country alluded to in our last chapter, in order to avoid all chance of recognition in the town; but as this might have led them into more dangerous contact with some of the outlying parties of Indians, who were known to prowl around the fort at night, this plan had been abandoned for the more circuitous and safe passage by the village. Through this our little party now pursued their way, and without encountering aught to impede their progress. The simple mannered inhabitants had long since retired to rest, and neither light nor sound denoted the existence of man or beast within its precincts. At length they reached that part of the road which turned off abruptly in the direction of the Fleur de lis. The rude hut threw its dark shadows across their path, but all was still and deathlike as in the village they had just quitted. Presently, however, as they drew nearer, they beheld, reflected from one of the upper windows, a faint light that fell upon the ground immediately in front of the auberge; and, at intervals, the figure of a human being approaching and receding from it as if in the act of pacing the apartment.

An instinctive feeling of danger rose at the same moment to the hearts of the young officers; and each, obeying the same impulse, unfastened one of the large horn buttons of his blanket coat, and thrust his right hand into the opening.

"François, recollect your oath," hastily aspirated the elder, as he grasped the hand of their conductor rather in supplication than in threat; "if there be aught to harm us here, your own life will most assuredly pay the forfeit of your faith."

"It is noting but a womans," calmly returned the Canadian; "it is my Babette who is sorry at my loss. But I shall come and tell you directly."

He then stole gently round the corner of the hut, leaving his anxious companions in the rear of the little building, and completely veiled in the obscurity produced by the mingling shadows of the hut itself, and a few tall pear trees that overhung the paling of the orchard at some yards from the spot on which they stood.

They waited some minutes to hear the result of the Canadian's admittance into his dwelling; but although each with suppressed breathing sought to catch those sounds of welcome with which a daughter might be supposed to greet a parent so unexpectedly restored, they listened in vain. At length, however, while the ears of both were on the rack to drink in the tones of a human voice, a faint scream floated on the hushed air, and all again was still.

"Good!" whispered the elder of the officers; "that scream is sweeter to my ear than the softest accents of woman's love. It is evident the ordinary tones of speech cannot find their way to us here from the front of the hut. The faintness of yon cry, which was unquestionably that of a female, is a convincing proof of it."

"Hist!" urged his companion, in the same almost inaudible whisper, "what sound was that?"

Both again listened attentively, when the noise was repeated. It came from the orchard, and resembled the sound produced by the faint crash of rotten sticks and leaves under the cautious but unavoidably rending tread of a human foot. At intervals it ceased, as if the person treading, alarmed at his own noise, was apprehensive of betraying his approach; and then recommenced, only to be checked in the same manner. Finally it ceased altogether.

For upwards of five minutes the young men continued to listen for a renewal of the sound, but nothing was now audible, save the short and fitful gusts of a rising wind among the trees of the orchard.

"It must have been some wild animal in search of its prey," again whispered the younger officer; "had it been a man, we should have heard him leap the paling before this."

"By Heaven, we are betrayed, – here he is," quickly rejoined the other, in the same low tone. "Keep close to the hut, and stand behind me. If my dagger fail, you must try your own. But fire not, on your life, unless there be more than two, for the report of a pistol will be the destruction of ourselves and all that are dear to us."

Each with uplifted arm now stood ready to strike, even while his heart throbbed with a sense of danger, that had far more than the mere dread of personal suffering or death to stimulate to exertion in self-defence. Footsteps were now distinctly heard stealing round that part of the hut which bordered on the road; and the young men turned from the orchard, to which their attention had previously been directed, towards the new quarter whence they were intruded upon.

It was fortunate this mode of approach had been selected. That part of the hut which rested on the road was so exposed as to throw the outline of objects into strong relief, whereas in the direction of the thickly wooded orchard all was impenetrable gloom. Had the intruder stolen unannounced upon the alarmed but determined officers by the latter route, the dagger of the first would in all probability have been plunged to its hilt in his bosom. As it was, each had sufficient presence of mind to distinguish, as it now doubled the corner of the hut, and reposed upon the road, the stout square-set figure of the Canadian. The daggers were instantly restored to their sheaths, and each, for the first time since the departure of their companion, respired freely.

"It is quite well," whispered the latter as he approached. "It was my poor Babette, who tought I was gone to be kill. She scream so loud, as if she had seen my ghost. But we must wait a few minute in de house, and you shall see how glad my girl is to see me once again."

"Why this delay, François? why not start directly?" urged the taller officer; "we shall never clear the river in time; and if the dawn catches us in the waters of the Détroit, we are lost for ever."

"But you see I am not quite prepare yet," was the answer. "I have many tings to get ready for de canoe, which I have not use for a long times. But you shall not wait ten minute, if you do not like. Dere is a good fire, and Babette shall give you some ting to eat while I get it all ready."

The young men hesitated. The delay of the Canadian, who had so repeatedly urged the necessity for expedition while in the fort, had, to say the least of it, an appearance of incongruity. Still it was evident, if disposed to harm them, he had full opportunity to do so without much risk of effectual opposition from themselves. Under all circumstances, therefore, it was advisable rather to appear to confide implicitly in his truth, than, by manifesting suspicion, to pique his self-love, and neutralize whatever favourable intentions he might cherish in their behalf. In this mode of conduct they were confirmed, by a recollection of the sacredness attached by the religion of their conductor to the oath so solemnly pledged on the symbol of the cross, and by a conviction of the danger of observation to which they stood exposed, if, as they had apprehended, it was actually a human footstep they had heard in the orchard. This last recollection suggested a remark.

"We heard a strange sound within the orchard, while waiting here for your return," said the taller officer; "it was like the footstep of a man treading cautiously over rotten leaves and branches. How do you account for it?"

"Oh, it was my pigs," replied the Canadian, without manifesting the slightest uneasiness at the information. "They run about in de orchard for de apples what blows down wid de wind."

"It could not be a pig we heard," pursued his questioner; "but another thing, François, before we consent to enter the hut, – how will you account to your daughter for our presence? and what suspicion may she not form at seeing two armed strangers in company with you at this unseasonable hour."

"I have tell her," replied the Canadian, "dat I have bring two friends, who go wid me in de canoe to shoot de ducks for two tree days. You know, sir, I go always in de fall to kill de ducks wid my friends, and she will not tink it strange."

"You have managed well, my brave fellow; and now we follow you in confidence. But in the name of Heaven, use all possible despatch, and if money will lend a spur to your actions, you shall have plenty of it when our enterprise has been accomplished."

Our adventurers followed their conductor in the track by which he had so recently rejoined them. As they turned the corner of the hut, the younger, who brought up the rear, fancied he again heard a sound in the direction of the orchard, resembling that of one lightly leaping to the ground. A gust of wind, however, passing rapidly at the moment through the dense foliage, led him to believe it might have been produced by the sullen fall of one of the heavy fruits it had detached in its course. Unwilling to excite new and unnecessary suspicion in his companion, he confined the circumstance to his own breast, and followed into the hut.

After ascending a flight of about a dozen rude steps, they found themselves in a small room, furnished with no other ceiling than the sloping roof itself, and lighted by an unwieldy iron lamp, placed on a heavy oak table, near the only window with which the apartment was provided. This latter had suffered much from the influence of time and tempest; and owing to the difficulty of procuring glass in so remote a region, had been patched with slips of paper in various parts. The two corner and lower panes of the bottom sash were out altogether, and pine shingles, such as are used even at the present day for covering the roofs of dwelling houses, had been fitted into the squares, excluding air and light at the same time. The centre pane of this tier was, however, clear and free from flaw of every description. Opposite to the window blazed a cheerful wood fire, recently supplied with fuel; and at one of the inner corners of the room was placed a low uncurtained bed, that exhibited marks of having been lain in since it was last made. On a chair at its side were heaped a few dark-looking garments, the precise nature of which were not distinguishable at a cursory and distant glance.

Such were the more remarkable features of the apartment into which our adventurers were now ushered. Both looked cautiously around on entering, as if expecting to find it tenanted by spirits as daring as their own; but, with the exception of the daughter of their conductor, whose moist black eyes expressed, as much by tears as by smiles, the joy she felt at this unexpected return of her parent, no living object met their enquiring glance. The Canadian placed a couple of rush-bottomed chairs near the fire, invited his companions to seat themselves until he had completed his preparation for departure, and then, desiring Babette to hasten supper for the young hunters, quitted the room and descended the stairs.

Two

THE POSITION of the young men was one of embarrassment; for while the daughter, who was busied in executing the command of her father, remained in the room, it was impossible they could converse together without betraying the secret of their country, and, as a result of this, the falsehood of the character under which they appeared. Long residence in the country had, it is true, rendered the patois of that class of people whom they personated familiar to one, but the other spoke only the pure and native language of which it was a corruption. It might have occurred to them at a cooler moment, and under less critical circumstances, that, even if their disguise had been penetrated, it was unlikely a female, manifesting so much lively affection for her parent, would have done aught to injure those with whom he had evidently connected himself. But the importance attached to their entire security from danger left them but little room for reflections of a calming character, while a doubt of that security remained.

One singularity struck them both. They had expected the young woman, urged by a natural curiosity, would have commenced a conversation, even if they did not; and he who spoke the patois was prepared to sustain it as well as his anxious and overcharged spirit would enable him; and as he was aware the morning had furnished sufficient incident of fearful interest, he had naturally looked for a verbal re-enactment of the harrowing and dreadful scene. To their surprise, however, they both remarked that, far from evincing a desire to enter into conversation, the young woman scarcely ever looked at them, but lingered constantly near the table, and facing the window. Still, to avoid an appearance of singularity on their own parts as far as possible, the elder of the officers motioned to his companion, who, following his example, took a small pipe and some tobacco from a compartment in his shot pouch, and commenced puffing the wreathing smoke from his lips, – an occupation, more than any other, seeming to justify their silence.

The elder officer sat with his back to the window, and immediately in front of the fire; his companion, at a corner of the rude hearth, and in such a manner that, without turning his head, he could command every part of the room at a glance. In the corner facing him stood the bed already described. A faint ray of the fire-light fell on some minute object glittering in the chair, the contents of which were heaped up in disorder. Urged by that wayward curiosity, which is sometimes excited, even under circumstances of the greatest danger and otherwise absorbing interest, the young man kicked the hickory log that lay nearest to it with his mocassined foot, and produced a bright crackling flame, the reflection of which was thrown entirely upon the object of his gaze; it was a large metal button, on which the number of his regiment was distinctly visible. Unable to check his desire to know further, he left his seat, to examine the contents of the chair. As he moved across the room, he fancied he heard a light sound from without; his companion, also, seemed to manifest a similar impression by an almost imperceptible start; but the noise was so momentary, and so fanciful, neither felt it worth his while to pause upon the circumstance. The young officer now raised the garments from the chair: they consisted of a small grey great-coat, and trowsers, a waistcoat of coarse white cloth, a pair of worsted stockings, and the half-boots of a boy; the whole forming the drum-boy's equipment, worn by the wretched wife of Halloway when borne senseless into the hut on that fatal morning. Hastily quitting a dress that called up so many dreadful recollections, and turning to his companion with a look that denoted apprehension, lest he too should have beheld these melancholy remembrances of the harrowing scene, the young officer hastened to resume his seat. In the act of so doing, his eye fell upon the window, at which the female still lingered. Had a blast from Heaven struck his sight, the terror of his soul could not have been greater. He felt his cheek to pale, and his hair to bristle beneath his cap, while the checked blood crept slowly and coldly, as if its very function had been paralysed; still he had presence of mind sufficient not to falter in his step, or to betray, by any extraordinary movement, that his eye had rested on any thing hateful to behold.

His companion had emptied his first pipe, and was in the act of refilling it, when he resumed his seat. He was evidently impatient at the delay of the Canadian, and already were his lips opening to give utterance to his disappointment, when he felt his foot significantly pressed by that of his friend. An instinctive sense of something fearful that was to ensue, but still demanding caution on his part, prevented him from turning hastily round to know the cause. Satisfied, however, there was danger, though not of an instantaneous character, he put his pipe gently by, and stealing his hand under his coat, again grasped the hilt of his dagger. At length he slowly and partially turned his head, while his eyes inquiringly demanded of his friend the cause of his alarm.

Partly to aid in concealing his increasing paleness, and partly with a view to render it a medium for the conveyance of subdued sound, the hand of the latter was raised to his face in such a manner that the motion of his lips could not be distinguished from behind.

"We are betrayed," he scarcely breathed. "If you can command yourself, turn and look at the window; but for

God's sake arm yourself with resolution, or look not at all: first draw the hood over your head, and without any appearance of design. Our only chance of safety lies in this, – that the Canadian may still be true, and that our disguise may not be penetrated."

In despite of his native courage, – and this had often been put to honourable proof, – he, thus mysteriously addressed, felt his heart to throb violently. There was something so appalled in the countenance of his friend – something so alarming in the very caution he had recommended – that a vague dread of the horrible reality rushed at once to his mind, and for a moment his own cheek became ashy pale, and his breathing painfully oppressed. It was the natural weakness of the physical man, over which the moral faculties had, for an instant, lost their directing power. Speedily recovering himself, the young man prepared to encounter the alarming object which had already so greatly intimidated his friend. Carefully drawing the blanket hood over his head, he rose from his seat, and, with the energetic movement of one who has formed some desperate determination, turned his back to the fireplace, and threw his eyes rapidly and eagerly upon the window. They fell only on the rude patchwork of which it was principally composed. The female had quitted the room.

"You must have been deceived," he whispered, keeping his eye still bent upon the window, and with so imperceptible a movement of the lips that sound alone could have betrayed he was speaking, – "I see nothing to justify your alarm. Look again."

The younger officer once more directed his glance towards the window, and with a shuddering of the whole person, as he recollected what had met his eye when he last looked upon it. "It is no longer there, indeed," he returned in the same scarcely audible tone. "Yet I could not be mistaken; it was between those two corner squares of wood in the lower sash."

"Perhaps it was merely a reflection produced by the lamp on the centre pane," rejoined his friend, still keeping his eye riveted on the suspicious point.

"Impossible! but I will examine the window from the spot on which I stood when I first beheld it."

Again he quitted his seat, and carelessly crossed the room. As he returned he threw his glance upon the pane, when, to his infinite horror and surprise, the same frightful vision presented itself.

"God of Heaven!" he exclaimed aloud, and unable longer to check the ebullition of his feelings, – "what means this? – Is my brain turned? and am I the sport of my own delusive fancy? – Do you not see it *now*?"

No answer was returned. His friend stood mute and motionless, with his left hand grasping his gun, and his right thrust into the waist of his coat. His eye grew upon the window, and his chest heaved, and his cheek paled and flushed alternately with the subdued emotion of his heart. A human face was placed close to the unblemished glass, and every feature was distinctly revealed by the lamp that still lay upon the table. The glaring eye was fixed on the taller of the officers; but though the expression was unfathomably guileful, there was nothing that denoted any thing like a recognition of the party. The brightness of the wood fire had so far subsided as to throw the interior of the room into partial obscurity, and under the disguise of his hood it was impossible for one without to distinguish the features of the taller officer. The younger, who was scarcely an object of attention, passed comparatively unnoticed.

Fatigued and dimmed with the long and eager tension of its nerves, the eye of the latter now began to fail him. For a moment he closed it; and when again it fell upon the window, it encountered nothing but the clear and glittering pane. For upwards of a minute he and his friend still continued to rivet their gaze, but the face was no longer visible.

Why is it that what is called the "human face divine" is

sometimes gifted with a power to paralyse, that the most loathsome reptile in the creation cannot attain? Had a hyena or cougar of the American forest, roaring for prey, appeared at that window, ready to burst the fragile barrier, and fasten its talons in their hearts, its presence would not have struck such sickness to the soul of our adventurers as did that human face. It is that man, naturally fierce and inexorable, is alone the enemy of his own species. The solution of this problem – this glorious paradox in nature, we leave to profounder philosophers to resolve. Sufficient for us be it to know, and to deplore that it is so.

Footsteps were now heard upon the stairs; and the officers, aroused to a full sense of their danger, hastily and silently prepared themselves for the encounter.

"Drop a bullet into your gun," whispered the elder, setting the example himself. "We may be obliged to have recourse to it at last. Yet make no show of hostility unless circumstances satisfy us we are betrayed; then, indeed, all that remains for us will be to sell our lives as dearly as we can. Hist! he is here."

The door opened; and at the entrance, which was already filled up in the imaginations of the young men with a terrible and alarming figure, appeared one whose return had been anxiously and long desired. It was a relief, indeed, to their gallant but excited hearts to behold another than the form they had expected; and although, for the moment, they knew not whether the Canadian came in hostility or in friendship, each quitted the attitude of caution into which he had thrown himself, and met him midway in his passage through the room. There was nothing in the expression of his naturally open and good-humoured countenance to denote he was at all aware of the causes for alarm that had operated so powerfully on themselves. He announced with a frank look and unfaltering voice every thing was in readiness for their departure.

The officers hesitated; and the taller fixed his eyes upon those of mine host, as if his gaze would have penetrated to the innermost recesses of his heart. Could this be a refinement of his treachery? and was he really ignorant of the existence of the danger which threatened them? Was it not more probable his object was to disarm their fears, that they might be given unprepared and, therefore, unresisting victims to the ferocity of their enemies? Aware as he was, that they were both well provided with arms, and fully determined to use them with effect, might not his aim be to decoy them to destruction without, lest the blood spilt under his roof, in the desperation of their defence, should hereafter attest against him, and expose him to the punishment he would so richly merit? Distracted by these doubts, the young men scarcely knew what to think or how to act; and anxious as they had previously been to quit the hut, they now considered the moment of their doing so would be that of their destruction. The importance of the enterprise on which they were embarked was such as to sink all personal considerations. If they had felt the influence of intimidation on their spirits, it arose less from any apprehension of consequences to themselves, than from the recollection of the dearer interests involved in their perfect security from discovery.

"François," feelingly urged the taller officer, again adverting to his vow, "you recollect the oath you so solemnly pledged upon the cross of your Saviour. Tell me, then, as you hope for mercy, have you taken that oath only that you might the more securely betray us to our enemies? What connection have you with them at this moment? and who is *he* who stood looking through that window not ten minutes since?"

"As I shall hope for mercy in my God," exclaimed the Canadian with unfeigned astonishment, "I have not see nobody. But what for do you tink so? It is not just. I have given my oat to serve you, and I shall do it."

There was candour both in the tone and countenance of the man as he uttered these words, half in reproach, half in justification; and the officers no longer doubted.

"You must forgive our suspicions at a moment like the present," soothingly observed the younger; "yet, François, your daughter saw and exchanged signals with the person we mean. She left the room soon after he made his appearance. What has become of her?"

The Canadian gave a sudden start, looked hastily round, and seemed to perceive for the first time the girl was absent. He then put a finger to his lip to enjoin silence, advanced to the table, and extinguished the light. Desiring his companions, in a low whisper, to tread cautiously and follow, he now led the way with almost noiseless step to the entrance of the hut. At the threshold of the door were placed a large well-filled sack, a light mast and sail, and half a dozen paddles. The latter burden he divided between the officers, on whose shoulders he carefully balanced them. The sack he threw across his own; and without expressing even a regret that an opportunity of bidding adieu to his child was denied him, hastily skirted the paling of the orchard until, at the further extremity, he had gained the high road.

The heavens were obscured by passing clouds driven rapidly by the wind, during the short pauses of which our adventurers anxiously and frequently turned to listen if they were pursued. Save the rustling of the trees that lined the road, and the slight dashing of the waters on the beach, however, no sound was distinguishable. At length they gained the point whence they were to start. It was the fatal bridge, the events connected with which were yet so painfully fresh in their recollection.

"Stop one minutes here," whispered the Canadian, throwing his sack upon the sand near the mouth of the lesser river; "my canoe is chain about twenty yards up de bridge. I shall come to you directly." Then cautioning the officers to keep themselves concealed under the bridge, he moved hastily under the arch, and disappeared in the dark shadow which it threw across the rivulet.

The extremities of the bridge rested on the banks of the little river in such a manner as to leave a narrow passage along the sands immediately under the declination of the arch. In accordance with the caution of their conductor, the officers had placed themselves under it; and with their backs slightly bent forward to meet the curvature of the bridge, so that no ray of light could pass between their bodies and the fabric itself, now awaited the arrival of the vessel on which their only hope depended. We shall not attempt to describe their feelings on finding themselves, at that lone hour of the night, immediately under a spot rendered fearfully memorable by the tragic occurrences of the morning. The terrible pursuit of the fugitive, the execution of the soldier, the curse and prophecy of his maniac wife, and, above all, the forcible abduction and threatened espousal of that unhappy woman by the formidable being who seemed to have identified himself with the evils with which they stood menaced, – all rushed with rapid tracery on the mind, and excited the imagination, until each, filled with a sentiment not unallied to superstitious awe, feared to whisper forth his thoughts, lest in so doing he should invoke the presence of those who had principally figured in the harrowing and revolting scene.

"Did you not hear a noise?" at length whispered the elder, as he leaned himself forward, and bent his head to the sand, to catch more distinctly a repetition of the sound.

"I did; there again! It is upon the bridge, and not unlike the step of one endeavouring to tread lightly. It may be some wild beast, however."

"We must not be taken by surprise," returned his companion. "If it be a man, the wary tread indicates consciousness of our presence. If an animal, there can be no harm in setting our fears at rest."

Cautiously stealing from his lurking-place, the young officer emerged into the open sands, and in a few measured noiseless strides gained the extremity of the bridge. The dark shadow of something upon its centre caught his eye, and a low sound like that of a dog lapping met his ear. While his gaze yet lingered on the shapeless object, endeavouring to give it a character, the clouds which had so long obscured it passed momentarily from before the moon, and disclosed the appalling truth. It was a wolf-dog lapping up from the earth, in which they were encrusted, the blood and brains of the unfortunate Frank Halloway.

Sick and faint at the disgusting sight, the young man rested his elbow on the railing that passed along the edge of the bridge, and, leaning his head on his hand for a moment, forgot the risk of exposure he incurred, in the intenseness of the sorrow that assailed his soul. His heart and imagination were already far from the spot on which he stood, when he felt an iron hand upon his shoulder. He turned, shuddering with an instinctive knowledge of his yet unseen visitant, and beheld standing over him the terrible warrior of the Fleur de lis.

"Ha, ha, ha!" laughed the savage in a low triumphant tone, "the place of our meeting is well timed, though somewhat singular, it must be confessed. Nay," he fiercely added, grasping as in a vice the arm that was already lifted to strike him, "force me not to annihilate you on the spot. Ha! hear you the cry of my wolf-dog?" as that animal now set up a low but fearful howl; "it is for your blood he asks, but your hour is not yet come."

"No, by Heaven, is it not!" exclaimed a voice; a rapid and rushing sweep was heard through the air for an instant, and then a report like a stunning blow. The warrior released his grasp – placed his hand upon his tomahawk, but without strength to remove it from his belt – tottered a pace or two backwards – and then fell, uttering a cry of mingled pain and disappointment, at his length upon the earth.

"Quick, quick to our cover!" exclaimed the younger officer, as a loud shout was now heard from the forest in reply to the yell of the fallen warrior. "If François come not, we are lost; the howl of that wolf-dog alone will betray us, even if his master should be beyond all chance of recovery."

"Desperate diseases require desperate remedies," was the reply; "there is little glory in destroying a helpless enemy, but the necessity is urgent, and we must leave nothing to chance." As he spoke, he knelt upon the huge form of the senseless warrior, whose scalping knife he drew from its sheath, and striking a firm and steady blow, quitted not the weapon until he felt his hand reposing on the chest of his enemy.

The howl of the wolf-dog, whose eyes glared like two burning coals through the surrounding gloom, was now exchanged to a fierce and snappish bark. He made a leap at the officer while in the act of rising from the body; but his fangs fastened only in the chest of the shaggy coat, which he wrung with the strength and fury characteristic of his peculiar species. This new and ferocious attack was fraught with danger little inferior to that which they had just escaped, and required the utmost promptitude of action. The young man seized the brute behind the neck in a firm and vigorous grasp, while he stooped upon the motionless form over which this novel struggle was maintained, and succeeded in making himself once more master of the scalping knife. Half choked by the hand that unflinchingly grappled with him, the savage animal quitted his hold and struggled violently to free himself. This was the critical moment. The officer drew the heavy sharp blade, from the handle to the point, across the throat of the infuriated beast, with a force that divided the principal artery. He made a desperate leap upwards, spouting his blood over his destroyer, and then fell gasping across the body of his master. A low growl, intermingled with faint attempts to bark, which the rapidly oozing life rendered more and more indistinct, succeeded; and at length nothing but a gurgling sound was distinguishable.

Meanwhile the anxious and harassed officers had regained their place of concealment under the bridge, where they listened with suppressed breathing for the slightest sound to indicate the approach of the canoe. At intervals they fancied they could hear a noise resembling the rippling of water against the prow of a light vessel, but the swelling cries of the rushing band, becoming at every instant more distinct, were too unceasingly kept up to admit of their judging with accuracy.

They now began to give themselves up for lost, and many and bitter were the curses they inwardly bestowed on the Canadian, when the outline of a human form was seen advancing along the sands, and a dark object upon the water. It was their conductor, dragging the canoe along, with all the strength and activity of which he was capable.

"What the devil have you been about all this time, François?" exclaimed the taller officer, as he bounded to meet him. "Quick, quick, or we shall be too late. Hear you not the blood-hounds on their scent?" Then seizing the chain in his hand, with a powerful effort he sent the canoe flying through the arch to the very entrance of the river. The burdens that had been deposited on the sands were hastily flung in, the officers stepping lightly after. The Canadian took the helm, directing the frail vessel almost noiselessly through the water, and with such velocity, that when the cry of the disappointed savages was heard resounding from the bridge, it had already gained the centre of the Détroit.

Three

TWO DAYS had succeeded to the departure of the officers from the fort, but unproductive of any event of importance. About daybreak, however, on the morning of the third, the harassed garrison were once more summoned to arms, by an alarm from the sentinels planted in the rear of the works; a body of Indians they had traced and lost at intervals, as they wound along the skirt of the forest, in their progress from their encampment, were at length developing themselves in force near the bomb proof. With a readiness which long experience and watchfulness had rendered in some degree habitual to them, the troops flew to their respective posts; while a few of the senior officers, among whom was the governor, hastened to the ramparts to reconnoitre the strength and purpose of their enemies. It was evident the views of these latter were not immediately hostile; for neither were they in their war paint, nor were their arms of a description to carry intimidation to a disciplined and fortified soldiery. Bows, arrows, tomahawks, war clubs, spears, and scalping knives, constituted their warlike equipments, but neither rifle nor firearms of any kind were discernible. Several of their leaders, distinguishable by a certain haughty carriage and commanding gesticulation, were collected within the elevated bomb-proof; apparently holding a short but important conference apart from their people, most of whom stood or lay in picturesque attitudes around the ruin.

These also had a directing spirit. A tall and noble looking warrior, wearing a deer-skin hunting frock closely girded around his loins, appeared to command the deference of his colleagues, claiming profound attention when he spoke himself, and manifesting his assent or dissent to the apparently expressed opinions of the lesser chiefs, merely by a slight movement of the head.

"There he is indeed!" exclaimed Captain Erskine, speaking as one who communes with his own thoughts, while he kept his telescope levelled on the form of the last warrior; "looking just as noble as when, three years ago, he opposed himself to the progress of the first English detachment that had ever penetrated to this part of the world. What a pity such a fine fellow should be so desperate and determined an enemy!"

"True; you were with Major Rogers on that expedition," observed the governor, in a tone now completely divested of the haughtiness which formerly characterised his address to his officers. "I have often heard him speak of it. You had many difficulties to contend against, if I recollect."

"We had indeed, sir," returned the frank-hearted Erskine, dropping the glass from his eye. "So many, in fact, that more than once, in the course of our progress through the wilderness, did I wish myself at head-quarters with my company. Never shall I forget the proud and determined expression of Ponteac's countenance, when he told Rogers, in his figurative language, 'he stood in the path in which he travelled.' "

"Thank Heaven, he at least stands not in the path in which *others* travel," musingly rejoined the governor. "But what sudden movement is that within the ruin?"

"The Indians are preparing to show a white flag," shouted an artillery-man from his station in one of the embrasures below.

The governor and his officers received this intelligence without surprise; the former took the glass from Captain Erskine, and coolly raised it to his eye. The consultation had ceased; and the several chiefs, with the exception of their leader and two others, were now seen quitting the bomb-proof to join their respective tribes. One of those who remained, sprang upon an elevated fragment of the ruin, and uttered a prolonged cry, the purport of which, – and it was fully understood from its peculiar nature, – was to claim attention from the fort. He then received from the hands of the other chief a long spear, to the end of which was attached a piece of white linen. This he waved several times above his head; then stuck the barb of the spear firmly into the projecting fragment. Quitting his elevated station, he next stood at the side of the Ottawa chief, who had already assumed the air and attitude of one waiting to observe in what manner his signal would be received.

"A flag of truce in all its bearings, by Jupiter!" remarked Captain Erskine. "Ponteac seems to have acquired a few lessons since we first met."

"This is evidently the suggestion of some European," observed Major Blackwater; "for how should he understand any thing of the nature of a white flag? Some of those vile spies have put him up to this."

"True enough, Blackwater; and they appear to have found an intelligent pupil," observed Captain Wentworth. "I was curious to know how he would make the attempt to approach us; but certainly never once dreamt of his having recourse to so civilised a method. Their plot works well, no doubt; still we have the counter-plot to oppose to it."

"We must foil them with their own weapons," remarked the governor, "even if it be only with a view to gain time. Wentworth, desire one of your bombardiers to hoist the large French flag on the staff."

The order was promptly obeyed. The Indians made a simultaneous movement expressive of their satisfaction; and in the course of a minute, the tall warrior, accompanied by nearly a dozen inferior chiefs, was seen slowly advancing across the common, towards the group of officers.

"What generous confidence the fellow has, for an Indian!" observed Captain Erskine, who could not dissemble his admiration of the warrior. "He steps as firmly and as proudly within reach of our muskets, as if he was leading in the war-dance."

"How strange," mused Captain Blessington, "that one who meditates so deep a treachery, should have no apprehension of it in others!"

"It is a compliment to the honour of our flag," observed the governor, "which it must be our interest to encourage. If, as you say, Erskine, the man is really endowed with generosity, the result of this affair will assuredly call it forth."

"If it prove otherwise, sir," was the reply, "we must only attribute his perseverance to the influence which that terrible warrior of the Fleur de lis is said to exercise over his better feelings. By the by, I see nothing of him among this flag of truce party. It could scarcely be called a violation of faith to cut off such a rascally renegade. Were he of the number of those advancing, and Valletort's rifle within my reach, I know not what use I might not be tempted to make of the last."

Poor Erskine was singularly infelicitous in touching, and ever unconsciously, on a subject sure to give pain to more than one of his brother officers. A cloud passed over the brow of the governor, but it was one that originated more in sorrow than in anger. Neither had he time to linger on the painful recollections hastily and confusedly called up by the allusion made to this formidable and mysterious being, for the attention of all was now absorbed by the approaching Indians. With a bold and confiding carriage the fierce Ponteac moved at the head of his little party, nor hesitated one moment in his course, until he got near the brink of the ditch, and stood face to face with the governor, at a distance that gave both parties not only the facility of tracing the expression of each other's features, but of conversing without effort. There he made a sudden stand, and thrusting his spear into the earth, assumed an attitude as devoid of apprehension as if he had been in the heart of his own encampment.

"My father has understood my sign," said the haughty chief. "The warriors of a dozen tribes are far behind the path the Ottawa has just travelled; but when the red skin comes unarmed, the hand of the Saganaw is tied behind his back."

"The strong hold of the Saganaw is his safeguard," replied the governor, adopting the language of the Indian. "When the enemies of his great father come in strength, he knows how to disperse them; but when a warrior throws himself unarmed into his power, he respects his confidence, and his arms hang rusting at his side."

"The talk of my father is big," replied the warrior, with a scornful expression that seemed to doubt the fact of so much indifference as to himself; "but when it is a great chief who directs the nations, and that chief his sworn enemy, the temptation to the Saganaw may be strong."

"The Saganaw is without fear," emphatically rejoined the governor; "he is strong in his own honour; and he would rather die under the tomahawk of the red skin, than procure a peace by an act of treachery."

The Indian paused; cold, calm looks of intelligence passed between him and his followers, and a few indistinct and guttural sentences were exchanged among themselves.

"But our father asks not why our mocassins have brushed the dew from off the common," resumed the chief; "and yet it is long since the Saganaw and the red skin have spoken to each other, except through the war whoop. My father must wonder to see the great chief of the Ottawa without the hatchet in his hand."

"The hatchet often wounds those who use it unskilfully," calmly returned the governor. "The Saganaw is not blind. The Ottawas, and the other tribes, find the war paint heavy on their skins. They see that my young men are not to be conquered, and they have sent the great head of all the nations to sue for peace."

In spite of the habitual reserve and self-possession of his race, the haughty warrior could not repress a movement of impatience at the bold and taunting language of his enemy, and for a moment there was a fire in his eye that told how willingly he would have washed away the insult in his blood. The same low guttural exclamations that had previously escaped their lips, marked the sense entertained of the remark by his companions.

"My father is right," pursued the chief, resuming his self-command; "the Ottawas, and the other tribes, ask for peace, but not because they are afraid of war. When they strike the hatchet into the war post, they leave it there until their enemies ask them to take it out."

"Why come they now, then, to ask for peace?" was the cool demand.

The warrior hesitated, evidently at a loss to give a reply that could reconcile the palpable contradiction of his words.

"The rich furs of our forests have become many," he at length observed, "since we first took up the hatchet against the Saganaw; and every bullet we keep for our enemies is a loss to our trade. We once exchanged furs with the children of our father of the pale flag. They gave us, in return, guns, blankets, powder, ball, and all that the red man requires in the hunting season. These are all expended; and my young men would deal with the Saganaw as they did with the French."

"Good; the red skins would make peace; and although the arm of the Saganaw is strong, he will not turn a deaf ear to their desire."

"All the strong holds of the Saganaw, except two, have fallen before the great chief of the Ottawas!" proudly returned the Indian, with a look of mingled scorn and defiance. "They, too, thought themselves beyond the reach of our tomahawks; but they were deceived. In less than a single moon nine of them have fallen, and the tents of my young warriors are darkened with their scalps; but this is past. If the red skin asks for peace, it is because he is tired of seeing the blood of the Saganaw on his tomahawk. Does my father hear?"

"We will listen to the great chief of the Ottawas, and hear what he has to say," returned the governor, who, as well as the officers at his side, could with difficulty conceal their disgust and sorrow at the dreadful intelligence thus imparted of the fates of their companions. "But peace," he pursued with dignity, "can only be made in the council room, and under the sacred pledge of the calumet. The great chief has a wampum belt on his shoulder, and a calumet in his hand. His aged warriors, too, are at his side. What says the Ottawa? Will he enter? If so, the gate of the Saganaw shall be open to him."

The warrior started; and for a moment the confidence that had hitherto distinguished him seemed to give place to an apprehension of meditated treachery. He, however, speedily recovered himself, and observed emphatically, "It is the great head of all the nations whom my father invites to the council seat. Were he to remain in the hands of the Saganaw, his young men would lose their strength. They would bury the hatchet for ever in despair, and hide their faces in the laps of their women."

"Does the Ottawa chief see the pale flag on the strong hold of his enemies? While that continues to fly, he is safe as if he were under the cover of his own wigwam. If the Saganaw could use guile like the fox" (and this was said with marked emphasis), "what should prevent him from cutting off the Ottawa and his chiefs, even where they now stand?"

A half smile of derision passed over the dark cheek of the Indian. "If the arm of an Ottawa is strong," he said, "his foot is not less swift. The short guns of the chiefs of the Saganaw" (pointing to the pistols of the officers) "could not reach us; and before the voice of our father could be raised, or his eye turned, to call his warriors to his side, the Ottawa would be already far on his way to the forest."

"The great chief of the Ottawas shall judge better of the

Saganaw," returned the governor. – "He shall see that his young men are ever watchful of their posts: – Up, men, and show yourselves."

A second or two sufficed to bring the whole of Captain Erskine's company, who had been lying flat on their faces, to their feet on the rampart. The Indians were evidently taken by surprise, though they evinced no fear. The low and guttural "Ugh!" was the only expression they gave to their astonishment, not unmingled with admiration.

But, although the chiefs preserved their presence of mind, the sudden appearance of the soldiers had excited alarm among their warriors, who, grouped in and around the bomb-proof, were watching every movement of the conferring parties, with an interest proportioned to the risk they conceived their head men had incurred in venturing under the very walls of their enemies. Fierce yells were uttered; and more than a hundred dusky warriors, brandishing their tomahawks in air, leaped along the skirt of the common, evidently only awaiting the signal of their great chief, to advance and cover his retreat. At the command of the governor, however, the men had again suddenly disappeared from the surface of the rampart; so that when the Indians finally perceived their leader stood unharmed and unmolested, on the spot he had previously occupied, the excitement died away, and they once more assumed their attitude of profound attention.

"What thinks the great chief of the Ottawas now?" asked the governor; – "did he imagine that the young white men lie sleeping like beavers in their dams, when the hunter sets his traps to catch them? – did he imagine that they foresee not the designs of their enemies? and that they are not always on the watch to prevent them?"

"My father is a great warrior," returned the Indian; "and if his arm is full of strength, his head is full of wisdom. The chiefs will no longer hesitate; – they will enter the strong hold of the Saganaw, and sit with him in the council."

He next addressed a few words, and in a language not

understood by those upon the walls, to one of the younger of the Indians. The latter acknowledged his sense and approbation of what was said to him by an assentient and expressive "Ugh!" which came from his chest without any apparent emotion of the lips, much in the manner of a modern ventriloquist. He then hastened, with rapid and lengthened boundings, across the common towards his band. After the lapse of a minute or two from reaching them, another simultaneous cry arose, differing in expression from any that had hitherto been heard. It was one denoting submission to the will, and compliance with some conveyed desire, of their superior.

"Is the gate of the Saganaw open?" asked the latter, as soon as his ear had been greeted with the cry we have just named. "The Ottawa and the other great chiefs are ready; – their hearts are bold, and they throw themselves into the hands of the Saganaw without fear."

"The Ottawa chief knows the path," drily rejoined the governor: "when he comes in peace, it is ever open to him; but when his young men press it with the tomahawk in their hands, the big thunder is roused to anger, and they are scattered away like the leaves of the forest in the storm. Even now," he pursued, as the little band of Indians moved slowly round the walls, "the gate of the Saganaw opens for the Ottawa and the other chiefs."

"Let the most vigilant caution be used every where along the works, but especially in the rear," continued the governor, addressing Captain Blessington, on whom the duty of the day had devolved. "We are safe, while their chiefs are with us; but still it will be necessary to watch the forest closely. We cannot be too much on our guard. The men had better remain concealed, every twentieth file only standing up to form a look-out chain. If any movement of a suspicious nature be observed, let it be communicated by the discharge of a single musket, that the drawbridge may be raised on the instant." With the delivery of these brief instructions he quitted the rampart with the majority of his officers.

Meanwhile, hasty preparations had been made in the mess-room to receive the chiefs. The tables had been removed, and a number of clean rush mats, manufactured, after the Indian manner, into various figures and devices, spread carefully upon the floor. At the further end from the entrance was placed a small table and chair, covered with scarlet cloth. This was considerably elevated above the surface of the floor, and intended for the governor. On either side of the room, near these, were ranged a number of chairs for the accommodation of the inferior officers.

Major Blackwater received the chiefs at the gate. With a firm, proud step, rendered more confident by his very unwillingness to betray any thing like fear, the tall, and, as Captain Erskine had justly designated him, the noble-looking Ponteac trod the yielding planks that might in the next moment cut him off from his people for ever. The other chiefs, following the example of their leader, evinced the same easy fearlessness of demeanour, nor glanced once behind them to see if there was any thing to justify the apprehension of hidden danger.

The Ottawa was evidently mortified at not being received by the governor in person. "My father is not here!" he said fiercely to the major: – "how is this? The Ottawa and the other chiefs are kings of all their tribes. The head of one great people should be received only by the head of another great people!"

"Our father sits in the council-hall," returned the major. "He has taken his seat, that he may receive the warriors with becoming honour. But I am the second chief, and our father has sent me to receive them."

To the proud spirit of the Indian this explanation scarcely sufficed. For a moment he seemed to struggle, as if endeavouring to stifle his keen sense of an affront put upon him. At length he nodded his head haughtily and condescendingly, in token of assent; and gathering up his noble form, and swelling out his chest, as if with a view to strike terror as well as admiration into the hearts of those by whom he expected to be surrounded, stalked majestically forward at the head of his confederates.

An indifferent observer, or one ignorant of these people, would have been at fault; but those who understood the workings of an Indian's spirit could not have been deceived by the tranquil exterior of these men. The rapid, keen, and lively glance – the suppressed sneer of exultation – the half start of surprise – the low, guttural, and almost inaudible "Ugh!" – all these indicated the eagerness with which, at one sly but compendious view, they embraced the whole interior of a fort which it was of such vital importance to their future interests they should become possessed of, yet which they had so long and so unsuccessfully attempted to subdue. As they advanced into the square, they looked around, expecting to behold the full array of their enemies; but, to their astonishment, not a soldier was to be seen. A few women and children only, in whom curiosity had overcome a natural loathing and repugnance to the savages, were peeping from the windows of the block houses. Even at a moment like the present, the fierce instinct of these latter was not to be controlled. One of the children, terrified at the wild appearance of the warriors, screamed violently, and clung to the bosom of its mother for protection. Fired at the sound, a young chief raised his hand to his lips, and was about to peal forth his terrible war whoop in the very centre of the fort, when the eye of the Ottawa suddenly arrested him.

Four

THERE WERE few forms of courtesy observed by the warriors towards the English officers on entering the council room. Ponteac, who had collected all his native haughtiness into one proud expression of look and figure, strode in without taking the slightest notice even of the governor. The other chiefs imitated his example, and all took their seats upon the matting in the order prescribed by their rank among the tribes, and their experience in council. The Ottawa chief sat at the near extremity of the room, and immediately facing the governor. A profound silence was observed for some minutes after the Indians had seated themselves, during which they proceeded to fill their pipes. The handle of that of the Ottawa chief was decorated with numerous feathers fancifully disposed.

"This is well," at length observed the governor. "It is long since the great chiefs of the nations have smoked the sweet grass in the council hall of the Saganaw. What have they to say, that their young men may have peace to hunt the beaver, and to leave the print of their mocassins in the country of the Buffalo? – What says the Ottawa chief?"

"The Ottawa chief is a great warrior," returned the other, haughtily; and again repudiating, in the indomitableness of his pride, the very views that a more artful policy had first led him to avow. "He has already said that, within a single moon, nine of the strong holds of the Saganaw have fallen into his hands, and that the scalps of the white men fill the tents of his warriors. If the red skins wish for peace, it is because they are sick with spilling the blood of their enemies. Does my father hear?"

"The Ottawa has been cunning, like the fox," calmly returned the governor. "He went with deceit upon his lips, and said to the great chiefs of the strong holds of the Saganaw, – 'You have no more forts upon the lakes; they have all fallen before the red skins: they gave themselves into our hands; and we spared their lives, and sent them down to the great towns near the salt lake.' But this was false: the chiefs of the Saganaw, believing what was said to them, gave up their strong holds; but their lives were not spared, and the grass of the Canadas is yet moist with their blood. Does the Ottawa hear?"

Amazement and stupefaction sat for a moment on the features of the Indians. The fact was as had been stated; and yet, so completely had the several forts been cut off from all communication, it was deemed almost impossible one could have received tidings of the fate of the other, unless conveyed through the Indians themselves.

"The spies of the Saganaw have been very quick to escape the vigilance of the red skins," at length replied the Ottawa; "yet they have returned with a lie upon their lips. I swear by the Great Spirit, that nine of the strong holds of the Saganaw have been destroyed. How could the Ottawa go with deceit upon his lips, when his words were truth?"

"When the red skins said so to the warriors of the last forts they took, they said true; but when they went to the first, and said that all the rest had fallen, they used deceit. A great nation should overcome their enemies like warriors, and not seek to beguile them with their tongues under the edge of the scalping knife!"

"Why did the Saganaw come into the country of the red skins?" haughtily demanded the chief. "Why did they take our hunting grounds from us? Why have they strong places encircling the country of the Indians, like a belt of wampum round the waist of a warrior?"

"This is not true," rejoined the governor. "It was not the

Saganaw, but the warriors of the pale flag, who first came and took away the hunting grounds, and built the strong places. The great father of the Saganaw had beaten the great father of the pale flag quite out of the Canadas, and he sent his young men to take their place and to make peace with the red skins, and to trade with them, and to call them brothers."

"The Saganaw was false," retorted the Indian. "When a chief of the Saganaw came for the first time with his warriors into the country of the Ottawas, the chief of the Ottawas stood in his path, and asked him why, and from whom, he came? That chief was a bold warrior, and his heart was open, and the Ottawa liked him; and when he said he came to be friendly with the red skins, the Ottawa believed him, and he shook him by the hand, and said to his young men, 'Touch not the life of a Saganaw; for their chief is the friend of the Ottawa chief, and his young men shall be the friends of the red warriors.' Look," he proceeded, marking his sense of the discovery by another of those ejaculatory "Ughs!" so expressive of surprise in an Indian, "at the right hand of my father I see a chief," pointing to Captain Erskine, "who came with those of the Saganaw, who first entered the country of the Détroit; – ask that chief if what the Ottawa says is not true. When the Saganaw said he came only to remove the warriors of the pale flag, that he might be friendly and trade with the red skins, the Ottawa received the belt of wampum he offered, and smoked the pipe of peace with him, and he made his men bring bags of parched corn to his warriors who wanted food, and he sent to all the nations on the lakes, and said to them, 'The Saganaw must pass unhurt to the strong hold on the Détroit.' But for the Ottawa, not a Saganaw would have escaped; for the nations were thirsting for their blood, and the knives of the warriors were eager to open their scalps. Ask the chief who sits at the right hand of my father," he again energetically repeated, "if what the Ottawa says is not true."

"What the Ottawa says is true," rejoined the governor;

"for the chief who sits on my right hand has often said that, but for the Ottawa, the small number of the warriors of the Saganaw must have been cut off; and his heart is big with kindness to the Ottawa for what he did. But if the great chief meant to be friendly, why did he declare war after smoking the pipe of peace with the Saganaw? Why did he destroy the wigwams of the settlers, and carry off the scalps even of their weak women and children? All this has the Ottawa done; and yet he says that he wished to be friendly with my young men. But the Saganaw is not a fool. He knows the Ottawa chief had no will of his own. On the right hand of the Ottawa sits the great chief of the Delawares, and on his left the great chief of the Shawanees. They have long been the sworn enemies of the Saganaw; and they came from the rivers that run near the salt lake to stir up the red skins of the Détroit to war. They whispered wicked words in the ear of the Ottawa chief, and he determined to take up the bloody hatchet. This is a shame to a great warrior. The Ottawa was a king over all the tribes in the country of the fresh lakes, and yet he weakly took council like a woman from another."

"My father lies!" fiercely retorted the warrior, half springing to his feet, and involuntarily putting his hand upon his tomahawk. "If the settlers of the Saganaw have fallen," he resumed in a calmer tone, while he again sank upon his mat, "it is because they did not keep their faith with the red skins. When they came weak, and were not yet secure in their strong holds, their tongues were smooth and full of soft words; but when they became strong under the protection of their thunder, they no longer treated the red skins as their friends, and they laughed at them for letting them come into their country. But," he pursued, elevating his voice, "the Ottawa is a great chief, and he will be respected." Then adverting in bitterness to the influence supposed to be exercised over him, – "What my father has said is false. The Shawanees and the Delawares are great nations; but the Ottawas are greater than any, and their chiefs are full of wisdom. The Shawanees and the Delawares had no talk with the Ottawa chief to make him do what his own wisdom did not tell him."

"Then, if the talk came not from the Shawanees and the Delawares, it came from the spies of the warriors of the pale flag. The great father of the French was angry with the great father of the Saganaw, because he conquered his warriors in many battles; and he sent wicked men to whisper lies of the Saganaw into the ears of the red skins, and to make them take up the hatchet against them. There is a tall spy at this moment in the camp of the red skins," he pursued with earnestness, and yet paling as he spoke. "It is said he is the bosom friend of the great chief of the Ottawas. But I will not believe it. The head of a great nation would not be the friend of a spy – of one who is baser than a dog. His people would despise him; and they would say, 'Our chief is not fit to sit in council, or to make war; for he is led by the word of a pale face who is without honour.' "

The swarthy cheek of the Indian reddened, and his eye kindled into fire. "There is no spy, but a great warrior, in the camp of the Ottawas," he fiercely replied. "Though he came from the country that lies beyond the salt lake, he is now a chief of the red skins, and his arm is mighty, and his heart is big. Would my father know why he has become a chief of the Ottawas?" he pursued with scornful exultation. "When the strong holds of the Saganaw fell, the tomahawk of the 'white warrior' drank more blood than that of a red skin, and his tent is hung around with poles bending under the weight of the scalps he has taken. When the great chief of the Ottawas dies, the pale face will lead his warriors, and take the first seat in the council. The Ottawa chief is his friend."

"If the pale face be the friend of the Ottawa," pursued the governor, in the hope of obtaining some particular intelligence in regard to this terrible and mysterious being, "why is he not here to sit in council with the chiefs? Perhaps," he proceeded tauntingly, as he fancied he perceived a disinclination on the part of the Indian to account for the absence of the warrior, "the pale face is not worthy to take his place among the head men of the council. His arm may be strong like that of a warrior, but his head may be weak like that of a woman; or, perhaps, he is ashamed to show himself before the pale faces, who have turned him out of their tribe."

"My father lies!" again unceremoniously retorted the warrior. "If the friend of the Ottawa is not here, it is because his voice cannot speak. Does my father recollect the bridge on which he killed his young warrior? Does he recollect the terrible chase of the pale face by the friend of the Ottawa? Ugh!" he continued, as his attention was now diverted to another object of interest, "that pale face was swifter than any runner among the red skins, and for his fleetness he deserved to live to be a great hunter in the Canadas; but fear broke his heart, – fear of the friend of the Ottawa chief. The red skins saw him fall at the feet of the Saganaw without life, and they saw the young warriors bear him off in their arms. Is not the Ottawa right?" The Indian paused, threw his eye rapidly along the room, and then, fixing it on the governor, seemed to wait with deep but suppressed interest for his reply.

"Peace to the bones of a brave warrior!" seriously and evasively returned the governor: "the pale face is no longer in the land of the Canadas, and the young warriors of the Saganaw are sorry for his loss; but what would the Ottawa say of the bridge? and what has the pale warrior, the friend of the Ottawa, to do with it?"

A gleam of satisfaction pervaded the countenance of the Indian, as he eagerly bent his ear to receive the assurance that the fugitive was no more; but when allusion was again made to the strange warrior, his brow became overcast, and he replied with mingled haughtiness and anger, –

"Does my father ask? He has dogs of spies among the settlers of the pale flag, but the tomahawk of the red skins will find them out, and they shall perish even as the Saganaw themselves. Two nights ago, when the warriors of the Ottawas were returning from their scout upon the common, they heard the voice of Onondato, the great wolf-dog of the friend of the Ottawa chief. The voice came from the bridge where the Saganaw killed his young warrior, and it called upon the red skins for assistance. My young men gave their war cry, and ran like wild deer to destroy the enemies of their chief; but when they came, the spies had fled, and the voice of Onondato was low and weak as that of a new fawn; and when the warriors came to the other end of the bridge, they found the pale chief lying across the road and covered over with blood. They thought he was dead, and their cry was terrible; for the pale warrior is a great chief, and the Ottawas love him; but when they looked again, they saw that the blood was the blood of Onondato, whose throat the spies of the Saganaw had cut, that he might not hunt them and give them to the tomahawk of the red skins."

Frequent glances, expressive of their deep interest in the announcement of this intelligence, passed between the governor and his officers. It was clear the party who had encountered the terrible warrior of the Fleur de lis were not spies (for none were employed by the garrison), but their adventurous companions who had so recently quitted them. This was put beyond all doubt by the night, the hour, and the not less important fact of the locality; for it was from the bridge described by the Indian, near which the Canadian had stated his canoe to be chained, they were to embark on their perilous and uncertain enterprise. The question of their own escape from danger in this unlooked for collision with so powerful and ferocious an enemy, and of the fidelity of the Canadian, still remained involved in doubt, which it might be imprudent, if not dangerous, to seek to have resolved by any direct remark on the subject to the keen and observant warrior. The governor removed this difficulty by artfully observing, –

"The great chief of the Ottawas has said they were the spies of the Saganaw who killed the pale warrior. His young men have found them, then; or how could he know they were spies?"

"Is there a warrior among the Saganaw who dares to show himself in the path of the red skins, unless he come in strength and surrounded by his thunder?" was the sneering demand. "But my father is wrong, if he supposes the friend of the Ottawa is killed. No," he pursued fiercely, "the dogs of spies could not kill him; they were afraid to face so terrible a warrior. They came behind him in the dark, and they struck him on the head like cowards and foxes as they were. The warrior of the pale face, and the friend of the Ottawa chief, is sick, but not dead. He lies without motion in his tent, and his voice cannot speak to his friend to tell him who were his enemies, that he may bring their scalps to hang up within his wigwam. But the great chief will soon be well, and his arm will be stronger than ever to spill the blood of the Saganaw as he has done before."

"The talk of the Ottawa chief is strange," returned the governor, emphatically and with dignity. "He says he comes to smoke the pipe of peace with the Saganaw, and yet he talks of spilling their blood as if it was water from the lake. What does the Ottawa mean?"

"Ugh!" exclaimed the Indian, in his surprise. "My father is right, but the Ottawa and the Saganaw have not yet smoked together. When they have, the hatchet will be buried for ever. Until then, they are still enemies."

During this long and important colloquy of the leading parties, the strictest silence had been preserved by the remainder of the council. The inferior chiefs had continued deliberately puffing the smoke from their curled lips, as they sat cross-legged on their mats, and nodding their heads at intervals in confirmation of the occasional appeal made by the rapid glance of the Ottawa, and uttering their guttural "Ugh!" whenever any observation of the parlant parties touched their feelings, or called forth their surprise. The officers had been no less silent and attentive listeners, to a conversation on the issue of which hung so many dear and paramount interests. A pause in the conference gave them an opportunity of commenting in a low tone on the communication made, in the strong excitement of his pride, by the Ottawa chief, in regard to the terrible warrior of the Fleur de lis; who, it was evident, swayed the councils of the Indians, and consequently exercised an influence over the ultimate destinies of the English, which it was impossible to contemplate without alarm. It was evident to all, from whatsoever cause it might arise, this man cherished a rancour towards certain individuals in the fort, inducing an anxiety in its reduction scarcely equalled by that entertained on the part of the Indians themselves. Beyond this, however, all was mystery and doubt; nor had any clue been given to enable them to arrive even at a well founded apprehension of the motives which had given birth to the vindictiveness of purpose, so universally ascribed to him even by the savages themselves.

The chiefs also availed themselves of this pause in the conversation of the principals, to sustain a low and animated discussion. Those of the Shawanee and Delaware nations were especially earnest; and, as they spoke across the Ottawa, betrayed, by their vehemence of gesture, the action of some strong feeling upon their minds, the precise nature of which could not be ascertained from their speech at the opposite extremity of the room. The Ottawa did not deign to join in their conversation, but sat smoking his pipe in all the calm and forbidding dignity of a proud Indian warrior conscious of his own importance.

"Does the great chief of the Ottawas, then, seek for peace in his heart at length?" resumed the governor; "or is he come to the strong hold of Détroit, as he went to the other strong holds, with deceit on his lips?"

The Indian slowly removed his pipe from his mouth, fixed his keen eye searchingly on that of the questioner for nearly a minute, and then briefly and haughtily said, "The Ottawa chief has spoken."

"And do the great chiefs of the Shawanees, and the great chiefs of the Delawares, and the great chiefs of the other nations, ask for peace also?" demanded the governor. "If so, let them speak for themselves, and for their warriors."

We will not trespass on the reader, on whom we have already inflicted too much of this scene, by a transcript of the declarations of the inferior chiefs. Suffice it to observe, each in his turn avowed motives similar to those of the Ottawa for wishing the hatchet might be buried for ever, and that their young men should mingle once more in confidence, not only with the English troops, but with the settlers, who would again be brought into the country at the cessation of hostilities. When each had spoken, the Ottawa passed the pipe of ceremony, with which he was provided, to the governor.

The latter put it to his lips, and commenced smoking. The Indians keenly, and half furtively, watched the act; and looks of deep intelligence, that escaped not the notice of the equally anxious and observant officers, passed among them.

"The pipe of the great chief of the Ottawas smokes well," calmly remarked the governor; "but the Ottawa chief, in his hurry to come and ask for peace, has made a mistake. The pipe and all its ornaments are red like blood: it is the pipe of war, and not the pipe of peace. The great chief of the Ottawas will be angry with himself; he has entered the strong hold of the Saganaw, and sat in the council, without doing any good for his young men. The Ottawa must come again."

A deep but subdued expression of disappointment passed over the features of the chiefs. They watched the countenances of the officers, to see whether the substitution of one pipe for the other had been attributed, in their estimation, to accident or design. There was nothing, however, to indicate the slightest doubt of their sincerity.

"My father is right," replied the Indian, with an appearance of embarrassment, which, whether natural or feigned, had nothing suspicious in it. "The great chief of the Ottawas has been foolish, like an old woman. The young chiefs of his tribe will laugh at him for this. But the

Ottawa chief will come again, and the other chiefs with him, for, as my father sees, they all wish for peace; and that my father may know all the nations wish for peace, as well as their head men, the warriors of the Ottawa, and of the Shawanee, and of the Delaware, shall play at ball upon the common, to amuse his young men, while the chiefs sit in council with the chiefs of the Saganaw. The red skins shall come naked, and without their rifles and their tomahawks; and even the squaws of the warriors shall come upon the common, to show the Saganaw they may be without fear. Does my father hear?"

"The Ottawa chief says well," returned the governor; "but will the pale friend of the Ottawa come also to take his seat in the council hall? The great chief has said the pale warrior has become the second chief among the Ottawas; and that when he is dead, the pale warrior will lead the Ottawas, and take the first seat in the council. He, too, should smoke the pipe of peace with the Saganaw, that they may know he is no longer their enemy."

The Indian hesitated, uttering merely his quick ejaculatory "Ugh!" in expression of his surprise at so unexpected a requisition. "The pale warrior, the friend of the Ottawa, is very sick," he at length said; "but if the Great Spirit should give him back his voice before the chiefs come again to the council, the pale face will come too. If my father does not see him then, he will know the friend of the Ottawa chief is very sick."

The governor deemed it prudent not to press the question too closely, lest in so doing he should excite suspicion, and defeat his own object. "When will the Ottawa and the other chiefs come again?" he asked; "and when will their warriors play at ball upon the common, that the Saganaw may see them and be amused?"

"When the sun has travelled so many times," replied Ponteac, holding up three fingers of his left hand. "Then will the Ottawa and the other chiefs bring their young warriors and their women."

"It is too soon," was the reply; "the Saganaw must have

time to collect their presents, that they may give them to the young warriors who are swiftest in the race, and the most active at the ball. The great chief of the Ottawas, too, must let the settlers of the pale flag, who are the friends of the red skins, bring in food for the Saganaw, that a great feast may be given to the chiefs, and to the warriors, and that the Saganaw may make peace with the Ottawas and the other nations as becomes a great people. In twice so many days," holding up three of his fingers in imitation of the Indian, "the Saganaw will be ready to receive the chiefs in council, that they may smoke the pipe of peace, and bury the hatchet for ever. What says the great chief of the Ottawas?"

"It is good," was the reply of the Indian, his eye lighting up with deep and exulting expression. "The settlers of the pale flag shall bring food to the Saganaw. The Ottawa chief will send them, and he will desire his young men not to prevent them. In so many days, then," indicating with his fingers, "the great chiefs will sit again in council with the Saganaw, and the Ottawa chief will not be a fool to bring the pipe he does not want."

With this assurance the conference terminated. Ponteac raised his tall frame from the mat on which he had been squatted, nodded condescendingly to the governor, and strode haughtily into the square or area of the fort. The other chiefs followed his example; and to Major Black-water was again assigned the duty of accompanying them without the works. The glance of the savages, and that of Ponteac in particular, was less wary than at their entrance. Each seemed to embrace every object on which the eye could rest, as if to fix its position indelibly in his memory. The young chief, who had been so suddenly and oppor-tunely checked while in the very act of pealing forth his terrible war whoop, again looked up at the windows of the block house, in quest of those whom his savage instinct had already devoted in intention to his tomahawk, but they were no longer there. Such was the silence that reigned every where, the fort appeared to be tenanted only by the few men of the guard, who lingered near their stations, attentively watching the Indians, as they passed towards the gate. A very few minutes sufficed to bring the latter once more in the midst of their warriors, whom, for a few moments, they harangued earnestly, when the whole body again moved off in the direction of their encampment.

Five

THE WEEK that intervened between the visit of the chiefs and the day appointed for their second meeting in council, was passed by the garrison in perfect freedom from alarm, although, as usual, in diligent watchfulness and preparations for casualties. In conformity with his promise, the Indian had despatched many of the Canadian settlers, with such provisions as the country then afforded, to the governor, and these, happy to obtain the gold of the troops in return for what they could conveniently spare, were not slow in availing themselves of the permission. Dried bears' meat, venison, and Indian corn, composed the substance of these supplies, which were in sufficient abundance to produce a six weeks' increase to the stock of the garrison. Hitherto they had been subsisting, in a great degree, upon salt provisions; the food furtively supplied by the Canadians being necessarily, from their dread of detection, on so limited a scale, that a very small portion of the troops had been enabled to profit by it. This, therefore, was an important and unexpected benefit, derived from the falling in of the garrison with the professed views of the savages; and one which, perhaps, few officers would, like Colonel de Haldimar, have possessed the forethought to have secured. But although it served to relieve the animal wants of the man, there was little to remove his moral inquietude. Discouraged by the sanguinary character of the warfare in which they seemed doomed to be for ever engaged, and harassed by constant watchings, – seldom taking off their clothes for weeks together, – the men had gradually been losing their energy of spirit, in the contemplation of the almost irremediable evils by which they were beset; and looked forward with sad and disheartening conviction to a fate, that all things tended to prove to them was unavoidable, however the period of its consummation might be protracted. Among the officers, this dejection, although proceeding from a different cause, was no less prevalent; and notwithstanding they sought to disguise it before their men, when left to themselves, they gave unlimited rein to a despondency hourly acquiring strength, as the day fixed on for the second council with the Indians drew near.

At length it came, that terrible and eventful day, and, as if in mockery of those who saw no beauty in its golden beams, arrayed in all the gorgeous softness of its autumnal glory. Sad and heavy were the hearts of many within that far distant and isolated fort, as they rose, at the first glimmering of light above the horizon, to prepare for the several duties assigned them. All felt the influence of a feeling that laid prostrate the moral energies even of the boldest: but there was one young officer in particular, who exhibited a dejection, degenerating almost into stupefaction; and more than once, when he received an order from his superior, hesitated as one who either heard not, or, in attempting to perform it, mistook the purport of his instructions, and executed some entirely different duty. The countenance of this officer, whose attenuated person otherwise bore traces of languor and debility, but too plainly marked the abstractedness and terror of his mind, while the set stiff features and contracted muscles of the face contributed to give an expression of vacuity, that one who knew him not might have interpreted unfavourably. Several times, during the inspection of his company at the early parade, he was seen to raise his head, and throw forward his ear, as if expecting to catch the echo of some horrible and appalling cry, until the men themselves remarked, and commented, by interchange of looks, on the singular conduct of their officer, whose thoughts had evidently no connection with the duty he was performing, or the spot on which he stood.

When this customary inspection had been accomplished, – how imperfectly, has been seen, – and the men dismissed from their ranks, the same young officer was observed, by one who followed his every movement with interest, to ascend that part of the rampart which commanded an unbroken view of the country westward, from the point where the encampment of the Indians was supposed to lie, down to the bridge on which the terrible tragedy of Halloway's death had been so recently enacted. Unconscious of the presence of two sentinels, who moved to and fro near their respective posts, on either side of him, the young officer folded his arms, and gazed in that direction for some minutes, with his whole soul riveted on the scene. Then, as if overcome by recollections called up by that on which he gazed, he covered his eyes hurriedly with his hands, and betrayed, by the convulsed movement of his slender form, he was weeping bitterly. This paroxysm past, he uncovered his face, sank with one knee upon the ground, and upraising his clasped hands, as if in appeal to his God, seemed to pray deeply and fervently. In this attitude he continued for some moments, when he became sensible of the approach of an intruder. He raised himself from his knee, turned, and beheld one whose countenance was stamped with a dejection scarcely inferior to his own. It was Captain Blessington.

"Charles, my dear Charles!" exclaimed the latter hurriedly, as he laid his hand upon the shoulder of the emaciated De Haldimar, "consider you are not alone. For God's sake, check this weakness! There are men observing you on every side, and your strange manner has already been the subject of remark in the company."

"When the heart is sick, like mine," replied the youth, in a tone of fearful despondency, "it is alike reckless of forms, and careless of appearances. I trust, however," and here spoke the soldier, "there are few within this fort who will believe me less courageous, because I have been seen to bend my knee in supplication to my God. I did not think that *you*, Blessington, would have been the first to condemn the act."

"I condemn it, Charles! you mistake me, indeed you do," feelingly returned his captain, secretly pained at the mild reproach contained in the concluding sentence; "but there are two things to be considered. In the first instance, the men, who are yet in ignorance of the great evils with which we are threatened, may mistake the cause of your agitation; you were in tears just now, Charles, and the sentinels must have remarked it as well as myself. I would not have them to believe that one of their officers was affected by the anticipation of coming disaster, in a way their own hearts are incapable of estimating. You understand me, Charles? I would not have them too much discouraged by an example that may become infectious."

"I *do* understand you, Blessington," and a forced and sickly smile played for a moment over the wan yet handsome features of the young officer; "you would not have me appear a weeping coward in their eyes."

"Nay, dear Charles, I did not say it."

"But you meant it, Blessington; yet, think not," – and he warmly pressed the hand of his captain, – "think not, I repeat, I take your hint in any other than the friendly light in which it was intended. That I have been no coward, however, I hope I have given proof more than once before the men, most of whom have known me from my very cradle; yet, whatever they may think, is to me, at this moment, a matter of utter indifference. Blessington," and again the tears rolled from his fixed eyes over his cheek, while he pointed with his finger to the western horizon, "I have neither thought nor feeling for myself; my whole heart lies buried there. Oh, God of Heaven!" he pursued after a pause, and again raising his eyes in supplication, "avert the dreadful destiny that awaits my beloved sister."

"Charles, Charles, if only for that sister's sake, then,

calm an agitation which, if thus indulged in, will assuredly
destroy you. All will yet be well. The delay obtained by
your father has been sufficient for the purpose proposed.
Let us hope for the best: if we are deceived in our expectation, it will then be time enough to indulge in a grief,
which could scarcely be exceeded, were the fearful misgivings of your mind to be realised before your eyes."

"Blessington," returned the young officer, – and his features exhibited the liveliest image of despair, – "all hope
has long since been extinct within my breast. See you yon
theatre of death?" he mournfully pursued, pointing to the
fatal bridge, which was thrown into full relief against the
placid bosom of the Détroit: "recollect you the scene that
was acted on it? As for me, it is ever present to my mind, –
it haunts me in my thoughts by day, and in my dreams by
night. I shall never forget it while memory is left to curse
me with the power of retrospection. On the very spot on
which I now stand was I borne in a chair, to witness the
dreadful punishment; you see the stone at my feet, I
marked it by that. I saw you conduct Halloway to the
centre of the bridge; I beheld him kneel to receive his
death; I saw, too, the terrible race for life, that interrupted
the proceedings; I marked the sudden upspring of Halloway to his feet upon the coffin, and the exulting waving of
his hand, as he seemed to recognise the rivals for mastery
in that race. Then was heard the fatal volley, and I saw the
death-struggle of him who had saved my brother's life. I
could have died, too, at that moment; and would to Providence I had! but it was otherwise decreed. My aching
interest was, for a moment, diverted by the fearful chase
now renewed upon the height; and, in common with those
around me, I watched the efforts of the pursuer and the
pursued with painful earnestness and doubt as to the final
result. Ah, Blessington, why was not this all? The terrible
shriek, uttered at the moment when the fugitive fell, apparently dead, at the feet of the firing party, reached us
even here. I felt as if my heart must have burst, for I knew
it to be the shriek of poor Ellen Halloway, – the suffering

wife, – the broken-hearted woman who had so recently, in all the wild abandonment of her grief, wetted my pillow, and even my cheek, with her burning tears, while supplicating an intercession with my father for mercy, which I knew it would be utterly fruitless to promise. Oh, Blessington," pursued the sensitive and affectionate young officer, "I should vainly attempt to paint all that passed in my mind at that dreadful moment. Nothing but the depth of my despair gave me strength to support the scene throughout. I saw the frantic and half-naked woman glide like a phantom past the troops, dividing the air with the rapidity of thought. I knew it to be Ellen; for the discovery of her exchange of clothes with one of the drum boys of the grenadiers was made soon after you left the fort. I saw her leap upon the coffin, and, standing over the body of her unhappy husband, raise her hands to heaven in adjuration, and my heart died within me. I recollected the words she had spoken on a previous occasion, during the first examination of Halloway, and I felt it to be the prophetic denunciation, then threatened, that she was now uttering on all the race of De Haldimar. I saw no more, Blessington. Sick, dizzy, and with every faculty of my mind annihilated, I turned away from the horrid scene, and was again borne to my room. I tried to give vent to my overcharged heart in tears; but the power was denied me, and I sank at once into that stupefaction which you have since remarked in me, and which has been increasing every hour. What additional cause I have had for the indulgence of this confirmed despondency you are well acquainted with. It is childish, it is unsoldierlike, I admit: but, alas! that dreadful scene is eternally before my eyes, and absorbs my mind, to the exclusion of every other feeling. I have not a thought or a care but for the fate that too certainly awaits those who are most dear to me; and if this be a weakness, it is one I shall never have the power to shake off. In a word, Blessington, I am heart-broken."

Captain Blessington was deeply affected; for there was a solemnity in the voice and manner of the young officer that carried conviction to the heart; and it was some moments before he could so far recover himself as to observe, –

"That scene, Charles, was doubtless a heart-rending one to us all; for I well recollect, on turning to remark the impression made on my men when the wretched Ellen Halloway pronounced her appalling curse, to have seen the large tears coursing each other over the furrowed cheeks of some of our oldest soldiers: and if *they* could feel thus, how much more acute must have been the grief of those immediately interested in its application!"

"*Their* tears were not for the denounced race of De Haldimar," returned the youth, – "they were shed for their unhappy comrade – they were wrung from their stubborn hearts by the agonising grief of the wife of Halloway."

"That this was the case in part, I admit," returned Captain Blessington. "The feelings of the men partook of a mixed character. It was evident that grief for Halloway, compassion for his wife, secret indignation and, it may be, disgust at the severity of your father, and sorrow for his innocent family, who were included in that denunciation, predominated with equal force in their hearts at the same moment. There was an expression that told how little they would have pitied any anguish of mind inflicted on their colonel, provided his children, whom they loved, were not to be sacrificed to its accomplishment."

"You admit, then, Blessington, although indirectly," replied the young De Haldimar in a voice of touching sorrow, "that the consummation of the sacrifice *is* to be looked for. Alas! it is that on which my mind perpetually lingers; yet, Heaven knows, my fears are not for myself."

"You mistake me, dearest Charles. I look upon the observations of the unhappy woman as the ravings of a distracted mind – the last wild outpourings of a broken heart, turning with animal instinct on the hand that has inflicted its death-blow."

"Ah, why did she except no one member of that family!" said the unhappy De Haldimar, pursuing rather the chain of his reflections than replying to the observation of his captain. "Had the weight of her malediction fallen on all else than my adored sister, I could have borne the infliction, and awaited the issue with resignation, if not without apprehension. But my poor gentle and unoffending Clara, – alike innocent of the cause, and ignorant of the effect, – what had she done to be included in this terrible curse? – she, who, in the warm and generous affection of her nature, had ever treated Ellen Halloway rather as a sister than as the dependant she always appeared." Again he covered his eyes with his hands, to conceal the starting tears.

"De Haldimar," said Captain Blessington reprovingly, but mildly, "this immoderate grief is wrong – it is unmanly, and should be repressed. I can feel and understand the nature of your sorrow; but others may not judge so favourably. We shall soon be summoned to fall in; and I would not that Mr. Delme, in particular, should notice an emotion he is so incapable of understanding."

The hand of the young officer dropped from his face to the hilt of his sword. His cheek became scarlet; and even through the tears which he half choked himself to command, there was an unwonted flashing from his blue eye, that told how deeply the insinuation had entered his into heart.

"Think you, Captain Blessington," he proudly retorted, "there is an officer in the fort who should dare to taunt me with my feelings as you have done? I came here, sir, in the expectation I should be alone. At a fitting hour I shall be found where Captain Blessington's subaltern should be – with his company."

"De Haldimar – dear De Haldimar, forgive me!" returned his captain. "Heaven knows I would not, on any consideration, wantonly inflict pain on your sensitive heart. My design was to draw you out of this desponding humour; and with this view I sought to arouse your pride, but certainly not to wound your feelings. De Haldimar," he concluded, with marked expression, "you must not, indeed, feel offended with one who has known and esteemed you from very boyhood. Friendship and interest in your deep affliction of spirit alone brought me here – the same feelings prompted my remark. Do you not believe me?"

"I do," impressively returned the young man, grasping the hand that was extended to him in amity. "It is I, rather, Blessington, who should ask you to forgive my petulance; but, indeed, indeed," and again his tone faltered, and his eye was dimmed, "I am more wretched even than I am willing to confess. Pardon my silly conduct – it was but the vain and momentary flashing of the soldier's spirit impatient of an assumed imputation, and the man less than the profession is to be taxed with it. But it is past; and already do you behold me once more the tame and apprehensive being I must ever continue until all is over."

"What can I possibly urge to console one who seems so willing to nurse into conviction all the melancholy imaginings of a diseased mind," observed Captain Blessington, in a voice that told how deeply he felt for the situation of his young friend. "Recollect, dearest Charles, the time that has been afforded to our friends. More than a week has gone by since they left the fort, and a less period was deemed sufficient for their purpose. Before this they must have gained their destination. In fact, it is my positive belief they have; for there could be nothing to detect them in their disguise. Had I the famous lamp of Aladdin," he pursued, in a livelier tone, "over the history of which Clara and yourself used to spend so many hours in childhood, I have no doubt I could show them to you quietly seated within the fort, recounting their adventures to Clara and her cousin, and discoursing of their absent friends."

"Would to Heaven you had the power to do so!" replied De Haldimar, smiling faintly at the conceit, while a ray of hope beamed for a moment upon his sick soul; "for then, indeed, would all my fears for the present be at rest. But you forget, Blessington, the encounter stated to have taken place between them and that terrible stranger near the bridge. Besides, is it not highly probable the object of their expedition was divined by that singular and mysterious being, and that means have been taken to intercept their passage? If so, all hope is at an end."

"Why persevere in viewing only the more sombre side of the picture?" returned his friend. "In your anxiety to anticipate evil, Charles, you have overlooked one important fact. Ponteac distinctly stated that his ruffian friend was still lying deprived of consciousness and speech within his tent, and yet two days had elapsed since the encounter was said to have taken place. Surely we have every reason then to infer they were beyond all reach of pursuit, even admitting, what is by no means probable, the recovery of the wretch immediately after the return of the chiefs from the council."

A gleam of satisfaction, but so transient as to be scarcely noticeable, passed over the pale features of the youthful De Haldimar. He looked his thanks to the kind officer who was thus solicitous to tender him consolation; and was about to reply, when the attention of both was diverted by the report of a musket from the rear of the fort. Presently afterwards, the word was passed along the chain of sentinels upon the ramparts, that the Indians were issuing in force from the forest upon the common near the bomb-proof. Then was heard, as the sentinel at the gate delivered the pass-word, the heavy roll of the drum summoning to arms.

"Ha! here already!" said Captain Blessington, as, glancing towards the forest, he beheld the skirt of the wood now alive with dusky human forms: "Ponteac's visit is earlier than we had been taught to expect; but we are as well prepared to receive him now, as later; and, in fact, the sooner the interview is terminated, the sooner we shall know what we have to depend upon. Come, Charles, we must join the company, and let me entreat you to evince less despondency before the men. It is hard, I know, to sustain an artificial character under such disheartening circumstances; still, for example's sake, it must be done."

"What I can I will do, Blessington," rejoined the youth, as they both moved from the ramparts; "but the task is, in truth, one to which I find myself wholly unequal. How do I know that, even at this moment, my defenceless, terrified, and innocent sister may not be invoking the name and arm of her brother to save her from destruction."

"Trust in Providence, Charles. Even although our worst apprehensions be realised, as I fervently trust they will not, your sister may be spared. The Canadian could not have been unfaithful, or we should have learnt something of his treachery from the Indians. Another week will confirm us in the truth or fallacy of our impressions. Until then, let us arm our hearts with hope. Trust me, we shall yet see the laughing eyes of Clara fill with tears of affection, as I recount to her all her too sensitive and too desponding brother has suffered for her sake."

De Haldimar made no reply. He deeply felt the kind intention of his captain, but was far from cherishing the hope that had been recommended. He sighed heavily, pressed the arm, on which he leaned, in gratitude for the motive, and moved silently with his friend to join their company below the rampart.

Six

MEANWHILE the white flag had again been raised by the Indians upon the bomb-proof; and this having been readily met by a corresponding signal from the fort, a numerous band of savages now issued from the cover with which their dark forms had hitherto been identified, and spread themselves far and near upon the common. On this occasion they were without arms, offensive or defensive, of any kind, if we may except the knife which was always carried at the girdle, and which constituted a part rather of their necessary dress than of their warlike equipment. These warriors might have been about five hundred in number, and were composed chiefly of picked men from the nations of the Ottawas, the Delawares, and the Shawanees; each race being distinctly recognisable from the others by certain peculiarities of form and feature which individualised, if we may so term it, the several tribes. Their only covering was the legging before described, composed in some instances of cloth, but principally of smoked deerskin, and the flap that passed through the girdle around the loins, by which the straps attached to the leggings were secured. Their bodies, necks, and arms were, with the exception of a few slight ornaments, entirely naked; and even the blanket, that served them as a couch by night and a covering by day, had, with one single exception, been dispensed with, apparently with a view to avoid any thing like encumbrance in their approaching sport. Each individual was provided with a stout sapling of about three feet in length, curved, and flattened at the root extremity, like that used at the Irish hurdle; which game, in fact, the manner of ball-playing among the Indians in every way resembled.

Interspersed among these warriors were a nearly equal number of squaws. These were to be seen lounging carelessly about in small groups, and were of all ages; from the hoary-headed, shrivelled-up hag, whose eyes still sparkled with a fire that her lank and attenuated frame denied, to the young girl of twelve, whose dark and glowing cheek, rounded bust, and penetrating glance, bore striking evidence of the precociousness of Indian beauty. These latter looked with evident interest on the sports of the younger warriors, who, throwing down their hurdles, either vied with each other in the short but incredibly swift foot-race, or indulged themselves in wrestling and leaping; while their companions, abandoned to the full security they felt to be attached to the white flag waving on the fort, lay at their lazy length upon the sward, ostensibly following the movements of the several competitors in these sports, but in reality with heart and eye directed solely to the fortification that lay beyond. Each of these females, in addition to the machecoti, or petticoat, which in one solid square of broad-cloth was tightly wrapped around the loins, also carried a blanket loosely thrown around the person, but closely confined over the shoulders in front, and reaching below the knee. There was an air of constraint in their movements, which accorded ill with the occasion of festivity for which they were assembled; and it was remarkable, whether it arose from deference to those to whom they were slaves, as well as wives and daughters, or from whatever other cause it might be, none of them ventured to recline themselves upon the sward in imitation of the warriors.

When it had been made known to the governor that the Indians had begun to develope themselves in force upon the common unarmed, yet redolent with the spirit that was to direct their mediated sports, the soldiers were dismissed from their respective companies to the ramparts; where they were now to be seen, not drawn up in formidable and hostile array, but collected together in careless groups, and simply in their side-arms. This reciprocation of confidence on the part of the garrison was acknowledged by the Indians by marks of approbation, expressed as much by the sudden and classic disposition of their fine forms into attitudes strikingly illustrative of their admiration and pleasure, as by the interjectional sounds that passed from one to the other of the throng. From the increased alacrity with which they now lent themselves to the preparatory and inferior amusements of the day, it was evident their satisfaction was complete.

Hitherto the principal chiefs had, as on the previous occasion, occupied the bomb-proof; and now, as then, they appeared to be deliberating among themselves, but evidently in a more energetic and serious manner. At length they separated, when Ponteac, accompanied by the chiefs who had attended him on the former day, once more led in the direction of the fort. The moment of his advance was the signal for the commencement of the principal game. In an instant those of the warriors who lay reclining on the sward sprang to their feet, while the wrestlers and racers resumed their hurdles, and prepared themselves for the trial of mingled skill and swiftness. At first they formed a dense group in the centre of the common; and then, diverging in two equal files both to the right and to the left of the immediate centre, where the large ball was placed, formed an open chain, extending from the skirt of the forest to the commencement of the village. On the one side were ranged the Delawares and the Shawanees, and on the other the more numerous nation of the Ottawas. The women of these several tribes, apparently much interested in the issue of an amusement in which the manliness and activity of their respective friends were staked, had gradually and imperceptibly gained the front of the fort, where they were now huddled in groups at about twenty paces from the drawbridge, and bending eagerly forward to command the movements of the ball-players.

In his circuit round the walls, Ponteac was seen to re-mark the confiding appearance of the unarmed soldiery with a satisfaction that was not sought to be disguised; and from the manner in which he threw his glance along each face of the rampart, it was evident his object was to embrace the numerical strength collected there. It was moreover observed, when he passed the groups of squaws on his way to the gate, he addressed some words in a strange tongue to the elder matrons of each.

Once more the dark warriors were received at the gate by Major Blackwater; and, as with firm but elastic tread, they moved across the square, each threw his fierce eyes rapidly and anxiously around, and with less of conceal-ment in his manner than had been manifested on the former occasion. On every hand the same air of naked-ness and desertion met their gaze. Not even a soldier of the guard was to be seen; and when they cast their eyes upwards to the windows of the blockhouses, they were found to be tenantless as the area through which they passed. A gleam of fierce satisfaction pervaded the swarthy countenances of the Indians; and the features of Ponteac, in particular, expressed the deepest exultation. Instead of leading his party, he now brought up the rear; and when arrived in the centre of the fort, he, without any visible cause for the accident, stumbled, and fell to the earth. The other chiefs for a moment lost sight of their ordinary gravity, and marked their sense of the circum-stance by a prolonged sound, partaking of the mingled character of a laugh and a yell. Startled at the cry, Major Blackwater, who was in front, turned to ascertain the cause. At that moment Ponteac sprang lightly again to his feet, responding to the yell of his confederates by another even more startling, fierce, and prolonged than their own. He then stalked proudly to the head of the party, and even preceded Major Blackwater into the council room.

In this rude theatre of conference some changes had

been made since their recent visit, which escaped not the observation of the quick-sighted chiefs. Their mats lay in the position they had previously occupied, and the chairs of the officers were placed as before, but the room itself had been considerably enlarged. The slight partition terminating the interior extremity of the mess-room, and dividing it from that of one of the officers, had been removed; and midway through this, extending entirely across, was drawn a curtain of scarlet cloth, against which the imposing figure of the governor, elevated as his seat was above those of the other officers, was thrown into strong relief. There was another change, that escaped not the observation of the Indians, and that was, not more than one half of the officers who had been present at the first conference being now in the room. Of these latter, one had, moreover, been sent away by the governor the moment the chiefs were ushered in.

"Ugh!" ejaculated the proud leader, as he took his seat unceremoniously, and yet not without reluctance, upon the mat. "The council-room of my father is bigger than when the Ottawa was here before, yet the number of his chiefs is not so many."

"The great chief of the Ottawas knows that the Saganaw has promised the red skins a feast," returned the governor. "Were he to leave it to his young warriors to provide it, he would not be able to receive the Ottawa like a great chief, and to make peace with him as he could wish."

"My father has a great deal of cloth, red, like the blood of a pale face," pursued the Indian, rather in demand than in observation, as he pointed with his finger to the opposite end of the room. "When the Ottawa was here last, he did not see it."

"The great chief of the Ottawas knows that the great father of the Saganaw has a big heart to make presents to the red skins. The cloth the Ottawa sees there is sufficient to make leggings for the chiefs of all the nations."

Apparently satisfied with this reply, the fierce Indian

uttered one of his strong guttural and assentient "ughs," and then commenced filling the pipe of peace, correct on the present occasion in all its ornaments, which was handed to him by the Delaware chief. It was remarked by the officers this operation took up an unusually long portion of his time, and that he frequently turned his ear, like a horse stirred by the huntsman's horn, with quick and irrepressible eagerness towards the door.

"The pale warrior, the friend of the Ottawa chief, is not here," said the governor, as he glanced his eye along the semicircle of Indians. "How is this? Is his voice still sick, that he cannot come; or has the great chief of the Ottawas forgotten to tell him?"

"The voice of the pale warrior is still sick, and he cannot speak," replied the Indian. "The Ottawa chief is very sorry; for the tongue of his friend the pale face is full of wisdom."

Scarcely had the last words escaped his lips, when a wild shrill cry from without the fort rang on the ears of the assembled council, and caused a momentary commotion among the officers. It arose from a single voice, and that voice could not be mistaken by any who had heard it once before. A second or two, during which the officers and chiefs kept their eyes intently fixed on each other, passed anxiously away, and then nearer to the gate, apparently on the very drawbridge itself, was pealed forth the wild and deafening yell of a legion of devilish voices. At that sound, the Ottawa and the other chiefs sprang to their feet, and their own fierce cry responded to that yet vibrating on the ears of all. Already were their gleaming tomahawks brandished wildly over their heads, and Ponteac had even bounded a pace forward to reach the governor with the deadly weapon, when, at the sudden stamping of the foot of the latter upon the floor, the scarlet cloth in the rear was thrown aside, and twenty soldiers, their eyes glancing along the barrels of their levelled muskets, met the startled gaze of the astonished Indians.

An instant was enough to satisfy the keen chief of the

true state of the case. The calm composed mien of the officers, not one of whom had even attempted to quit his seat, amid the din by which his ears were so alarmingly assailed, – the triumphant, yet dignified, and even severe expression of the governor's countenance; and, above all, the unexpected presence of the prepared soldiery, – all these at once assured him of the discovery of his treachery, and the danger that awaited him. The necessity for an immediate attempt to join his warriors without, was now obvious to the Ottawa; and scarcely had he conceived the idea before it was sought to be executed. In a single spring he gained the door of the mess-room, and, followed eagerly and tumultuously by the other chiefs, to whose departure no opposition was offered, in the next moment stood on the steps of the piazza that ran along the front of the building whence he had issued.

The surprise of the Indians on reaching this point, was now too powerful to be dissembled; and, incapable either of advancing or receding, they remained gazing on the scene before them with an air of mingled stupefaction, rage, and alarm. Scarcely ten minutes had elapsed since they had proudly strode through the naked area of the fort; and yet, even in that short space of time, its appearance had been entirely changed. Not a part was there now of the surrounding buildings that was not redolent with human life, and hostile preparation. Through every window of the officers' low rooms, was to be seen the dark and frowning muzzle of a field-piece, bearing upon the gateway; and behind these were artillerymen, holding their lighted matches, supported again by files of bayonets, that glittered in their rear. In the blockhouses the same formidable array of field-pieces and muskets was visible; while from the four angles of the square, as many heavy guns, that had been artfully masked at the entrance of the chiefs, seemed ready to sweep away every thing that should come before them. The guard-room near the gate presented the same hostile front. The doors of this, as well as of the other buildings, had been firmly secured within; but from every window affording cover to the troops, gleamed a line of bayonets rising above the threatening field pieces, pointed, at a distance of little more than twelve feet, directly upon the gateway. In addition to his musket, each man of the guard moreover held a hand grenade, provided with a short fuze that could be ignited in a moment from the matches of the gunners, and with immediate effect. The soldiers in the block-houses were similarly provided.

Almost magic as was the change thus suddenly effected in the appearance of the garrison, it was not the most interesting feature in the exciting scene. Choking up the gateway, in which they were completely wedged, and crowding the drawbridge, a dense mass of dusky Indians were to be seen casting their fierce glances around; yet paralysed in their movements by the unlooked-for display of a resisting force, threatening instant annihilation to those who should attempt either to advance or to recede. Never, perhaps, were astonishment and disappointment more forcibly depicted on the human countenance, than as they were now exhibited by these men, who had already, in imagination, secured to themselves an easy conquest. They were the warriors who had so recently been engaged in the manly yet innocent exercise of the ball; but, instead of the harmless hurdle, each now carried a short gun in one hand and a gleaming tomahawk in the other. After the first general yelling heard in the council-room, not a sound was uttered. Their burst of rage and triumph had evidently been checked by the unexpected manner of their reception, and they now stood on the spot on which the further advance of each had been arrested, so silent and motionless, that, but for the rolling of their dark eyes, as they keenly measured the insurmountable barriers that were opposed to their progress, they might almost have been taken for a wild group of statuary.

Conspicuous at the head of these was he who wore the blanket; a tall warrior, on whom rested the startled eye of every officer and soldier who was so situated as to behold him. His face was painted black as death; and as he stood under the arch of the gateway, with his white turbaned head towering far above those of his companions, this formidable and mysterious enemy might have been likened to the spirit of darkness presiding over his terrible legions.

In order to account for the extraordinary appearance of the Indians, armed in every way for death, at a moment when neither gun nor tomahawk was apparently within miles of their reach, it will be necessary to revert to the first entrance of the chiefs into the fort. The fall of Ponteac had been the effect of design; and the yell pealed forth by him, on recovering his feet, as if in taunting reply to the laugh of his comrades, was in reality a signal intended for the guidance of the Indians without. These, now following up their game with increasing spirit, at once changed the direction of their line, bringing the ball nearer to the fort. In their eagerness to effect this object, they had overlooked the gradual secession of the unarmed troops, spectators of their sport from the ramparts, until scarcely more than twenty stragglers were left. As they neared the gate, the squaws broke up their several groups, and forming a line on either hand of the road leading to the drawbridge, appeared to separate solely with a view not to impede the action of the players. For an instant a dense group collected around the ball, which had been driven to within a hundred yards of the gate, and fifty hurdles were crossed in their endeavours to secure it, when the warrior, who formed the solitary exception to the multitude, in his blanket covering, and who had been lingering in the extreme rear of the party, came rapidly up to the spot where the well-affected struggle was maintained. At his approach, the hurdles of the others players were withdrawn, when, at a single blow from his powerful arm, the ball was seen flying into the air in an oblique direction, and was for a moment lost altogether to the view. When it again met the eye, it was descending perpendicularly into the very centre of the fort.

With the fleetness of thought now commenced a race that had ostensibly for its object the recovery of the lost ball; and in which, he who had driven it with such resistless force outstripped them all. Their course lay between the two lines of squaws; and scarcely had the head of the bounding Indians reached the opposite extremity of those lines, when the women suddenly threw back their blankets, and disclosed each a short gun and a tomahawk. To throw away their hurdles and seize upon these, was the work of an instant. Already, in imagination, was the fort their own; and, such was the peculiar exultation of the black and turbaned warrior, when he felt the planks of the drawbridge bending beneath his feet, all the ferocious joy of his soul was pealed forth in the terrible cry which, rapidly succeeded by that of the other Indians, had resounded so fearfully through the council-room. What their disappointment was, when, on gaining the interior, they found the garrison prepared for their reception, has already been shown.

"Secure that traitor, men!" exclaimed the governor, advancing into the square, and pointing to the black warrior, whose quick eye was now glancing on every side, to discover some assailable point in the formidable defences of the troops.

A laugh of scorn and derision escaped the lips of the warrior. "Is there a man – are there any ten men, even with Governor de Haldimar at their head, who will be bold enough to attempt it?" he asked. "Nay!" he pursued, stepping boldly a pace or two in front of the wondering savages, – "here I stand singly, and defy your whole garrison!"

A sudden movement among the soldiers in the guard-room announced they were preparing to execute the order of their chief. The eye of the black warrior sparkled with ferocious pleasure; and he made a gesture to his followers, which was replied to by the sudden tension of their hitherto relaxed forms into attitudes of expectance and preparation.

"Stay, men; quit not your cover for your lives!" commanded the governor, in a loud deep voice: – "keep the barricades fast, and move not."

A cloud of anger and disappointment passed over the features of the black warrior. It was evident the object of his bravado was to draw the troops from their defences, that they might be so mingled with their enemies as to render the cannon useless, unless friends and foes (which was by no means probable) should alike be sacrificed. The governor had penetrated the design in time to prevent the mischief.

In a moment of uncontrollable rage, the savage warrior aimed his tomahawk at the head of the governor. The latter stepped lightly aside, and the steel sank with such force into one of the posts supporting the piazza, that the quivering handle snapped close off at its head. At that moment, a single shot, fired from the guard-house, was drowned in the yell of approbation which burst from the lips of the dark crowd. The turban of the warrior was, however, seen flying through the air, carried away by the force of the bullet which had torn it from his head. He himself was unharmed.

"A narrow escape for us both, Colonel de Haldimar," he observed, as soon as the yell had subsided, and with an air of the most perfect unconcern. "Had my tomahawk obeyed the first impulse of my heart, I should have cursed myself and died: as it is, I have reason to avoid all useless exposure of my own life, at present. A second bullet may be better directed; and to die, robbed of my revenge, would ill answer the purpose of a life devoted to its attainment. Remember my pledge!"

At the hasty command of the governor, a hundred muskets were raised to the shoulders of his men; but, before a single eye could glance along the barrel, the formidable and active warrior had bounded over the heads of the nearest Indians into a small space that was left unoccupied; when, stooping suddenly to the earth, he disappeared altogether from the view of his enemies. A slight movement in the centre of the numerous band crowding the gateway, and extending even beyond the bridge, was now discernible: it was like the waving of a field of standing corn, through which some animal rapidly winds its tortuous course, bending aside as the object advances, and closing again when it has passed. After the lapse of a minute, the terrible warrior was seen to spring again to his feet, far in the rear of the band; and then, uttering a fierce shout of exultation, to make good his retreat towards the forest.

Meanwhile, Ponteac and the other chiefs of the council continued rooted to the piazza on which they had rushed at the unexpected display of the armed men behind the scarlet curtain. The loud "Waugh" that burst from the lips of all, on finding themselves thus foiled in their schemes of massacre, had been succeeded, the instant afterwards, by feelings of personal apprehension, which each, however, had collectedness enough to disguise. Once the Ottawa made a movement as if he would have cleared the space that kept him from his warriors; but the emphatical pointing of the finger of Colonel de Haldimar to the levelled muskets of the men in the block-houses prevented him, and the attempt was not repeated. It was remarked by the officers, who also stood on the piazza, close behind the chiefs, when the black warrior threw his tomahawk at the governor, a shade of displeasure passed over the features of the Ottawa; and that, when he found the daring attempt was not retaliated on his people, his countenance had been momentarily lighted up with a satisfied expression, apparently marking his sense of the forbearance so unexpectedly shown.

"What says the great chief of the Ottawas now?" asked the governor calmly, and breaking a profound silence that had succeeded to the last fierce yell of the formidable being just departed. "Was the Saganaw not right, when he said the Ottawa came with guile in his heart, and with a lie upon his lips? But the Saganaw is not a fool, and he can read the thoughts of his enemies upon their faces, and long before their lips have spoken."

"Ugh!" ejaculated the Indian; "my father is a great chief, and his head is full of wisdom. Had he been feeble, like the other chiefs of the Saganaw, the strong hold of the Détroit must have fallen, and the red skins would have danced their war-dance round the scalps of his young men, even in the council-room where they came to talk of peace."

"Does the great chief of the Ottawas see the big thunder of the Saganaw?" pursued the governor: "if not, let him open his eyes and look. The Saganaw has but to move his lips, and swifter than the lightning would the pale faces sweep away the warriors of the Ottawa, even where they now stand: in less time than the Saganaw is now speaking, would they mow them down like the grass of the Prairie."

"Ugh!" again exclaimed the chief, with mixed doggedness and fierceness: "if what my father says is true, why does he not pour out his anger upon the red skins?"

"Let the great chief of the Ottawas listen," replied the governor with dignity. "When the great chiefs of all the nations that are in league with the Ottawas came last to the council, the Saganaw knew that they carried deceit in their hearts, and that they never meant to smoke the pipe of peace, or to bury the hatchet in the ground. The Saganaw might have kept them prisoners, that their warriors might be without a head; but he had given his word to the great chief of the Ottawas, and the word of a Saganaw is never broken. Even now, while both the chiefs and the warriors are in his power, he will not slay them, for he wishes to show the Ottawa the desire of the Saganaw is to be friendly with the red skins, and not to destroy them. Wicked men from the Canadas have whispered lies in the ear of the Ottawa; but a great chief should judge for himself, and take council only from the wisdom of his own heart. The Ottawa and his warriors may go," he resumed, after a short pause; "the path by which they came is again open to them. Let them depart in peace; the big thunder of the Saganaw shall not harm them."

The countenance of the Indian, who had clearly seen the danger of his position, wore an expression of surprise which could not be dissembled: low exclamations passed between him and his companions; and, then pointing to the tomahawk that lay half buried in the wood, he said, doubtingly, –

"It was the pale face, the friend of the great chief of the Ottawas, who struck the hatchet at my father. The Ottawa is not a fool to believe the Saganaw can sleep without revenge."

"The great chief of the Ottawas shall know us better," was the reply. "The young warriors of the Saganaw might destroy their enemies where they now stand, but they seek not their blood. When the Ottawa chief takes council from his own heart, and not from the lips of a cowardly dog of a pale face, who strikes his tomahawk and then flies, his wisdom will tell him to make peace with the Saganaw, whose warriors are without treachery, even as they are without fear."

Another of those deep interjectional "ughs" escaped the chest of the proud Indian.

"What my father says is good," he returned; "but the pale face is a great warrior, and the Ottawa chief is his friend. The Ottawa will go."

He then addressed a few sentences, in a tongue unknown to the officers, to the swarthy and anxious crowd in front. These were answered by a low, sullen, yet assentient grunt, from the united band, who now turned, though with justifiable caution and distrust, and recrossed the drawbridge without hinderance from the troops. Ponteac waited until the last Indian had departed, and then making a movement to the governor, which, with all its haughtiness, was meant to mark his sense of the forbearance and good faith that had been manifested, once more stalked proudly and calmly across the area, followed by the remainder of the chiefs. The officers who were with the governor ascended to the ramparts, to follow their movements; and it was not before their report had been made, that the Indians were immerging once more into the heart of the forest, the troops were withdrawn from their formidable defences, and the gate of the fort again firmly secured.

Seven

WHILE THE reader is left to pause over the rapid succession of incidents resulting from the mysterious entrance of the warrior of the Fleur de lis into the English fort, be it our task to explain the circumstances connected with the singular disappearance of Captain de Haldimar, and the melancholy murder of his unfortunate servant.

It will be recollected that the ill-fated Halloway, in the course of his defence before the court-martial, distinctly stated the voice of the individual who had approached his post, calling on the name of Captain de Haldimar, on the night of the alarm, to have been that of a female, and that the language in which they subsequently conversed was that of the Ottawa Indians. This was strictly the fact; and the only error into which the unfortunate soldier had fallen, had reference merely to the character and motives of the party. He had naturally imagined, as he had stated, it was some young female of the village, whom attachment for his officer had driven to the desperate determination of seeking an interview; nor was this impression at all weakened by the subsequent discourse of the parties in the Indian tongue, with which it was well known most of the Canadians, both male and female, were more or less conversant. The subject of that short, low, and hurried conference was, indeed, one that well warranted the singular intrusion; and, in the declaration of Halloway, we have already seen the importance and anxiety attached by the young officer to the communication. Without waiting to repeat the motives assigned for his departure, and the prayers and expostulations to which he had recourse to overcome the determination and sense of duty of the unfortunate sentinel, let us pass at once to the moment when, after having cleared the ditch, conjointly with his faithful follower, in the manner already shown, Captain de Haldimar first stood side by side with his midnight visitant.

The night, it has elsewhere been observed, was clear and starry, so that objects upon the common, such as the rude stump that here and there raised its dark low head above the surface, might be dimly seen in the distance. To obviate the danger of discovery by the sentinels, appeared to be the first study of the female; for, when Captain de Haldimar, followed by his servant, had reached the spot on which she stood, she put the forefinger of one hand to her lips, and with the other pointed to his booted foot. A corresponding signal showed that the lightness of the material offered little risk of betrayal. Donellan, however, was made to doff his heavy ammunition shoes; and, with this precaution, they all stole hastily along, under the shadows of the projecting ramparts, until they had gained the extreme rear. Here the female suddenly raised her tall figure from the stooping position in which she, as well as her companions, had performed the dangerous circuit; and, placing her finger once more significantly on her lips, led in the direction of the bomb-proof, unperceived by the sentinels, most of whom, it is probable, had, up to the moment of the alarm subsequently given, been too much overcome by previous watching and excitement to have kept the most vigilant look-out.

Arrived at the skirt of the forest, the little party drew up within the shadow of the ruin, and a short and earnest dialogue ensued, in Indian, between the female and the officer. This was succeeded by a command from the latter to his servant, who, after a momentary but respectful expostulation, which, however, was utterly lost on him to whom it was addressed, proceeded to divest himself of his humble apparel, assuming in exchange the more elegant uniform of his superior. Donellan, who was also of the grenadiers, was remarkable for the resemblance he bore, in figure, to Captain de Haldimar; wanting, it is true, the grace and freedom of movement of the latter, but still presenting an outline which, in an attitude of profound repose, might, as it subsequently did, have set even those who were most intimate with the officer at fault.

"This is well," observed the female, as the young man proceeded to induct himself in the grey coat of his servant, having previously drawn the glazed hat close over his waving and redundant hair: "if the Saganaw is ready, Oucanasta will go."

"Sure, and your honour does not mane to lave me behind!" exclaimed the anxious soldier, as his captain now recommended him to stand closely concealed near the ruin until his return. "Who knows what ambuscade the she-divil may not lade your honour into; and thin who will you have to bring you out of it?"

"No, Donellan, it must not be: I first intended it, as you may perceive by my bringing you out; but the expedition on which I am going is of the utmost importance to us all, and too much precaution cannot be taken. I fear no ambuscade, for I can depend on the fidelity of my guide; but the presence of a third person would only embarrass, without assisting me in the least. You must remain behind; the woman insists upon it, and there is no more to be said."

"To ould Nick with the ugly winch, for her pains!" half muttered the disappointed soldier to himself. "I wish it may be as your honour says; but my mind misgives me sadly that evil will come of this. Has your honour secured the pistols?"

"They are here," returned his captain, placing a hand on either chest. "And now, Donellan, mark me: I know nothing that can detain me longer than an hour; at least the woman assures me, and I believe her, that I may be back then; but it is well to guard against accidents. You must continue here for the hour, and for the hour only. If I come not then, return to the fort without delay, for the rope must be removed, and the gate secured, before Halloway is relieved. The keys you will find in the pocket of my uniform: when you have done with them, let them be hung up in their proper place in the guard-room. My father must not know either that Halloway suffered me to pass the gate, or that you accompanied me."

"Lord love us! your honour talks as if you nivir would return, giving such a heap of orders!" exclaimed the startled man; "but if I go back alone, as I trust in heaven I shall not, how am I to account for being dressed in your honour's rigimintals?"

"I tell you, Donellan," impatiently returned the officer, "that I shall be back; but I only wish to guard against accidents. The instant you get into the fort, you will take off my clothes and resume your own. Who the devil is to see you in the uniform, unless it be Halloway?"

"If the Saganaw would not see the earth red with the blood of his race, he will go," interrupted the female. "Oucanasta can feel the breath of the morning fresh upon her cheek, and the council of the chiefs must be begun."

"The Saganaw is ready, and Oucanasta shall lead the way," hastily returned the officer. "One word more, Donellan;" and he pressed the hand of his domestic kindly: "should I not return, you must, without committing Halloway or yourself, cause my father to be apprised that the Indians meditate a deep and treacherous plan to get possession of the fort. What that plan is, I know not yet myself, neither does this woman know; but she says that I shall hear it discussed unseen, even in the heart of their own encampment. All you have to do is acquaint my father with the existence of danger. And now be cautious: above all things, keep close under the shadow of the bomb-proof; for there are scouts constantly prowling about the common, and the glittering of the uniform in the starlight may betray you."

"But why may I not follow your honour?" again urged the faithful soldier; "and where is the use of my remaining here to count the stars, and hear the 'All's well!' from the fort, when I could be so much better employed in guarding your honour from harm? What sort of protection can that Ingian woman afford, who is of the race of our bitterest enemies, them cursed Ottawas, and your honour venturing, too, like a spy into the very heart of the bloodhounds? Ah, Captain de Haldimar, for the love of God, do not trust yourself alone with her, or I am sure I shall never see your honour again!"

The last words (unhappily too prophetic) fell only on the ear of him who uttered them. The female and the officer had already disappeared round an abrupt angle of the bomb-proof; and the soldier, as directed by his master, now drew up his tall figure against the ruin, where he continued for a period immovable, as if he had been planted there in his ordinary character of sentinel, listening, until they eventually died away in distance, to the receding footsteps of his master; and then ruminating on the several apprehensions that crowded on his mind, in regard to the probable issue of his adventurous project.

Meanwhile, Captain de Haldimar and his guide trod the mazes of the forest, with an expedition that proved the latter to be well acquainted with its bearings. On quitting the bomb-proof, she had struck into a narrow winding path, less seen than felt in the deep gloom pervading the wood, and with light steps bounded over obstacles that lay strewed in their course, emitting scarcely more sound than would have been produced by the slimy crawl of its native rattlesnake. Not so, however, with the less experienced tread of her companion. Wanting the pliancy of movement given to it by the light mocassin, the booted foot of the young officer, despite all of his precaution, fell heavily to the ground, producing such a rustling among the dried leaves, that, had an Indian ear been lurking any where around, his approach must inevitably have been betrayed. More than once, too, neglecting to follow the injunction of his companion, who moved in a stooping posture, with her head bent over her chest, his hat was caught in the closely matted branches, and fell sullenly and heavily to the earth, evidently much to the discomfiture of his guide.

At length they stood on the verge of a dark and precipitous ravine, the abrupt sides of which were studded with underwood, so completely interwoven, that all passage appeared impracticable. What, however, seemed an insurmountable obstacle, proved, in reality, an inestimable advantage; for it was by clinging to this, in imitation of the example set him by his companion, the young officer was prevented from rolling into an abyss, the depth of which was lost in the profound obscurity that pervaded the scene. Through the bed of this dark dell rolled a narrow stream, so imperceptible to the eye in the "living darkness," and so noiseless in its course, that it was not until warned by his companion he stood on the very brink of it, Captain de Haldimar was made sensible of its existence. Both cleared it at a single bound, in which the activity of the female was not the least conspicuous, and, clambering up the opposite steep, secured their footing, by the aid of the same underwood that had assisted them in their descent.

On gaining the other summit, which was not done without detaching several loose stones from their sandy bed, they again fell into the path, which had been lost sight of in traversing the ravine. They had proceeded along this about half a mile, when the female suddenly stopped, and pointing to a dim and lurid atmosphere that now began to show itself between the thin foliage, whispered that in the opening beyond stood the encampment of the Indians. She then seated herself on the trunk of a fallen tree, that lay at the side of the almost invisible path they had hitherto pursued, and motioning to her companion to unboot himself, proceeded to unlace the fastenings of her mocassins.

"The foot of the Saganaw must fall like the night dew on the prairie," she observed: "the ear of the red skin is quicker than the lightning, and he will know that a pale face is near, if he hear but his tread upon a blade of grass."

Gallantry in the civilised man is a sentiment that never wholly abandons him; and in whatever clime he may be thrown, or under whatever circumstances he may be placed, – be it called forth by white or by blackamoor, – it is certain to influence his conduct: it is a refinement, of that instinctive deference to the weaker sex, which nature has implanted in him for the wisest of purposes; and which, while it tends to exalt those to whom its influence is extended, fails not to reflect a corresponding lustre on himself.

The young officer had, at the first suggestion of his guide, divested himself of his boots, prepared to perform the remainder of the journey merely in his stockings, but his companion now threw herself on her knees before him, and, without further ceremony, proceeded to draw over his foot one of the mocassins she had just relinquished.

"The feet of the Saganaw are soft as those of a young child," she remarked, in a voice of commiseration; "but the mocassins of Oucanasta shall protect them from the thorns of the forest."

This was too un-European, – too much reversing the established order of things, to be borne patiently. As if he had felt the dignity of his manhood offended by the proposal, the officer drew his foot hastily back, declaring, as he sprang from the log, he did not care for the thorns, and could not think of depriving a female, who must be much more sensible of pain than himself.

Oucanasta, however, was not to be outdone in politeness. She calmly reseated herself on the log, drew her right foot over her left knee, caught one of the hands of her companion, and placing it upon the naked sole, desired him to feel how impervious to attack of every description was that indurated portion of the lower limb.

This practical argument was not without its weight, and had more effect in deciding the officer than a volume of remonstrance. Most men love to render tribute to a delicate and pretty foot. Some, indeed, go so far as to connect every thing feminine with these qualities, and to believe that nothing can be feminine without them. For our parts, we confess, that, although no enemies to a pretty foot, it is by no means a *sine qua non* in our estimate of female perfection; being in no way disposed, where the head and heart are gems, to undervalue these in consideration of any deficiency in the heels. Captain de Haldimar probably thought otherwise; for when he had passed his unwilling hand over the foot of Oucanasta, which, whatever her face might have been, was certainly any thing but delicate, and encountered numerous ragged excrescences and raspy callosities that set all symmetry at defiance, a wonderful revolution came over his feelings, and, secretly determining the mocassins would be equally well placed on his own feet, he no longer offered any opposition.

This important point arranged, the officer once more followed his guide in silence. Gradually the forest, as they advanced, became lighter with the lurid atmosphere before alluded to; and at length, through the trees, could be indistinctly seen the Indian fires from which it proceeded. The young man was now desired by his conductress to use the utmost circumspection in making the circuit of the wood, in order to gain a position immediately opposite to the point where the path they had hitherto pursued terminated in the opening. This, indeed, was the most dangerous and critical part of the undertaking. A false step, or the crackling of a decayed branch beneath the foot, would have been sufficient to betray proximity, in which case his doom was sealed.

Fortunate did he now deem himself in having yielded to the counsel of his guide. Had he retained his unbending boot, it must have crushed whatever it pressed; whereas, the pliant mocassin, yielding to the obstacles it encountered, enabled him to pass noiselessly over them. Still, while exempt from danger on this score, another, scarcely less perplexing, became at every instant more obvious; for, as they drew nearer to the point which the female sought to gain, the dim light of the half-slumbering fires fell so immediately upon their path, that had a single human eye been turned in that direction, their discovery was inevitable. It was with a beating heart, to which mere personal fear, however, was a stranger, that Captain de Haldimar performed this concluding stage of his adventurous course; but, at a moment when he considered detection unavoidable, and was arming himself with resolution to meet the event, the female suddenly halted, placing, in the act, the trunk of an enormous beech between her companion and the dusky forms within, whose very breathing could be heard by the anxious officer. Without uttering a word, she took his hand, and, drawing him gently forward, disappeared altogether from his view. The young man followed, and in the next moment found himself in the bowelless body of the tree itself; into which, on the side of the encampment, both light and sound were admitted by a small aperture formed by the natural decay of the wood.

The Indian pressed her lips to the ear of her companion, and rather breathed than said, – "The Saganaw will see and hear every thing from this in safety; and what he hears let him treasure in his heart. Oucanasta must go. When the council is over she will return, and lead him back to his warriors."

With this brief intimation she departed, and so noiselessly, that the young officer was not aware of her absence until some minutes of silence had satisfied him she must be gone. His first care then was to survey, through the aperture that lay in a level with his eye, the character of the scene before him. The small plain, in which lay the encampment of the Indians, was a sort of oasis of the forest, girt round with a rude belt of underwood, and somewhat elevated, so as to present the appearance of a mound, constructed on the first principles of art. This was thickly although irregularly studded with tents, some of which were formed of large coarse mats thrown over poles disposed in a conical shape, while others were more rudely composed of the leafy branches of the forest.

Within these groups of human forms lay, wrapped in their blankets, stretched at their lazy length. Others, with their feet placed close to the dying embers of their fires, diverged like so many radii from their centre, and lay motionless in sleep, as if life and consciousness were wholly extinct. Here and there was to be seen a solitary warrior securing, with admirable neatness, and with delicate ligatures formed of the sinew of the deer, the guiding feather, or fashioning the bony barb of his long arrow; while others, with the same warlike spirit in view, employed themselves in cutting and greasing small patches of smoked deerskin, which were to secure and give a more certain direction to the murderous bullet. Among the warriors were interspersed many women, some of whom might be seen supporting in their laps the heavy heads of their unconscious helpmates, while they occupied themselves, by the firelight, in parting the long black matted hair, and maintaining a destructive warfare against the pigmy inhabitants of that dark region. These signs of life and activity in the body of the camp generally were, however, but few and occasional; but, at the spot where Captain de Haldimar stood concealed, the scene was different. At a few yards from the tree stood a sort of shed, composed of tall poles placed upright in the earth, and supporting a roof formed simply of rude boughs, the foliage of which had been withered by time. This simple edifice might be about fifty feet in circumference. In the centre blazed a large fire that had been newly fed, and around this were assembled a band of swarthy warriors, some twenty or thirty in number, who, by their proud, calm, and thoughtful bearing, might at once be known to be chiefs.

The faces of most of these were familiar to the young officer, who speedily recognised them for the principals of the various tribes Ponteac had leagued in arms against his enemies. That chief himself, ever remarkable for his haughty eye and commanding gesture, was of the number of those present; and, a little aloof from his inferiors, sat, with his feet stretched towards the fire, and half reclining on his side in an attitude of indolence; yet with his mind evidently engrossed by deep and absorbing thought. From some observations that distinctly met his ear, Captain de Haldimar gathered, the party were only awaiting the arrival of an important character, without whose presence the leading chief was unwilling the conference should begin. The period of the officer's concealment had just been long enough to enable him to fix all these particulars in his mind, when suddenly the faint report of a distant rifle was heard echoing throughout the wood. This was instantly succeeded by a second, that sounded more sharply on the ear; and then followed a long and piercing cry, that brought every warrior, even of those who slept, quickly to his feet.

An anxious interval of some minutes passed away in the fixed and listening attitudes, which the chiefs especially had assumed, when a noise resembling that of some animal forcing its way rapidly through the rustling branches, was faintly heard in the direction in which the shots had been fired. This gradually increased as it evidently approached the encampment, and then, distinctly, could be heard the light yet unguarded boundings of a human foot. At every moment the rustling of the underwood, rapidly divided by the approaching form, became more audible; and so closely did the intruder press upon the point in which Captain de Haldimar was concealed, that that officer, fancying he had been betrayed, turned hastily round, and, grasping one of the pistols he had secreted in his chest, prepared himself for a last and deadly encounter. An instant or two was sufficient to re-assure him. The form glided hastily past, brushing the tree with its garments in its course, and clearing, at a single bound, the belt of underwood that divided the encampment from the tall forest, stood suddenly among the group of anxious and expectant chiefs.

This individual, a man of tall stature, was powerfully made. He wore a jerkin, or hunting-coat, of leather; and his arms were, a rifle which had every appearance of having just been discharged, a tomahawk reeking with blood, and a scalping-knife, which, in the hurry of some recent service it had been made to perform, had missed its sheath, and was thrust naked into the belt that encircled his loins. His countenance wore an expression of malignant triumph; and as his eye fell on the assembled throng, its self-satisfied and exulting glance seemed to give them to understand he came not without credentials to recommend him to their notice. Captain de Haldimar was particularly struck by the air of bold daring and almost insolent recklessness pervading every movement of this man; and it was difficult to say whether the haughtiness of bearing peculiar to Ponteac himself, was not exceeded by that of this herculean warrior.

By the body of chiefs his appearance had been greeted with a mere general grunt of approbation; but the countenance of the leader expressed a more personal interest. All seemed to expect he had something of moment to communicate; but as it was not consistent with the dignity of Indian etiquette to enquire, they waited calmly until it should please their new associate to enter on the history of his exploits. In pursuance of an invitation from Ponteac, he now took his seat on the right hand of that chief, and immediately facing the tree, from which Captain de Haldimar, strongly excited both by the reports of the shots that had been fired, and the sight of the bloody tomahawk of the recently arrived Indian, gazed earnestly and anxiously on the swarthy throng.

Glancing once more triumphantly round the circle, who sat smoking their pipes in calm and deliberative silence, the latter now observed the eye of a young chief, who sat opposite to him, intently riveted on his left shoulder. He raised his hand to the part, withdrew it, looked at it, and found it wet with blood. A slight start of surprise betrayed his own unconsciousness of the accident; yet, secretly vexed at the discovery which had been made, and urged probably by one of his wayward fits, he demanded haughtily and insultingly of the young chief, if that was the first time he had ever looked on the blood of a warrior.

"Does my brother feel pain?" was the taunting reply. "If he is come to us with a trophy, it is not without being dearly bought. The Saganaw has spilt his blood."

"The weapons of the Saganaw, like those of the smooth face of the Ottawa, are without sting," angrily retorted the other. "They only prick the skin like a thorn; but when Wacousta drinks the blood of his enemy," and he glanced his eye fiercely at the young man, "it is the blood next his heart."

"My brother has always big words upon his lips," returned the young chief, with a scornful sneer at the implied threat against himself. "But where are his proofs?"

For a moment the eye of the party thus challenged kindled into flame, while his lips were firmly compressed together; and as he half bent himself forward, to scan with greater earnestness the features of his questioner, his right hand sank to his left side, tightly grasping the handle of his scalping-knife. The action was but momentary. Again he drew himself up, puffed the smoke deliberately from his bloody tomahawk, and, thrusting his right hand into his bosom, drew leisurely forth a reeking scalp, which he tossed insolently across the fire into the lap of the young chief. A loud and general "ugh!" testified the approbation of the assembled group, at the unequivocal answer thus given to the demand of the youth. The eye of the huge warrior sparkled with a deep and ferocious exultation.

"What says the smooth face of the Ottawas now?" he demanded, in the same insolent strain. "Does it make his heart sick to look upon the scalp of a great chief?"

The young man quietly turned the horrid trophy over several times in his hand, examining it attentively in every part. Then tossing it back with contemptuous coolness to its owner, he replied –

"The eyes of my brother are weak with age. He is not cunning, like a red skin. The Ottawa has often seen the Saganaw in their fort, and he knows their chiefs have fine hair like women; but this is like the bristles of the fox.

My brother has not slain a great chief, but a common warrior."

A flush of irrepressible and threatening anger passed over the features of the vast savage.

"Is it for a boy," he fiercely asked, "whose eyes know not yet the colour of blood, to judge of the enemies that fall by the tomahawk of Wacousta? but a great warrior never boasts of actions that he does not achieve. It is the son of the great chief of the Saganaw whom he has slain. If the smooth face doubts it, and has courage to venture, even at night, within a hundred yards of the fort, he will see a Saganaw without a scalp; and he will know that Saganaw by his dress – the dress," he pursued, with a low emphatic laugh, "that Oucanasta, the sister of the smooth face, loved so much to look upon."

Quicker than thought was the upspringing of the young Indian to his feet. With a cheek glowing, an eye flashing, and his gleaming tomahawk whirling rapidly round his head, he cleared at a single bound the fire that separated him from his insulter. The formidable man who had thus wantonly provoked the attack, was equally prompt in meeting it. At the first movement of the youth, he too had leapt to his feet, and brandished the terrible weapon that served in the double capacity of pipe and hatchet. A fierce yell escaped the lips of each, as they thus met in close and hostile collision, and the scene for the moment promised to be one of the most tragic character; but before either could find an assailable point on which to rest his formidable weapon, Ponteac himself had thrown his person between them, and in a voice of thunder commanded the instant abandonment of their purpose. Exasperated even as they now mutually were, the influence of that authority, for which the great chief of the Ottawas was well known, was not without due effect on the combatants. His anger was principally directed against the assailant, on whom the tones of his reproving voice produced a change the intimidation of his powerful opponent could never have effected. The young chief dropped the point of his toma-hawk, bowed his head in submission, and then resuming his seat, sat during the remainder of the night with his arms folded, and his head bent in silence over his chest.

"Our brother has done well," said Ponteac, glancing approvingly at him who had exhibited the reeking trophy, and whom he evidently favoured. "He is a great chief, and his words are truth. We heard the report of his rifle, and we also heard the cry that told he had borne away the scalp of an enemy. But we will think of this to-morrow. Let us now commence our talk."

Our readers will readily imagine the feelings of Captain de Haldimar during this short but exciting scene. From the account given by the warrior, there could be no doubt the murdered man was the unhappy Donellan; who, prob-ably, neglecting the caution given him, had exposed him-self to the murderous aim of this fierce being, who was apparently a scout sent for the purpose of watching the movements of the garrison. The direction of the firing, the allusion made to the regimentals, nay, the scalp itself, which he knew from the short crop to be that of a soldier, and fancied he recognised from its colour to be that of his servant, formed but too conclusive evidence of the fact; and, bitterly and deeply, as he gazed on this melancholy proof of the man's sacrifice of life to his interest, did he repent that he had made him the companion of his adven-ture, or that, having done so, he had not either brought him away altogether, or sent him instantly back to the fort. Commiseration for the fate of the unfortunate Donellan naturally induced a spirit of personal hostility towards his destroyer; and it was with feelings strongly excited in fa-vour of him whom he now discovered to be the brother of his guide, that he saw him spring fiercely to the attack of his gigantic opponent. There was an activity about the young chief amply commensurate with the greater physi-cal power of his adversary; while the manner in which he wielded his tomahawk, proved him to be any thing but the novice in the use of the formidable weapon the other had represented him. It was with a feeling of disappointment, therefore, which the peculiarity of his own position could not overcome, he saw Ponteac interpose himself between the parties.

Presently, however, a subject of deeper and more absorbing interest than even the fate of his unhappy follower engrossed every faculty of his mind, and riveted both eye and ear in painful tension to the aperture in his hiding-place. The chiefs had resumed their places, and the silence of a few minutes had succeeded to the fierce affray of the warriors, when Ponteac, in a calm and deliberate voice, proceeded to state he had summoned all the heads of the nations together, to hear a plan he had to offer for the reduction of the last remaining forts of their enemies, Michillimackinac and Détroit. He pointed out the tediousness of the warfare in which they were engaged; the desertion of the hunting grounds by their warriors; and their consequent deficiency in all those articles of European traffic which they were formerly in the habit of receiving in exchange for their furs. He dwelt on the beneficial results that would accrue to them all in the event of the reduction of those two important fortresses; since, in that case, they would be enabled to make such terms with the English as would secure them considerable advantages; while, instead of being treated with the indignity of a conquered people, they would be enabled to command respect from the imposing attitude this final crowning of their successes would enable them to assume. He stated that the prudence and vigilance of the commanders of these two unreduced fortresses were likely long to baffle, as had hitherto been the case, every open attempt at their capture; and admitted he had little expectation of terrifying them into a surrender by the same artifice that had succeeded with the forts on the Ohio and the lower lakes. The plan, however, which he had to propose, was one he felt assured would be attended with success. He would disclose that plan, and the great chiefs should give it the advantage of their deliberation.

Captain de Haldimar was on the rack. The chief had gradually dropped his voice as he explained his plan, until at length it became so low, that undistinguishable sounds alone reached the ear of the excited officer. For a moment he despaired of making himself fully master of the important secret; but in the course of the deliberation that ensued, the blanks left unsupplied in the discourse of the leader were abundantly filled up. It was what the reader has already seen. The necessities of the Indians were to be urged as a motive for their being tired of hostilities. A peace was to be solicited; a council held; a ball-playing among the warriors proposed, as a mark of their own sincerity and confidence during that council; and when the garrison, lulled into security, should be thrown entirely off their guard, the warriors were to seize their guns and tomahawks, with which (the former cut short, for the better concealment of their purpose) their women would be provided, rush in, under pretext of regaining their lost ball, when a universal massacre of men, women, and children was to ensue, until nothing wearing the garb of a Saganaw should be left.

It would be tedious to follow the chief through all the minor ramifications of his subtle plan. Suffice it they were of a nature to throw the most wary off his guard; and so admirably arranged was every part, so certain did it appear their enemies must give into the snare, that the oldest chiefs testified their approbation with a vivacity of manner and expression little wont to characterize the deliberative meetings of these reserved people. But deepest of all was the approval of the tall warrior who had so recently arrived. To him had the discourse of the leader been principally directed, as one whose counsel and experience were especially wanting to confirm him in his purpose. He was the last who spoke; but, when he did, it was with a force – an energy – that must have sunk every objection, even if the plan had not been so perfect and unexceptionable in its concoction as to have precluded a possibility of all negative argument. During the delivery of his animated speech, his swarthy countenance kindled into fierce and rapidly varying expression. A thousand dark and complicated passions evidently struggled at his heart; and as he dwelt leisurely and emphatically on the sacrifice of human life that must inevitably attend the adoption of the proposed measure, his eye grew larger, his chest expanded, nay, his very nostril appeared to dilate with unfathomably guileful exultation. Captain de Haldimar thought he had never gazed on any thing wearing the human shape half so atrociously savage.

Long before the council was terminated, the inferior warriors, who had been so suddenly aroused from their slumbering attitudes, had again retired to their tents, and stretched their lazy length before the embers of their fires. The weary chiefs now prepared to follow their example. They emptied the ashes from the bowls of their pipe-tomahawks, replaced them carefully at their side, rose, and retired to their respective tents. Ponteac and the tall warrior alone remained. For a time they conversed earnestly together. The former listened attentively to some observations made to him by his companion, in the course of which, the words "chief of the Saganaw – fort – spy – enemy," and two or three others equally unconnected, were alone audible to the ear of him who so attentively sought to catch the slightest sound. He then thrust his hand under his hunting-coat, and, as if in confirmation of what he had been stating, exhibited a coil of rope and the glossy boot of an English officer. Ponteac uttered one of his sharp ejaculating "ughs!" and then rising quickly from his seat, followed by his companion, soon disappeared in the heart of the encampment.

Eight

HOW SHALL we attempt to paint all that passed through the mind of Captain de Haldimar during this important conference of the fierce chiefs? – where find language to convey the cold and thrilling horror with which he listened to the calm discussion of a plan, the object of which was the massacre, not only of a host of beings endeared to him by long communionship of service, but of those who were wedded to his heart by the dearer ties of affection and kindred? As Ponteac had justly observed, the English garrisons, strong in their own defences, were little likely to be speedily reduced, while their enemies confined themselves to overt acts of hostility; but, against their insidious professions of amity who could oppose a sufficient caution? His father, the young officer was aware, had all along manifested a spirit of conciliation towards the Indians, which, if followed up by the government generally, must have had the effect of preventing the cruel and sanguinary war that had so recently desolated this remote part of the British possessions. How likely, therefore, was it, having this object always in view, he should give in to the present wily stratagem, where such plausible motives for the abandonment of their hostile purpose were urged by the perfidious chiefs! From the few hasty hints already given him by his guide, – that kind being, who evidently sought to be the saviour of the devoted garrisons, – he had gathered that a deep and artful plan was to be submitted to the chiefs by their leader; but little did he imagine it was of the finished nature it now proved to be. Any other than the present attempt, the vigilance and prudence of his experienced father, he felt, would have rendered abortive; but there was so much speciousness in the pleas that were to be advanced in furtherance of their assumed object, he could not but admit the almost certainty of their influence, even on him.

Sick and discouraged as he was at the horrible perspective thus forced on his mental view, the young officer had not, for some moments, presence of mind to reflect that the danger of the garrison existed only so long as he should be absent from it. At length, however, the cheering recollection came, and with it the mantling rush of blood, to his faint heart. But, short was the consoling hope: again he felt dismay in every fibre of his frame; for he now reflected, that although his opportune discovery of the meditated scheme would save one fort, there was no guardian angel to extend, as in this instance, its protecting influence to the other; and within that other there breathed those who were dearer far to him than his own existence; – beings, whose lives were far more precious to him than any even in the garrison of which he was a member. His sister Clara, whom he loved with a love little inferior to that of his younger brother; and one, even more dearly loved than Clara, – Madeline de Haldimar, his cousin and affianced bride, – were both inmates of Michillimackinac, which was commanded by the father of the latter, a major in the —— regiment. With Madeline de Haldimar he had long since exchanged his vows of affection; and their nuptials, which were to have taken place about the period when the present war broke out, had only been suspended because all communication between the two posts had been entirely cut off by the enemy.

Captain de Haldimar had none of the natural weakness and timidity of character which belonged to the gentler and more sensitive Charles. Sanguine and full of enterprise, he seldom met evils half way; but when they did

come, he sought to master them by the firmness and collectedness with which he opposed his mind to their infliction. If his heart was now racked with the most acute
suffering – his reason incapacitated from exercising its
calm deliberative power, the seeming contradiction arose
not from any deficiency in his character, but was attributable wholly to the extraordinary circumstances of the
moment.

It was a part of the profound plan of the Ottawa chief,
that it should be essayed on the two forts on the same day;
and it was a suggestion of the murderer of poor Donellan,
that a parley should be obtained, through the medium of a
white flag, the nature of which he explained to them, as it
was understood among their enemies. If invited to the
council, then they were to enter, or not, as circumstances
might induce; but, in any case, they were to go unprovided
with the pipe of peace, since this could not be smoked
without violating every thing held most sacred among
themselves. The red, or war-pipe, was to be substituted as
if by accident; and, for the success of the deception, they
were to presume on the ignorance of their enemies. This,
however, was not important, since the period of their first
parley was to be the moment chosen for the arrangement
of a future council, and the proposal of a ball-playing
upon the common. Three days were to be named as the
interval between the first conference of Ponteac with the
governor and the definitive council which was to ensue;
during which, however, it was so arranged, that, before the
lip of a red skin should touch the pipe of peace, the ball-
players should rush in and massacre the unprepared soldiery, while the chiefs despatched the officers in council.

It was the proximity of the period allotted for the execution of their cruel scheme that mainly contributed to the
dismay of Captain de Haldimar. The very next day was
appointed for carrying into effect the first part of the
Indian plan: and how was it possible that a messenger,
even admitting he should elude the vigilance of the enemy,
could reach the distant post of Michillimackinac within

the short period on which hung the destiny of that devoted fortress. In the midst of the confused and distracting images that now crowded on his brain, came at length one thought, redolent with the brightest colourings of hope. On his return to the garrison, the treachery of the Indians being made known, the governor might so far, and with a view of gaining time, give in to the plan of his enemies, as to obtain such delay as would afford the chance of communication between the forts. The attempt, on the part of those who should be selected for this purpose, would, it is true, be a desperate one: still it must be made; and, with such incentives to exertion as he had, how willingly would he propose his own services!

The more he dwelt on this mode of defeating the subtle designs of the enemy, the more practicable did it appear. Of his own safe return to the fort he entertained not a doubt; for he knew and relied on the Indian woman, who was bound to him by a tie of gratitude, which her conduct that night evidently denoted to be superior even to the interests of her race. Moreover, as he had approached the encampment unnoticed while the chiefs were yet awake to every thing around them, how little probability was there of his return being detected while all lay wrapped in the most profound repose. It is true that, for a moment, his confidence deserted him as he recurred to the earnest dialogue of the two Indians, and the sudden display of the rope and boot, the latter of which articles he had at once recognised to be one of those he had so recently worn; but his apprehensions on that score were again speedily set to rest, when he reflected, had any suspicion existed in the minds of these men that an enemy was lurking near them, a general alarm would have been spread, and hundreds of warriors despatched to scour the forest.

The night was now rapidly waning away, and already the cold damp air of an autumnal morning was beginning to make itself felt. More than half an hour had elapsed since the departure of Ponteac and his companion, and yet Oucanasta came not. With a sense of the approach of day came new and discouraging thoughts, and, for some minutes, the mind of the young officer became petrified with horror, as he reflected on the bare possibility of his escape being intercepted. The more he lingered on this apprehension, the more bewildered were his ideas; and already, in horrible perspective, he beheld the destruction of his nearest and dearest friends, and the host of those who were humbler followers, and partakers in the same destiny. Absolutely terrified with the misgivings of his own heart, he, in the wildness and unconnectedness of his purpose, now resolved to make the attempt to return alone, although he knew not even the situation of the path he had so recently quitted. He had actually moved a pace forward on his desperate enterprise, when he felt a hand touching the extended arm with which he groped to find the entrance to his hiding-place. The unexpected collision sent a cold shudder through his frame; and such was the excitement to which he had worked himself up, it was not without difficulty he suppressed an exclamation, that must inevitably have sealed his doom. The soft tones of Oucanasta's voice re-assured him.

"The day will soon dawn," she whispered; "the Saganaw must go."

With the return of hope came the sense of all he owed to the devotedness of this kind woman. He grasped the hand that still lingered on his own, pressed it affectionately in his own, and then placed it in silence on his throbbing heart. The breathing of Oucanasta became deeper, and the young officer fancied he could feel her trembling with agitation. Again, however, and in a tone of more subdued expression, she whispered that he must go.

There was little urging necessary to induce a prompt compliance with the hint. Cautiously emerging from his concealment, Captain de Haldimar now followed close in the rear of his guide, who took the same circuit of the forest to reach the path that led towards the fort. This they speedily gained, and then pursued their course in silence, until they at length arrived at the log where the exchange of mocassins had been made.

"Here the Saganaw may take breath," she observed, as she seated herself on the fallen tree; "the sleep of the red skin is sound, and there is no one upon the path but Oucanasta."

Anxious as he felt to secure his return to the fort, there was an implied solicitation in the tones of her to whom he owed so much, that prevented Captain de Haldimar from offering an objection, which he feared might be construed into slight.

For a moment or two the Indian remained with her arms folded, and her head bent over her chest; and then, in a low, deep, but tremulous voice, observed, –

"When the Saganaw saved Oucanasta from perishing in the angry waters, there was a girl of the pale faces with him, whose skin was like the snows of the Canadian winter, and whose hair was black like the fur of the squirrel. Oucanasta saw," she pursued, dropping her voice yet lower, "that the Saganaw was loved by the pale girl, and her own heart was very sick, for the Saganaw had saved her life, and she loved him too. But she knew she was very foolish, and that an Indian girl could never be the wife of a handsome chief of the Saganaw; and she prayed to the Great Spirit of the red skins to give her strength to over-come her feelings; but the Great Spirit was angry with her, and would not hear her." She paused a moment, and then abruptly demanded, "Where is that pale girl now?"

Captain de Haldimar had often been rallied, not only by his brother-officers, but even by his sister and Madeline de Haldimar herself, on the conquest he had evidently made of the heart of this Indian girl. The event to which she had alluded had taken place several months previous to the breaking out of hostilities. Oucanasta was directing her frail bark, one evening, along the shores of the Détroit, when one of those sudden gusts of wind, so frequent in these countries, upset the canoe, and left its pilot struggling amid the waves. Captain de Haldimar, who happened to be on the bank at the moment with his sister and cousin, was an eye-witness of her danger, and instantly flew down the steep to her assistance. Being an excellent swimmer, he was not long in gaining the spot, where, exhausted with the exertion she had made, and encumbered with her awkward machecoti, the poor girl was already on the point of perishing. But for his timely assistance, indeed, she must have sunk to the bottom; and, since that period, the grateful being had been remarked for the strong but unexpressed attachment she felt for her deliverer. This, however, was the first moment Captain de Haldimar became acquainted with the extent of feelings, the avowal of which not a little startled and surprised, and even annoyed him. The last question, however, suggested a thought that kindled every fibre of his being into expectancy, – Oucanasta might be the saviour of those he loved; and he felt that, if time were but afforded her, she would. He rose from the log, dropped on one knee before the Indian, seized both her hands with eagerness, and then in tones of earnest supplication whispered, –

"Oucanasta is right: the pale girl with the skin like snow, and hair like the fur of the squirrel, is the bride of the Saganaw. Long before he saved the life of Oucanasta, he knew and loved that pale girl. She is dearer to the Saganaw than his own blood; but she is in the fort beyond the great lake, and the tomahawks of the red skins will destroy her; for the warriors of that fort have no one to tell them of their danger. What says the red girl? will she go and save the lives of the sister and the wife of the Saganaw."

The breathing of the Indian became deeper; and Captain de Haldimar fancied she sighed heavily, as she replied, –

"Oucanasta is but a weak woman, and her feet are not swift like those of a runner among the red skins; but what the Saganaw asks, for his sake she will try. When she has seen him safe to his own fort, she will go and prepare herself for the journey. The pale girl shall lay her head on the bosom of the Saganaw, and Oucanasta will try to rejoice in her happiness."

In the fervour of his gratitude, the young officer caught the drooping form of the generous Indian wildly to his heart; his lips pressed hers, and during the kiss that followed, the heart of the latter bounded and throbbed, as if it would have passed from her own into the bosom of her companion.

Never was a kiss less premeditated, less unchaste. Gratitude, not passion, had called it forth; and had Madeline de Haldimar been near at the moment, the feeling that had impelled the seeming infidelity to herself would have been regarded as an additional claim on her affection. On the whole, however, it was a most unfortunate and ill-timed kiss, and, as is often the case under such circumstances, led to the downfall of the woman. In the vivacity of his embrace, Captain de Haldimar had drawn his guide so far forward upon the log, that she lost her balance, and fell with a heavy and reverberating crash among the leaves and dried sticks that were strewed thickly around.

Scarcely a second elapsed when the forest was alive with human yells, that fell achingly on the ears of both; and bounding warriors were heard on every hand, rapidly dividing the dense underwood they encountered in their pursuit.

Quick as thought the Indian had regained her feet. She grasped the hand of her companion; and hurrying, though not without caution, along the path, again stood on the brow of the ravine through which they had previously passed.

"The Saganaw must go alone," she whispered. "The red skins are close upon our trail, but they will find only an Indian woman, when they expect a pale face. Oucanasta will save her friend."

Captain de Haldimar did as he was desired. Clinging to the bushes that lined the face of the precipitous descent, he managed once more to gain the bed of the ravine. For a moment he paused to listen to the sounds of his pursuers, whose footsteps were now audible on the eminence he had just quitted; and then, gathering himself up for the leap that was to enable him to clear the rivulet, he threw himself heavily forward. His feet alighted upon an elevated and yielding substance, that gave way with a crashing sound that echoed far and near throughout the forest, and he felt himself secured as if in a trap. Although despairing of escape, he groped with his hands to discover what it was that thus detained him, and found he had fallen through a bark canoe, the bottom of which had been turned upwards. The heart of the fugitive now sank within him: there could be no doubt that his retreat was intercepted. The canoe had been placed there since he last passed through the ravine: and it was evident, from the close and triumphant yell that followed the rending of the frail bark, such a result had been anticipated.

Stunned as he was by the terrific cries of the savages, and confused as were his ideas, Captain de Haldimar had still presence of mind to perceive the path itself offered him no further security. He therefore quitted it altogether, and struck, in an oblique direction, up the opposite face of the ravine. Scarcely had he gone twenty yards, when he heard the voices of several Indians conversing earnestly near the canoe he had just quitted; and presently afterwards he could distinctly hear them ascending the opposite brow of the ravine by the path he recently congratulated himself on having abandoned. To advance or to recede was now equally impracticable; for, on every side, he was begirt by enemies, into whose hands a single false step must inevitably betray him. What would he not have given for the presence of Oucanasta, who was so capable of advising him in this difficulty! but, from the moment of his descending into the ravine, he had utterly lost sight of her.

The spot on which he now rested was covered with thick brushwood, closely interwoven at their tops, but affording sufficient space beneath for a temporary close concealment; so that, unless some Indian should touch him with his foot, there was little seeming probability of his being discovered by the eye. Under this he crept, and lay, breathless and motionless, with his head raised from the ground, and his ear on the stretch for the slightest noise. For several minutes he remained in this position, vainly seeking to catch the sound of a voice, or the fall of a footstep; but the most deathlike silence had succeeded to the fierce yellings that had so recently rent the forest. At times he fancied he could distinguish faint noises in the direction of the encampment; and so certain was he of this, he at length came to the conclusion that the Indians, either baffled in their search, had relinquished the pursuit, or, having encountered Oucanasta, had been thrown on a different scent. His first intention had been to lie concealed until the following night, when the warriors, no longer on the alert, should leave the path once more open to him; but now that the conviction of their return was strong on his mind, he changed his determination, resolving to make the best of his way to the fort with the aid of the approaching dawn. With this view he partly withdrew his body from beneath its canopy of underwood; but, scarcely had he done so, when a hundred tongues, like the baying of so many blood-hounds, again rent the air with their wild cries, which seemed to rise up from the very bowels of the earth, and close to the appalled ear of the young officer.

Scarcely conscious of what he did, Captain de Haldimar grasped one of his pistols, for he fancied he felt the hot breathing of human life upon his cheek. With a sickly sensation of fear, he turned to satisfy himself whether it was not an illusion of his heated imagination. What, however, was his dismay, when he beheld bending over him a dark and heavy form, the outline of which alone was distinguishable in the deep gloom in which the ravine remained enveloped! Desperation was in the heart of the excited officer: he cocked his pistol; but scarcely had the sharp ticking sound floated on the air, when he felt a powerful hand upon his chest; and, with as much facility as if he had been a child, was he raised by that invisible hand to his feet. A dozen warriors now sprang to the assistance of their comrade, when the whole, having disarmed and bound their prisoner, led him back in triumph to their encampment.

Nine

THE FIRES of the Indians were nearly now extinct; but the faint light of the fast dawning day threw a ghastly, sickly, hue over the countenances of the savages, which rendered them even more terrific in their war paint. The chiefs grouped themselves immediately around their prisoner, while the inferior warriors, forming an outer circle, stood leaning their dark forms upon their rifles, and following, with keen and watchful eye, every movement of their captive. Hitherto the unfortunate officer had been too much engrossed by his despair to pay any immediate attention to the individual who had first discovered and seized him. It was sufficient for him to know all hope of the safety of the garrison had perished with his captivity: and, with that recklessness of life which often springs from the very consciousness of inability to preserve it, he now sullenly awaited the death which he expected at each moment would be inflicted. Suddenly his ear was startled by an interrogatory, in English, from one who stood behind him.

With a movement of surprise, Captain de Haldimar turned to examine his questioner. It was the dark and ferocious warrior who had exhibited the scalp of his ill-fated servant. For a moment the officer fixed his eyes firmly and unshrinkingly on those of the savage, seeking to reconcile the contradiction that existed between his dress and features and the purity of the English he had just spoken. The other saw his drift, and, impatient of the scrutiny, again repeated, as he fiercely pulled the strong leathern thong by which the prisoner now found himself secured to his girdle, –

"Who and what are you? – whence come you? – and for what purpose are you here?" Then, as if struck by some sudden recollection, he laid his hand upon the shoulder of his victim; and, while his eye grew upon his features, he pursued, in a tone of vehemence, – "Ha! by Heaven, I should know that face! – the cursed lines of the blood of De Haldimar are stamped upon that brow! But stay, one proof and I am satisfied." While he yet spoke he dashed the menial hat of his captive to the earth, put aside his hair, and then, with fiendish exultation, pursued, – "It is even so. Do you recollect the battle of the plains of Abraham, Captain de Haldimar? – Recollect you the French officer who aimed so desperately at your life, and whose object was defeated by a soldier of your regiment? I am that officer: my victim escaped me then, but not for ever. The hour of vengeance is nearly now arrived, and your capture is the pledge of my success. Hark, how the death-cry of all his hated race will ring in madness on your father's ear!"

Amazement, stupefaction, and horror, filled the mind of the wretched officer at this extraordinary declaration. He perfectly recollected that the individual who had evinced so much personal hostility on the occasion alluded to, was indeed a man wearing the French uniform, although at the head of a band of savages, and of a stature and strength similar to those of him who now so fiercely avowed himself the bitter and deadly foe of all his race. If this were so, and his tone and language left little room for doubt, the doom of the ill-fated garrison was indeed irrevocably sealed. This mysterious enemy evidently possessed great influence in the councils of the Indians; and while the hot breath of his hatred continued to fan the flame of fierce hostility that had been kindled in the bosom of Ponteac, whose particular friend he appeared to be, there would be no end to the atrocities that must follow. Great, however, as was the dismay of Captain de Haldimar, who, exhausted with the adventures of the night, presented a ghastly image of anxiety and fatigue, it was impossible for him to repress the feelings of indignation with which the language of this fierce man had inspired him.

"If you are in reality a French officer," he said, "and not an Englishman, as your accent would denote, the sentiments you have now avowed may well justify the belief, that you have been driven with ignominy from a service which your presence must eternally have disgraced. There is no country in Europe that would willingly claim you for its subject. Nay, even the savage race, with whom you are now connected, would, if apprised of your true nature, spurn you as a thing unworthy to herd even with their wolf-dogs."

A fierce sardonic laugh burst from the lips of the warrior, but this was so mingled with rage as to give an almost devilish expression to his features.

"Ignominy – ignominy!" he repeated, while his right hand played convulsively with the handle of his tomahawk; "is it for a De Haldimar to taunt me with ignominy? Fool!" he pursued, after a momentary pause, "you have sealed your doom." Then abruptly quitting the handle of his weapon, he thrust his hand into his bosom, and again drawing forth the reeking scalp of Donellan, he dashed it furiously in the face of his prisoner. "Not two hours since," he exclaimed, "I cheered myself with the thought that the scalp of a De Haldimar was in my pouch. Now, indeed, do I glory in my mistake. The torture will be a more fitting death for you."

Had an arm of the insulted soldier been at liberty, the offence would not have gone unavenged even there; for such was the desperation of his heart, that he felt he could have hugged the death struggle with his insolent captor, notwithstanding the fearful odds, nor quitted him until one or both should have paid the debt of fierce enmity with life. As it was he could only betray, by his flashing eye, excited look, and the impatient play of his foot upon the ground, the deep indignation that consumed his heart.

The tall savage exulted in the mortification he had awakened, and as his eye glanced insolently from head to foot along his enemy, its expression told how much he laughed at the impotence of his anger. Suddenly, however, a change passed over his features. The mocassin of the officer had evidently attracted his attention, and he now demanded, in a more serious and imperative tone, –

"Ha! what means this disguise? Who is the wretch whom I have slain, mistaking him for a nobler victim; and how comes it that an officer of the English garrison appears here in the garb of a servant? By heaven, it is so! you are come as a spy into the camp of the Indians to steal away the councils of the chiefs. Speak, what have you heard?"

With these questions returned the calm and self-possession of the officer. He at once saw the importance of his answer, on which hung not merely his own last faint chance of safety, but that also of his generous deliverer. Struggling to subdue the disgust which he felt at holding converse with this atrocious monster, he asked in turn, –

"Am I then the only one whom the warriors have overtaken in their pursuit?"

"There was a woman, the sister of that boy," and he pointed contemptuously to the young chief who had so recently assailed him, and who now, in common with his followers, stood impatiently listening to a colloquy that was unintelligible to all. "Speak truly, was *she* not the traitress who conducted you here?"

"Had you found me here," returned the officer, with difficulty repressing his feelings, "there might have been some ground for the assertion; but surely the councils of the chiefs could not be overheard at the distant point at which you discovered me."

"Why then were you there in this disguise? – and who is he," again holding up the bloody scalp, "whom I have despoiled of this?"

"There are few of the Ottawa Indians," returned Captain de Haldimar, "who are ignorant I once saved that young woman's life. Is it then so very extraordinary an attachment should have been the consequence? The man whom you slew was my servant. I had brought him out with me for protection during my interview with the woman, and I exchanged my uniform with him for the same purpose. There is nothing in this, however, to warrant the supposition of my being a spy."

During the delivery of these more than equivocal sentences, which, however, he felt were fully justified by circumstances, the young officer had struggled to appear calm and confident; but, despite of his exertions, his consciousness caused his cheek to colour, and his eye to twinkle, beneath the searching glance of his ferocious enemy. The latter thrust his hand into his chest, and slowly drew forth the rope he had previously exhibited to Ponteac.

"Do you think me a fool, Captain de Haldimar," he observed, sneeringly, "that you expect so paltry a tale to be palmed successfully on my understanding? An English officer is not very likely to run the risk of breaking his neck by having recourse to such a means of exit from a besieged garrison, merely to intrigue with an Indian woman, when there are plenty of soldiers' wives within, and that too at an hour when he knows the scouts of his enemies are prowling in the neighbourhood. Captain de Haldimar," he concluded, slowly and deliberately, "you have lied."

Despite of the last insult, his prisoner remained calm. The very observation that had just been made afforded him a final hope of exculpation, which, if it benefited not himself, might still be of service to the generous Oucanasta.

"The onus of such language," he observed coolly and with dignity, "falls not on him to whom it is addressed, but on him who utters it. Yet one who professes to have been himself a soldier, must see in this very circumstance a proof of my innocence. Had I been sent out as a spy to reconnoitre the movements, and to overhear the councils of our enemies, the gate would have been open for my egress; but that rope is in itself an evidence I must have stolen forth unknown to the garrison."

Whether it was that the warrior had his own particular reasons for attaching truth to this statement, or that he merely pretended to do so, Captain de Haldimar saw with secret satisfaction his last argument was conclusive.

"Well, be it so," retorted the savage, while a ferocious smile passed over his swarthy features; "but, whether you have been here as a spy, or have merely ventured out in prosecution of an intrigue, it matters not. Before the sun has travelled far in the meridian you die; and the tomahawk of your father's deadly foe – of – of – of Wacousta, as I am called, shall be the first to drink your blood."

The officer made a final effort at mercy. "Who or what you are, or whence your hatred of my family, I know not," he said; "but surely I have never injured you: wherefore, then, this insatiable thirst for my blood? If you are, indeed, a Christian and a soldier, let your heart be touched with humanity, and procure my restoration to my friends. You once attempted my life in honourable combat, why not wait, then, until a fitting opportunity shall give not a bound and defenceless victim to your steel, but one whose resistance may render him a conquest worthy of your arm?"

"What! and be balked of the chance of my just revenge? Hear me, Captain de Haldimar," he pursued, in that low, quick, deep tone that told all the strong excitement of his heart: – "I have, it is true, no particular enmity to yourself, further than that you are a De Haldimar; but hell does not supply a feeling half so bitter as my enmity to your proud father; and months, nay years, have I passed in the hope of such an hour as this. For this have I forsworn my race, and become – what you now behold me – a savage both in garb and character. But this matters not," he continued, fiercely and impatiently, "your doom is sealed; and before another sun has risen, your stern father's gaze shall be blasted with the sight of the mangled carcase of his first born. Ha! ha! ha!" and he laughed low and exultingly; "even now I think I see him withering, if heart so hard can wither, beneath this proof of my un-dying hate."

"Fiend! – monster! – devil!" exclaimed the excited offi-cer, now losing sight of all considerations of prudence in the deep horror inspired by his captor: – "Kill me – torture me – commit any cruelty on me, if such be your savage will; but outrage not humanity by the fulfilment of your last disgusting threat. Suffer not a father's heart to be agonised – a father's eye to be blasted – with a view of the mangled remains of him to whom he has given life."

Again the savage rudely pulled the thong that bound his prisoner to his girdle, and removing his tomahawk from his belt, and holding its sullied point close under the eye of the former, exclaimed, as he bent eagerly over him, –

"See you this, Captain de Haldimar? At the still hour of midnight, while you had abandoned your guard to revel in the arms of your Indian beauty, I stole into the fort by means of the same rope that you had used in quitting it. Unseen by the sentinels I gained your father's apartment. It was the first time we had met for twenty years; and I do believe that had the very devil presented himself in my place, he would have been received with fewer marks of horror. Oh, how that proud man's eye twinkled beneath this glittering blade! He attempted to call out, but my look paralysed his tongue, and cold drops of sweat stole rapidly down his brow and cheek. Then it was that my seared heart once more beat with the intoxication of triumph. Your father was alone and unarmed, and throughout the fort not a sound was to be heard, save the distant tread of the sentinels. I could have laid him dead at my feet at a single blow, and yet have secured my retreat. But no, that was not my object. I came to taunt him with the promise of my revenge – to tell him the hour of my triumph was approaching fast; and, ha!" he concluded, laughing hideously as he passed his large rude hand through the wavy hair of the now uncovered officer, "this is, indeed, a fair and unexpected first earnest of the full redemption of my pledge. No – no!" he continued, as if talking to himself, "he must not die. Tantulus-like, he shall have death ever apparently within his grasp; but, until all his race have perished before his eyes, he shall not attain it."

Hitherto the Indians had preserved an attitude of calm, listening to the interrogatories put to the prisoner with that wonder and curiosity with which a savage people hear a language different from their own; and marking the several emotions that were elicited in the course of the animated colloquy of the pale faces. Gradually, however, they became impatient under its duration; and many of them, in the excitement produced by the fierce manner of him who was called Wacousta, fixed their dark eyes upon the captive, while they grasped the handles of their toma-hawks, as if they would have disputed with the former the privilege of dying his weapon first in his blood. When they saw the warrior hold up his menacing blade to the eye of his victim, while he passed his hand through the redundant hair, they at once inferred the sacrifice was about to be completed, and rushing furiously forward, they bounded, and leaped, and yelled, and brandished their own weapons in the most appalling manner.

Already had the unhappy officer given himself up for lost; fifty bright tomahawks were playing about his head at the same instant, and death – that death which is never without terror to the young, however brave they may be in the hour of generous conflict – seemed to have arrived at last. He raised his eyes to Heaven, committing his soul to his God in the same silent prayer that he offered up for the preservation of his friends and comrades; and then bending them upon the earth, summoned all his collectedness and courage to sustain him through the trial. At the very moment, however, when he expected to feel the crashing steel within his brain, he felt himself again violently pulled by the thong that secured his hands. In the next instant he was pressed close to the chest of his vast enemy, who, with one arm encircling his prisoner, and the other brandishing his fierce blade in rapid evolutions round his head, kept the yelling band at bay, with the evident unshaken determination to maintain his sole and acknowledged right to the disposal of his captive.

For several moments the event appeared doubtful; but, notwithstanding his extreme agility in the use of a weapon, in the management of which he evinced all the dexterity of the most practised native, the odds were fearfully against Wacousta; and while his flashing eye and swelling chest betrayed his purpose rather to perish himself than suffer the infringement of his claim, it was evident that numbers must, in the end, prevail against him. On an appeal to Ponteac, however, of which he now suddenly bethought himself, the authority of the latter was successfully exerted, and he was again left in the full and undisturbed possession of his prisoner.

A low and earnest conversation now ensued among the chiefs, in which, as before, Wacousta bore a principal part. When this was terminated, several Indians approached the unhappy officer, and unfastening the thong with which his hands were firmly and even painfully girt, deprived him both of coat, waistcoat, and shirt. He was then bound a second time in the same manner, his body besmeared with paint, and his head so disguised as to give him the caricature semblance of an Indian warrior. When these preparations were completed, he was led to the tree in which he had been previously concealed, and there firmly secured. Meanwhile Wacousta, at the head of a numerous band of warriors, had departed once more in the direction of the fort.

With the rising of the sun now vanished all traces of the mist that had fallen since the early hours of morning, leaving the unfortunate officer ample leisure to survey the difficulties of his position. He had fancied, from the course taken by his guide the previous night, that the plain or oasis, as we have elsewhere termed it, lay in the very heart of the forest; but that route now proved to have been circuitous. The tree to which he was bound was one of a slight belt, separating the encampment from the open grounds which extended towards the river, and which was so thin and scattered on that side as to leave the clear silver waters of the Détroit visible at intervals. Oh, what would he not have given, at that cheering sight, to have had his limbs free, and his chance of life staked on the swiftness of his flight! While he had imagined himself begirt by interminable forest, he felt as one whose very thought to elude those who were, in some degree, the deities of that wild scene, must be paralysed in its first conception. But here was the vivifying picture of civilised nature. Corn fields, although trodden down and destroyed – dwelling houses, although burnt or dilapidated – told of the existence of those who were of the same race with himself; and notwithstanding these had perished even as he must perish, still there was something in the aspect of the very ruins of their habitations which, contrasted with the solemn gloom of the forest, carried a momentary and indefinable consolation to his spirit. Then there was the ripe and teeming orchard, and the low whitewashed cabin of the Canadian peasant, to whom the officers of charity, and the duties of humanity, were no strangers; and who, although the secret enemies of his country, had no motive for personal hostility towards himself. Then, on the river itself, even at that early hour, was to be seen, fastened to the long stake driven into its bed, or secured by the rude anchor of stone appended to a cable of twisted bark, the light canoe or clumsy periagua of the peasant fisherman, who, ever and anon, drew up from its deep bosom the shoal-loving pickerel or pike, or white or black bass, or whatever other tenant of these waters might chance to affix itself to the traitorous hook. It is true that his view of these objects was only occasional and indistinct; but his intimate acquaintance with the localities beyond brought every thing before Captain de Haldimar's eye; and even while he sighed to think they were for ever cut off from his reach, he already, in idea, followed the course of flight he should pursue were the power but afforded him.

From this train of painful and exciting thought the wretched captive was aroused, by a faint but continued yelling in a distant part of the forest, and in the direction that had been taken by Wacousta and his warriors. Then, after a short interval, came the loud booming of the cannon of the fort, carried on with a spirit and promptitude that told of some pressing and dangerous emergency, and fainter afterwards the sharp shrill reports of the rifles, bearing evidence the savages were already in close collision with the garrison. Various were the conjectures that passed rapidly through the mind of the young officer, during a firing that had called almost every Indian in the encampment away to the scene of action, save the two or three young Ottawas who had been left to guard his own person, and who lay upon the sward near him, with head erect and ear sharply set, listening to the startling sounds of conflict. What the motive of the hurried departure of the Indians was he knew not; but he had conjectured the object of the fierce Wacousta was to possess himself of the uniform in which his wretched servant was clothed, that no mistake might occur in his identity, when its true owner should be exhibited in it, within view of the fort, mangled and disfigured, in the manner that fierce and mysterious man had already threatened. It was exceedingly probable the body of Donellan had been mistaken for his own, and that in the anxiety of his father to prevent the Indians from carrying it off, the cannon had been directed to open upon them. But if this were the case, how were the reports of the rifles, and the fierce yellings that continued, save at intervals, to ring throughout the forest to be accounted for? The bullets of the Indians evidently could not reach the fort, and they were too wily, and attached too much value to their ammunition, to risk a shot that was not certain of carrying a wound with it. For a moment the fact itself flashed across his mind, and he attributed the fire of small arms to the attack and defence of a party that had been sent out for the purpose of securing the body, supposed to be his own; yet, if so, again how was he to account for his not hearing the report of a single musket? His ear was too well practised not to know the sharp crack of the rifle from the heavy dull discharge of the musket, and as yet the former only had been distinguishable, amid the intervals that ensued between each sullen booming of the cannon. While this impression continued on the mind of the anxious officer, he caught, with the avidity of desperation, at the faint and improbable idea that his companions might be able to penetrate to his place of concealment, and procure his liberation; but when he found the firing, instead of drawing nearer, was confined to the same spot, and even more fiercely kept up by the Indians towards the close, he again gave way to his despair, and resigning himself to his fate, no longer sought comfort in vain speculation as to its cause. His ear now caught the report of the last shell as it exploded, and then all was still and hushed, as if what he had so recently heard was but a dream.

The first intimation given him of the return of the savages was the death howl, set up by the women within the encampment. Captain de Haldimar turned his eyes, instinct with terror, towards the scene, and beheld the warriors slowly issuing from the opposite side of the forest into the plain, and bearing in silence the dead and stiffened forms of those who had been cut down by the destructive fire from the fort. Their mien was sullen and revengeful, and more than one dark and gleaming eye did he encounter turned upon him, with an expression that seemed to say a separate torture should avenge the death of each of their fallen comrades.

The early part of the morning wore away in preparation for the interment of the slain. These were placed in rows under the council shed, where they were attended by their female relatives, who composed the features and confined the limbs, while the gloomy warriors dug, within the limit of the encampment, rude graves, of a depth just sufficient to receive the body. When these were completed, the dead were deposited, with the usual superstitious ceremonies of these people, in their several receptacles, after which a mound of earth was thrown up over each, and the whole covered with round logs, so disposed as to form a tomb of semicircular shape: at the head of each grave was finally planted a pole, bearing various devices in paint, intended to illustrate the warlike achievements of the defunct parties.

Captain de Haldimar had followed the course of these proceedings with a beating heart; for too plainly had he read in the dark and threatening manner both of men and women, that the retribution about to be wreaked upon himself would be terrible indeed. Much as he clung to life, and bitterly as he mourned his early cutting off from the affections hitherto identified with his existence, his wretchedness would have been less, had he not been overwhelmed by the conviction that, with him, must perish every chance of the safety of those, the bare recollection of whom made the bitterness of death even more bitter. Harrowing as were these reflections, he felt that immediate destruction, since it could not be avoided, would be rather a blessing than otherwise. But such, evidently, was not the purpose of his relentless enemy. Every species of torment which his cruel invention could supply would, he felt convinced, be exercised upon his frame; and with this impression on his mind, it would have required sterner nerves than his, not to have shrunk from the very anticipation of so dreadful an ordeal.

It was now noon, and yet no visible preparation was making for the consummation of the sacrifice. This, Captain de Haldimar imputed to the absence of the fierce Wacousta, whom he had not seen since the return of the warriors from their skirmish. The momentary disappearance of this extraordinary and ferocious man was, however, fraught with no consolation to his unfortunate prisoner, who felt he was only engaged in taking such measures as would render not only his destruction more certain, but his preliminary sufferings more complicated and protracted. While he was thus indulging in fruitless speculation as to the motive for his absence, he fancied he heard the report of a rifle, succeeded immediately afterwards by the war-whoop, at a considerable distance, and in the direction of the river. In this impression he was confirmed, by the sudden upstarting to their feet of the young Indians to whose custody he had been committed, who now advanced to the outer edge of the belt of forest, with the apparent object of obtaining a more unconfined view of the open ground that lay beyond. The rapid gliding of spectral forms from the interior of the encampment in the same direction, denoted, moreover, that the Indians generally had heard, and were attracted by the same sound.

Presently afterwards, repeated "waughs!" and "Wacousta! – Wacousta!" from those who had reached the extreme skirt of the forest, fell on the dismayed ear of the young officer. It was evident, from the peculiar tones in which these words were pronounced, that they beheld that warrior approaching them with some communication of interest; and, sick at heart, and filled with irrepressible dismay, Captain de Haldimar felt his pulse to throb more violently as each moment brought his enemy nearer to him.

A startling interest was now created among the Indians; for, as the savage warrior neared the forest, his lips pealed forth that peculiar cry which is meant to announce some intelligence of alarm. Scarcely had its echoes died away in the forest, when the whole of the warriors rushed from the encampment towards the clearing. Directed by the sound, Captain de Haldimar bent his eyes upon the thin skirt of wood that lay immediately before him, and at intervals could see the towering form of that vast warrior bounding, with incredible speed, up the sloping ground that led from the town towards the forest. A ravine lay before him; but this he cleared, with a prodigious effort, at a single leap;

and then, continuing his way up the slope, amid the low guttural acclamations of the warriors at his extraordinary dexterity and strength, finally gained the side of Ponteac, then leaning carelessly against a tree at a short distance from the prisoner.

A low and animated conversation now ensued between these two important personages, which at moments assumed the character of violent discussion. From what Captain de Haldimar could collect, the Ottawa chief was severely reproving his friend for the inconsiderate ardour which had led him that morning into collision with those whom it was their object to lull into security by a careful avoidance of hostility, and urging the possibility of their plan being defeated in consequence. He moreover obstinately refused the pressing request of Wacousta, in regard to some present enterprise which the latter had just suggested, the precise nature of which, however, Captain de Haldimar could not learn. Meanwhile, the rapid flitting of numerous forms to and from the encampment, arrayed in all the fierce panoply of savage warfare, while low exclamations of excitement occasionally caught his ear, led the officer to infer, strange and unusual as such an occurrence was, that either the detachment already engaged, or a second, was advancing on their position. Still, this offered little chance of security for himself; for more than once, during his long conference with Ponteac, had the fierce Wacousta bent his eye in ferocious triumph on his victim, as if he would have said, – "Come what will – whatever be the result – you, at least, shall not escape me." Indeed, so confident did the latter feel that the instant of attack would be the signal of his own death, that, after the first momentary and instinctive cheering of his spirit, he rather regretted the circumstance of their approach; or, if he rejoiced at all, it was only because it afforded him the prospect of immediate death, instead of being exposed to all the horror of a lingering and agonising suffering from the torture.

While the chiefs were yet earnestly conversing, the

alarm cry, previously uttered by Wacousta, was repeated, although in a low and subdued tone, by several of the Indians who stood on the brow of the eminence. Ponteac started suddenly to the same point; but Wacousta continued for a moment or two rooted to the spot on which he stood, with the air of one in doubt as to what course he should pursue. He then abruptly raised his head, fixed his dark and menacing eye on his captive, and was already in the act of approaching him, when the earnest and repeated demands for his presence, by the Ottawa chief, drew him once more to the outskirt of the wood.

Again Captain de Haldimar breathed freely. The presence of that fierce man had been a clog upon the vital functions of his heart; and, to be relieved from it, even at a moment like the present, when far more important interests might be supposed to occupy his mind, was a gratification, of which not even the consciousness of impending death could wholly deprive him. From the continued pressing of the Indians towards one particular point in the clearing, he now conjectured, that, from that point, the advance of the troops was visible. Anxious to obtain even a momentary view of those whom he deemed himself fated never more to mingle with in this life, he raised himself upon his feet, and stretched his neck and bent his eager glance in the direction by which Wacousta had approached; but, so closely were the dark warriors grouped among the trees, he found it impossible. Once or twice, however, he thought he could distinguish the gleaming of the English bayonets in the bright sunshine, as they seemed to file off in a parallel line with the ravine. Oh, how his generous heart throbbed at that moment; and how ardently did he wish that he could have stood in the position of the meanest soldier in those gallant ranks! Perhaps his own brave and devoted grenadiers were of the number, burning with enthusiasm to be led against the captors or destroyers of their officer; and this thought added to his wretchedness still more.

While the unfortunate prisoner, thus strongly excited,

bent his whole soul on the scene before him, he fancied he heard the approach of a cautious footstep. He turned his head as well as his confined position would admit, and beheld, close behind him, a dark Indian, whose eyes alone were visible above the blanket in which his person was completely enveloped. His right arm was uplifted, and the blade of a scalping knife glittered in his hand. A cold shudder ran through the veins of the young officer, and he closed his eyes, that he might not see the blow which he felt was about to be directed at his heart. The Indian glanced hurriedly yet cautiously around, to see if he was observed; and then, with the rapidity of thought, divided, first the thongs that secured the legs, and then those which confined the arms of the defenceless captive. When Captain de Haldimar, full of astonishment at finding himself once more at liberty, again unclosed his eyes, they fell on the not unhandsome features of the young chief, the brother of Oucanasta.

"The Saganaw is the prisoner of Wacousta," said the Indian hastily; "and Wacousta is the enemy of the young Ottawa chief. The warriors of the pale faces are there" (and he pointed directly before him). "If the Saganaw has a bold heart and a swift foot, he may save his life:" and, with this intimation, he hurried away in the same cautious manner, and was in the next instant seen making a circuit to arrive at the point at which the principal strength of the Indians was collected.

The position of Captain de Haldimar had now attained its acmé of interest; for on his own exertions alone depended every thing that remained to be accomplished. With wonderful presence of mind he surveyed all the difficulties of his course, while he availed himself at the same moment of whatever advantages were within his grasp. On the approach of Wacousta, the young Indians, to whose custody he had been committed, had returned to their post; but no sooner had that warrior, obeying the call of Ponteac, again departed, than they once more flew to the extreme skirt of the forest, after first satisfying themselves the ligatures which confined their prisoner were secure. Either with a view of avoiding unnecessary encumbrance in their course, or through hurry and inadvertence, they had left their blankets near the foot of the tree. The first thought of the officer was to seize one of these; for, in order to gain the point whence his final effort to join the detachment must be made, it was necessary he should pass through the body of scattered Indians who stood immediately in his way; and the disguise of the blanket could alone afford him a reasonable chance of moving unnoticed among them. Secretly congratulating himself on the insulting mockery that had inducted his upper form in the disguising war-paint of his enemies, he now drew the protecting blanket close up to his eyes; and then, with every nerve braced up, every faculty of mind and body called into action, commenced his dangerous enterprise.

He had not, however, taken more than two or three steps in advance, when, to his great discomfiture and alarm, he beheld the formidable Wacousta approaching from a distance, evidently in search of his prisoner. With the quickness of thought he determined on his course. To appear to avoid him would be to excite the suspicion of the fierce warrior; and, desperate as the alternative was, he resolved to move undeviatingly forward. At each step that drew him nearer to his enemy, the beating of his heart became more violent; and had it not been for the thick coat of paint in which he was invested, the involuntary contraction of the muscles of his face must inevitably have betrayed him. Nay, even as it was, had the keen eye of the warrior fallen on him, such was the agitation of the officer, he felt he must have been discovered. Happily, however, Wacousta, who evidently took him for some inferior warrior hastening to the point where his fellows were already assembled, passed without deigning to look at him, and so close, their forms almost touched. Captain de Haldimar now quickened his pace. It was evident there was no time to be lost; for Wacousta, on finding him gone, would at once give the alarm, when a hundred warriors would be ready on the instant to intercept his flight. Taking the precaution to disguise his walk by turning in his toes after the Indian manner, he reached, with a beating heart, the first of the numerous warriors who were collected within the belt of forest, anxiously watching the movements of the detachment in the plain below. To his infinite joy he found that each was too much intent on what was passing in the distance, to heed any thing going on near themselves; and when he at length gained the extreme opening, and stood in a line with those who were the farthest advanced, without having excited a single suspicion in his course, he could scarcely believe the evidence of his senses.

Still the most difficult part of the enterprise remained to be completed. Hitherto he had moved under the friendly cover of the underwood, the advantage of which had been to conceal that part of his regimental trousers which the blanket left exposed; and if he moved forward into the clearing, the quick glance of an Indian would not be slow in detecting the difference between these and his own ruder leggings. There was no alternative now but to commence his flight from the spot on which he stood; and for this he prepared himself. At one rapid and comprehensive view he embraced the immediate localities before him. On the other side of the ravine he could now distinctly see the English troops, either planning, as he conceived, their own attack, or waiting in the hope of drawing the Indians from their cover. It was evident that to reach them the ravine must be crossed, unless the more circuitous route by the bridge, which was hid from his view by an intervening hillock, should be preferred; but as the former had been cleared by Wacousta in his ascent, and was the nearest point by which the detachment could be approached, to this did he now direct his undivided attention.

While he yet paused with indecision, at one moment fancying the time for starting was not yet arrived, and at the next that he had suffered it to pass away, the powerful and threatening voice of Wacousta was heard proclaiming the escape of his captive. Low but expressive exclamations from the warriors marked their sense of the importance of the intelligence; and many of them hastily dispersed themselves in pursuit. This was the critical moment for action: for, as the anxious officer had rather wished than expected, those Indians who had been immediately in front, and whose proximity he most dreaded, were among the number of those who dashed into the heart of the forest – Captain de Haldimar now stood alone, and full twenty paces in front of the nearest of the savages. For a moment he played with his mocassined foot to satisfy himself, of the power and flexibility of its muscles, and then committing himself to his God, dashed the blanket suddenly from his shoulders, and, with eye and heart fixed on the distant soldiery, darted down the declivity with a speed of which he had never yet believed himself capable. Scarcely, however, had his fleeing form appeared in the opening, when a tremendous and deafening yell rent the air, and a dozen wild and naked warriors followed instantly in pursuit. Attracted by that yell, the terrible Wacousta, who had been seeking his victim in a different quarter, bounded forward to the front with an eye flashing fire, and a brow compressed into the fiercest hate; and so stupendous were his efforts, so extraordinary was his speed, that had it not been for the young Ottawa chief, who was one of the pursuing party, and who, under the pretence of assisting in the recapture of the prisoner, sought every opportunity of throwing himself before, and embarrassing the movements of his enemy, it is highly probable the latter would have succeeded. Despite of these obstacles, however, the fierce Wacousta, who had been the last to follow, soon left the foremost of his companions far behind him; and but for his sudden fall, while in the very act of seizing the arm of his prisoner, his gigantic efforts must have been crowned with the fullest success. But the reader has already seen how miraculously

Captain de Haldimar, reduced to the last stage of debility, as much from inanition as from the unnatural efforts of his flight, finally accomplished his return to the detachment.

Ten

AT THE WESTERN extremity of the lake Huron, and almost washed by the waters of that pigmy ocean, stands the fort of Michillimackinac. Constructed on a smaller scale, and garrisoned by a less numerical force, the defences of this post, although less formidable than those of the Détroit, were nearly similar, at the period embraced by our story, both in matter and in manner. Unlike the latter fortress, however, it boasted none of the advantages afforded by culture; neither, indeed, was there a single spot in the immediate vicinity that was not clad in the eternal forest of these regions. It is true, that art and laborious exertion had so far supplied the deficiencies of nature as to isolate the fort, and throw it under the protecting sweep of its cannon; but, while this afforded security, it failed to produce any thing like a pleasing effect to the eye. The very site on which the fortress now stood had at one period been a portion of the wilderness that every where around was only terminated by the sands on the lake shore: and, although time and the axe of the pioneer had in some degree changed its features, still there was no trace of that blended natural scenery that so pleasingly diversified the vicinity of the sister fort. Here and there, along the imperfect clearing, and amid the dark and thickly studded stumps of the felled trees, which in themselves were sufficient to give the most lugubrious character to the scene, rose the rude log cabin of the settler; but, beyond this, cultivation appeared to have lost her power in proportion with the difficulties she had to encounter. Even the two Indian villages, L'Arbre-Croche and Chabouiga, situate about a mile from the fort, with which they formed nearly an equilateral triangle, were hid from the view of the garrison by the dark dense forest, in the heart of which they were embedded.

Lakeward the view was scarcely less monotonous; but it was not, as in the rear, that monotony which is never occasionally broken in upon by some occurrence of interest. If the eye gazed long and anxiously for the white sail of the well known armed vessel, charged at stated intervals with letters and tidings of those whom time, and distance, and danger, far from estranging, rendered more dear to the memory, and bound more closely to the heart, it was sure of being rewarded at last; and then there was no picture on which it could love to linger so well as that of the silver waves bearing that valued vessel in safety to its wonted anchorage in the offing. Moreover, the light swift bark canoes of the natives often danced joyously on its surface; and while the sight was offended at the savage, skulking among the trees of the forest, like some dark spirit moving cautiously in its course of secret destruction, and watching the moment when he might pounce unnoticed on his unprepared victim, it followed, with momentary pleasure and excitement, the activity and skill displayed by the harmless paddler, in the swift and meteor-like race that set the troubled surface of the Huron in a sheet of hissing foam. Nor was this all. When the eye turned wood-ward, it fell heavily, and without interest, upon a dim and dusky point, known to enter upon savage scenes and unexplored countries; whereas, whenever it reposed upon the lake, it was with an eagerness and energy that embraced the most vivid recollections of the past, and led the imagination buoyantly over every well-remembered scene that had previously been traversed, and which must be traversed again before the land of the European could be pressed once more. The forest, in a word, formed, as it were, the gloomy and impenetrable walls of the prison-house, and the bright lake that lay before it the only portal through which happiness and liberty could be again secured.

The principal entrance into the fort, which presented four equal sides of a square, was from the forest; but, immediately opposite to this, and behind the apartments of the commanding officer, there was another small gate that opened upon the lake shore; but which, since the investment of the place, had been kept bolted and locked, with a precaution befitting the danger to which the garrison was exposed. Still, there were periods, even now, when its sullen hinges were to be heard moaning on the midnight breeze; for it served as a medium of communication between the besieged and others who were no less critically circumstanced than themselves.

The very day before the Indians commenced their simultaneous attack on the several posts of the English, the only armed vessel that had been constructed on these upper lakes, serving chiefly as a medium of communication between Détroit and Michillimackinac, had arrived with despatches and letters from the former fort. A well-concerted plan of the savages to seize her in her passage through the narrow waters of the river Sinclair had only been defeated by the vigilance of her commander; but, ever since the breaking out of the war, she had been imprisoned within the limits of the Huron. Laborious indeed was the duty of the devoted crew. Several attempts had been renewed by the Indians to surprise them; but, although their little fleets stole cautiously and noiselessly, at the still hour of midnight, to the spot where, at the last expiring rays of twilight, they had beheld her carelessly anchored, and apparently lulled into security, the subject of their search was never to be met with. No sooner were objects on the shore rendered indistinct to the eye, than the anchor was silently weighed, and, gliding wherever the breeze might choose to carry her, the light bark was made to traverse the lake, with every sail set, until dawn. None, however, were suffered to slumber in the presumed security afforded by this judicious flight. Every man was at his post; and, while a silence so profound was preserved, that the noise of a falling pin might have been heard upon her decks, every thing was in readiness to repel an attack of their enemies, should the vessel, in her course, come accidentally in collision with their pigmy fleets. When morning broke, and no sign of their treacherous foes was visible, the vessel was again anchored, and the majority of the crew suffered to retire to their hammocks, while the few whose turn of duty it chanced to be, kept a vigilant look-out, that, on the slightest appearance of alarm, their slumbering comrades might again be aroused to energy and action.

Severe and harassing as had been the duty on board this vessel for many months, – at one moment exposed to the assaults of the savages, at another assailed by the hurricanes that are so prevalent and so dangerous on the American lakes, – the situation of the crew was even less enviable than that of the garrison itself. What chiefly contributed to their disquietude, was the dreadful consciousness that, however their present efforts might secure a temporary safety, the period of their fall was only protracted. A few months more must bring with them all the severity of the winter of those climes, and then, blocked up in a sea of ice, – exposed to all the rigour of cold, – all the miseries of hunger, – what effectual resistance could they oppose to the numerous bands of Indians who, availing themselves of the defenceless position of their enemies, would rush from every quarter to their destruction.

At the outset of these disheartening circumstances the officer had summoned his faithful crew together, and pointing out the danger and uncertainty of their position, stated that two chances of escape still remained to them. The first was, by an attempt to accomplish the passage of the river Sinclair during some dark and boisterous night, when the Indians would be least likely to suspect such an intention: it was at this point that the efforts of their enemies were principally to be apprehended; but if, under cover of storm and darkness, they could accomplish this difficult passage, they would easily gain the Détroit, and thence pass into lake Erie, at the further extremity of which they might, favoured by Providence, effect a landing, and penetrate to the inhabited parts of the colony of New York. The other alternative was, – and he left it to themselves to determine, – to sink the vessel on the approach of winter, and throw themselves into the fort before them, there to await and share the destiny of its gallant defenders.

With the generous enthusiasm of their profession, the noble fellows had determined on the latter course. With their officer they fully coincided in opinion, that their ultimate hopes of life depended on the safe passage of the Sinclair; for it was but too obvious, that soon or late, unless some very extraordinary revolution should be effected in the intentions of the Indians, the fortress must be starved into submission. Still, as it was tolerably well supplied with provisions, this gloomy prospect was remote, and they were willing to run all chances with their friends on shore, rather than desert them in their extremity. The determination expressed by them, therefore, was, that when they could no longer keep the lake in safety, they would, if the officer permitted it, scuttle the vessel, and attempt an entrance into the fort, where they would share the fate of the troops, whatever it might chance to be.

No sooner was this resolution made known, than their young commander sought an opportunity of communicating with the garrison. This, however, was no very easy task; for, so closely was the fort hemmed in by the savages, it was impossible to introduce a messenger within its walls; and so sudden had been the cutting off of all communication between the vessel and the shore, that the thought had not even occurred to either commander to establish the most ordinary intelligence by signal. In this dilemma recourse was had to an ingenious expedient. The dispatches of the officer were enclosed in one of the long tin tubes in which were generally deposited the maps and charts of the schooner, and to this, after having been carefully soldered, was attached an inch rope of several hundred fathoms in length: the case was then put into one of the ship's guns, so placed as to give it the elevation of a mortar; thus prepared, advantage was taken of a temporary absence of the Indians to bring the vessel within half a mile of the shore, and when the attention of the garrison, naturally attracted by this unusual movement, was sufficiently awakened, that opportunity was chosen for the discharge of the gun; and as the quantity of powder had been proportionably reduced for the limited range, the tube was soon safely deposited within the rampart. The same means were adopted in replying; and one end of the rope remaining attached to the schooner, all that was necessary was to solder up the tube as before, and throw it over the ramparts upon the sands, whence it was immediately pulled over her side by the watchful mariners.

As the dispatch conveyed to the garrison, among other subjects of interest, bore the unwelcome intelligence that the supplies of the crew were nearly expended, an arrangement was proposed by which, at stated intervals, a more immediate communication with the former might be effected. Whenever, therefore, the wind permitted, the vessel was kept hovering in sight during the day, beneath the eyes of the savages, and on the approach of evening an unshotted gun was discharged, with a view of drawing their attention more immediately to her movements; every sail was then set, and under a cloud of canvass the course of the schooner was directed towards the source of the Sinclair, as if an attempt to accomplish that passage was to be made during the night. No sooner, however, had the darkness fairly set in, than the vessel was put about, and, beating against the wind, generally contrived to reach the offing at a stated hour, when a boat, provided with muffled oars, was sent off to the shore. This ruse had several times deceived the Indians, and it was on these occasions that the small gate to which we have alluded was opened, for the purpose of conveying the necessary supplies.

The buildings of the fort consisted chiefly of block-houses, the internal accommodations of which were fully in keeping with their rude exterior, being but indifferently provided with the most ordinary articles of comfort, and fitted up as the limited resources of that wild and remote district could supply. The best and most agreeably situated of these, if a choice could be made, was that of the commanding officer. This building rose considerably above the others, and overhanging that part of the rampart which skirted the shores of the Huron, commanded a full view of the lake, even to its extremity of frowning and belting forest.

To this block-house there were two staircases; the principal leading to the front entrance from the barrack-square, the other opening in the rear, close under the rampart, and communicating by a few rude steps with the small gate that led upon the sands. In the lower part of this building, appropriated by the commanding officer to that exclusive purpose, the official duties of his situation were usually performed; and on the ground-floor a large room, that extended from front to rear of the block-house on one side of the passage, had formerly been used as a hall of council with the Indian chiefs. The floor above this comprised both his own private apartments and those set apart for the general use of the family; but, above all, and preferable from their cheerful view over the lake, were others, which had been reserved for the exclusive accommodation of Miss de Haldimar. This upper floor consisted of two sleeping apartments, with a sitting-room, the latter extending the whole length of the block-house and opening immediately upon the lake, from the only two windows with which that side of the building was provided. The principal staircase led into one of the bed-rooms, and both of the latter communicated immediately with the sitting-room, which again, in its turn, opened, at the opposite extremity, on the narrow staircase that led to the rear of the block-house.

The furniture of this apartment, which might be taken as a fair sample of the best the country could afford, was wild, yet simple, in the extreme. Neat rush mats, of an oblong square, and fantastically put together, so as to exhibit in the weaving of the several coloured reeds both figures that were known to exist in the creation, and those which could have no being save in the imagination of their framers, served as excellent substitutes for carpets, while rush bottomed chairs, the product of Indian ingenuity also, occupied those intervals around the room that were unsupplied by the matting. Upon the walls were hung numerous specimens both of the dress and of the equipments of the savages, and mingled with these were many natural curiosities, the gifts of Indian chiefs to the commandant at various periods before the war.

Nothing could be more unlike the embellishments of a modern European boudoir than those of this apartment, which had, in some degree, been made the sanctum of its present occupants. Here was to be seen the scaly carcass of some huge serpent, extending its now harmless length from the ceiling to the floor – there an alligator, stuffed after the same fashion; and in various directions the skins of the beaver, the marten, the otter, and an infinitude of others of that genus, filled up spaces that were left unsupplied by the more ingenious specimens of Indian art. Head-dresses tastefully wrought in the shape of the crowning bays of the ancients, and composed of the gorgeous feathers of the most splendid of the forest birds – bows and quivers handsomely, and even elegantly ornamented with that most tasteful of Indian decorations, the stained quill of the porcupine; war clubs of massive iron wood, their handles covered with stained horsehair and feathers curiously mingled together – machecotis, hunting coats, mocassins, and leggings, all worked in porcupine quill, and fancifully arranged, – these, with many others, had been called into requisition to bedeck and relieve the otherwise rude and naked walls of the apartment.

Nor did the walls alone reflect back the picture of savage ingenuity, for on the various tables, the rude polish of which was hid from view by the simple covering of green baize, which moreover constituted the garniture of the windows, were to be seen other products of their art. Here stood upon an elevated stand a model of a bark canoe, filled with its complement of paddlers carved in wood and dressed in full costume; the latter executed with such singular fidelity of feature, that although the speaking figures sprung not from the experienced and classic chisel of the sculptor but from the rude scalping knife of the savage, the very tribe to which they belonged could be discovered at a glance by the European who was conversant with the features of each: then there were handsomely ornamented vessels made of the birch bark, and filled with the delicate sugars which the natives extract from the maple tree in early spring; these of all sizes, even to the most tiny that could well be imagined, were valuable rather as exquisite specimens of the neatness with which those slight vessels could be put together, sewn as they were merely with strips of the same bark, than from any intrinsic value they possessed. Covered over with fantastic figures, done either in paint, or in quill work artfully interwoven into the fibres of the bark, they presented, in their smooth and polished surface, strong evidence of the address of the savages in their preparation of this most useful and abundant produce of the country. Interspersed with these, too, were numerous stands filled with stuffed birds, some of which combined in themselves every variety and shade of dazzling plumage; and numerous rude cases contained the rarest specimens of the American butterfly, most of which were of sizes and tints that are no where equalled in Europe. One solitary table alone was appropriated to whatever wore a transatlantic character in this wild and museum-like apartment. On this lay a

Spanish guitar, a few pieces of old music, a collection of English and French books, a couple of writing-desks, and, scattered over the whole, several articles of unfinished needle-work.

Such was the apartment in which Madeline and Clara de Haldimar were met at the moment we have selected for their introduction to our readers. It was the morning of that day on which the second council of the chiefs, the result of which has already been seen, was held at Détroit. The sun had risen bright and gorgeously above the adjacent forest, throwing his golden beams upon the calm glassy waters of the lake; and now, approaching rapidly towards the meridian, gradually diminished the tall bold shadows of the block-houses upon the shore. At the distance of about a mile lay the armed vessel so often alluded to; her light low hull dimly seen in the hazy atmosphere that danced upon the waters, and her attenuated masts and sloping yards, with their slight tracery of cordage, recalling rather the complex and delicate ramifications of the spider's web, than the elastic yet solid machinery to which the lives of those within had so often been committed in sea and tempest. Upon the strand, and close opposite to the small gate which now stood ajar, lay one of her boats, the crew of which had abandoned her with the exception only of a single individual, apparently her cockswain, who, with the tiller under his arm, lay half extended in the stern-sheets, his naked chest exposed, and his tarpaulin hat shielding his eyes from the sun while he indulged in profound repose. These were the only objects that told of human life. Every where beyond the eye rested on the faint outline of the forest, that appeared like the softened tracing of a pencil at the distant junction of the waters with the horizon.

The windows that commanded this prospect were now open; and through that which was nearest to the gate, half reclined the elegant, slight, and somewhat petite form of a female, who, with one small and delicately formed hand supporting her cheek, while the other played almost unconsciously with an open letter, glanced her eye alternately, and with an expression of joyousness, towards the vessel that lay beyond, and the point in which the source of the Sinclair was known to lie. It was Clara de Haldimar.

Presently the vacant space at the same window was filled by another form, but of less girlish appearance – one that embraced all the full rich contour of the Medicean Venus, and a lazy languor in its movements that harmonised with the speaking outlines of the form, and without which the beauty of the whole would have been at variance and imperfect. Neither did the face belie the general expression of the figure. The eyes, of a light hazel, were large, full, and somewhat prominent – the forehead broad, high, and redolent with an expression of character – and the cheek rich in that peculiar colour which can be likened only to the downy hues of the peach, and is, in itself, a physical earnest of the existence of deep, but not boisterous – of devoted, but not obtrusive affections; an impression that was not, in the present instance, weakened by the full and pouting lip, and the rather heavy formation of the lower face. The general expression, moreover, of a countenance which, closely analysed, could not be termed beautiful, marked a mind at once ardent in its conceptions, and steady and resolute in its silent accomplishments of purpose. She was of the middle height.

Such was the person of Madeline de Haldimar; but attractive, or rather winning, as were her womanly attributes, her principal power lay in her voice, – the beauty, nay, the voluptuousness of which nothing could surpass. It was impossible to listen to the slow, full, rich, deep, and melodious tones that fell trembling from her lips upon the ear, and not feel, aye shudder, under all their fascination on the soul. In such a voice might the Madonna of Raphael have been supposed to offer up her supplications from the gloomy precincts of the cloister. No wonder that Frederick de Haldimar loved her, and loved her with all the intense devotedness of his own glowing heart. His cousin was to him a divinity whom he worshipped in the innermost recesses of his being; and his, in return, was the only ear in which the accents of that almost superhuman voice had breathed the thrilling confession of an attachment, which its very tones announced could be deep and imperishable as the soul in which it had taken root. Often in the hours that preceded the period when they were to have been united heart and mind and thought in one common destiny, would he start from her side, his brain whirling with very intoxication, and then obeying another wild impulse, rush once more into her embrace; and clasping his beloved Madeline to his heart, entreat her again to pour forth all the melody of that confession in his enraptured ear. Artless and unaffected as she was generous and impassioned, the fond and noble girl never hesitated to gratify him whom alone she loved; and deep and fervent was the joy of the soldier, when he found that each passionate entreaty, far from being met with caprice, only drew from the lips of his cousin warmer and more affectionate expressions of her attachment. Such expressions, coming from any woman, must have been rapturous and soothing in the extreme; but, when they flowed from a voice whose very sound was melody, they acted on the heart of Captain de Haldimar with a potency that was as irresistible as the love itself which she inspired.

Such was the position of things just before the commencement of the Indian war. Madeline de Haldimar had been for some time on a visit to Détroit, and her marriage with her cousin was to have taken place within a few days. The unexpected arrival of intelligence from Michillimackinac that her father was dangerously ill, however, retarded the ceremony; and, up to the present period, their intercourse had been completely suspended. If Madeline de Haldimar was capable of strong attachment to her lover, the powerful ties of nature were no less deeply rooted in her heart, and commiseration and anxiety for her father now engrossed every faculty of her mind. She entreated her cousin to defer the solemnisation of their nuptials until her parent should be pronounced out of danger, and, having obtained his consent to the delay, instantly set off for Michillimackinac, accompanied by her cousin Clara, whom she had prevailed on the governor to part with until her own return. Hostilities were commenced very shortly afterwards, and, although Major de Haldimar speedily recovered from his illness, the fair cousins were compelled to share the common imprisonment of the garrison.

When Miss de Haldimar joined her more youthful cousin at the window, through which the latter was gazing thoughtfully on the scene before her, she flung her arm around her waist with the protecting manner of a mother. The mild blue eyes of Clara met those that were fastened in tenderness upon her, and a corresponding movement on her part brought the more matronly form of her cousin into close and affectionate contact with her own.

"Oh, Madeline, what a day is this!" she exclaimed, "and how often on my bended knees have I prayed to Heaven that it might arrive! Our trials are ended at last, and happiness and joy are once more before us. There is the boat that is to conduct us to the vessel, which, in its turn, is to bear me to the arms of my dear father, and you to those of the lover who adores you. How beautiful does that fabric appear to me now! Never did I feel half the pleasure in surveying it I do at this moment."

"Dear, dear girl!" exclaimed Miss de Haldimar, and she pressed her closer and in silence to her heart: then, after a slight pause, during which the mantling glow upon her brow told how deeply she desired the reunion alluded to by her cousin – "that, indeed, will be an hour of happiness to us both, Clara; for irrevocably as our affections have been pledged, it would be silly in the extreme to deny that I long most ardently to be restored to him who is already my husband. But, tell me," she concluded, with an archness of expression that caused the long-lashed eyes of her companion to sink beneath her own, "are you quite sincere in your own case? I know how deeply you love your father and your brothers, but do these alone occupy your attention? Is there not a certain friend of Charles whom you have some little curiosity to see also?"

"How silly, Madeline!" and the cheek of the young girl became suffused with a deeper glow; "you know I have never seen this friend of my brother, how then can I possibly feel more than the most ordinary interest in him? I am disposed to like him, certainly, for the mere reason that Charles does; but this is all."

"Well, Clara, I will not pretend to decide; but certain it is, this is the last letter you received from Charles, and that it contains the strongest recommendations of his friend to your notice. Equally certain is it, that scarcely a day has passed, since we have been shut up here, that you have not perused and re-perused it half a dozen times. Now, as I am confessedly one who should know something of these matters, I must be suffered to pronounce these are strong symptoms, to say the very least. Ah! Clara, that blush declares you guilty. – But, who have we here? Middleton and Baynton."

The eyes of the cousins now fell upon the ramparts immediately under the window. Two officers, one apparently on duty for the day, were passing at the moment; and, as they heard their names pronounced, stopped, looked up, and saluted the young ladies with that easy freedom of manner, which, unmixed with either disrespect or effrontery, so usually characterises the address of military men.

"What a contrast, by heaven!" exclaimed he who wore the badge of duty suspended over his chest, throwing himself playfully into a theatrical attitude, expressive at once of admiration and surprise, while his eye glanced intelligently over the fair but dissimilar forms of the cousins. "Venus and Psyche in the land of the Pottowatamies by all that is magnificent! Come, Middleton, quick, out with that eternal pencil of yours, and perform your promise."

"And what may that promise be?" asked Clara, laughingly, and without adverting to the hyperbolical compliment of the dark-eyed officer who had just spoken.

"You shall hear," pursued the lively captain of the

guard. "While making the tour of the ramparts just now, to visit my sentries, I saw Middleton leaning most sentimentally against one of the boxes in front, his note-book in one hand and his pencil in the other. Curious to discover the subject of his abstraction, I stole cautiously behind him, and saw that he was sketching the head of a tall and rather handsome squaw, who, in the midst of a hundred others, was standing close to the gateway watching the preparations of the Indian ball-players. I at once taxed him with having lost his heart; and rallying him on his bad taste in devoting his pencil to any thing that had a red skin, never combed its hair, and turned its toes in while walking, pronounced his sketch to be an absolute fright. Well, will you believe what I have to add? The man absolutely flew into a tremendous passion with me, and swore that she was a Venus, a Juno, a Minerva, a beauty of the first water in short; and finished by promising, that when I could point out any woman who was superior to her in personal attraction, he would on the instant write no less than a dozen consecutive sonnets in her praise. I now call upon him to fulfil his promise, or maintain the superiority of his Indian beauty."

Before the laughing Middleton could find time to reply to the light and unmeaning rattle of his friend, the quick low roll of a drum was heard from the front. The signal was understood by both officers, and they prepared to depart.

"This is the hour appointed for the council," said Captain Baynton, looking at his watch, "and I must be with my guard, to receive the chiefs with becoming honour. How I pity you, Middleton, who will have the infliction of one of their great big talks, as Murphy would call it, dinned into your ear for the next two hours at least! Thank heaven, my tour of duty exempts me from that; and by way of killing an hour, I think I shall go and carry on a flirtation with your Indian Minerva, alias Venus, alias Juno, while you are discussing the affairs of the nation with closed doors. But hark! there is the assembly drum again. We must be off. Come, Middleton, come. – Adieu!" waving his hand to the cousins, "we shall meet at dinner."

"What an incessant talker Baynton is!" observed Miss de Haldimar, as the young men now disappeared round an angle of the rampart; "but he has reminded me of what I had nearly forgotten, and that is to give orders for dinner. My father has invited all the officers to dine with him to day, in commemoration of the peace which is being concluded. It will be the first time we shall have all met together since the commencement of this cruel war, and we must endeavour, Clara, to do honour to the feast."

"I hope," timidly observed her cousin, shuddering as she spoke, "that none of those horrid chiefs will be present, Madeline; for, without any affectation of fear whatever, I feel that I could not so far overcome my disgust as to sit at the same table with them. There was a time, it is true, when I thought nothing of these things; but, since the war, I have witnessed and heard so much of their horrible deeds, that I shall never be able to endure the sight of an Indian face again. Ah!" she concluded, turning her eyes upon the lake, while she clung more closely to the embrace of her companion; "would to Heaven, Madeline, that we were both at this moment gliding in yonder vessel, and in sight of my father's fort!"

Eleven

THE EYES of Miss de Haldimar followed those of her cousin, and rested on the dark hull of the schooner, with which so many recollections of the past and anticipations of the future were associated in their minds. When they had last looked upon it, all appearance of human life had vanished from its decks; but now there was strong evidence of unusual bustle and activity. Numerous persons could be seen moving hastily to and fro, their heads just peering above the bulwarks; and presently they beheld a small boat move from the ship's side, and shoot rapidly ahead, in a direct line with the well-known bearings of the Sinclair's source. While they continued to gaze on this point, following the course of the light vessel, and forming a variety of conjectures as to the cause of a movement, especially remarkable from the circumstance of the commander being at that moment in the fort, whither he had been summoned to attend the council, another and scarcely perceptible object was dimly seen, at the distance of about half a mile in front of the boat. With the aid of a telescope, which had formed one of the principal resources of the cousins during their long imprisonment, Miss de Haldimar now perceived a dark and shapeless mass moving somewhat heavily along the lake, and in a line with the schooner and the boat. This was evidently approaching; for each moment it loomed larger upon the hazy water, increasing in bulk in the same proportion that the departing skiff became less distinct: still, it was impossible to discover, at that distance, in what manner it was propelled. Wind there was none, not as much as would have changed the course of a feather dropping through space; and, except where the dividing oars of the boatmen had agitated the waters, the whole surface of the lake was like a sea of pale and liquid gold.

At length the two dark bodies met, and the men in the boat were seen to lie upon their oars, while one in the stern seemed to be in the act of attaching a rope to the formless matter. For a few moments there was a cessation of all movement; and then again the active and sturdy rowing of the boatmen was renewed, and with an exertion of strength even more vigorous than that they had previously exhibited. Their course was now directed towards the vessel; and, as it gradually neared that fabric, the rope by which the strange-looking object was secured, could be distinctly though faintly seen with the telescope. It was impossible to say whether the latter, whatever it might be, was urged by some invisible means, or merely floated in the wake of the boat; for, although the waters through which it passed ran rippling and foaming from their course, this effect might have been produced by the boat which preceded it. As it now approached the vessel, it presented the appearance of a dense wood of evergreens, the overhanging branches of which descended close to the water's edge, and baffled every attempt of the cousins to discover its true character. The boat had now arrived within a hundred yards of the schooner, when a man was seen to rise from its bows, and, putting both his hands to his mouth, after the manner of sailors in hailing, to continue in that position for some moments, apparently conversing with those who were grouped along the nearest gangway. Then were observed rapid movements on the decks; and men were seen hastening aloft, and standing out upon the foremast yards. This, however, had offered no interruption to the exertions of the boatmen, who still kept plying with a vigour that set even the sail-less vessel in motion, as the foaming water, thrown from their bending oar-blades, dashed angrily against her prow. Soon afterwards both the boat and her prize disappeared on the opposite side of the schooner, which, now lying with her broadside immediately on a line with the shore, completely hid them from the further view of the cousins.

"Look! – Look!" said Clara, clinging sensitively and with alarm to the almost maternal bosom against which she reposed, while she pointed with her finger to another dark mass that was moving through the lake in a circular sweep from the point of wood terminating the clearing on the right of the fort.

Miss de Haldimar threw the glass on the object to which her attention was now directed. It was evidently some furred animal, and presented all the appearance either of a large water-rat or a beaver, the latter of which it was pronounced to be as a nearer approach rendered its shape more distinct. Ever and anon, too, it disappeared altogether under the water; and, when it again came in sight, it was always several yards nearer. Its course, at first circuitous, at length took a direct line with the stern of the boat, where the sailor who was in charge still lay extended at his drowsy length, his tarpaulin hat shading his eyes, and his arms folded over his uncovered and heaving chest, while he continued to sleep as profoundly as if he had been comfortably berthed in his hammock in the middle of the Atlantic.

"What a large bold animal it is," remarked Clara, in the tone of one who wishes to be confirmed in an impression but indifferently entertained. "See how close it approaches the boat! Had that lazy sailor but his wits about him, he might easily knock it on the head with his oar. It is – it is a beaver, Madeline; I can distinguish its head even with the naked eye."

"Heaven grant it may be a beaver," answered Miss de Haldimar, in a voice so deep and full of meaning, that it made her cousin startle and turn paler even than before. "Nay, Clara, dearest, command yourself, nor give way to what may, after all, prove a groundless cause of alarm. Yet, I know not how it is, my heart misgives me sadly; for I like not the motions of this animal, which are strangely and unusually bold. But this is not all: a beaver or a rat might ruffle the mere surface of the water, yet this leaves behind it a deep and gurgling furrow, as if the element had been ploughed to its very bottom. Observe how the lake is agitated and discoloured wherever it has passed. Moreover, I dislike this sudden bustle on board the schooner, knowing, as I do, there is not an officer present to order the movements now visibly going forward. The men are evidently getting up the anchor; and see how her sails are loosened, apparently courting the breeze, as if she would fly to avoid some threatened danger. Would to Heaven this council scene were over; for I do, as much as yourself, dearest Clara, distrust these cruel Indians!"

A significant gesture from her trembling cousin again drew her attention from the vessel to the boat. The animal, which now exhibited the delicate and glossy fur of the beaver, had gained the stern, and remained stationary within a foot of her quarter. Presently the sailor made a sluggish movement, turning himself heavily on his side, and with his face towards his curious and daring visitant. In the act the tarpaulin hat had fallen from his eyes, but still he awoke not. Scarcely had he settled himself in his new position, when, to the infinite horror of the excited cousins, a naked human hand was raised from beneath the surface of the lake, and placed upon the gunwale of the boat. Then rose slowly, and still covered with its ingenious disguise, first the neck, then the shoulders, and finally the form, even to the midwaist, of a dark and swarthy Indian, who, stooping low and cautiously over the sailor, now reposed the hand that had quitted the gunwale upon his form, while the other was thrust searchingly into the belt encircling his waist.

Miss de Haldimar would have called out, to apprise the unhappy man of his danger; but her voice refused its office, and her cousin was even less capable of exertion than herself. The deep throbbings of their hearts were now audible to each; for the dreadful interest they took in the scene, had excited their feelings to the most intense stretch of agony. At the very moment, however, when, with almost suspended animation, they expected to see the knife of the savage driven into the chest of the sleeping and unsuspecting sailor, the latter suddenly started up, and, instinct with the full sense of the danger by which he was menaced, in less time than we take to describe it, seized the tiller of his rudder, the only available instrument within his reach, and directing a powerful blow at the head of his amphibious enemy, laid him, without apparent life or motion, across the boat.

"Almighty God! what can this mean?" exclaimed Miss de Haldimar, as soon as she could recover her presence of mind. "There is some fearful treachery in agitation; and a cloud now hangs over all, that will soon burst with irresistible fury on our devoted heads. Clara, my love," and she conducted the almost fainting girl to a seat, "wait here until I return. The moment is critical, and my father must be apprised of what we have seen. Unless the gates of the fort be instantly closed, we are lost."

"Oh, Madeline, leave me not alone," entreated the sinking Clara. "We will go together. Perhaps I may be of service to you below."

"The thought is good; but have you strength and courage to face the dark chiefs in the council-room. If so, hasten there, and put my father on his guard, while I fly across the parade, and warn Captain Baynton of the danger."

With these words she drew the arm of her agitated cousin within her own, and rapidly traversing the apartment, gained the bed-room which opened close upon the head of the principal staircase. Already were they descending the first steps, when a loud cry, that sent a thrill of terror through their blood, was heard from without the fort. For a moment Miss de Haldimar continued irresolute; and leaning against the rude balustrade for support, passed her hand rapidly across her brow, as if to collect her scattered energies. The necessity for prompt and immediate action was, however, evident; and she alone was capable of exertion. Speechless with alarm, and trembling in every joint, the unhappy Clara had now lost all command of her limbs; and, clinging close to the side of her cousin, by her wild looks alone betrayed consciousness had not wholly deserted her. The energy of despair lent more than woman's strength to Miss de Haldimar. She caught the fainting girl in her arms, retraced her way to the chamber, and depositing her burden on the bed, emphatically enjoined her on no account to move until her return. She then quitted the room, and rapidly descended the staircase.

For some moments all was still and hushed as the waveless air; and then again a loud chorus of shouts was heard from the ramparts of the fort. The choked breathing of the young girl became more free, and the blood rushed once more from her oppressed heart to the extremities. Never did tones of the human voice fall more gratefully on the ear of mariner cast on some desert island, than did those on that of the highly excited Clara. It was the loud laugh of the soldiery, who, collected along the line of rampart in front, were watching the progress of the ball-players. Cheered by the welcome sounds, she raised herself from the bed to satisfy her eye her ear had not deceived her. The windows of both bed-chambers looked immediately on the barrack square, and commanded a full view of the principal entrance. From that at which she now stood, the revived but still anxious girl could distinctly see all that was passing in front. The ramparts were covered with soldiers, who, armed merely with their bayonets, stood grouped in careless attitudes – some with their wives leaning on their arms – others with their children up-raised, that they might the better observe the enlivening sports without – some lay indolently with their legs overhanging the works – others, assuming pugilistic attitudes, dealt their harmless blows at each other, – and all were blended together, men, women, and children, with that heedlessness of thought that told how little of distrust existed within their breasts. The soldiers of the guard, too, exhibited the same air of calm and unsuspecting confidence; some walking to and fro within the square, while the greater portion either mixed with their comrades above, or, with arms folded, legs carelessly crossed, and pipe in mouth, leant lazily against the gate, and gazed beyond the lowered drawbridge on the Indian games.

A mountain weight seemed to have been removed from the breast of Clara at this sight, as she now dropped upon her knees before the window, and raised her hands in pious acknowledgement to Heaven.

"Almighty God, I thank thee," she fervently exclaimed, her eye once more lighting up, and her cheek half suffused with blushes at her late vague and idle fears; while she embraced, at a single glance, the whole of the gladdening and inspiriting scene.

While her soul was yet upturned whither her words had gone before, her ears were again assailed by sounds that curdled her blood, and made her spring to her feet as if stricken by a bullet through the heart, or powerfully touched by some electric fluid. It was the well-known and devilish war-cry of the savages, startling the very air through which it passed, and falling like a deadly blight upon the spirit. With a mechanical and desperate effort at courage, the unhappy girl turned her eyes below, and there met images of death in their most appalling shapes. Hurry and confusion and despair were every where visible; for a band of Indians were already in the fort, and these, fast succeeded by others, rushed like a torrent into the square, and commenced their dreadful work of butchery. Many of the terrified soldiers, without thinking of drawing their bayonets, flew down the ramparts in order to gain their respective block-houses for their muskets: but these every where met death from the crashing tomahawk, short rifle, or gleaming knife; – others who had presence of mind sufficient to avail themselves of their only weapons of defence, rushed down in the fury of desperation on the yelling fiends, resolved to sell their lives as dearly as possible; and for some minutes an obstinate contest was maintained: but the vast superiority of the Indian numbers triumphed; and although the men fought with all the fierceness of despair, forcing their way to the blockhouses, their mangled corses strewed the area in every direction. Neither was the horrid butchery confined to these. Women clinging to their husbands for protection, and, in the recklessness of their despair, impeding the efforts of the latter in their self-defence – children screaming in terror, or supplicating mercy on their bended knees – infants clasped to their parents' breasts, – all alike sunk under the unpitying steel of the blood-thirsty savages. At the guard-house the principal stand had been made; for at the first rush into the fort, the men on duty had gained their station, and, having made fast the barricades, opened their fire upon the enemy. Mixed pêle-mêle as they were with the Indians, many of the English were shot by their own comrades, who, in the confusion of the moment, were incapable of taking a cool and discriminating aim. These, however, were finally overcome. A band of desperate Indians rushed upon the main door, and with repeated blows from their tomahawks and massive war clubs, succeeded in demolishing it, while others diverted the fire of those within. The door once forced, the struggle was soon over. Every man of the guard perished; and their scalpless and disfigured forms were thrown out to swell the number of those that already deluged the square with their blood.

Even amid all the horrors of this terrific scene, the agonised Clara preserved her consciousness. The very imminence of the danger endued her with strength to embrace it under all its most disheartening aspects; and she, whose mind had been wrought up to the highest pitch of powerful excitement by the mere preliminary threatenings, was comparatively collected under the catastrophe itself. Death, certain death, to all, she saw was inevitable;

and while her perception at once embraced the futility of all attempts at escape from the general doom, she snatched from despair the power to follow its gloomy details without being annihilated under their weight.

The confusion of the garrison had now reached its acmé of horror. The shrieks of women and the shrill cries of children, as they severally and fruitlessly fled from the death certain to overtake them in the end, – the cursings of the soldiers, the yellings of the Indians, the reports of rifles, and the crashings of tomahawks; – these, with the stamping of human feet in the death struggle maintained in the council-room below between the chiefs and the officers, and which shook the block-house to its very foundation, all mixed up in terrible chorus together, might have called up a not inapt image of hell to the bewildered and confounding brain. And yet the sun shone in yellow lustre, and all Nature smiled, and wore an air of calm, as if the accursed deed had had the sanction of Heaven, and the spirits of light loved to look upon the frightful atrocities then in perpetration.

In the first distraction of her spirit, Clara had utterly lost all recollection of her cousin; but now that she had, with unnatural desperation, brought her mind to bear upon the fiercest points of the grim reality, she turned her eye every where amid the scene of death in search of the form of her beloved Madeline, whom she did not remember to have seen cross the parade in pursuance of the purpose she had named. While she yet gazed fearfully from the window, loud bursts of mingled anguish and rage, that were almost drowned in the fiercer yells with which they were blended, ascended from the ground floor of the block-house. These had hitherto been suppressed, as if the desperate attack of the chiefs on the officers had been made with closed doors. Now, however, there was an evident outburst of all parties into the passage; and there the struggle appeared to be desperately and fearfully maintained. In the midst of that chaotic scene, the loud and piercing shriek of a female rose far above the discordant yell even of the savages. There was an instant of pause, and then the crashing of a skull was heard, and the confusion was greater than before, and shrieks, and groans, and curses, and supplications rent the air.

The first single shriek came from Madeline de Haldimar, and vibrated through every chord of the heart on which it sank. Scarcely conscious of what she did, Clara, quitting the window, once more gained the top of the staircase, and at the extremity of her voice called on the name of her cousin in the most piteous accents. She was answered by a loud shout from the yelling band; and presently bounding feet and screaming voices were heard ascending the stairs. The terrified girl fancied at the moment she heard a door open on the floor immediately below her, and some one dart suddenly up the flight communicating with the spot on which she stood. Without waiting to satisfy herself, she rushed with all the mechanical instinct of self-preservation back into her own apartment. As she passed the bed-room window, she glanced once more hastily into the area below, and there beheld a sight that, filling her soul with despair, paralysed all further exertion. A tall savage was bearing off the apparently lifeless form of her cousin through the combatants in the square, her white dress stained all over with blood, and her beautiful hair loosened and trailing on the ground. She followed with her burning eyes until they passed the drawbridge, and finally disappeared behind the intervening rampart, and then bowing her head between her hands, and sinking upon her knees, she reposed her forehead against the sill of the window, and awaited unshrinkingly, yet in a state of inconceivable agony, the consummation of her own unhappy destiny.

The sounds of ascending feet were now heard in the passage without; and presently, while the clangour of a thousand demons seemed to ring throughout the upper part of the building, a man rushed furiously into the room. The blood of the young girl curdled in her veins. She mechanically grasped the ledge of the window on which her aching head still reposed, and with her eyes firmly closed, to shut out from view the fiend whose sight she dreaded, even more than the death which threatened her, quietly awaited the blow that was to terminate at once her misery and her life. Scarcely, however, had the feet of the intruder pressed the sanctuary of her bedchamber, when the heavy door, strongly studded with nails, was pushed rapidly to, and bolt and lock were heard sliding into their several sockets. Before Clara could raise her head to discover the cause of this movement, she felt herself firmly secured in the grasp of an encircling arm, and borne hastily through the room. An instinctive sense of something worse even than death now flashed across the mind of the unhappy girl; and while she feared to unclose her eyes, she struggled violently to disengage herself.

"Clara! dear Miss de Haldimar, do you not know me?" exclaimed her supporter, while, placing her for a moment on a seat, he proceeded to secure the fastenings of the second door, that led from the bed-chamber into the larger apartment.

Re-assured by the tones of a voice which, even in that dreadful moment of trial and destruction, were familiar to her ear, the trembling girl opened her eyes wildly upon her protector. A slight scream of terror marked her painful sense of the recognition. It was Captain Baynton whom she beheld: but how unlike the officer who a few minutes before had been conversing with her from the ramparts. His fine hair, matted with blood, now hung loosely and disfiguringly over his eyes, and his pallid face and brow were covered with gore spots, the evident spatterings from the wounds of others; while a stream that issued from one side of his head attested he himself had not escaped unhurt in the cruel mêlée. A skirt and a lappel had been torn from his uniform, which, together with other portions of his dress, were now stained in various parts by the blood continually flowing from his wound.

"Oh, Captain Baynton," murmured the fainting girl, her whole soul sinking within her, as she gazed shudderingly on his person, "is there no hope for us? must we die?"

"No, by Heaven, not while I have strength to save you," returned the officer, with energy. "If the savages have not penetrated to the rear, we may yet escape. I saw the postern open just now, on my passage round the rampart, and the boat of the schooner upon the strand. Ha!" he exclaimed, as he flew to the window, and cast his eye rapidly below, "we are lost! The gate is still clear, and not an Indian to be seen; but the coward sailor is pulling for his life towards the vessel. But hold! another boat is now quitting the ship's side. See, how manfully they give themselves to the oars: in a few minutes they will be here. Come, Clara, let us fly!" and again he caught her in his arms, and bore her across the room. "Hark, hear you not the exulting yellings of the monsters? They are forcing the outer door: mark how they redouble their efforts to break it open! That passed, but one more barrier remains between us and inevitable and instant death."

"And my cousin, my uncle!" shrieked the unhappy girl, as the officer now bore her rapidly down the back staircase.

"Oh, ask me not!" exclaimed Baynton: "were I to linger again on all I have witnessed, I should go mad. All, all have perished! but, hark!"

A tremendous yell now bursting from the passage, announced at once, the triumph of the savages in having effected an entrance into the bed-room, and their disappointment at finding their pursuit baulked by a second door. Presently afterwards their heavy weapons were to be heard thundering at this new obstacle, in the most furious manner. This gave new stimulus to the exertions of the generous officer. Each winding of the staircase was familiar to him, and he now descended it with a rapidity which, considering the burden that reposed against his chest, could only have been inspired by his despair. The flight terminated at a door that led directly upon the rampart, without communicating with any of the passages of the building; and in this consisted the principal facility of escape: for, in order to reach them, the savages must either make the circuit of the block-house, or overtake them in the course they were now following. In this trying emergency, the presence of mind of the young officer, wounded and bleeding as he was, did not desert him. On quitting the larger apartment above, he had secured the outside fastenings of a small door at the top of the stairs, and having now gained the bottom, he took a similar precaution. All that remained was to unclose the bolts of the ponderous door that opened upon their final chance of escape: this was speedily done, but here the feelings of the officer were put to a severe test. A rude partition divided him from the fatal council-room; and while he undid the fastenings, the faint and dying groans of his butchered brother officers rung in his ears, even at the moment that he felt his feet dabbling in the blood that oozed through the imperfectly closed planks of which the partition was composed. As for Clara, she was insensible to all that was passing. From the moment of the Indian yell, announcing their entry into the bed-room, she had fainted.

The huge door came now creaking back upon its hinges, when the sounds of the yet unfinished conflict in front, which had hitherto been deadened in their descent through the remote staircase, rang once more fiercely and startlingly upon the ear. A single glance satisfied Captain Baynton the moment for exertion was come, and that the way to the lake shore, which, by some strange oversight, both the Indians and the men had overlooked, was perfectly clear. He clasped his unconscious burden closer to his chest, and then, setting his life upon the cast, hastened down the few steps that led to the rampart, and dashed rapidly through the postern; in the next minute he stood on the uttermost verge of the sands, unharmed and unfollowed. He cast his eyes anxiously along the surface of the lake; but such was the excitement and confusion of his mind, produced by the horrid recollection of the past scene, it was not until he had been abruptly hailed from it, he could see a boat, at the distance of about two hundred yards, the crew of which were lying on their oars. It was the long boat of the schooner, which, prevented from a nearer approach by a sand bar that ran along the lake to a considerable extent, had taken her station there to receive the fugitives. Two tall young men in the dress, yet having little the mien, of common sailors, were standing up in her stern; and one of these, with evident anxiety in his manner, called on Baynton by name to make the best of his way to the boat. At that moment a loud and frantic yell came from the block-house the latter had just quitted. In the wild impulse of his excited feelings, he answered with a cheer of defiance, as he turned to discover the precise point whence it proceeded. The windows of the apartment so recently occupied by the unhappy cousins, were darkened with savage forms, who now pealed forth their mingled fury and disappointment in the most terrific manner.

"Fly, fly, Baynton, or you are lost!" exclaimed the same voice from the boat; "the devils are levelling from the windows."

While he yet spake several shots came whizzing along the waters, and a spent ball even struck the now rapidly fleeing officer in the back; but the distance was too great for serious injury. The guns of the savages had been cut so short for their desperate enterprise, that they carried little further than a horse pistol.

Again, in the desperation of his feelings, and heedless of the danger he was drawing on himself and charge, the officer turned fiercely round and shouted, at his utmost lungs, a peal of triumph in the ears of his enemies. Scarcely, however, had the sounds escaped his lips, when two hideously painted Indians sprang through the postern, and, silent as the spectres they resembled, rushed down the sands, and thence into the lake. Loud shouts from the windows above were again pealed forth, and from the consternation visible on the features of those within the boat, the nearly exhausted Baynton learnt all the risk he incurred. Summoning all his strength, he now made the most desperate efforts to reach his friends. The lake was little more than knee deep from the shore to the bar, but, encumbered as he was, the difficulty opposed to his movements was immeasurably against him, and yet he seemed generously resolved rather to perish than relinquish his charge. Already were his pursuers, now closely followed by a numerous band, within twenty yards of him, when the two young men, each armed with a cutlass and pistol, sprang from the boat upon the sand bar: as the Indians came on they fired deliberately at them, but both missed their aim. Encouraged by this failure, the fearless devils dashed eagerly on, brandishing their gleaming tomahawks, but uttering not a sound. Already was the unfortunate Baynton within a few feet of the bar, when he felt that the savages were immediately upon him.

"Take, take, for God's sake take her!" he cried, as with a desperate effort he threw the light form of the still unconscious girl into the arms of one of the young men. "My strength is quite exhausted, and I can do no more."

For the first time a yell burst from the lips of the pursing savages, as they saw him, to whom the guardianship of the wretched Clara was now confided, suddenly spring from the sand bar into the lake, and in a few rapid strokes gain the side of the boat. Leaving the hapless Baynton to be disposed of by his companion, the foremost darted upon the bank, burning with disappointment, and resolved to immolate another victim. For a moment he balanced his tomahawk, and then, with the rapidity of thought, darted it at the covered head of the youth who still lingered on the bar. A well-timed movement of the latter averted the blow, and the whizzing steel passed harmlessly on. A gutteral "Ugh!" marked the disappointment of the Indian, now reduced to his scalping-knife; but before he could determine whether to advance or to retreat, his opponent had darted upon him, and, with a single blow from his cutlass, cleft his skull nearly asunder. The next instantaneous purpose of the victor was to advance to the rescue of the exhausted Baynton; but, when he turned to look for him, he saw the mangled form of what had once been that gallant and handsome officer floating, without life or motion, on the blood-stained surface of the Huron, while his fiendish murderer, calmly awaiting the approach of his companions, held up the reeking scalp, in triumph, to the view of the still yelling groups within the block-house.

"Noble, generous, self-devoted fellow!" exclaimed the youth, as he fixed his burning tearless eye for a moment on the unfortunate victim; "even you, then, are not spared to tell the horrid story of this butchery; yet is the fate of the fallen far, far more enviable than that of those who have survived this day." He then committed his cutlass to its sheath; and, leaping into the deep water that lay beyond the bar, was, in a few seconds, once more in the stern of the boat.

Meanwhile, the numerous band, who followed their two first fierce comrades into the lake, bounded rapidly forward; and, so active were their movements, that, at almost the same moment when the second of the youths had gained his temporary place of refuge, they stood yelling and screaming on the sand bar he had just quitted. Two or three, excited to desperation by the blood they had seen spilt, plunged unhesitatingly into the opposite depths of the lake; and the foremost of these was the destroyer of the ill-fated Baynton. With his bloody scalping-knife closely clutched between his teeth, and his tomahawk in his right hand, this fierce warrior buffeted the waves lustily with one arm, and, noiselessly as in the early part of his pursuit, urged his way towards the boat. In the stern of this a few planks from the schooner had been firmly lashed, to serve as a shield against the weapons of the savages, and was so arranged as to conceal all within while retiring from the shore. A small aperture had, however, been bored for the purpose of observing the movements of the enemy without risk. Through this an eye was now directed, while only the blades of the oars were to be seen projecting from the boat's sides as they reposed in their rowlocks. Encouraged by the seeming apathy and inertness of the crew, the swimming savages paused not to consider of consequences, but continued their daring course as if they had apprehended neither risk nor resistance. Presently a desperate splash was heard near the stern of the boat, and the sinuous form of the first savage was raised above the gunwale, his grim face looking devilish in its war-paint, and his fierce eyes gleaming and rolling like fire-balls in their sockets. Scarcely was he seen, however, when he had again disappeared. A blow from the cutlass that had destroyed his companion descended like lightning on his naked and hairless head; and, in the agony of death, he might be seen grinding his teeth against the knife which the instinctive ferocity of his nature forbade his relinquishing. A yell of fury burst from the savages on the bar, and presently a shower of bullets ran whistling through the air. Several were heard striking the rude rampart in the stern; but, although the boat was scarcely out of pistol-shot, the thickness of the wood prevented all injury to those within. Another fierce yell followed this volley; and then nearly a score of warriors, giving their guns in charge to their companions, plunged furiously into the water; and, with an air of the most infuriated determination, leaped rather than swam along its surface.

"Now, then, my lads, give way," said he at the look-out; "there are more than a dozen of the devils in full cry; and our only chance is in flight! Ha! another here!" as, turning to issue these directions, he chanced to see the dark hand of a savage at that moment grasping the gunwale of the boat, as if with a view to retard her movements until the arrival of his companions.

A heavy blow from his cutlass accompanied these words. The fingers, divided at their very roots, rolled to the bottom of the boat, and the carcase of the savage dropped, with a yell of anguish, far in the rear. The heavy oar-blades of the seamen now made play, dashing the lake away in sheets of foam; and, in less than five minutes, the heads of the swimming savages were seen mingling like so many rats upon the water, as they returned once more in disappointment from their fruitless pursuit.

Twelve

THE SUN had gone down, as he had risen, in all the gloriousness of his autumnal splendour, and twilight was now fast descending on the waters of the Huron. A slight breeze was just beginning to make itself felt from the land, the gradual rising of which was hailed by many an anxious heart, as the schooner, which had been making vain attempts to quit her anchorage during the day, now urged her light bows through the slightly curling element. A deathlike silence, interrupted only by the low gruff voice of a veteran seaman, as he issued, in technical language, the necessary orders for the management of the vessel, prevailed every where along her decks. The dress and general appearance of this individual announced him for a petty officer of the royal service; and it was evident, from the tone of authority with which he spoke, he was now in the enjoyment of a temporary command. The crew, consisting of about thirty souls, and chiefly veterans of the same class, were assembled along the gangways, each man wearing a brace of pistols in the belt, which, moreover, secured a naked cutlass around his loins; and these now lingered near the several guns that were thrown out from their gloomy looking ports, as if ready for some active service. But, although the arming of these men indicated hostile preparation, there was none of that buoyancy of movement and animation of feature to be observed, which so usually characterise the indomitable daring of the British sailor. Some stood leaning their heads pensively on their hands against the rigging and hammocks that were stowed away along the bulwarks, after the fashion of war ships in boarding; others, with arms tightly folded across their chests, spirted the tobacco juice thoughtfully from their closed teeth into the receding waters; while not a few gazed earnestly and despondingly on the burning fort in the distance, amid the rolling volumes of smoke and flame from which, ever and anon, arose the fiendish yell of those who, having already sacked, were now reducing it to ashes. Nor was this the only object of their attention. On the sand bank alluded to in our last chapter were to be dimly seen through the growing dusk, the dark outlines of many of the savages, who, frantic with rage at their inability to devote them to the same doom, were still unwilling to quit a spot which approached them nearest to the last surviving objects of their enmity. Around this point were collected numerous canoes, filled also with warriors; and, at the moment when the vessel, obeying the impulse given by her flowing sails, glided from her anchorage, these followed, scudding in her wake, and made a show of attacking her in the stern. The sudden yawing of the schooner, however, in bringing her tier of bristling ports into view, had checked the ardour of the pursuing fleet; and the discharge of a single gun, destroying in its course three of their canoes, and carrying death among those who directed them, had driven them back, in the greatest hurry and confusion, to their yelling and disappointed comrades.

The after-deck of the schooner presented a different, though not less sombre and discouraging, scene. On a pile of mattrasses lay the light and almost inanimate form of Clara de Haldimar; her fair and redundant hair overshadowing her pallid brow and cheek, and the dress she had worn at the moment of her escape from the fort still spotted with the blood of her generous but unfortunate preserver. Close at her side, with her hands clasped in his, while he watched the expression of deep suffering reflected from each set feature, and yet with the air of one pre-occupied with some other subject of painful interest, sat, on an empty shot-box, the young man in sailor's attire, whose cutlass had performed the double service of destroying his own immediate opponent, and avenging the death of the devoted Baynton. At the head of the rude couch, and leaning against a portion of the schooner's stern-work, stood his companion, who from delicacy appeared to have turned away his eyes from the group below, merely to cast them vacantly on the dark waters through which the vessel was now beginning to urge her course.

Such was the immediate position of this little party, when the gun fired at the Indians was heard booming heavily along the lake. The loud report, in exciting new sources of alarm, seemed to have dissipated the spell that had hitherto chained the energies and perception of the still weak, but now highly excited girl.

"Oh, Captain Baynton, where are we?" she exclaimed, starting up suddenly in terror, and throwing her arms around him who sat at her side, as if she would have clung to him for protection. "Is the horrid massacre not finished yet? Where is Madeline? where is my cousin? Oh, I cannot leave the fort without her."

"Ha! where indeed is she?" exclaimed the youth, as he clasped his trembling and scarcely conscious burden to his chest, "Almighty God, where is she?" Then, after a short pause, and in a voice of tender but exquisite anguish, "Clara, my beloved sister, do you not know me? It is not Baynton but your brother, who now clasps you to his breaking heart."

A deluge of tears was the only answer of the wretched girl. They were the first she had shed, – the first marks of consciousness she had exhibited. Hitherto her heart had been oppressed; every fibre of her brain racked almost to bursting, and filled only with ghastly flitting visions of the dreadful horrors she had seen perpetrated, she had continued, since the moment of her fainting in the block-house, as one bereft of all memory of the past, or apprehension of the present. But now, the full outpouring of her grief relieved her overcharged brain and heart, even while the confused images floating before her recollection acquired a more tangible and painful character. She raised herself a moment from the chest on which her burning head reposed, looked stedfastly in the face that hung anxiously over her own, and saw indeed that it was her brother. She tried to speak, but she could not utter a word, for the memory of all that had occurred that fatal morning rushed with mountain weight upon her fainting spirit, and again she wept, and more bitterly than before.

The young man pressed her in silence to his chest; nor was it until she had given full vent to her grief, that he ventured to address her on the subject of his own immediate sorrows. At length, when she appeared somewhat more calm, he observed, in a voice broken by emotion, –

"Clara, dearest, what account have you to give me of Madeline? Has she shared the fate of all? or have you reason to suppose her life has been spared?"

Another burst of tears succeeded to these questions, for coupled with the name of her cousin arose all the horrid associations connected with her loss. As soon, however, as she could compose herself, she briefly stated all she had witnessed of the affair, from the moment when the boat of the schooner was seen to meet the strange looking object on the water, to that when she had beheld her ill-fated cousin borne away apparently lifeless in the arms of the tall Indian by whom she had been captured.

During this recital, the heart of Captain de Haldimar, – for it was he, – beat audibly against the cheek that still reposed on his breast; but when his sister had, in a faint voice, closed her melancholy narrative with the manner of her cousin's disappearance, he gave a sudden start, uttering at the same time an exclamation of joy.

"Thank God, she still lives!" he cried, pressing his sister once more in fondness to his heart; then turning to his companion, who, although seemingly abstracted, had been a silent and attentive witness of the scene, – "By

Heaven! Valletort, there is yet a hope. She it was indeed whom we saw borne out of the fort, and subsequently made to walk by the cruel Indian who had charge of her."

"Valletort, Valletort," murmured Clara unconsciously, her sick heart throbbing with she knew not what. "How is this, Frederick? – Where, then, is Captain Baynton? and how came you here?"

"Alas! Clara, poor Baynton is no more. Even at the moment when he confided the unconscious burden, preserved at the peril of his own life, to the arms of Sir Everard here, he fell beneath the tomahawk of a pursuing savage. Poor, noble, generous Baynton," he continued, mournfully; "to him, indeed, Clara, are you indebted for your life; yet was it purchased at the price of his own."

Again the pained and affectionate girl wept bitterly, and her brother proceeded: –

"The strange object you saw on the lake, my love, was nothing more than a canoe disguised with leafy boughs, in which Sir Everard Valletort and myself, under the guidance of old François of the Fleur de lis, whom you must recollect, have made the dangerous passage of the Sinclair in the garb of duck hunters, – which latter we had only discarded on reaching the schooner, in order to assume another we conceived better suited to our purpose. Alas!" and he struck his hand violently against his brow, "had we made directly for the shore without touching the vessel at all, there might have been time to save those we came to apprise of their danger. Do you not think there was, Valletort?"

"Most assuredly not," returned his companion, anxious to remove the impression of self-blame that existed in the mind of Captain de Haldimar. "From the moment of our reaching the schooner, which lay immediately in our route, to that when the shout was raised by the savages as they rushed into the fort, there was scarcely an interval of three minutes; and it would have required a longer period to have enabled us even to gain the shore."

"Thank, thank you for that!" exclaimed the officer,

drawing himself up with the air of one who breathes more freely. "I would not, for the wealth and honours of the united world, that such a cause for self-reproach should linger on my mind. By Heaven! it would break my heart to think we had been in time to save them, and yet had lost the opportunity through even one moment of neglect." Then turning once more to his sister, – "Now, Clara, that I see you in safety, I have another sacred duty to perform. I must leave you, but not alone."

"What mean you, Frederick?" exclaimed his agitated sister, clinging more closely to his embrace. "Scarce have we met, and you talk of leaving me. Oh, whither would you go?"

"Surely, my love," and he spoke half reproachfully, although with tenderness of accent, "my meaning must be obvious. But what do I say? You know it not. Madeline still lives. We saw her, as we pulled towards the shore, led across the clearing in the direction of Chabouiga. Hear me, then: the canoe in which we came is still towing from the vessel's stern, and in this do I mean to embark, without further loss of time, in search of her who is dearer to me than existence. I know," he pursued with emotion, "I have but little hope of rescuing, even if I do succeed in finding her; but at least I shall not have to suffer under the self-reproach of having neglected the only chance that now lies within my reach. If she be doomed to die, I shall then have nothing left to live for —— except you, Clara," he concluded, after a pause, pressing the weeping girl to his heart, as he remarked how much she seemed pained by the declaration.

Having placed his sister once more on the couch, and covered her with a cloak that had been brought from the cabin of the unfortunate commander, Captain de Haldimar now rose from his humble seat, and grasping the hand of his friend, –

"Valletort," he said, "I commit this dear girl to your keeping. Hitherto we have been equal sharers in an enterprise having for its object the preservation of our mutual companions and friends. At present, interests of a more personal nature occupy my attention; and to these must I devote myself alone. I trust you will reach Détroit in safety; and when you have delivered my unfortunate sister into the arms of her father, you will say to him from me, I could not survive the loss of that being to whom I had sworn eternal fidelity and affection. François must be my only companion on this occasion. Nay," he continued, pointing to his sister, in answer to the rising remonstrance of the baronet, "will you desert the precious charge I have confided to your keeping? Recollect, Valletort," in a more subdued tone, "that besides yourself, there will be none near her but rude and uneducated sailors; – honest men enough in their way, it is true; but not the sort of people to whom I should like to confide my poor sister."

The warm and silent pressure by Sir Everard of his hand announced his participation in the sentiment; and Captain de Haldimar now hastened forward to apprise the Canadian of his purpose. He found mine host of the Fleur de lis seated in the forecastle of the schooner; and with an air of the most perfect unconcern discussing a substantial meal, consisting of dried uncooked venison, raw onions, and Indian corn bread, the contents of a large bag or wallet that lay at his feet. No sooner, however, had the impatient officer communicated his design, asking at the same time if he might expect his assistance in the enterprise, than the unfinished meal of the Canadian was discontinued, the wallet refilled, and the large greasy clasp-knife with which the portions had been separated, closed and thrust into a pocket of his blanket coat.

"I shall go to de devils for you, capitaine, if we must," he said, as he raised his portly form, not without effort, from the deck, slapping the shoulder of the officer at the same time somewhat rudely with his hand. There was nothing, however, offensively familiar in this action. It expressed merely the devotedness of heart with which the man lent himself to the service to which he had pledged himself, and was rather complimentary than otherwise to him to whom it was directed. Captain de Haldimar took it in the light in which we have just shown it, and he grasped and shook the rough hand of the Canadian with an earnestness highly gratifying to the latter.

Every thing was now in readiness for their departure. The canoe, still covered with its streaming boughs, was drawn close up to the gangway, and a few hasty necessaries thrown in. While this was passing, the officer had again assumed his disguise of a duck-hunter; and he now appeared in the blanket costume in which we introduced Sir Everard and himself at the opening of this volume.

"If I may be so bold as to put in my oar, your honour," – said the veteran boatswain, on whom the command of the schooner had fallen, as he now advanced, rolling his quid in his mouth, and dropping his hat on his shoulder, while the fingers of the hand which clutched it were busily occupied in scratching his bald head, – "if I may be so bold, there is another chap here as might better sarve your honour's purpose than that 'ere fat Canadian, who seems to think only of stuffing while his betters are fasting."

"And who is he, my good Mullins?" asked Captain de Haldimar.

"Why, that 'ere Ingian, your honour, as began the butchery in the fort, yonder, by trying to kill Jack Fuller while he laid asleep this morning, waiting for the captain in the jolly boat. Jack never seed him coming, until he felt his black hands upon his throat, and then he ups with the tiller at his noddle, and sends him floundering across the boat's thwarts like a flat-fish. I thought, your honour, seeing as how I have got the command of the schooner, of tying him up to the mainmast, and giving him two or three round dozen or so, and then sending him to swim among the mascannungy with a twenty-four pound shot in his neckcloth; but, seeing as how your honour is going among them savages agin, I thought as how some good might be done with him, if your honour could contrive to keep him in tow, and close under your lee quarter, to prevent his escape."

"At all events," returned the officer, after a pause of some moments, during which he appeared to be deliberating on his course of action, "it may be dangerous to keep him in the vessel; and yet, if we take him ashore, he may be the means of our more immediate destruction; unless, indeed, as you observe, he can be so secured as to prevent the possibility of escape: but that I very much doubt indeed. Where is he, Mullins? I should like to see and question him."

"He shall be up, your honour, in no time," replied the sailor, once more resuming his hat, and moving a pace or two forward. Then addressing two or three men in the starboard gangway in the authoritative tone of command: – "Bear a hand there, my men, and cast off the lashings of that black Ingian, and send him aft, here, to the officer."

The order was speedily executed. In a few minutes the Indian stood on the quarter-deck, his hands firmly secured behind, and his head sunk upon his chest in sullen despondency. In the increasing gloom in which objects were now gradually becoming more and more indistinct, it was impossible for Captain de Haldimar to distinguish his features; but there was something in the outline of the Indian's form that impressed him with the conviction he had seen it before. Advancing a pace or two forward, he pronounced, in an emphatic and audible whisper, the name of "Oucanasta!"

The Indian gave an involuntary start, – uttered a deep interjectional "Ugh!" – and, raising his head from his chest, fixed his eye heavily on the officer.

"Hookynaster! – Hookynaster!" growled Jack Fuller, who had followed to hear the examination of his immediate captive: "why, your honour, that jaw-breaking name reminds me as how the chap had a bit of paper when I chucked him into the jolly boat, stuck in his girdle. It was covered over with pencil-marks, as writing like; but all was rubbed out agin, except some such sort of a name as that."

"Where is it? – what have you done with it?" hastily asked Captain de Haldimar.

"Here, in my backy-box, your honour. I kept it safe, thinking as how it might sarve to let us know all about it afterwards."

The sailor now drew from the receptacle just named a dirty piece of folded paper, deeply impregnated with the perfume of stale and oft rechewed quids of coarse tobacco; and then, with the air of one conscious of having "rendered the state some service," hitched up his trowsers with one hand, while with the other he extended the important document.

To glance his eye hurriedly over the paper by the light of a dark lanthorn that had meanwhile been brought upon deck, unclasp his hunting-knife, and divide the ligatures of the captive, and then warmly press his liberated hands within his own, were, with Captain de Haldimar, but the work of a minute.

"Holloa! which the devil way does the wind blow now?" muttered Fuller, the leer of self-satisfaction that had hitherto played in his eye rapidly giving place to an air of seriousness and surprise; an expression that was not at all diminished by an observation from his new commander.

"I tell you what it is, Jack," said the latter, impressively; "I don't pretend to have more gumption than my messmates; but I can see through a millstone as clear as any man as ever heaved a lead in these here lakes; and may I never pipe boatswain's whistle again, if you ar'n't, some how or other, in the wrong box. That 'ere Ingian's one of us!"

The feelings of Captain de Haldimar may easily be comprehended by our readers, when, on glancing at the paper, he found himself confirmed in the impression previously made on him by the outline of the captive's form. The writing, nearly obliterated by damp, had been rudely traced by his own pencil on a leaf torn from his pocket-book on the night of his visit to the Indian encampment, and at the moment when, seated on the fatal log, Oucanasta had generously promised her assistance in at least rescuing his betrothed bride. They were addressed to Major de Haldimar, and briefly stated that a treacherous plan was in contemplation by the enemy to surprise the fort, which the bearer, Oucanasta (the latter word strongly marked), would fully explain, if she could possibly obtain access within. From the narrative entered into by Clara, who had particularly dwelt on the emotions of fear that had sprung up in her own and cousin's heart by the sudden transformation of a supposed harmless beaver into a fierce and threatening savage, he had no difficulty in solving the enigma.

The Indian, in whom he had recognised the young chief who had saved him from the fury of Wacousta, had evidently been won upon by his sister to perform a service which offered so much less difficulty to a warrior than to a woman; and it was clear, that, finding all other means of communication with the fort, undiscovered by his own people, impracticable, he had availed himself of the opportunity, when he saw the boat waiting on the strand, to assume a disguise so well adapted to insure success. It was no remarkable thing in these countries, to see both the beaver and the otter moving on the calm surface of the waters in the vicinity of the forts, even at mid-day; and occupied as the Indians were, to a man, at that moment with their cruel projects, it was by no means likely that their attention should have been called off from these to so apparently unimportant a circumstance. The act that had principally alarmed the cousins, and terminated, as we have seen, in the sudden attack of the sailor, had evidently been misconceived. The hand supposed to be feeling for the heart of the sluggard, had, in all probability, been placed on his chest with a view to arouse him from his slumber; while that which was believed to have been dropped to the handle of his knife, was, in reality, merely seeking the paper that contained the announcement, which, if *then* delivered, might have saved the garrison.

Such was the train of conjecture that now passed through the mind of the officer; but, although he thus placed the conduct of the Indian in the most favourable light, his impression received no confirmation from the lips of the latter. Sullen and doggedly, notwithstanding the release from his bonds, the Ottawa hung his head upon his chest, with his eyes riveted on the deck, and obstinately refused to answer every question put to him by his deliverer. This, however, did not the less tend to confirm Captain de Haldimar in his belief. He knew enough of the Indian character, to understand the indignant and even revengeful spirit likely to be aroused by the treatment the savage had met with in return for his intended services. He was aware that, without pausing to reflect on the fact, that the sailor, ignorant of his actual purpose, could merely have seen in him an enemy in the act of attempting his life, the chief would only consider and inflame himself over the recollection of the blow inflicted; and that, with the true obstinacy of his race, he would rather suffer captivity or death itself, than humble the haughty pride of his nature, by condescending to an explanation with those by whom he felt himself so deeply injured. Still, even amid all his own personal griefs, – griefs that rendered the boon in some degree at present valueless, – Captain de Haldimar could not forget that the youth, no matter by what motive induced, had rescued him from a dreadful death on a previous occasion. With the generous warmth, therefore, of a grateful mind, he now sought to impress on the Indian the deep sense of obligation under which he laboured; explaining at the same time the very natural error into which the sailor had fallen, and concluding with a declaration that he was free to quit the vessel in the canoe in which he himself was about to take his departure for the shore, in search of her whom his sister had pledged herself, at all hazards, to save.

The address of the officer, touching and impressive as language ever is that comes from the heart, was not altogether without effect on the Indian. Several times he interrupted him with a short, quick, approving "Ugh!" and when he at length received the assurance that he was no longer a prisoner, he raised his eyes rapidly, although without moving his head, to the countenance of his deliverer. Already were his lips opening to speak for the first time, when the attention of the group around him was arrested by his giving a sudden start of surprise. At the same moment he raised his head, stretched his neck, threw forward his right ear, and, uttering a loud and emphatic "Waugh!" pointed with his finger over the bows of the vessel.

All listened for upwards of a minute in mute suspense; and then a faint and scarcely distinguishable sound was heard in the direction in which he pointed. Scarcely had it floated on the air, when a shrill, loud, and prolonged cry, of peculiar tendency, burst hurriedly and eagerly from the lips of the captive; and, spreading over the broad expanse of water, seemed to be re-echoed back from every point of the surrounding shore.

Great was the confusion that followed this startling yell on the decks of the schooner. "Cut the hell-fiend down!" – "Chuck him overboard!" – "We are betrayed!" – "Every man to his gun!" – "Put the craft about!" were among the numerous exclamations that now rose simultaneously from at least twenty lips, and almost drowned the loud shriek that burst again from the wretched Clara de Haldimar.

"Stop, Mullins! – Stop, men!" shouted Captain de Haldimar, firmly, as the excited boatswain, with two or three of his companions, now advanced with the intention of laying violent hands on the Indian. "I will answer for his fidelity with my life. If he be false, it will be time enough to punish him afterwards; but let us calmly await the issue like men. Hear me," he proceeded, as he remarked their incredulous, uncertain, and still threatening air; – "this Indian saved me from the tomahawks of his tribe not a week ago; and, even now, he has become our captive in the act of taking a note from me to the garrison, to warn them of their danger. But for that slumbering fool," he added, bitterly, pointing to Fuller, who slept when he should have watched, "yon fort would not now have been what it is, – a mass of smoking ruins. He has an ocean of blood upon his soul, that all the waters of the Huron can never wash out!"

Struck by the vehement manner of the officer, and the disclosure he had just made, the sailors sunk once more into inaction and silence. The boatswain alone spoke.

"I thought, your honour, as how Jack Fuller, who sartainly is a better hand at a snooze than a watch, had got into a bit of a mess; but, shiver my topsails, if I think it's quite fair to blame him, neither, for clapping a stopper on the Ingian's cable, seeing as how he was expecting a shot between wind and water. Still, as the chap turns out to be an honest chap, and has saved your honour's life above all, I don't much care if I give him a grip. Here, old fellow, tip us your fist!"

Without seeming to understand that his cry had been productive of general and intense alarm throughout the vessel, the Indian had viewed the sudden rushing of the crew towards him as an act of gratuitous hostility; and, without shrinking from the attack, had once more resumed his original air of dogged sullenness. It was evident to him, from the discussion going on, that some violence, about to be offered to his person, had only been prevented by the interference of the officer. With the natural haughtiness of his savage nature, he therefore rejected the overtures of the sailor, whose hand he had observed among the first that were raised against him.

While the angry boatswain was yet rolling his quid within his capacious jaws, racking his brain for the strongest language wherein to give vent to his indignation, his ears were suddenly saluted by a low but clear "Hilloa!" from the bows of the schooner.

"Ay, ay!" was the brief response.

"There's something approaching us ahead, on the weather fore quarter," continued the same voice, which was that of the man on the look-out.

The most profound silence now pervaded the deck. Every individual, including Captain de Haldimar and the boatswain, had flown to the gangway of the quarter indicated, which was on the side occupied by the couch of the unfortunate Clara. Presently a noise like that produced by a single paddle rapidly dividing the water, was heard by every anxious ear. Night had long since thrown her mantle over the surrounding waste; and all that was to be seen reflected from the bosom of the gradually darkening river, scarcely ruffled by the yet incipient breeze, were a few straggling stars, that here and there appeared in the overcast heavens. Hitherto no object could be discovered by those who strained their eyes eagerly and painfully through the gloom, although the sounds became at each moment more distinct. It was evident the party, guided by the noise of the rippling waves that fell from the bows of the schooner, was enabled to follow up a course, the direct clue to which had been indicated by the cry of the captive. Every man stood near his gun on the starboard battery, and the burning matches hanging over their respective buckets ready to be seized at a moment's notice. Still, but little room for apprehension existed; for the practised ear of the mariners could easily tell that a solitary bark alone approached; and of one, or even ten, they entertained no fear. Suddenly, as the course of the vessel was now changed a point to windward, – a movement that brought her bows more off the adjacent shore, – the sound, in which all were more or less interested, was heard not more than twenty yards off, and in a line with the gangway at which the principal of the crew were assembled. In the next minute the low hull of a canoe came in sight, and then a tall and solitary human figure was seen in the stern, bending alternately to the right and to the left, as the paddle was rapidly and successively changed from side to side.

Another deep and exulting "Ugh!" was now heaved from the chest of the Indian, who stood calmly on the spot on which he had first rested, while Fuller prepared a coil of rope to throw to the active steersman.

"Avast there, Jack!" growled the boatswain, addressing the sailor; "how can the stranger keep the bow of his craft on, and grapple at the same time? Just pass one end of the coil round your waist, and swing yourself gently into her."

The head of the canoe was now near enough for the purpose. The sailor did as he was desired, having previously divested himself of his shoes, and leaping forward, alighted on what appeared to be a bundle of blankets stowed away in her bows. No sooner, however, had he secured his footing, when with another desperate leap, and greatly to the astonishment of all around, he bounded once more to the deck of the schooner, his countenance exhibiting every mark of superstitious alarm. In the act of quitting the canoe he had spurned her violently several feet from the vessel, which the silent steersman was again making every effort to reach.

"Why what the devil's the matter with you now?" exclaimed the rough boatswain, who, as well as Captain de Haldimar and the rest of the crew, had quitted the gangway to learn the cause of this extraordinary conduct. "Damn my eyes, if you ar'n't worse scared than when the Ingian stood over you in the jolly boat."

"Scared, ay, to be sure I am; and so would you be scared too, if you'd a see'd what I did. May I never touch the point at Portsmouth, if I a'n't seen her ghost."

"Where? – whose ghost? – what ghost? – what do you mean, Jack?" exclaimed several of the startled men in the same breath, while the superstitious dread so common to mariners drew them still closer in the group that encircled their companion.

"Well, then, as I am a miserable sinner," returned the man, impressively, and in a low tone, "I see'd in the bows of the canoe, – and the hand that steered it was not made of flesh and blood like ours, – what do you think? – the ghost of —— "

Captain de Haldimar heard no more. At a single bound he had gained the ship's side. He strained his eyes anxiously over the gangway in search of the canoe, but it was gone. A death-like silence throughout the deck followed the communication of the sailor, and in that pause the sound of the receding boat could be heard, not urged, as it had approached, by one paddle, but by two. The heart of the officer throbbed almost to suffocation; and his firmness, hitherto supported by the manly energies of his nature, now failed him quite. Heedless of appearances, regardless of being overlooked, he tottered like a drunken man for support against the mainmast. For a moment or two he leant his head upon his hand, with the air of one immersed in the most profound abstraction; while the crew, at once alarmed and touched by the deep distress into which this mysterious circumstance had plunged him, stood silently and respectfully watching his emotion. Suddenly he started from his attitude of painful repose, like one awaking from a dream, and demanded what had become of the Indian.

Every one looked around, but the captive was nowhere to be seen. Search was made below, both in the cabin and in the fore decks, and men were sent up aloft to see if he had secreted himself in the rigging; but all returned, stating he was nowhere to be found. He had disappeared from the vessel altogether, yet no one knew how; for he had not been observed to stir from the spot on which he had first planted himself. It was plain, however, he had joined the mysterious party in the canoe, from the fact of the second paddle having been detected; and all attempts at pursuit, without endangering the vessel on the shallows, whither the course of the fugitives was now directed, was declared by the boatswain utterly impracticable.

The announcement of the Indian's disappearance seemed to put the climax to the despair of the unfortunate officer. – "Then is our every hope lost!" he groaned aloud, as, quitting the centre of the vessel, he slowly traversed the deck, and once more stood at the side of his no less unhappy and excited sister. For a moment or two he remained with his arms folded across his chest, gazing on the dark outline of her form; and then, in a wild paroxysm of silent, tearless grief, threw himself suddenly on the edge of the couch, and clasping her in a long close embrace to his audibly beating heart, lay like one bereft of all sense and consciousness of surrounding objects.

WACOUSTA

Volume III

One

THE NIGHT passed away without further event on board the schooner, yet in all the anxiety that might be supposed incident to men so perilously situated. Habits of long-since acquired superstition, too powerful to be easily shaken off, moreover contributed to the dejection of the mariners, among whom there were not wanting those who believed the silent steersman was in reality what their comrade had represented, – an immaterial being, sent from the world of spirits to warn them of some impending evil. What principally gave weight to this impression were the repeated asseverations of Fuller, during the sleepless night passed by all on deck, that what he had seen was no other, could be no other, than a ghost! exhibiting in its hueless, fleshless cheek, the well-known lineaments of one who was supposed to be no more: and, if the story of their comrade had needed confirmation among men in whom faith in, rather than love for, the marvellous was a constitutional ingredient, the terrible effect that seemed to have been produced on Captain de Haldimar by the same mysterious visitation would have been more than conclusive. The very appearance of the night, too, favoured the delusion. The heavens, comparatively clear at the moment when the canoe approached the vessel, became suddenly enveloped in the deepest gloom at its departure, as if to enshroud the course of those who, having so mysteriously approached, had also so unaccountably disappeared. Nor

had this threatening state of the atmosphere the counter-
balancing advantage of storm and tempest to drive them
onward through the narrow waters of the Sinclair, and
enable them, by anticipating the pursuit of their enemies,
to shun the Scylla and Charybdis that awaited their more
leisure advance. The wind increased not; and the disappointed seamen remarked, with dismay, that their craft
scarcely made more progress than at the moment when
she first quitted her anchorage.

It was now near the first hours of day; and although,
perhaps, none slept, there were few who were not apparently at rest, and plunged in the most painful reflections.
Still occupying her humble couch, and shielded from the
night air merely by the cloak that covered her own blood-
stained garments, lay the unhappy Clara, her deep groans
and stifled sobs bursting occasionally from her pent-up
heart, and falling on the ears of the mariners like sounds
of fearful import, produced by the mysterious agency that
already bore such undivided power over their thoughts.
On the bare deck, at her side, lay her brother, his face
turned upon the planks, as if to shut out all objects from
eyes he had not the power to close; and, with one arm
supporting his heavy brow, while the other, cast around the
restless form of his beloved sister, seemed to offer protection and to impart confidence, even while his lips denied
the accents of consolation. Seated on an empty hen-coop
at their head, was Sir Everard Valletort, his back reposing
against the bulwarks of the vessel, his arms folded across
his chest, and his eyes bent mechanically on the man at
the helm, who stood within a few paces of him, – an
attitude of absorption, which he, ever and anon, changed
to one of anxious and enquiring interest, whenever the
agitation of Clara was manifested in the manner already
shown.

The main deck and forecastle of the vessel presented a
similar picture of mingled unquietness and repose. Many
of the seamen might be seen seated on the gun-carriages,
with their cheeks pressing the rude metal that served

them for a pillow. Others lay along the decks, with their heads resting on the elevated hatches; while not a few, squatted on their haunches with their knees doubled up to their very chins, supported in that position the aching head that rested between their rough and horny palms. A first glance might have induced the belief that all were buried in the most profound slumber; but the quick jerking of a limb, – the fitful, sudden shifting of a position, – the utter absence of that deep breathing which indicates the unconsciousness of repose, and the occasional spirting of tobacco juice upon the deck, – all these symptoms only required to be noticed, to prove the living silence that reigned throughout was not born either of apathy or sleep.

At the gangway at which the canoe had approached now stood the individual already introduced to our readers as Jack Fuller. The same superstitious terror that caused his flight had once more attracted him to the spot where the subject of his alarm first appeared to him; and, without seeming to reflect that the vessel, in her slow but certain progress, had left all vestige of the mysterious visitant behind, he continued gazing over the bulwarks on the dark waters, as if he expected at each moment to find his sight stricken by the same appalling vision. It was at the moment when he had worked up his naturally dull imagination to its highest perception of the supernatural, that he was joined by the rugged boatswain, who had passed the greater part of the night in pacing up and down the decks, watching the aspect of the heavens, and occasionally tauting a rope or squaring a light yard, unassisted, as the fluttering of the canvass in the wind rendered the alteration necessary.

"Well, Jack!" bluntly observed the latter in a gruff whisper that resembled the suppressed growling of a mastiff, "what the hell are ye thinking of now? – Not got over your flumbustification yet, that ye stand here, looking as sanctified as an old parson!"

"I'll tell ye what it is, Mr. Mullins," returned the sailor, in the same key; "you may make as much game on me as you like; but these here strange sort of doings are some-how quizzical; and, though I fears nothing in the shape of flesh and blood, still, when it comes to having to do with those as is gone to Davy Jones's locker like, it gives a fellow an all-overishness as isn't quite the thing. You understand me?"

"I'm damned if I do!" was the brief but energetic rejoinder.

"Well, then," continued Fuller, "if I must out with it, I must. I think that 'ere Ingian must have been the devil, or how could he come so sudden and unbeknownst upon me, with the head of a 'possum: and then, agin, how could he get away from the craft without our seeing him? and how came the ghost on board of the canoe?"

"Avast there, old fellow; you means not the head of a 'possum, but a beaver: but that 'ere's all nat'r'l enough, and easily 'counted for; but you hav'n't told us whose ghost it was, after all."

"No; the captain made such a spring to the gunwale, as frighted it all out of my head: but come closer, Mr. Mullins, and I'll whisper it in your ear. – Hark! what was that?"

"I hears nothing," said the boatswain, after a pause.

"It's very odd," continued Fuller; "but I thought as how I heard it several times afore you came."

"There's something wrong, I take it, in your upper story, Jack Fuller," coolly observed his companion; "that 'ere ghost has quite capsized you."

"Hark, again!" repeated the sailor. "Didn't you hear it then? A sort of a groan like."

"Where, in what part?" calmly demanded the boat-swain, though in the same suppressed tone in which the dialogue had been carried on.

"Why, from the canoe that lies alongside there. I heard it several times afore."

"Well, damn my eyes, if you a'rn't turned a real coward at last," politely remarked Mr. Mullins. "Can't the poor fat devil of a Canadian snooze a bit in his hammock, without putting you so completely out of your reckoning?"

"The Canadian – the Canadian!" hurriedly returned Fuller: "why, don't you see him there, leaning with his back to the mainmast, and as fast asleep as if the devil himself couldn't wake him?"

"Then it was the devil, you heard, if you like," quaintly retorted Mullins: "but bear a hand, and tell us all about this here ghost."

"Hark, again! what was that?" once more enquired the excited sailor.

"Only a gust of wind passing through the dried boughs of the canoe," said the boatswain: "but since we can get nothing out of that crazed noddle of yours, see if you can't do something with your hands. That 'ere canoe running alongside, takes half a knot off the ship's way. Bear a hand then, and cast off the painter, and let her drop astern, that she may follow in our wake. Hilloa! what the hell's the matter with the man now?"

And well might he ask. With his eyeballs staring, his teeth chattering, his body half bent, and his arms thrown forward, yet pendent as if suddenly arrested in that position while in the act of reaching the rope, the terrified sailor stood gazing on the stern of the canoe; in which, by the faint light of the dawning day, was to be seen an object well calculated to fill the least superstitious heart with terror and dismay. Through an opening in the foliage peered the pale and spectral face of a human being, with its dull eyes bent fixedly and mechanically upon the vessel. In the centre of the wan forehead was a dark incrustation, as of blood covering the superficies of a newly closed wound. The pallid mouth was partially unclosed, so as to display a row of white and apparently lipless teeth; and the features were otherwise set and drawn, as those of one who is no longer of earth. Around the head was bound a covering so close, as to conceal every part save the face; and once or twice a hand was slowly raised, and pressed upon the blood spot that dimmed the passing fairness of the brow. Every other portion of the form was invisible.

"Lord have mercy upon us!" exclaimed the boatswain, in a voice that, now elevated to more than its natural tone, sounded startlingly on the stillness of the scene; "sure enough it is, indeed, a ghost!"

"Ha! do you believe me now?" returned Fuller, gaining confidence from the admission of his companion, and in the same elevated key. "It is, as I hope to be saved, the ghost I see'd afore."

The commotion on deck was now every where universal. The sailors started to their feet, and, with horror and alarm visibly imprinted on their countenances, rushed tumultuously towards the dreaded gangway.

"Make way – room, fellows!" exclaimed a hurried voice; and presently Captain de Haldimar, who had bounded like lightning from the deck, appeared with eager eye and excited cheek among them. To leap into the bows of the canoe, and disappear under the foliage, was the work of a single instant. All listened breathlessly for the slightest sound; and then every heart throbbed with the most undefinable emotions, as his lips were heard giving utterance to the deep emotion of his own spirit, –

"Madeline, oh, my own lost Madeline!" he exclaimed with almost frantic energy of passion: "do I then press you once more in madness to my doting heart? Speak, speak to me – for God's sake speak, or I shall go mad! Air, air, – she wants air only – she cannot be dead."

These last words were succeeded by the furious rending asunder of the fastenings that secured the boughs, and presently the whole went overboard, leaving revealed the tall and picturesque figure of the officer; whose left arm encircled while it supported the reclining and powerless form of one who well resembled, indeed, the spectre for which she had been mistaken, while his right hand was busied in detaching the string that secured a portion of the covering round her throat. At length it fell from her shoulders; and the well known form of Madeline de Haldimar, clad even in the vestments in which they had been wont to see her, met the astonished gaze of the excited seamen. Still there were some who doubted it was the corporeal woman whom they beheld; and several of the crew who were catholics even made the sign of the cross as the supposed spirit was now borne up the gangway in the arms of the pained yet gratified De Haldimar: nor was it until her feet were seen finally resting on the deck, that Jack Fuller could persuade himself it was indeed Miss de Haldimar, and not her ghost, that lay clasped to the heart of the officer.

With the keen rush of the morning air upon her brow returned the suspended consciousness of the bewildered Madeline. The blood came slowly and imperceptibly to her cheek; and her eyes, hitherto glazed, fixed, and inexpressive, looked enquiringly, yet with stupid wonderment, around. She started from the embrace of her lover, gazed alternately at his disguise, at himself, and at Clara; and then passing her hand several times rapidly across her brow, uttered an hysteric scream, and threw herself impetuously forward on the bosom of the sobbing girl; who, with extended arms, parted lips, and heaving bosom, sat breathlessly awaiting the first dawn of the returning reason of her more than sister.

We should vainly attempt to paint all the heart-rending misery of the scene exhibited in the gradual restoration of Miss de Haldimar to her senses. From a state of torpor, produced by the freezing of every faculty into almost idiotcy, she was suddenly awakened to all the terrors of the past; and the deep intonations of her rich voice were heard only in expressions of agony, that entered into the most iron-hearted of the assembled seamen; while they drew from the bosom of her gentle and sympathising cousin fresh bursts of desolating grief. Imagination itself would find difficulty in supplying the harrowing effect upon all, when, with upraised hands, and on her bended knees, her large eyes turned wildly up to heaven, she invoked in deep and startling accents the terrible retribution of a just God on the inhuman murderers of her father, with whose life-blood her garments were profusely saturated; and then, with hysteric laughter, demanded why she alone had been singled out to survive the bloody tragedy. Love and affection, hitherto the first principles of her existence, then found no entrance into her mind. Stricken, broken-hearted, stultified to all feeling save that of her immediate wretchedness, she thought only of the horrible scenes through which she had passed; and even he, whom at another moment she could have clasped in an agony of fond tenderness to her beating bosom, – he to whom she had pledged her virgin faith, and was bound by the dearest of human ties, – he whom she had so often longed to behold once more, and had thought of, the preceding day, with all the tenderness of her impassioned and devoted soul, – even he did not, in the first hours of her terrible consciousness, so much as command a single passing regard. All the affections were for a period blighted in her bosom. She seemed as one devoted, without the power of resistance, to a grief which calcined and preyed upon all other feelings of the mind. One stunning and annihilating reflection seemed to engross every principle of her being; nor was it for hours after she had been restored to life and recollection that a deluge of burning tears, giving relief to her heart and a new direction to her feelings, enabled her at length to separate the past from, and in some degree devote herself to, the present. Then, indeed, for the first time did she perceive and take pleasure in the presence of her lover; and clasping her beloved and weeping Clara to her heart, thank her God, in all the fervour of true piety, that she at least had been spared to shed a ray of comfort on her distracted spirit. But we will not pain the reader by dwelling on a scene that drew tears even from the rugged and flint-nerved boatswain himself; for, although we should linger on it with minute anatomical detail, no powers of language we possess could convey the transcript as it should be. Pass we on, therefore, to the more immediate incidents of our narrative.

The day now rapidly developing, full opportunity was afforded the mariners to survey the strict nature of their position. To all appearance they were yet in the middle of the lake, for around them lay the belting sweep of forest that bounded the perspective of the equidistant circle, of which their bark was the focus or immediate centre. The wind was dying gradually away, and when at length the sun rose, in all his splendour, there was scarce air enough in the heavens to keep the sails from flapping against the masts, or to enable the vessel to obey her helm. In vain was the low and peculiar whistle of the seamen heard, ever and anon, in invocation of the departing breeze. Another day, calm and breathless as the preceding, had been chartered from the world of light; and their hearts failed them, as they foresaw the difficulty of their position, and the almost certainty of their retreat being cut off. It was while labouring under the disheartening consciousness of danger, peculiar to all, that the anxious boatswain summoned Captain de Haldimar and Sir Everard Valletort, by a significant beck of the finger, to the side of the deck opposite to that on which still lay the suffering and nearly broken-hearted girls.

"Well, Mullins, what now?" enquired the former, as he narrowly scanned the expression of the old man's features: "that clouded brow of yours, I fear me, bodes no agreeable information."

"Why, your honour, I scarcely knows what to say about it; but seeing as I'm the only officer in the ship, now our poor captain is killed, God bless him! I thought I might take the liberty to consult with your honours as to the best way of getting out of the jaws of them sharks of Ingians; and two heads, as the saying is, is always better than one."

"And now you have the advantage of three," observed the officer, with a sickly smile; "but I fear, Mullins, that if your own be not sufficient for the purpose, ours will be of little service. You must take counsel from your own experience and knowledge of nautical matters."

"Why, to be sure, your honour," and the sailor rolled his

quid from one cheek to the other, "I think I may say as how I'll venture to steer the craft with any man on the Canada lakes, and bring her safe into port too; but seeing as how I'm only a petty officer, and not yet recommended by his worship the governor for the full command, I thought it but right to consult with my superiors, not as to the management of the craft, but the best as is to be done. What does your honour think of making for the high land over the larboard bow yonder, and waiting for the chance of the night-breeze to take us through the Sinclair?"

"Do whatever you think best," returned the officer. "For my part, I scarcely can give an opinion. Yet how are we to get there? There does not appear to be a breath of wind."

"Oh, that's easily managed; we have only to brail and furl up a little, to hide our cloth from the Ingians, and then send the boats a-head to tow the craft, while some of us lend a hand at her own sweeps. We shall get close under the lee of the land afore night, and then we must pull up agin along shore, until we get within a mile or so of the head of the river."

"But shall we not be seen by our enemies?" asked Sir Everard; "and will they not be on the watch for our movements, and intercept our retreat?"

"Now that's just the thing, your honour, as they're not likely to do, if so be as we bears away for yon headlands. I knows every nook and sounding round the lake; and odd enough if I didn't, seeing as how the craft circumnavigated it, at least, a dozen times since we have been cooped up here. Poor Captain Danvers! (may the devil damn his murderers, I say, though it does make a commander of me for once;) he used always to make for that 'ere point, whenever he wished to lie quiet; for never once did we see so much as a single Ingian on the headland. No, your honour, they keeps all at t'other side of the lake, seeing as how that is the main road from Mackina' to Détroit."

"Then, by all means, do so," eagerly returned Captain de Haldimar. "Oh, Mullins! take us but safely through, and if the interest of my father can procure you a king's commission, you shall not want it, believe me."

"And if half my fortune can give additional stimulus to exertion, it shall be shared, with pleasure, between yourself and crew," observed Sir Everard.

"Thank your honours, – thank your honours," said the boatswain, somewhat electrified by these brilliant offers. "The lads may take the money, if they like; all I cares about is the king's commission. Give me but a swab on my shoulder, and the money will come fast enough of itself. But, still, shiver my topsails, if I wants any bribery to make me do my duty; besides, if 'twas only for them poor girls alone, I would go through fire and water to sarve them. I'm not very chicken-hearted in my old age, your honours, but I don't recollect the time when I blubbered so much as I did when Miss Madeline come aboard. But I can't bear to think of it; and now let us see and get all ready for towing."

Every thing now became bustle and activity on board the schooner. The matches, no longer required for the moment, were extinguished, and the heavy cutlasses and pistols unbuckled from the loins of the men, and deposited near their respective guns. Light forms flew aloft, and, standing out upon the yards, loosely furled the sails that had previously been hauled and clewed up; but, as this was an operation requiring little time in so small a vessel, those who were engaged in it speedily glided to the deck again, ready for a more arduous service. The boats had, meanwhile, been got forward, and into these the sailors sprang, with an alacrity that could scarcely have been expected from men who had passed not only the preceding night, but many before it, in utter sleeplessness and despair. But the imminence of the danger, and the evident necessity existing for exertion, aroused them to new energy; and the hitherto motionless vessel was now made to obey the impulse given by the tow ropes of the boats, in a manner that proved their crews to have entered on their toil with the determination of men, resolved to devote themselves in earnest to their task. Nor was the spirit of action confined to these. The long sweeps of the schooner had been shipped, and such of the crew as remained on board laboured effectually at them, – a service, in which they were essentially aided, not only by mine host of the Fleur de lis, but by the young officers themselves.

At mid-day the headlands were seen looming largely in the distance, while the immediate shores of the ill-fated fortress were momentarily, and in the same proportion, disappearing under the dim line of horizon in the rear. More than half their course, from the spot whence they commenced towing, had been completed, when the ha-rassed men were made to quit their oars, in order to par-take of the scanty fare of the vessel, consisting chiefly of dried bear's meat and venison. Spirit of any description they had none; but, unlike their brethren of the Atlantic, when driven to extremities in food, they knew not what it was to poison the nutritious properties of the latter by sipping the putrid dregs of the water-cask, in quantities scarce sufficient to quench the fire of their parched pal-ates. Unslaked thirst was a misery unknown to the mari-ners of these lakes: it was but to cast their buckets deep into the tempting element, and water, pure, sweet, and grateful as any that ever bubbled from the moss-clad fountain of sylvan deity, came cool and refreshing to their lips, neutralising, in a measure, the crudities of the coars-est food. It was to this inestimable advantage the crew of the schooner had been principally indebted for their health, during the long series of privation, as far as related to fresh provisions and rest, to which they had been sub-jected. All appeared as vigorous in frame, and robust in health, as at the moment when they had last quitted the waters of the Détroit; and but for the inward sinking of the spirit, reflected in many a bronzed and furrowed brow, there was little to show they had been exposed to any very extraordinary trials.

Their meal having been hastily dispatched, and sweet-ened by a draught from the depths of the Huron, the seamen once more sprang into their boats, and devoted themselves, heart and soul, to the completion of their task, pulling with a vigour that operated on each and all with a tendency to encouragement and hope. At length the vessel, still impelled by her own sweeps, gradually approached the land; and at rather more than an hour before sunset was so near that the moment was deemed arrived when, without danger of being perceived, she might be run up along the shore to the point alluded to by the boatswain. Little more than another hour was occupied in bringing her to her station; and the red tints of departing day were still visible in the direction of the ill-fated fortress of Michillimackinac, when the sullen rumbling of the cable, following the heavy splash of the anchor, announced the place of momentary concealment had been gained.

The anchorage lay between two projecting headlands; to the outermost extremities of which were to be seen, overhanging the lake, the stately birch and pine, connected at their base by an impenetrable brushwood, extending to the very shore, and affording the amplest concealment, except from the lake side and the banks under which the schooner was moored. From the first quarter, however, little danger was incurred, as any canoes the savages might send in discovery of their course, must unavoidably be seen the moment they appeared over the line of the horizon, while, on the contrary, their own vessel, although much larger, resting on and identified with the land, must be invisible, except on a very near approach. In the opposite direction they were equally safe; for, as Mullins had truly remarked, none, save a few wandering hunters, whom chance occasionally led to the spot, were to be met with in a part of the country that lay so completely out of the track of communication between the fortresses. It was, however, but to double the second headland in their front, and they came within view of the Sinclair, the head of which was situated little more than a league beyond the spot where they now lay. Thus secure for the present, and waiting only for the rising of the breeze, of which the setting sun had given promise, the sailors once more snatched their hasty refreshment, while two of their number were sent aloft to keep a vigilant look-out along the circuit embraced by the enshrouding headlands.

During the whole of the day the cousins had continued on deck clasped in each other's arms, and shedding tears of bitterness, and heaving the most heart-rending sobs at intervals, yet but rarely conversing. The feelings of both were too much oppressed to admit of the utterance of their grief. The vampire of despair had banqueted on their hearts. Their vitality had been sucked, as it were, by its cold and bloodless lips; and little more than the withered rind, that had contained the seeds of so many affections, had been left. Often had Sir Everard and De Haldimar paused momentarily from the labour of their oars, to cast an eye of anxious solicitude on the scarcely conscious girls, wishing, rather than expecting, to find the violence of their desolation abated, and that, in the full expansion of unreserved communication, they were relieving their sick hearts from the terrible and crushing weight of woe that bore them down. Captain de Haldimar had even once or twice essayed to introduce the subject himself, in the hope that some fresh paroxysm, following their disclosures, would remove the horrible stupefaction of their senses; but the wild look and excited manner of Madeline, whenever he touched on the chord of her affliction, had as often caused him to desist.

Towards the evening, however, her natural strength of character came in aid of his quiescent efforts to soothe her; and she appeared not only more composed, but more sensible of the impression produced by surrounding objects. As the last rays of the sun were tinging the horizon, she drew up her form in a sitting position against the bulwarks, and, raising her clasped hands to heaven, while her eyes were bent long and fixedly on the distant west, appeared for some minutes wholly lost in that attitude of absorption. Then she closed her eyes; and through the swollen lids came coursing, one by one, over her quivering cheek, large tears, that seemed to scald a furrow where they passed. After this she became more calm – her respiration more free; and she even consented to taste the humble meal which the young man now offered for the third time. Neither Clara nor herself had eaten food since the preceding morning; and the weakness of their frames contributed not a little to the increasing despondency of their spirits; but, notwithstanding several attempts previously made, they had rejected what was offered them, with insurmountable loathing. When they had now swallowed a few morsels of the sliced venison ham, prepared with all the delicacy the nearly exhausted resources of the vessel could supply, accompanied by a small portion of the cornbread of the Canadian, Captain de Haldimar prevailed on them to swallow a few drops of the spirit that still remained in the canteen given them by Erskine on their departure from Détroit. The genial liquid sent a kindling glow to their chilled hearts, and for a moment deadened the pungency of their anguish; and then it was that Miss de Haldimar entered briefly on the horrors she had witnessed, while Clara, with her arm encircling her waist, fixed her dim and swollen eyes, from which a tear ever and anon rolled heavily to her lap, on those of her beloved cousin.

Two

WITHOUT borrowing the affecting language of the unhappy girl – a language rendered even more touching by the peculiar pathos of her tones, and the searching agony of spirit that burst at intervals through her narrative – we will merely present our readers with a brief summary of what was gleaned from her melancholy disclosure. On bearing her cousin to the bed-room, after the terrifying yell first heard from without the fort, she had flown down the front stairs of the block-house, in the hope of reaching the guard-room in time to acquaint Captain Baynton with what she and Clara had witnessed from their window. Scarcely, however, had she gained the exterior of the building, when she saw that officer descending from a point of the rampart immediately on her left, and almost in a line with the block-house. He was running to overtake and return the ball of the Indian players, which had, at that moment, fallen into the centre of the fort, and was now rolling rapidly away from the spot on which Miss de Haldimar stood. The course of the ball led the pursuing officer out of the reach of her voice; and it was not until he had overtaken and thrown it again over the rampart, she could succeed in claiming his attention. No sooner, however, had he heard her hurried statement, than, without waiting to take the orders of his commanding officer, he prepared to join his guard, and give directions for the immediate closing of the gates. But the opportunity was now lost. The delay occasioned by the chase and recovery of the ball had given the Indians time to approach the gates in a body, while the unsuspicious soldiery looked on without so much as dreaming to prevent them; and Captain Baynton had scarcely moved forward in execution of his purpose, when the yelling fiends were seen already possessing themselves of the drawbridge, and exhibiting every appearance of fierce hostility. Wild, maddened at the sight, the almost frantic Madeline, alive only to her father's danger, rushed back towards the council-room, whence the startling yell from without had already been echoed, and where the tramp of feet, and the clashing of weapons, were distinguishable.

Cut off from his guard, by the rapid inundation of warriors, Captain Baynton had at once seen the futility of all attempts to join the men, and his first impression evidently had been to devote himself to the preservation of the cousins. With this view he turned hastily to Miss de Haldimar, and hurriedly naming the back staircase of the block-house, urged her to direct her flight to that quarter. But the excited girl had neither consideration nor fear for herself; she thought only of her father: and, even while the fierceness of contest was at its height within, she suddenly burst into the council-room. The confusion and horror of the scene that met her eyes no language can render: blood was flowing in every direction, and dying and dead officers, already stripped of their scalps, were lying strewed about the room. Still the survivors fought with all the obstinacy of despair, and many of the Indians had shared the fate of their victims. Miss de Haldimar attempted to reach her father, then vigorously combating with one of the most desperate of the chiefs; but, before she could dart through the intervening crowd, a savage seized her by the hair, and brandished a tomahawk rapidly over her neck. At that moment Captain Baynton sent his glittering blade deep into the heart of the Indian, who, relinquishing his grasp, fell dead at the feet of his intended victim. The devoted officer then threw his left arm around her waist, and, parrying with his sword-arm the blows of those who sought to intercept his flight, dragged his reluctant burden towards the door. Hotly pressed by the remaining officers, nearly equal in number, the Indians were now compelled to turn and defend themselves in front, when Captain Baynton took that opportunity of getting once more into the corridor, not, however, without having received a severe wound immediately behind the right ear, and leaving a skirt and lappel of his uniform in the hands of two savages who had successively essayed to detain him. At that moment the band without had succeeded in forcing open the door of the guard-room; and the officer saw, at a glance, there was little time left for decision. In hurried and imploring accents he besought Miss de Haldimar to forget every thing but her own danger, and to summon resolution to tear herself from the scene: but prayer and entreaty, and even force, were alike employed in vain. Clinging firmly to the rude balustrades, she refused to be led up the staircase, and wildly resisting all his efforts to detach her hands, declared she would again return to the scene of death, in which her beloved parent was so conspicuous an actor. While he was yet engaged in this fruitless attempt to force her from the spot, the door of the council-room was suddenly burst open, and a group of bleeding officers, among whom was Major de Haldimar, followed by their yelling enemies, rushed wildly into the passage, and, at the very foot of the stairs where they yet stood, the combat was renewed. From that moment Miss de Haldimar lost sight of her generous protector. Meanwhile the tumult of execrations, and groans, and yells, was at its height; and one by one she saw the unhappy officers sink beneath weapons yet reeking with the blood of their comrades, until not more than three or four, including her father and the commander of the schooner, were left. At length Major de Haldimar, overcome by exertion, and faint from wounds, while his wild eye darted despairingly on his daughter, had his sword-arm desperately wounded, when the blade dropped to the earth, and a dozen weapons glittered above his head. The wild shriek that had startled Clara then burst from the agonised heart of her maddened cousin, and she darted forward to cover her father's head with her arms. But her senses failed her in the attempt; and the last thing she recollected was falling over the weltering form of Middleton, who pressed her, as she lay there, in the convulsive energy of death, to his almost pulseless heart.

A vague consciousness of being raised from the earth, and borne rapidly through the air, came over her even in the midst of her insensibility, but without any definite perception of the present, or recollection of the past, until she suddenly, when about midway between the fort and the point of wood that led to Chabouiga, opened her eyes, and found herself in the firm grasp of an Indian, whose features, even in the hasty and fearful glance she cast at the countenance, she fancied were not unfamiliar to her. Not another human being was to be seen in the clearing at that moment; for all the savages, including even the women assembled outside, were now within the fort assisting in the complex horrors of murder, fire, and spoliation. In the wild energy of returning reason and despair, the wretched girl struggled violently to free herself; and so far with success, that the Indian, whose strength was evidently fast failing him, was compelled to quit his hold, and suffer her to walk. No sooner did Miss de Haldimar feel her feet touching the ground, when she again renewed her exertions to free herself, and return to the fort; but the Indian held her firmly secured by a leathern thong he now attached to her waist, and every attempt proved abortive. He was evidently much disconcerted at her resistance; and more than once she expected, and almost hoped, the tomahawk at his side would be made to revenge him for the test to which his patience was subjected: but Miss de Haldimar looked in vain for the expression of ferocity and impatience that might have been expected from him at such a moment. There was an air of mournfulness, and even kindness, mingled with severity, on his smooth brow that harmonised ill with the horrible atrocities in which he had, to all appearance, covered as he was with blood, been so recent and prominent an actor. The Indian remarked her surprise; and then looking hurriedly, yet keenly, around, and finding no living being near them, suddenly tore the shirt from his chest, and emphatically pronouncing the names "Oucanasta," "De Haldimar," disclosed to the still struggling captive the bosom of a woman. After which, pointing in the direction of the wood, and finally towards Détroit, she gave Miss de Haldimar to understand that was the course intended to be pursued.

In a moment the resistance of the latter ceased. She at once recognised the young Indian woman whom her cousin had rescued from death: and aware, as she was, of the strong attachment that had subsequently bound her to her preserver, she was at no loss to understand how she might have been led to devote herself to the rescue of one whom, it was probable, she knew to be his affianced wife. Once, indeed, a suspicion of a different nature crossed her mind; for the thought occurred to her she had only been saved from the general doom to be made the victim of private revenge – that it was only to glut the jealous vengeance of the woman at a more deliberative hour, she had been made a temporary captive. The apprehension, however, was no sooner formed than extinguished. Bitterly, deeply as she had reason to abhor the treachery and cunning of the dark race to which her captor belonged, there was an expression of openness and sincerity, and even imploringness, in the countenance of Oucanasta, which, added to her former knowledge of the woman, at once set this fear at rest, inducing her to look upon her rather in the character of a disinterested saviour, than in that of a cruel and vindictive enemy, goaded on to the indulgence of malignant hate by a spirit of rivalry and revenge. Besides, even were her cruellest fears to be realised, what could await her worse than the past? If she could even succeed in getting away, it would only be to return upon certain death; and death only could await her, however refined the tortures accompanying its infliction, in the event of her quietly following and yielding herself up to the guidance of one who offered this slight consolation, at least, that she was of her own sex. But Miss de Haldimar was willing to attribute more generous motives to the Indian; and fortified in her first impression, she signified by signs, that seemed to be perfectly intelligible to her companion, she appreciated her friendly intentions, and confided wholly in her.

No longer checked in her efforts, Oucanasta now directed her course towards the wood, still holding the thong that remained attached to Miss de Haldimar's waist, probably with a view to deceive any individuals from the villages on whom they might chance to fall, into a belief that the English girl was in reality her prisoner. No sooner, however, had they entered the depths of the forest, when, instead of following the path that led to Chabouiga, Oucanasta took a direction to the left, and then moving nearly on a parallel line with the course of the lake, continued her flight as rapidly as the rude nature of the underwood, and the unpractised feet of her companion, would permit. They had travelled in this manner for upwards of four hours, without meeting a breathing thing, or even so much as exchanging a sound between themselves, when, at length, the Indian stopped at the edge of a deep cavern-like excavation in the earth, produced by the tearing up, by the wild tempest, of an enormous pine. Into this she descended, and presently reappeared with several blankets, and two light painted paddles. Then unloosing the thong from the waist of the exhausted girl, she proceeded to disguise her in one of the blankets in the manner already shown, securing it over the head, throat, and shoulders with the badge of captivity, now no longer necessary for her purpose. She then struck off at right angles from the course they had previously pursued; and in less than twenty minutes both stood on the lake shore, apparently at a great distance from the point whence they had originally set out. The Indian gazed for a moment anxiously before her; and then, with an exclamation, evidently meant to convey a sense of pleasure and satisfaction, pointed forward upon the lake. Miss de Haldimar followed, with eager and aching eyes, the direction of her finger, and beheld the well-known schooner evidently urging her flight towards the entrance of the Sinclair. Oh, how her sick heart seemed ready to burst at that moment! When she had last gazed upon it was from the window of her favourite apartment; and even while she held her beloved Clara clasped fondly in her almost maternal embrace, she had dared to indulge the fairest images that ever sprung into being at the creative call of woman's fancy. How bitter had been the reverse! and what incidents to fill up the sad volume of the longest life of sorrow and bereavement had not Heaven awarded her in lieu! In one short hour the weight of a thousand worlds had fallen on and crushed her heart; and when and how was the panacea to be obtained to restore one moment's cessation from suffering to her agonised spirit? Alas! she felt at that moment, that, although she should live a thousand years, the bitterness and desolation of her grief must remain. From the vessel she turned her eyes away upon the distant shore, which it was fast quitting, and beheld a column of mingled flame and smoke towering far above the horizon, and attesting the universal wreck of what had so long been endeared to her as her home. And she had witnessed all this, and yet had strength to survive it!

The courage of the unhappy girl had hitherto been sustained by no effort of volition of her own. From the moment when, discovering a friend in Oucanasta, she had yielded herself unresistingly to the guidance of that generous creature, her feelings had been characterised by an obtuseness strongly in contrast with the high excitement that had distinguished her previous manner. A dreamy recollection of some past horror, it is true, pursued her during her rapid and speechless flight; but any analysis of the causes conducing to that horror, her subjugated faculties were unable to enter upon. Even as one who, under the influence of incipient slumber, rejects the fantastic images that rise successively and indistinctly to the slothful brain, until, at length, they weaken, fade, and gradually die away, leaving nothing but a formless and confused picture of the whole; so was it with Miss de Haldimar. Had she been throughout alive to the keen recollections associated with her flight, she could not have stirred a foot in furtherance of her own safety, even if she would. The mere instinct of self-preservation would never have won one so truly devoted to the generous purpose of her deliverer, had not the temporary stupefaction of her mind prevented all desire of opposition. It is true, in the moment of her discovery of the sex of Oucanasta, she had been able to exercise her reflecting powers; but they were only in connection with the present, and wholly abstract and separate from the past. She had followed her conductor almost without consciousness, and with such deep absorption of spirit, that she neither once conjectured whither they were going, nor what was to be the final issue of their flight. But now, when she stood on the lake shore, suddenly awakened, as if by some startling spell, to every harrowing recollection, and with her attention assisted by objects long endeared, and rendered familiar to her gaze – when she beheld the vessel that had last borne her across the still bosom of the Huron, fleeing for ever from the fortress where her arrival had been so joyously hailed – when she saw that fortress itself presenting the hideous spectacle of a blackened mass of ruins fast crumbling into nothingness – when, in short, she saw nothing but what reminded her of the terrific past, the madness of reason returned, and the desolation of her heart was complete. And then, again, when she thought of her generous, her brave, her beloved, and too unfortunate father, whom she had seen perish at her feet – when she thought of her own gentle Clara, and the sufferings and brutalities to which, if she yet lived, she must inevitably be exposed, and of the dreadful fate of the garrison altogether, the most menial of whom was familiar to her memory, brought up, as she had been, among them from her childhood – when she dwelt on all these things, a faintness, as of death, came over her, and she sank without life on the beach. Of what passed afterwards she had no recollection. She neither knew how she had got into the canoe, nor what means the Indian had taken to secure her approach to the schooner. She had no consciousness of having been removed to the bark of the Canadian, nor did she even remember having risen and gazed through the foliage on the vessel at her side; but she presumed, the chill air of morning having partially restored pulsation, she had moved instinctively from her recumbent position to the spot in which her spectre-like countenance had been perceived by Fuller. The first moment of her returning reason was that when, standing on the deck of the schooner, she found herself so unexpectedly clasped to the heart of her lover.

Twilight had entirely passed away when Miss de Haldimar completed her sad narrative; and already the crew, roused to exertion by the swelling breeze, were once more engaged in weighing the anchor, and setting and trimming the sails of the schooner, which latter soon began to shoot around the concealing headland into the opening of the Sinclair. A deathlike silence prevailed throughout the decks of the little bark, as her bows, dividing the waters of the basin that formed its source, gradually immerged into the current of that deep but narrow river; so narrow, indeed, that from its centre the least active of the mariners might have leaped without difficulty to either shore. This was the most critical part of the dangerous navigation. With a wide sea-board, and full command of their helm, they had nothing to fear; but so limited was the passage of this river, it was with difficulty the yards and masts of the schooner could be kept disengaged from the projecting boughs of the dense forest that lined the adjacent shores to their very junction with the water. The darkness of the night, moreover, while it promised to shield them from the observation of the savages, contributed greatly to perplex their movements; for such was the abruptness with which the river wound itself round in various directions, that it required a man constantly on the alert at the bows to apprise the helmsman of the course he should steer, to avoid collision with the shores. Canopies of weaving branches met in various directions far above their heads, and through these the schooner glided with a silence that might have called up the idea of a Stygian freight. Meanwhile, the men stood anxiously to their guns, concealing the matches in their water-buckets as before; and, while they strained both ear and eye through the surrounding gloom to discover the slightest evidence of danger, grasped the handles of their cutlasses with a firm hand, ready to unsheathe them at the first intimation of alarm.

At the suggestion of the boatswain, who hinted at the necessity of having cleared decks, Captain de Haldimar had prevailed on his unfortunate relatives to retire to the small cabin arranged for their reception; and here they were attended by an aged female, who had long followed the fortunes of the crew, and acted in the twofold character of laundress and sempstress. He himself, with Sir Everard, continued on deck watching the progress of the vessel with an anxiety that became more intense at each succeeding hour. Hitherto their course had been unimpeded, save by the obstacles already enumerated; and they had now, at about an hour before dawn, gained a point that promised a speedy termination to their dangers and perplexities. Before them lay a reach in the river, enveloped in more than ordinary gloom, produced by the continuous weaving of the tops of the overhanging trees; and in the perspective, a gleam of relieving light, denoting the near vicinity of the lake that lay at the opposite extremity of the Sinclair, whose name it also bore. This was the narrowest part of the river; and so approximate were its shores, that the vessel in her course could not fail to come in contact both with the obtruding foliage of the forest and the dense bullrushes skirting the edge of either bank.

"If we get safe through this here place," said the boatswain, in a rough whisper to his anxious and attentive auditors, "I think as how I'll venture to answer for the craft. I can see daylight dancing upon the lake already. Ten minutes more and she will be there." Then turning to the man at the helm, – "Keep her in the centre of the stream, Jim. Don't you see you're hugging the weather shore?"

"It would take the devil himself to tell which is the centre," growled the sailor, in the same suppressed tone. "One might steer with one's eyes shut in such a queer place as this, and never be no worser off than with them open."

"Steady her helm, steady," rejoined Mullins, "it's as dark as pitch, to be sure, but the passage is straight as an arrow, and with a steady helm you can't miss it. Make for the light ahead."

"Abaft there!" hurriedly and loudly shouted the man on the look-out at the bows, "there's a tree lying across the river, and we're just upon it."

While he yet spoke, and before the boatswain could give such instructions as the emergency required, the vessel suddenly struck against the obstacle in question; but the concussion was not of the violent nature that might have been anticipated. The course of the schooner, at no one period particularly rapid, had been considerably checked since her entrance into the gloomy arch, in the centre of which her present accident had occurred; so that it was without immediate injury to her hull and spars she had been thus suddenly brought to. But this was not the most alarming part of the affair. Captain de Haldimar and Sir Everard both recollected, that, in making the same passage, not forty-eight hours previously, they had encountered no obstacle of the kind, and a misgiving of danger rose simultaneously to the hearts of each. It was, however, a thing of too common occurrence in these countries, where storm and tempest were so prevalent and partial, to create more than a mere temporary alarm; for it was quite as probable the barrier had been interposed by some fitful outburst of Nature, as that it arose from design on the part of their enemies: and when the vessel had continued stationary for some minutes, without the prepared and expectant crew discovering the slightest indication of attack, the former impression was preserved by the officers – at least avowedly to those around.

"Bear a hand, my lads, and cut away," at length ordered the boatswain, in a low but clear tone; "half a dozen at each end of the stick, and we shall soon clear a passage for the craft."

A dozen sailors grasped their axes, and hastened forward to execute the command. They sprang lightly from the entangled bows of the schooner, and diverging in equal numbers moved to either extremity of the fallen tree.

"This is sailing through the heart of the American forest with a vengeance," muttered Mullins, whose annoyance at their detention was strongly manifested as he paced up and down the deck. "Shiver my topsails, if it isn't bad enough to clear the Sinclair at any time, much more so when one's running for one's life, and not a whisper's length from one's enemies. Do you know, Captain," abruptly checking his movement, and familiarly placing his hand on the shoulder of De Haldimar, "the last time we sailed through this very reach I couldn't help telling poor Captain Danvers, God rest his soul, what a nice spot it was for an Ingian ambuscade, if they had only gumption enough to think of it."

"Hark!" said the officer, whose heart, eye, and ear were painfully on the alert, "what rustling is that we hear overhead?"

"It's Jack Fuller, no doubt, your honour; I sent him up to clear away the branches from the main topmast rigging." Then raising his head, and elevating his voice, "Hilloa! aloft there!"

The only answer was a groan, followed by a deeper commotion among the rustling foliage.

"Why, what the devil's the matter with you now Jack?" pursued the boatswain, in a voice of angry vehemence.

"Are ye scared at another ghost, and be damned to you, that ye keep groaning there after that fashion?"

At that moment a heavy dull mass was heard tumbling through the upper rigging of the schooner towards the deck, and presently a human form fell at the very feet of the small group, composed of the two officers and the individual who had last spoken.

"A light, a light!" shouted the boatswain; "the foolish chap has lost his hold through fear, and ten to one if he hasn't cracked his skull-piece for his pains. Quick there with a light, and let's see what we can do for him."

The attention of all had been arrested by the sound of the falling weight, and as one of the sailors now advanced, bearing a dark lantern from below, the whole of the crew, with the exception of those employed on the fallen tree, gathered themselves in a knot around the motionless form of the prostrate man. But no sooner had their eyes encountered the object of their interest, when each individual started suddenly and involuntarily back, baring his cutlass, and drawing forth his pistol, the whole presenting a group of countenances strongly marked by various shades of consternation and alarm, even while their attitudes were those of men prepared for some fierce and desperate danger. It was indeed Fuller whom they had beheld, but not labouring, as the boatswain had imagined, under the mere influence of superstitious fear. He was dead, and the blood flowing from a deep wound, inflicted by a sharp instrument in his chest, and the scalped head, too plainly told the manner of his death, and the danger that awaited them all.

A pause ensued, but it was short. Before any one could find words to remark on the horrible circumstance, the appalling war-cry of the savages burst loudly from every quarter upon the ears of the devoted crew. In the desperation of the moment, several of the men clutched their cutlasses between their teeth, and seizing the concealed matches, rushed to their respective stations at the guns. It was in vain the boatswain called out to them, in a voice of stern authority, to desist, intimating that their only protection lay in the reservation of the fire of their batteries. Goaded and excited, beyond the power of resistance, to an impulse that set all subordination at defiance, they applied the matches, and almost at the same instant the terrific discharge of both broadsides took place, rocking the vessel to the water's edge, and reverberating, throughout, the confined space in which she lay, like the deadly explosion of some deeply excavated mine.

Scarcely had the guns been fired, when the seamen became sensible of their imprudence. The echoes were yet struggling to force a passage through the dense forest, when a second yell of the Indians announced the fiercest joy and triumph, unmixed by disaster, at the result; and then the quick leaping of many forms could be heard, as they divided the crashing underwood, and rushed forward to close with their prey. It was evident, from the difference of sound, their first cry had been pealed forth while lying prostrate on the ground, and secure from the bullets, whose harmless discharge that cry was intended to provoke; for now the voices seemed to rise progressively from the earth, until they reached the level of each individual height, and were already almost hotly breathing in the ears of those they were destined to fill with illimitable dismay.

"Shiver my topsails, but this comes of disobeying orders," roared the boatswain, in a voice of mingled anger and vexation. "The Ingians are quite as cunning as ourselves, and arn't to be frighted that way. Quick, every cutlass and pistol to his gangway, and let's do our best. Pass the word forward for the axemen to return to quarters."

Recovered from their first paroxysm of alarm, the men at length became sensible of the presence of a directing power, which, humble as it was, their long habits of discipline had taught them to respect, and, headed on the one side by Captain de Haldimar, and on the other by Sir Everard Valletort, neither of whom, however, entertained the most remote chance of success, flew, as commanded, to their respective gangways. The yell of the Indians had again ceased, and all was hushed into stillness; but as the anxious and quicksighted officers gazed over the bulwarks, they fancied they could perceive, even through the deep gloom that every where prevailed, the forms of men, resting in cautious and eager attitudes, on the very verge of the banks, and at a distance of little more than half pistol shot. Every heart beat with expectancy, – every eye was riveted intently in front, to watch and meet the first movements of their foes, but not a sound of approach was audible to the equally attentive ear. In this state of aching suspense they might have continued about five minutes, when suddenly their hearts were made to quail by a third cry, that came, not as previously, from the banks of the river, but from the very centre of their own decks, and from the topmast and riggings of the schooner. So sudden and unexpected too was this fresh danger, that before the two parties had time to turn, and assume a new posture of defence, several of them had already fallen under the butchering blades of their enemies. Then commenced a desperate but short conflict, mingled with yellings, that again were answered from every point; and rapidly gliding down the pendant ropes, were to be seen the active and dusky forms of men, swelling the number of the assailants, who had gained the deck in the same noiseless manner, until resistance became almost hopeless.

"Ha! I hear the footsteps of our lads at last," exclaimed Mullins exultingly to his comrades, as he finished despatching a third savage with his sturdy weapon. "Quick, men, quick, up with hatchet and cutlass, and take them in the rear. If we are to die, let's die —— " game, he would perhaps have added, but death arrested the word upon his lips; and his corpse rolled along the deck, until its further progress was stopped by the stiffened body of the unhappy Fuller.

Notwithstanding the fall of their brave leader, and the whoopings of their enemies, the flagging spirits of the

men were for a moment excited by the announcement of
the return even of the small force of the axemen, and they
defended themselves with a courage and determination
worthy of a better result; but when, by the lurid light of the
torches, now lying burning about the decks, they turned
and beheld not their companions, but a fresh band of
Indians, at whose pouch-belts dangled the reeking scalps
of their murdered friends, they at once relinquished the
combat as hopeless, and gave themselves unresistingly up
to be bound by their captors.

Meanwhile the cousins experienced a renewal of all
those horrors from which their distracted minds had been
temporarily relieved; and, petrified with alarm, as they lay
in the solitary berth that contained them both, endured
sufferings infinitely more terrible than death itself. The
early part of the tumult they had noticed almost without
comprehending its cause, and but for the terrific cry of the
Indians that had preceded them, would have mistaken the
deafening broadsides for the blowing up of the vessel, so
tremendous and violent had been the concussion. Nay,
there was a moment when Miss de Haldimar felt a pang of
deep disappointment and regret at the misconception; for,
with the fearful recollection of past events, so strongly
impressed on her bleeding heart, she could not but acknowledge, that to be engulfed in one general and disastrous explosion, was mercy compared with the alternative
of falling into the hands of those to whom her loathing
spirit had been too fatally taught to deny even the com-
monest attributes of humanity. As for Clara, she had not
the power to think, or to form a conjecture on the subject:
– she was merely sensible of a repetition of the horrible
scenes from which she had so recently been snatched, and
with a pale cheek, a fixed eye, and an almost pulseless
heart, lay without motion in the inner side of the berth.
The piteous spectacle of her cousin's alarm lent a forced
activity to the despair of Miss de Haldimar, in whom
apprehension produced that strong energy of excitement
that sometimes gives to helplessness the character of true

courage. With the increasing clamour of appalling conflict on deck, this excitement grew at every moment stronger, until it finally became irrepressible, so that at length, when through the cabin windows there suddenly streamed a flood of yellow light, extinguishing that of the lamp that threw its flickering beams around the cabin, she flung herself impetuously from the berth, and, despite of the aged and trembling female who attempted to detain her, burst open the narrow entrance to the cabin, and rushed up the steps communicating with the deck.

The picture that here met her eyes was at once graphic and fearful in the extreme. On either side of the river lines of streaming torches were waved by dusky warriors high above their heads, reflecting the grim countenances, not only of those who bore them, but of dense groups in their rear, whose numbers were alone concealed by the foliage of the forest in which they stood. From the branches that wove themselves across the centre of the river, and the topmast and rigging of the vessel, the same strong yellow light, produced by the bark of the birch tree steeped in gum, streamed down upon the decks below, rendering each line and block of the schooner as distinctly visible as if it had been noon on the sunniest of those far distant lakes. The deck itself was covered with the bodies of slain men – sailors, and savages mixed together; and amid these were to be seen fierce warriors, reclining triumphantly and indolently on their rifles, while others were occupied in securing the arms of their captives with leathern thongs behind their backs. The silence that now prevailed was strongly in contrast with, and even more fearful than, the horrid shouts by which it had been preceded; and, but for the ghastly countenances of the captives, and the quick rolling eyes of the savages, Miss de Haldimar might have imagined herself the sport of some extraordinary and exciting illusion. Her glance over these prominent features in the tragedy had been cursory, yet accurate. It now rested on one that had more immediate and terrifying interest for herself. At a few paces in front of the companion ladder, and with their backs turned towards her, stood two individuals, whose attitudes denoted the purpose of men resolved to sell with their lives alone a passage to a tall fierce-looking savage, whose countenance betrayed every mark of triumphant and deadly passion, while he apparently hesitated whether his uplifted arm should stay the weapon it wielded. These individuals were Captain de Haldimar and Sir Everard Valletort; and to the former of these the attention of the savage was more immediately and exultingly directed; so much so, indeed, that Miss de Haldimar thought she could read in the ferocious expression of his features the death-warrant of her cousin. In the wild terror of the moment she gave a piercing scream that was answered by a hundred yelling voices, and rushing between her lover and his enemy, threw herself wildly and supplicatingly at the feet of the latter. Uttering a savage laugh, the monster spurned her from him with his foot, when, quick as thought, a pistol was discharged within a few inches of his face; but with a rapidity equal to that of his assailant, he bent aside his head, and the ball passed harmlessly on. The yell that followed was terrific; and while it was yet swelling into fulness, Captain de Haldimar felt an iron hand furiously grappling his throat, and, ere the grasp was relinquished, he again stood the bound and passive victim of the warrior of the Fleur de lis.

Three

THE INTERVAL that succeeded to the last council-scene of the Indians was passed by the officers of Détroit in a state of inexpressible anxiety and doubt. The fears entertained for the fate of their companions, who had set out in the perilous and almost forlorn hope of reaching Michillimackinac, in time to prevent the consummation of the threatened treachery, had, in some degree, if not wholly, been allayed by the story narrated by the Ottawa chief. It was evident, from his statement, the party had again met, and been engaged in fearful struggle with the gigantic warrior they had all so much reason to recollect; and it was equally apparent, that in that struggle they had been successful. But still, so many obstacles were likely to be opposed to their navigation of the several lakes and rivers over which lay their course, it was almost feared, even if they eventually escaped unharmed themselves, they could not possibly reach the fort in time to communicate the danger that awaited their friends. It is true, the time gained by Governor de Haldimar on the first occasion had afforded a considerable interval, of which advantage might be taken; but it was also, on the other hand, uncertain whether Ponteac had commanded the same delay in the council of the chiefs investing Michilli-mackinac, to which he had himself assented. Three days were sufficient to enable an Indian warrior to perform the journey by land; and it was chiefly on this vague and uncertain ground they based whatever little of hope was entertained on the subject.

It had been settled at the departure of the adventurers, that the instant they effected a communication with the schooner on Lake Huron, François should be immediately sent back, with instructions so to contrive the period of his return, that his canoe should make its appearance soon after daybreak at the nearest extremity of Hog Island, the position of which has been described in our introductory chapter. From this point a certain signal, that could be easily distinguished with the aid of a telescope, was to be made from the canoe, which, without being of a nature to attract the attention of the savages, was yet to be such as could not well be mistaken by the garrison. This was a precaution adopted, not only with the view of giving the earliest intimation of the result of the enterprise, but lest the Canadian should be prevented, by any closer investment on the part of the Indians, from communicating personally with the fort in the way he had been accustomed.

It will easily be comprehended therefore, that, as the period approached when they might reasonably look for the return of François, if he should return at all, the nervous anxiety of the officers became more and more developed. Upwards of a week had elapsed since the departure of their friends; and already, for the last day or two, their impatience had led them, at early dawn, and with beating hearts, to that quarter of the rampart which overlooked the eastern extremity of Hog Island. Hitherto, however, their eager watching had been in vain. As far as our recollection of the Canadian tradition of this story serves us, it must have been on the fourth night after the final discomfiture of the plans of Ponteac, and the tenth from the departure of the adventurers, that the officers were assembled in the mess-room, partaking of the scanty and frugal supper to which their long confinement had reduced them. The subject of their conversation, as it was ever of their thoughts, was the probable fate of their companions; and many and various, although all equally melancholy, were the conjectures offered as to the result. There was on the countenance of each, that deep and fixed expression of gloom, which, if it did not indicate any unmanliness of despair, told at least that hope was nearly extinct: but more especially was this remarkable in the young but sadly altered Charles de Haldimar, who, with a vacant eye and a pre-occupied manner, seemed wholly abstracted from the scene before him.

All was silence in the body of the fort. The men off duty had long since retired to rest in their clothes, and only the "All's well!" of the sentinels was heard at intervals of a quarter of an hour, as the cry echoed from mouth to mouth in the line of circuit. Suddenly, however, between two of those intervals, and during a pause in the languid conversation of the officers, the sharp challenge of a sentinel was heard, and then quick steps on the rampart, as of men hastening to the point whence the challenge had been given. The officers, whom this new excitement seemed to arouse into fresh activity, hurriedly quitted the room; and, with as little noise as possible, gained the spot where the voice had been heard. Several men were bending eagerly over the rampart, and, with their muskets at the recover, riveting their gaze on a dark and motionless object that lay on the verge of the ditch immediately beneath them.

"What have you here, Mitchell?" asked Captain Blessington, who was in command of the guard, and who had recognised the gruff voice of the veteran in the challenge just given.

"An American burnt log, your honour," muttered the soldier, "if one was to judge from its stillness; but if it is, it must have rolled there within the last minute; for I'll take my affidavy it wasn't here when I passed last in my beat."

"An American burnt log, indeed! it's some damned rascal of a spy, rather," remarked Captain Erskine. "Who knows but it may be our big friend, come to pay us a visit again? And yet he is not half long enough for him, either.

Can't you try and tickle him with the bayonet, any of you fellows, and see whether he is made of flesh and blood?"

Although this observation was made almost without object, it being totally impossible for any musket, even with the addition of its bayonet, to reach more than half way across the ditch, the several sentinels threw themselves on their chests, and, stretching over the rampart as far as possible, made the attempt to reach the suspicious looking object that lay beyond. No sooner, however, had their arms been extended in such a manner as to be utterly powerless, when the dark mass was seen to roll away in an opposite direction, and with such rapidity that, before the men could regain their feet and level their muskets, it had entirely disappeared from their view.

"Cleverly managed, to give the red skin his due," half laughingly observed Captain Erskine, while his brother officers continued to fix their eyes in astonishment on the spot so recently occupied by the strange object; "but what the devil could be his motive for lying there so long? Not playing the eaves-dropper, surely; and yet, if he meant to have picked off a sentinel, what was to have prevented him from doing it sooner?"

"He had evidently no arms," said Ensign Delme.

"No, nor legs either, it would appear," resumed the literal Erskine. "Curse me if I ever saw any thing in the shape of a human form bundled together in that manner."

"I mean he had no fire-arms – no rifle," pursued Delme.

"And if he had, he certainly would have rifled one of us of a life," continued the captain, laughing at his own conceit. "But come, the bird is flown, and we have only to thank ourselves for having been so egregiously duped. Had Valletort been here, he would have given a different account of him."

"Hist! listen!" exclaimed Lieutenant Johnstone, calling the attention of the party to a peculiar and low sound in the direction in which the supposed Indian had departed.

It was repeated, and in a plaintive tone, indicating a

desire to propitiate. Soon afterwards a human form was seen advancing slowly, but without show either of conceal-ment or hostility in its movements. It finally remained stationary on the spot where the dark and shapeless mass had been first perceived.

"Another Oucanasta for De Haldimar, no doubt," ob-served Captain Erskine, after a moment's pause. "These grenadiers carry every thing before them as well in love as in war."

The error of the good-natured officer was, however, obvious to all but himself. The figure, which was now distinctly traced in outline for that of a warrior, stood boldly and fearlessly on the brink of the ditch, holding up its left arm, in the hand of which dangled something that was visible in the starlight, and pointing energetically to this pendant object with the other.

A voice from one of the party now addressed the Indian in two several dialects, but without eliciting a reply. He either understood not, or would not answer the question proposed, but continued pointing significantly to the in-distinct object which he still held forth in an elevated position.

"The governor must be apprised of this," observed Captain Blessington to De Haldimar, who was his subalt-ern of the guard. "Hasten, Charles, to acquaint your fa-ther, and receive his orders."

The young officer willingly obeyed the injunction of his superior. A secret and indefinable hope rushed through his mind, that as the Indian came not in hostility, he might be the bearer of some communication from their friends; and he moved rapidly towards that part of the building occu-pied by his father.

The light of a lamp suspended over the piazza leading to the governor's rooms reflecting strongly on his regi-mentals, he passed unchallenged by the sentinels posted there, and uninterruptedly gained a door that opened on a narrow passage, at the further extremity of which was the sitting-room usually occupied by his parent. This again was entered from the same passage by a second door, the upper part of which was of common glass, enabling any one on the outside to trace with facility every object within when the place was lighted up.

A glance was sufficient to satisfy the youth his father was not in the room; although there was strong evidence he had not retired for the night. In the middle of the floor stood an oaken table, and on this lay an open writing desk, with a candle on each side, the wicks of which had burnt so long as to throw a partial gloom over the surrounding wainscotting. Scattered about the table and desk were a number of letters that had apparently been just looked at or read; and in the midst of these an open case of red morocco, containing a miniature. The appearance of these letters, thus left scattered about by one who was scrupulously exact in the arrangement of his papers, added to the circumstance of the neglected and burning candles, confirmed the young officer in an impression that his father, overcome by fatigue, had retired into his bedroom, and fallen unconsciously asleep. Imagining, therefore, he could not, without difficulty, succeed in making himself heard, and deeming the urgency of the case required it, he determined to wave the usual ceremony of knocking, and penetrate to his father's bedroom unannounced. The glass door being without fastening within, easily yielded to his pressure of the latch; but as he passed by the table, a strong and natural feeling of curiosity induced him to cast his eye upon the miniature. To his infinite surprise, nay, almost terror, he discovered it was that of his mother – the identical portrait which his sister Clara had worn in her bosom from infancy, and which he had seen clasped around her neck on the very deck of the schooner in which she sailed for Michillimackinac. He felt there could be no mistake, for only one miniature of the sort had ever been in possession of the family, and that the one just accounted for. Almost stupified at what he saw, and scarcely crediting the evidence of his senses, the young officer glanced his eye hurriedly along one of the open letters that lay around. It was in the well remembered hand-writing of his mother, and commenced, "Dear, dearest *Reginald*." After this followed expressions of endearment no woman might address except to an affianced lover, or the husband of her choice; and his heart sickened while he read. Scarcely, however, had he scanned half a dozen lines, when it occurred to him he was violating some secret of his parents; and, discontinuing the perusal with effort, he prepared to acquit himself of his mission.

On raising his eyes from the paper he was startled by the appearance of his father, who, with a stern brow and a quivering lip, stood a few paces from the table, apparently too much overcome by his indignation to be able to utter a sentence.

Charles de Haldimar felt all the awkwardness of his position. Some explanation of his conduct, however, was necessary; and he stammered forth the fact of the portrait having riveted his attention, from its striking resemblance to that in his sister's possession.

"And to what do these letters bear resemblance?" demanded the governor, in a voice that trembled in its attempt to be calm, while he fixed his penetrating eye on that of his son. "*They*, it appears, were equally objects of attraction with you."

"The letters were in the hand-writing of my mother; and I was irresistibly led to glance at one of them," replied the youth, with the humility of conscious wrong. "The action was involuntary, and no sooner committed than repented of. I am here, my father, on a mission of importance, which must account for my presence."

"A mission of importance!" repeated the governor, with more of sorrow than of anger in the tone in which he now spoke. "On what mission are you here, if it be not to intrude unwarrantably on a parent's privacy?"

The young officer's cheek flushed high, as he proudly answered: – "I was sent by Captain Blessington, sir, to take your orders in regard to an Indian who is now without the fort under somewhat extraordinary circumstances, yet evidently without intention of hostility. It is supposed he bears some message from my brother."

The tone of candour and offended pride in which this formal announcement of duty was made seemed to banish all suspicion from the mind of the governor; and he remarked, in a voice that had more of the kindness that had latterly distinguished his address to his son, "Was this, then, Charles, the *only* motive for your abrupt intrusion at this hour? Are you sure no inducement of private curiosity was mixed up with the discharge of your duty, that you entered thus unannounced? You must admit, at least, I found you employed in a manner different from what the urgency of your mission would seem to justify."

There was lurking irony in this speech; yet the softened accents of his father, in some measure, disarmed the youth of the bitterness he would have flung into his observation, – "That no man on earth, his parent excepted, should have dared to insinuate such a doubt with impunity."

For a moment Colonel de Haldimar seemed to regard his son with a surprised but satisfied air, as if he had not expected the manifestation of so much spirit, in one whom he had been accustomed greatly to undervalue.

"I believe you, Charles," he at length observed; "forgive the justifiable doubt, and think no more of the subject. Yet, one word," as the youth was preparing to depart; "you have read that letter" (and he pointed to that which had principally arrested the attention of the officer): "what impression has it given you of your mother? Answer me sincerely. *My* name," and his faint smile wore something of the character of triumph, "is not *Reginald*, you know."

The pallid cheek of the young man flushed at this question. His own undisguised impression was, that his mother had cherished a guilty love for another than her husband. He felt the almost impiety of such a belief, but he could not resist the conviction that forced itself on his mind; the letter in her handwriting spoke for itself; and though the idea was full of wretchedness, he was unable to conquer it.

Whatever his own inference might be, however, he could not endure the thought of imparting it to his father; he, therefore, answered evasively.

"Doubtless my mother had some dear relative of the name, and to him was this letter addressed; perhaps a brother, or an uncle. But I never knew," he pursued, with a look of appeal to his father, "that a second portrait of my mother existed. This is the very counter-part of Clara's."

"It may be the same," remarked the governor, but in a tone of indecision, that denied his faith in what he uttered.

"Impossible, my father. I accompanied Clara, if you recollect, as far as Lake Sinclair; and when I quitted the deck of the schooner to return, I particularly remarked my sister wore her mother's portrait, as usual, round her neck."

"Well, no matter about the portrait," hurriedly rejoined the governor; "yet, whatever your impression, Charles," and he spoke with a warmth that was far from habitual to him, "dare not to sully the memory of your mother by a doubt of her purity. An accident has given this letter to your inspection, but breathe not its contents to a human creature; above all, respect the being who gave you birth. Go, tell Captain Blessington to detain the Indian; I will join you immediately."

Strongly, yet confusedly, impressed with the singularity of the scene altogether, and more particularly with his father's strange admonition, the young officer quitted the room, and hastened to rejoin his companions. On reaching the rampart he found that the Indian, during his long absence, had departed; yet not without depositing, on the outer edge of the ditch, the substance to which he had previously directed their attention. At the moment of De Haldimar's approach, the officers were bending over the rampart, and, with straining eyes, endeavouring to make out what it was, but in vain; something was just perceptible in the withered turf, but what that something was no one could succeed in discovering.

"Whatever this be, we must possess ourselves of it,"

said Captain Blessington: "it is evident, from the energetic manner of him who left it, it is of importance. I think I know who is the best swimmer and climber of our party."

Several voices unanimously pronounced the name of "Johnstone."

"Any thing for a dash of enterprise," said that officer, whose slight wound had been perfectly healed. "But what do you propose that the swimmer and climber should do, Blessington?"

"Secure yon parcel, without lowering the drawbridge."

"What! and be scalped in the act? Who knows if it be not a trick after all, and that the rascal who placed it there is not lying within a few feet, ready to pounce upon me the instant I reach the bank."

"Never mind," said Erskine, laughingly, "we will revenge your death, my boy."

"Besides, consider the *nunquam non paratus*, Johnstone," slily remarked Lieutenant Leslie.

"What, again, Leslie?" energetically responded the young Scotsman. "Yet think not I hesitate, for I did but jest: make fast a rope round my loins, and I think I will answer for the result."

Colonel de Haldimar now made his appearance. Having heard a brief statement of the facts, and approving of the suggestion of Captain Blessington, a rope was procured, and made fast under the shoulders of the young officer, who had previously stripped himself of his uniform and shoes. He then suffered himself to drop gently over the edge of the rampart, his companions gradually lowering the rope, until a deep and gasping aspiration, such as is usually wrung from one coming suddenly in contact with cold water, announced he had gained the surface of the ditch. The rope was then slackened, to give him the unrestrained command of his limbs; and in the next instant he was seen clambering up the opposite elevation.

Although the officers, indulging in a forced levity, in a great degree meant to encourage their companion, had treated his enterprise with indifference, they were far from being without serious anxiety for the result. They had laughed at the idea, suggested by him, of being scalped; whereas, in truth, they entertained the apprehension far more powerfully than he did himself. The artifices resorted to by the savages, to secure an isolated victim, were so many and so various, that suspicion could not but attach to the mysterious occurrence they had just witnessed. Willing even as they were to believe their present visitor, whoever he was, came not in a spirit of enmity, they could not altogether divest themselves of a fear that it was only a subtle artifice to decoy one of them within the reach of their traitorous weapons. They, therefore, watched the movements of their companion with quickening pulses; and it was with a lively satisfaction they saw him, at length, after a momentary search, descend once more into the ditch, and, with a single powerful impulsion of his limbs, urge himself back to the foot of the rampart. Neither feet nor hands were of much service, in enabling him to scale the smooth and slanting logs that composed the exterior surface of the works; but a slight jerk of the well secured rope, serving as a signal to his friends, he was soon dragged once more to the summit of the rampart, without other injury than a couple of slight bruises.

"Well, what success?" eagerly asked Leslie and Captain Erskine in the same breath, as the dripping Johnstone buried himself in the folds of a capacious cloak procured during his absence.

"You shall hear," was the reply; "but first, gentlemen, allow me, if you please, to enjoy, with yourselves, the luxury of dry clothes. I have no particular ambition to contract an American ague fit just now; yet, unless you take pity on me, and reserve my examination for a future moment, there is every probability I shall not have a tooth left by to-morrow morning."

No one could deny the justice of the remark, for the teeth of the young man were chattering as he spoke. It was not, therefore, until after he had changed his dress, and swallowed a couple of glasses of Captain Erskine's never failing spirit, that they all repaired once more to the mess-room, when Johnstone anticipated all questions, by the production of the mysterious packet.

After removing several wrappers of bark, each of which was secured by a thong of deerskin, Colonel de Haldimar, to whom the successful officer had handed his prize, at length came to a small oval case of red morocco, precisely similar, in size and form, to that which had so recently attracted the notice of his son. For a moment he hesitated, and his cheek was observed to turn pale, and his hand to tremble; but quickly subduing his indecision, he hurriedly unfastened the clasp, and disclosed to the astonished view of the officers the portrait of a young and lovely woman, habited in the Highland garb.

Exclamations of various kinds burst from the lips of the group of officers. Several knew it to be the portrait of Mrs. de Haldimar; others recognised it from the striking likeness it bore to Clara and to Charles; all knew it had never been absent from the possession of the former since her mother's death; and feeling satisfied as they did that its extraordinary appearance among them, at the present moment, was an announcement of some dreadful disaster, their countenances wore an impress of dismay little inferior to that of the wretched Charles, who, agonized beyond all attempt at description, had thrown himself into a seat in the rear of the group, and sat like one bewildered, with his head buried in his hands.

"Gentlemen," at length observed Colonel de Haldimar, in a voice that proved how vainly his natural emotion was sought to be subdued by his pride, "this, I fear me, is an unwelcome token. It comes to announce to a father the murder of his child; to us all, the destruction of our last remaining friends and comrades."

"God forbid!" solemnly aspirated Captain Blessington. After a pause of a moment or two he pursued: "I know not why, sir; but my impression is, the appearance of this portrait, which we all recognise for that worn by Miss de Haldimar, bears another interpretation."

Colonel de Haldimar shook his head. – "I have but too much reason to believe," he observed, smiling in mournful bitterness, "it has been conveyed to us not in mercy but in revenge."

No one ventured to question why; for notwithstanding all were aware that in the mysterious ravisher of the wife of Halloway Colonel de Haldimar had a fierce and inexorable private enemy, no allusion had ever been made by that officer himself to the subject.

"Will you permit me to examine the portrait and envelopes, Colonel?" resumed Captain Blessington: "I feel almost confident, although I confess I have no other motive for it than what springs from a recollection of the manner of the Indian, that the result will bear me out in my belief the bearer came not in hostility but in friendship."

"By my faith, I quite agree with Blessington," said Captain Erskine; "for, in addition to the manner of the Indian, there is another evidence in favour of his position. Was it merely intended in the light in which you consider it, Colonel, the case or the miniature itself might have been returned, but certainly not the metal in which it is set. The savages are fully aware of the value of gold, and would not so easily let it slip through their fingers."

"And wherefore thus carefully wrapped up?" remarked Lieutenant Johnstone, "unless it had been intended it should meet with no injury on the way. I certainly think the portrait never would have been conveyed, in its present perfect state, by an enemy."

"The fellow seemed to feel, too, that he came in the character of one whose intentions claimed all immunity from harm," remarked Captain Wentworth. "He surely never would have stood so fearlessly on the brink of the ditch, and within pistol shot, had he not been conscious of rendering some service to those connected with us."

To these several observations of his officers, Colonel de Haldimar listened attentively; and although he made no reply, it was evident he felt gratified at the eagerness with which each sought to remove the horrible impression he had stated to have existed in his own mind. Meanwhile, Captain Blessington had turned and examined the miniature in fifty different ways, but without succeeding in discovering any thing that could confirm him in his original impression. Vexed and disappointed, he at length flung it from him on the table, and sinking into a seat at the side of the unfortunate Charles, pressed the hand of the youth in significant silence.

Finding his worst fears now confirmed, Colonel de Haldimar, for the first time, cast a glance towards his son, whose drooping head, and sorrowing attitude, spoke volumes to his heart. For a moment his own cheek blanched, and his eye was seen to glisten with the first tear ever witnessed there by those around him. Subduing his emotion, however, he drew up his person to its lordly height, as if that act reminded him the commander was not to be lost in the father, and quitting the room with a heavy brow and step, recommended to his officers the repose of which they appeared to stand so much in need. But not one was there who felt inclined to court the solitude of his pillow. No sooner were the footsteps of the governor heard dying away in the distance, when fresh lights were ordered, and several logs of wood heaped on the slackening fire. Around this the officers now grouped, and throwing themselves back in their chairs, assumed the attitudes of men seeking to indulge rather in private reflection than in personal converse.

The grief of the wretched Charles de Haldimar, hitherto restrained by the presence of his father, and encouraged by the touching evidences of interest afforded him by the ever-considerate Blessington, now burst forth audibly. No attempt was made by the latter officer to check the emotion of his young friend. Knowing his passionate fondness for his sister, he was not without fear that the sudden shock produced by the appearance of her miniature might destroy his reason, even if it affected not his life; and as the moment was now come when tears might be shed without exciting invidious remark in the only individual who was likely to make it, he sought to promote them as much as possible. Too much occupied in their own mournful reflections to bestow more than a passing notice on the weakness of their friend, the group round the fire-place scarcely seemed to have regarded his emotion.

This violent paroxysm past, De Haldimar breathed more freely; and, after listening to several earnest observations of Captain Blessington, who still held out the possibility of something favourable turning up, on a re-examination of the portrait by daylight, he was so far composed as to be able to attend to the summons of the sergeant of the guard, who came to say the relief were ready, and waiting to be inspected before they finally marched off. Clasping the extended hand of his captain between his own, with a pressure indicative of his deep gratitude, De Haldimar now proceeded to the discharge of his duty; and having caught up the portrait, which still lay on the table, and thrust it into the breast of his uniform, he repaired hurriedly to rejoin his guard, from which circumstances alone had induced his unusually long absence.

Four

THE REMAINDER of that night was passed by the unhappy De Haldimar in a state of indescribable wretchedness. After inspecting the relief, he had thrown himself on his rude guard-bed; and, drawing his cloak over his eyes, given full rein to the wanderings of his excited imagination. It was in vain the faithful old Morrison, who never suffered his master to mount a guard without finding some one with whom to exchange his tour of duty, when he happened not to be in orders himself, repeatedly essayed, as he sat stirring the embers of the fire, to enter into conversation with him. The soul of the young officer was sick, past the endurance even of that kind voice; and, more than once, he impetuously bade him be silent, if he wished to continue where he was; or, if not, to join his comrades in the next guard-room. A sigh was the only respectful but pained answer to these sharp remonstrances; and De Haldimar, all absorbed even as he was in his own grief, felt it deeply; for he knew the old man loved him, and he could not bear the idea of appearing to repay with slight the well-intentioned efforts of one whom he had always looked upon more as a dependant on his family than as the mere rude soldier. Still he could not summon courage to disclose the true nature of his grief, which the other merely ascribed to general causes and vague apprehensions of a yet unaccomplished evil. Morrison had ever loved his sister with an affection in no way inferior to that which he bore towards himself. He had also nursed her in childhood; and his memory was ever faithful to trace, as his tongue was to dwell on, those gentle and amiable qualities, which, strongly marked at an earlier period of her existence, had only undergone change, inasmuch as they had become matured and more forcibly developed in womanhood. Often, latterly, had the grey-haired veteran been in the habit of alluding to her; for he saw the subject was one that imparted a mournful satisfaction to the youth; and, with a tact that years, more than deep reading of the human heart, had given him, he ever made a point of adverting to their re-union as an event admitting not of doubt.

Hitherto the affectionate De Haldimar had loved to listen to these sounds of comfort; for, although they carried no conviction to his mind, impressed as he was with the terrible curse of Ellen Halloway, and the consequent belief that his family were devoted to some fearful doom, still they came soothingly and unctuously to his sick soul; and, all deceptive even as he felt them to be, he found they created a hope which, while certain to be dispelled by calm after-reflection, carried a momentary solace to his afflicted spirit. But, now that he had every evidence his adored sister was no more, and that the illusion of hope was past for ever, to have heard her name even mentioned by one who, ignorant of the fearful truth the events of that night had elucidated, was still ready to renew a strain every chord of which had lost its power of harmony, was repugnant beyond bearing to his heart. At one moment he resolved briefly to acquaint the old man with the dreadful fact, but unwillingness to give pain prevented him; and, moreover, he felt the grief the communication would draw from the faithful servitor of his family must be of so unchecked a nature as to render his own sufferings even more poignant than they were. Neither had he (independently of all other considerations) resolution enough to forego the existence of hope in another, even although it had passed entirely away from himself. It was for these reasons he had so harshly and (for him) unkindly checked the attempt of the old man at a conversation which he, at every moment, felt would be made to turn on the ill-fated Clara.

Miserable as he felt his position to be, it was not without satisfaction he again heard the voice of his serjeant summoning him to the inspection of another relief. This duty performed, and anxious to avoid the paining presence of his servant, he determined, instead of returning to his guard-room, to consume the hour that remained before day in pacing the ramparts. Leaving word with his subordinate, that, in the event of his being required, he might be found without difficulty, he ascended to that quarter of the works where the Indian had been first seen who had so mysteriously conveyed the sad token he still retained in his breast. It was on the same side with that particular point whence we have already stated a full view of the bridge with its surrounding scenery, together with the waters of the Détroit, where they were intersected by Hog Island, were distinctly commanded. At either of those points was stationed a sentinel, whose duty it was to extend his beat between the boxes used now rather as lines of demarcation than as places of temporary shelter, until each gained that of his next comrade, when they again returned to their own, crossing each other about half way: a system of precaution pursued by the whole of the sentinels in the circuit of the rampart.

The ostensible motive of the officer in ascending the works, was to visit his several posts; but no sooner had he found himself between the points alluded to, which happened to be the first in his course, than he seemed to be riveted there by a species of fascination. Not that there was any external influence to produce this effect, for the utmost stillness reigned both within and around the fort; and, but for the howling of some Indian wolf-dog in the distance, or the low and monotonous beat of their drums in the death-dance, there was nought that gave evidence of the existence of the dreadful enemy by whom they were beset. But the whole being of the acutely suffering De Haldimar was absorbed in recollections connected with the spot on which he stood. At one extremity was the point whence he had witnessed the dreadful tragedy of Halloway's death; at the other, that on which had been deposited the but too unerring record of the partial realisation of the horrors threatened at the termination of that tragedy; and whenever he attempted to pass each of these boundaries, he felt as if his limbs repugned the effort.

In the sentinels, his appearance among them excited but little surprise; for it was no uncommon thing for the officers of the guard to spend the greatest part of the night in visiting, in turn, the several more exposed points of the ramparts; and that it was now confined to one particular part, seemed not even to attract their notice. It was, therefore, almost wholly unremarked by his men, that the heart-stricken De Haldimar paced his quick and uncertain walk with an imagination filled with the most fearful forebodings, and with a heart throbbing with the most painful excitement. Hitherto, since the discovery of the contents of the packet, his mind had been so exclusively absorbed in stupifying grief for his sister, that his perception seemed utterly incapable of outstepping the limited sphere drawn around it; but now, other remembrances, connected with the localities, forced themselves upon his attention; and although, in all these, there was nothing that was not equally calculated to carry dismay and sorrow to his heart, still, in dividing his thoughts with the one supreme agony that bowed him down, they were rather welcomed than discarded. His mind was as a wheel, embracing grief within grief, multiplied to infinitude; and the wider and more diffusive the circle, the less powerful was the concentration of sickening heart and brain on that which was the more immediate axis of the whole.

Reminded, for the first time, as he pursued his measured but aimless walk, by the fatal portrait which he more than once pressed with feverish energy to his lips, of the singular discovery he had made that night in the apartments of his father, he was naturally led, by a chain of consecutive thought, into a review of the whole of the extraordinary scene. The fact of the existence of a second likeness of his mother was one that did not now fail to re-awaken all the unqualified surprise he had experienced at the first discovery. So far from having ever heard his father make the slightest allusion to this memorial of his departed mother, he perfectly recollected his repeatedly recommending to Clara the safe custody of a treasure, which, if lost, could never be replaced. What could be the motive for this mystery? – and why had he sought to impress him with the belief it was the identical portrait worn by his sister which had so unintentionally been exposed to his view? Why, too, had he evinced so much anxiety to remove from his mind all unfavourable impressions in regard to his mother? Why have been so energetic in his caution not to suffer a taint of impurity to attach to her memory? Why should he have supposed the possibility of such impression, unless there had been sufficient cause for it? In what, moreover, originated his triumphant expression of feature, when, on that occasion, he reminded him that *his* name was not Reginald? Who, then, was this Reginald? Then came the recollection of what had been repeated to him of the parting scene between Halloway and his wife. In addressing her ill-fated husband, she had named him Reginald. Could it be possible this was the same being alluded to by his father? But no; his youth forbade the supposition, being but two years older than his brother Frederick; yet might he not, in some way or other, be connected with the Reginald of the letter? Why, too, had his father shown such unrelenting severity in the case of this unfortunate victim? – a severity which had induced more than one remark from his officers, that it looked as if he entertained some personal feeling of enmity towards a man who had done so much for his family, and stood so high in the esteem of all who knew him.

Then came another thought. At the moment of his

execution, Halloway had deposited a packet in the hands of Captain Blessington; – could these letters – could that portrait be the same? Certain it was, by whatever means obtained, his father could not have had them long in his possession; for it was improbable letters of so old a date should have occupied his attention *now*, when many years had rolled over the memory of his mother. And then, again, what was the meaning of the language used by the implacable enemy of his father, that uncouth and ferocious warrior of the Fleur de lis, not only on the occasion of the execution of Halloway, but afterwards to his brother, during his short captivity; and, subsequently, when disguised as a black, he penetrated, with the band of Ponteac, into the fort, and aimed his murderous weapon at his father's head. What had made him the enemy of his family? and where and how had originated his father's connection with so extraordinary and so savage a being? Could he, in any way, be implicated with his mother? But no; there was something revolting, monstrous, in the thought: besides, had not his father stood forward the champion of her innocence? – had he not declared, with an energy carrying conviction with every word, that she was untainted by guilt? And would he have done this, had he had reason to believe in the existence of a criminal love for him who evidently was his mortal foe? Impossible.

Such were the questions and solutions that crowded on and distracted the mind of the unhappy De Haldimar, who, after all, could arrive at no satisfactory conclusion. It was evident there was a secret, – yet, whatever its nature, it was one likely to go down with his father to the grave; for, however humiliating the reflection to a haughty parent, compelled to vindicate the honour of a mother to her son, and in direct opposition to evidence that scarcely bore a shadow of misinterpretation, it was clear he had motives for consigning the circumstance to oblivion, which far outweighed any necessity he felt of adducing other proofs of her innocence than those which rested on his own simple yet impressive assertion.

In the midst of these bewildering doubts, De Haldimar heard some one approaching in his rear, whose footsteps he distinguished from the heavy pace of the sentinels. He turned, stopped, and was presently joined by Captain Blessington.

"Why, dearest Charles," almost querulously asked the kind officer, as he passed his arm through that of his subaltern, – "why will you persist in feeding this love of solitude? What possible result can it produce, but an utter prostration of every moral and physical energy? Come, come, summon a little fortitude; all may not yet be so hopeless as you apprehend. For my own part, I feel convinced the day will dawn upon some satisfactory solution of the mystery of that packet."

"Blessington, my dear Blessington!" – and De Haldimar spoke with mournful energy, – "you have known me from my boyhood, and, I believe, have ever loved me; seek not, therefore, to draw me from the present temper of my mind; deprive me not of an indulgence which, melancholy as it is, now constitutes the sole satisfaction I take in existence."

"By Heaven! Charles, I will not listen to such language. You absolutely put my patience to the rack."

"Nay, then, I will urge no more," pursued the young officer. "To revert, therefore, to a different subject. Answer me one question with sincerity. What were the contents of the packet you received from poor Halloway previous to his execution? and in whose possession are they now?"

Pleased to find the attention of his young friend diverted for the moment from his sister, Captain Blessington quickly rejoined, he believed the packet contained letters which Halloway had stated to him were of a nature to throw some light on his family connections. He had, however, transferred it, with the seal unbroken, as desired by the unhappy man, to Colonel de Haldimar.

An exclamation of surprise burst involuntarily from the lips of the youth. "Has my father ever made any allusion to that packet since?" he asked.

"Never," returned Captain Blessington; "and, I confess, his failing to do so has often excited my astonishment. But why do you ask?"

De Haldimar energetically pressed the arm of his captain, while a heavy sigh burst from his oppressed heart. "This very night, Blessington, on entering my father's apartment to apprise him of what was going on here, I saw, – I can scarcely tell you what, but certainly enough to convince me, from what you have now stated, Halloway was, in some degree or other, connected with our family. Tell me," he anxiously pursued, "was there a portrait enclosed with the letters?"

"I cannot state with confidence, Charles," replied his friend; "but if I might judge from the peculiar form and weight of the packet, I should be inclined to say not. Have you seen the letters, then?"

"I have seen certain letters which, I have reason to believe, are the same," returned De Haldimar. "They were addressed to 'Reginald;' and Halloway, I think you have told me, was so called by his unhappy wife."

"There can be little doubt they are the same," said Captain Blessington; "but what were their contents, and by whom written, that you deem they prove a connection between the unhappy soldier and your family?"

De Haldimar felt the blood rise into his cheek, at this natural but unexpected demand. "I am sure, Blessington," he replied, after a pause, "you will not think me capable of unworthy mystery towards yourself; but the contents of these letters are sacred, inasmuch as they relate only to circumstances connected with my father's family."

"This is singular indeed," exclaimed Captain Blessington, in a tone that marked his utter and unqualified astonishment at what had now been disclosed to him; "but surely, Charles," he pursued, "if the packet handed me by Halloway were the same you allude to, he would have caused the transfer to have been made before the period chosen by him for that purpose."

"But the name," pursued De Haldimar; "how are we to

separate the identity of the packets, when we recur to that name of 'Reginald?' "

"True," rejoined the musing Blessington; "there is a mystery in this that baffles all my powers of penetration. Were I in possession of the contents of the letters, I might find some clue to solve the enigma: but —— "

"You surely do not mean this as a reproach, Blessington?" fervently interrupted the youth. "More I dare not, cannot say, for the secret is not my own; and feelings, which it would be dishonour to outrage, alone bind me to silence. What little I have revealed to you even now, has been uttered in confidence. I hope you have so understood it."

"Perfectly, Charles. What you have stated, goes no further; but we have been too long absent from our guard, and I confess I have no particular fancy for remaining in this chill night-air. Let us return."

De Haldimar made no opposition, and they both prepared to quit the rampart. As they passed the sentinel stationed at that point where the Indian had been first seen, their attention was directed by him to a fire that now suddenly rose, apparently at a great distance, and rapidly increased in volume. The singularity of this occurrence riveted the officers for a moment in silent observation; until Captain Blessington at length ventured a remark, that, judging from the direction, and the deceptive nature of the element at night, he should incline to think it was the hut of the Canadian burning.

"Which is another additional proof, were any such wanting, that every thing is lost," mournfully urged the ever apprehensive De Haldimar. "François has been detected in rendering aid to our friends; and the Indians, in all probability, after having immolated their victim, are sacrificing his property to their rage."

During this exchange of opinions, the officers had again moved to the opposite point of the limited walk of the younger. Scarcely had they reached it, and before Captain Blessington could find time to reply to the fears of his friend, when a loud and distant booming like that of a cannon was heard in the direction of the fire. The alarm was given hastily by the sentinels, and sounds of preparation and arming were audible in the course of a minute or two every where throughout the fort. Startled by the report, which they had half inclined to imagine produced by the discharge of one of their own guns, the half slumbering officers had quitted the chairs in which they had passed the night in the mess-room, and were soon at the side of their more watchful companions, then anxiously listening for a repetition of the sound.

The day was just beginning to dawn, and as the atmosphere cleared gradually away, it was perceived the fire rose not from the hut of the Canadian, but at a point considerably beyond it. Unusual as it was to see a large fire of this description, its appearance became an object of minor consideration, since it might be attributed to some caprice or desire on the part of the Indians to excite apprehension in their enemies. But how was the report which had reached their ears to be accounted for? It evidently could only have been produced by the discharge of a cannon; and if so, where could the Indians have procured it? No such arm had recently been in their possession; and if it were, they were totally unacquainted with the manner of serving it.

As the day became more developed, the mystery was resolved. Every telescope in the fort had been called into requisition; and as they were now levelled in the direction of the fire, sweeping the line of horizon around, exclamations of surprise escaped the lips of several.

"The fire is at the near extremity of the wood on Hog Island," exclaimed Lieutenant Johnstone. "I can distinctly see the forms of a multitude of savages dancing round it with hideous gestures and menacing attitudes."

"They are dancing their infernal war dance," said Captain Wentworth. "How I should like to be able to discharge a twenty-four pound battery, loaded with grape, into the very heart of the devilish throng."

"Do you see any prisoners? – Are any of our friends among them?" eagerly and tremblingly enquired De Haldimar of the officer who had last spoken.

Captain Wentworth made a sweep of his glass along the shores of the island; but apparently without success. He announced that he could discover nothing but a vast number of bark canoes lying dry and upturned on the beach.

"It is an unusual hour for their war dance," observed Captain Blessington. "My experience furnishes me with no one instance in which it has not been danced previous to their retiring to rest."

"Unless," said Lieutenant Boyce, "they should have been thus engaged all night; in which case the singularity may be explained."

"Look, look," eagerly remarked Lieutenant Johnstone – "see how they are flying to their canoes, bounding and leaping like so many devils broke loose from their chains. The fire is nearly deserted already."

"The schooner – the schooner!" shouted Captain Erskine. "By Heaven, our own gallant schooner! see how beautifully she drives past the island. It was her gun we heard, intended as a signal to prepare us for her appearance."

A thrill of wild and indescribable emotion passed through every heart. Every eye was turned upon the point to which attention was now directed. The graceful vessel, with every stitch of canvass set, was shooting rapidly past the low bushes skirting the sands that still concealed her hull; and in a moment or two she loomed largely and proudly on the bosom of the Détroit, the surface of which was slightly curled with a north-western breeze.

"Safe, by Jupiter!" exclaimed the delighted Erskine, dropping the glass upon the rampart, and rubbing his hands together with every manifestation of joy.

"The Indians are in chase," said Lieutenant Boyce; "upwards of fifty canoes are following in the schooner's wake. But Danvers will soon give us an account of their Lilliputian fleet."

"Let the troops be held in readiness for a sortie, Mr. Lawson," said the governor, who had joined his officers just as the schooner cleared the island; "we must cover their landing, or, with this host of savages in pursuit, they will never effect it alive."

During the whole of this brief but exciting scene, the heart of Charles de Haldimar beat audibly. A thousand hopes and fears rushed confusedly on his mind, and he was as one bewildered by, and scarcely crediting what he saw. Could Clara, - could his cousin - could his brother - could his friend be on board? He scarcely dared to ask himself these questions; still it was with a fluttering heart, in which hope, however, predominated, that he hastened to execute an order of his captain, that bore immediate reference to his duty as subaltern of the guard.

Five

MEANWHILE the schooner dashed rapidly along, her hull occasionally hid from the view of those assembled on the ramparts by some intervening orchard or cluster of houses, but her tall spars glittering in their covering of white canvass, and marking the direction of her course. At length she came to a point in the river that offered no other interruption to the eye than what arose from the presence of almost all the inhabitants of the village, who, urged by curiosity and surprise, were to be seen crowding the intervening bank. Here the schooner was suddenly put about, and the English colours, hitherto concealed by the folds of the canvass, were at length discovered proudly floating in the breeze.

Immediately over the gateway of the fort there was an elevated platform, approached by the rampart, of which it formed a part, by some half dozen rude steps on either side; and on this platform was placed a long eighteen pounder, that commanded the whole extent of road leading from the drawbridge to the river. Hither the officers had all repaired, while the schooner was in the act of passing the town; and now that, suddenly brought up in the wind's eye, she rode leisurely in the offing, every movement on her decks was plainly discernible with the telescope.

"Where the devil can Danvers have hid all his crew?" first spoke Captain Erskine; "I count but half a dozen hands altogether on deck, and these are barely sufficient to work her."

"Lying concealed, and ready, no doubt, to give the canoes a warm reception," observed Lieutenant Johnstone; "but where can our friends be? Surely, if there, they would show themselves to us."

There was truth in this remark; and each felt discouraged and disappointed that they did not appear.

"There come the whooping hell fiends," said Major Blackwater. "By Heaven! the very water is darkened with the shadows of their canoes."

Scarcely had he spoken, when the vessel was suddenly surrounded by a multitude of savages, whose fierce shouts rent the air, while their dripping paddles, gleaming like silver in the rays of the rising sun, were alternately waved aloft in triumph, and then plunged into the troubled element, which they spurned in fury from their blades.

"What can Danvers be about? Why does he not either open his fire, or crowd sail and away from them?" exclaimed several voices.

"The detachment is in readiness, sir," said Mr. Lawson, ascending the platform, and addressing Major Blackwater.

"The deck, the deck!" shouted Erskine.

Already the eyes of several were bent in the direction alluded to by the last speaker, while those whose attention had been diverted by the approaching canoes glanced rapidly to the same point. To the surprise and consternation of all, the tall and well-remembered form of the warrior of the Fleur de lis was seen towering far above the bulwarks of the schooner; and with an expression in the attitude he had assumed, which no one could mistake for other than that of triumphant defiance. Presently he drew from the bosom of his hunting coat a dark parcel, and springing into the rigging of the mainmast, ascended with incredible activity to the point where the English ensign was faintly floating in the breeze. This he tore furiously away, and rending it into many pieces, cast the fragments into the silver element beneath him, on whose bosom they were seen to float among the canoes of the savages, many of whom possessed themselves, with eagerness, of the gaudy coloured trophies. The dark parcel was now unfolded by the active warrior, who, after having waved it several times round his head, commenced attaching it to the lines whence the English ensign had so recently been torn. It was a large black flag, the purport of which was too readily comprehended by the excited officers.

"D—n the ruffian! can we not manage to make that flag serve as his own winding sheet?" exclaimed Captain Erskine. "Come, Wentworth, give us a second edition of the sortie firing; I know no man who understands pointing a gun better than yourself, and this eighteen pounder might do some mischief."

The idea was instantly caught at by the officer of artillery, who read his consent in the eye of Colonel de Haldimar. His companions made way on either side; and several gunners, who were already at their stations, having advanced to work the piece at the command of their captain, it was speedily brought to bear upon the schooner.

"This will do, I think," said Wentworth, as, glancing his experienced eye carefully along the gun, he found it pointed immediately on the gigantic frame of the warrior. "If this chain-shot miss him, it will be through no fault of mine."

Every eye was now riveted on the mainmast of the schooner, where the warrior was still engaged in attaching the portentous flag. The gunner, who held the match, obeyed the silent signal of his captain; and the massive iron was heard rushing past the officers, bound on its murderous mission. A moment or two of intense anxiety elapsed; and when at length the rolling volumes of smoke gradually floated away, to the dismay and disappointment of all, the fierce warrior was seen standing apparently unharmed on the same spot in the rigging. The shot had, however, been well aimed, for a large rent in the outstretched canvass, close at his side, and about mid-height of his person, marked the direction it had taken. Again he tore away, and triumphantly waved the black flag around his head, while from his capacious lungs there burst yells of defiance and scorn, that could be distinguished for his own even at that distance. This done, he again secured the death symbol to its place; and gliding to the deck by a single rope, appeared to give orders to the few men of the crew who were to be seen; for every stitch of canvass was again made to fill, and the vessel, bounding forward before the breeze then blowing upon her quarter, shot rapidly behind the town, and was finally seen to cast anchor in the navigable channel that divides Hog Island from the shores of Canada.

At the discharge of the eighteen pounder, the river had been suddenly cleared, as if by magic, of every canoe; while, warned by the same danger, the groups of inhabitants, assembled on the bank, had rushed for shelter to their respective homes; so that, when the schooner disappeared, not a vestige of human life was to be seen along that vista so recently peopled with human forms. An order from Colonel de Haldimar to the adjutant, countermanding the sortie, was the first interruption to the silence that had continued to pervade the little band of officers; and two or three of these having hastened to the western front of the rampart, in order to obtain a more distinct view of the movements of the schooner, their example was speedily followed by the remainder, all of whom now quitted the platform, and repaired to the same point.

Here, with the aid of their telescopes, they again distinctly commanded a view of the vessel, which lay motionless close under the sandy beach of the island, and exhibiting all the technicalities of skill in the disposition of sails and yards peculiar to the profession. In vain, however, was every eye strained to discover, among the multitude of savages that kept momentarily leaping to her deck, the forms of those in whom they were most interested. A group of some half dozen men, apparently common sailors, and those, in all probability, whose services had been compelled in the working of the vessel, were the only evidences that civilised man formed a portion of that grotesque assemblage. These, with their arms evidently bound behind their backs, and placed on one of the gangways, were only visible at intervals, as the band of savages that surrounded them, brandishing their tomahawks around their heads, occasionally left an opening in their circle. The formidable warrior of the Fleur de lis was no longer to be seen, although the flag which he had hoisted still fluttered in the breeze.

"All is lost, then," ejaculated the governor, with a mournfulness of voice and manner that caused many of his officers to turn and regard him with surprise. "That black flag announces the triumph of my foe in the too certain destruction of my children. Now, indeed," he concluded in a lower tone, "for the first time, does the curse of Ellen Halloway sit heavily on my soul."

A deep sigh burst from one immediately behind him. The governor turned suddenly round, and beheld his son. Never did human countenance wear a character of more poignant misery than that of the unhappy Charles at the moment. Attracted by the report of the cannon, he had flown to the rampart to ascertain the cause, and had reached his companions only to learn the strong hope so recently kindled in his breast was fled for ever. His cheek, over which hung his neglected hair, was now pale as marble, and his lips bloodless and parted; yet, notwithstanding this intensity of personal sorrow, a tear had started to his eye, apparently wrung from him by this unusual expression of dismay in his father.

"Charles - my son - my only now remaining child," murmured the governor with emotion, as he remarked, and started at the deathlike image of the youth; "look not thus, or you will utterly unman me."

A sudden and involuntary impulse caused him to extend his arms. The young officer sprang forward into the proffered embrace, and sank his head upon the cheek of his father. It was the first time he had enjoyed that privilege since his childhood; and even overwhelmed as he was by his affliction, he felt it deeply.

This short but touching scene was witnessed by their companions, without levity in any, and with emotion by several. None felt more gratified at this demonstration of parental affection for the sensitive boy, than Blessington and Erskine.

"I cannot yet persuade myself," observed the former officer, as the colonel again assumed that dignity of demeanour which had been momentarily lost sight of in the ebullition of his feelings, – "I cannot yet persuade myself things are altogether so bad as they appear. It is true the schooner is in the possession of the enemy, but there is nothing to prove our friends are on board."

"If you had reason to know *him* into whose hands she has fallen, as I do, you would think differently Captain Blessington," returned the governor. "That mysterious being," he pursued, after a short pause, "would never have made this parade of his conquest, had it related merely to a few lives, which to him are of utter insignificance. The very substitution of yon black flag, in his insolent triumph, was the pledge of redemption of a threat breathed in my ear within this very fort: on what occasion I need not state, since the events connected with that unhappy night are still fresh in the recollections of us all. That he is my personal enemy, gentlemen, it would be vain to disguise from you; although who he is, or of what nature his enmity, it imports not now to enter upon. Suffice it, I have little doubt my children are in his power; but whether the black flag indicates they are no more, or that the tragedy is only in preparation, I confess I am at a loss to understand."

Deeply affected by the evident despondency that had dictated these unusual admissions on the part of their chief, the officers were forward to combat the inferences he had drawn: several coinciding in the opinion now expressed by Captain Wentworth, that the fact of the schooner having fallen into the hands of the savages by no means implied the capture of the fort whence she came; since it was not at all unlikely she had been chased during a calm by the numerous canoes into the Sinclair, where, owing to the extreme narrowness of the river, she had fallen an easy prey.

"Moreover," observed Captain Blessington, "it is highly improbable the ferocious warrior could have succeeded in capturing any others than the unfortunate crew of the schooner; for had this been the case, he would not have lost the opportunity of crowning his triumph by exhibiting his victims to our view in some conspicuous part of the vessel."

"This, I grant you," rejoined the governor, "to be one solitary circumstance in our favour; but may it not, after all, merely prove that our worst apprehensions are already realised?"

"He is not one, methinks, since vengeance seems his aim, to exercise it in so summary, and therefore merciful, a manner. Depend upon it, colonel, had any of those in whom we are more immediately interested, fallen into his hands, he would not have failed to insult and agonize us by an exhibition of his prisoners."

"You are right, Blessington," exclaimed Charles de Haldimar, in a voice that his choking feelings rendered almost sepulchral; "he is not one to exercise his vengeance in a summary and merciful manner. The deed is yet unaccomplished, for even now the curse of Ellen Halloway rings again in my ear, and tells me the atoning blood must be spilt on the grave of her husband."

The peculiar tone in which these words were uttered, caused every one present to turn and regard the speaker, for they recalled the prophetic language of the unhappy woman. There was now a wildness of expression in his handsome features, marking the mind utterly dead to hope, yet struggling to work itself up to passive endurance of the worst. Colonel de Haldimar sighed painfully, as he bent his eye half reproachfully on the dull and attenuated features of his son; and although he spoke not, his look betrayed the anguish that allusion had called up to his heart.

"Forgive me, my father," exclaimed the youth, grasping a hand that was reluctantly extended. "I meant it not in unkindness; but indeed I have ever had the conviction strongly impressed on my spirit. I know I appear weak, childish, unsoldierlike; yet can it be wondered at, when I have been so often latterly deceived by false hopes, that now my heart has room for no other tenant than despair. I am very wretched," he pursued, with affecting despondency; "in the presence of my companions do I admit it, but they all know how I loved my sister. Can they then feel surprise, that having lost not only her, but my brother and my friend, I should be the miserable thing I am."

Colonel de Haldimar turned away, much affected; and throwing his back against the sentry box near him, passed his hand over his eyes, and remained for a few moments motionless.

"Charles, Charles, is this your promise to me?" whispered Captain Blessington, as he approached and took the hand of his unhappy friend. "Is this the self-command you pledged yourself to exercise? For Heaven's sake, agitate not your father thus, by the indulgence of a grief that can have no other tendency than to render him equally wretched. Be advised by me, and quit the rampart. Return to your guard, and endeavour to compose yourself."

"Ha! what new movement is that on the part of the savages?" exclaimed Captain Erskine, who had kept his glass to his eye mechanically, and chiefly with a view of hiding the emotion produced in him by the almost infantine despair of the younger De Haldimar: "surely it is – yet, no, it cannot be – yes, see how they are dragging several prisoners from the wood to the beach. I can distinctly see a man in a blanket coat, and two others considerably taller, and apparently sailors. But look, behind them are two females in European dress. Almighty Heaven! there can be no doubt."

A painful pause ensued. Every other glass and eye was levelled in the same direction; and, even as Erskine had described it, a party of Indians were seen, by those who had the telescopes, conducting five prisoners towards a canoe that lay in the channel communicating from the island with the main land on the Détroit shore. Into the bottom of these they were presently huddled, so that only their heads and shoulders were visible above the gunwale of the frail bark. Presently a tall warrior was seen bounding from the wood towards the beach. The crowd of gesticulating Indians made way, and the warrior was seen to stoop and apply his shoulder to the canoe, one half of which was high and dry upon the sands. The heavily laden vessel obeyed the impetus with a rapidity that proved the muscular power of him who gave it. Like some wild animal, instinct with life, it lashed the foaming waters from its bows, and left a deep and gurgling furrow where it passed. As it quitted the shore, the warrior sprang lightly in, taking his station at the stern; and while his tall and remarkable figure bent nimbly to the movement, he dashed his paddle from right to left alternately in the stream, with a quickness that rendered it almost invisible to the eye. Presently the canoe disappeared round an intervening headland, and the officers lost sight of it altogether.

"The portrait, Charles; what have you done with the portrait?" exclaimed Captain Blessington, actuated by a sudden recollection, and with a trepidation in his voice and manner that spoke volumes of despair to the younger De Haldimar. "This is our only hope of solving the mystery. Quick, give me the portrait, if you have it."

The young officer hurriedly tore the miniature from the breast of his uniform, and pitched it through the interval that separated him from his captain, who stood a few feet off; but with so uncertain and trembling an aim, it missed the hand extended to secure it, and fell upon the very stone the youth had formerly pointed out to Blessington, as marking the particular spot on which he stood during the execution of Halloway. The violence of the fall separated the back of the frame from the picture itself, when suddenly a piece of white and crumpled paper, apparently part of the back of a letter, yet cut to the size and shape of the miniature, was exhibited to the view of all.

"Ha!" resumed the gratified Blessington, as he stooped to possess himself of the prize; "I knew the miniature would be found to contain some intelligence from our friends. It is only this moment it occurred to me to take it to pieces, but accident has anticipated my purpose. May the omen prove a good one! But what have we here?"

With some difficulty, the anxious officer now succeeded in making out the characters, which, in default of pen or pencil, had been formed by the pricking of a fine pin on the paper. The broken sentences, on which the whole of the group now hung with greedy ear, ran nearly as follows: – "All is lost. Michillimackinac is taken. We are prisoners, and doomed to die within eight and forty hours. Alas! Clara and Madeline are of our number. Still there is a hope, if my father deem it prudent to incur the risk. A surprise, well managed, may do much; but it must be tomorrow night; forty-eight hours more, and it will be of no avail. He who will deliver this is our friend, and the enemy of my father's enemy. He will be in the same spot at the same hour to-morrow night, and will conduct the detachment to wherever we may chance to be. If you fail in your enterprise, receive our last prayers for a less disastrous fate. God bless you all!"

The blood ran coldly through every vein during the perusal of these important sentences, but not one word of comment was offered by an individual of the group. No explanation was necessary. The captives in the canoe, the tall warrior in its stern, all sufficiently betrayed the horrible truth.

Colonel de Haldimar at length turned an enquiring look at his two captains, and then addressing the adjutant, asked –

"What companies are off duty to-day, Mr. Lawson?"

"Mine," said Blessington, with an energy that denoted how deeply rejoiced he felt at the fact, and without giving the adjutant time to reply.

"And mine," impetuously added Captain Erskine; "and, by G——! I will answer for them; they never embarked on a duty of the sort with greater zeal than they will on this occasion."

"Gentlemen, I thank you," said Colonel de Haldimar, with deep emotion, as he stepped forward and grasped in turn the hands of the generous-hearted officers. "To Heaven, and to your exertions, do I commit my children."

"Any artillery, colonel?" enquired the officer of that corps.

"No, Wentworth, no artillery. Whatever remains to be done, must be achieved by the bayonet alone, and under favour of the darkness. Gentlemen, again I thank you for this generous interest in my children – this forwardness in an enterprise on which depend the lives of so many dear friends. I am not one given to express warm emotion, but I do, indeed, appreciate this conduct deeply." He then moved away, desiring Mr. Lawson, as he quitted the rampart, to cause the men for this service to be got in instant readiness.

Following the example of their colonel, Captains Blessington and Erskine quitted the rampart also, hastening to satisfy themselves by personal inspection of the efficiency in all respects of their several companies; and in a few minutes, the only individual to be seen in that quarter of the works was the sentinel, who had been a silent and pained witness of all that had passed among his officers.

Six

DOUBTLESS, many of our readers are prepared to expect that the doom of the unfortunate Frank Halloway was, as an officer of his regiment had already hinted, the fruit of some personal pique and concealed motive of vengeance; and that the dénouement of our melancholy story will afford evidence of the governor's knowledge of the true character of him, who, under an assumed name, excited such general interest at his trial and death, not only among his military superiors, but those with whom his adverse destiny had more immediately associated him. It has already been urged to us, by one or two of our critical friends to whom we have submitted what has been thus far written in our tale, that, to explain satisfactorily and consistently the extreme severity of the governor, some secret and personally influencing motive must be assigned; but to these we have intimated, what we now repeat, – namely, that we hope to bear out our story, by natural explanation and simple deduction. Who Frank Halloway really was, or what the connection existing between him and the mysterious enemy of the family of De Haldimar, the sequel of our narrative will show; but whatever its nature, and however well founded the apprehension of the governor of the formidable being hitherto known as the warrior of the Fleur de lis, and however strong his conviction that the devoted Halloway and his enemy were in secret correspondence, certain it is, that, to the very hour of the death of the former, he knew him as no other than the simple private soldier.

To have ascribed to Colonel de Haldimar motives that would have induced his eagerly seeking the condemnation of an innocent man, either to gratify a thirst of vengeance, or to secure immunity against personal danger, would have been to have painted him, not only as a villain, but a coward. Colonel de Haldimar was neither; but, on the contrary, what is understood in worldly parlance and the generally received acceptation of the terms, a man of strict integrity and honour, as well as of the most undisputed courage. Still, he was a severe and a haughty man, – one whose military education had been based on the principles of the old school – and to whom the command of a regiment afforded a field for the exercise of an orthodox despotism, that could not be passed over without the immolation of many a victim on its rugged surface. Without ever having possessed any thing like acute feeling, his heart, as nature had formed it, was moulded to receive the ordinary impressions of humanity; and had he been doomed to move in the sphere of private life, if he had not been distinguished by any remarkable sensibilities, he would not, in all probability, have been conspicuous for any extraordinary cruelties. Sent into the army, however, at an early age, and with a blood not remarkable for its mercurial aptitudes, he had calmly and deliberately imbibed all the starched theories and standard prejudices which a mind by no means naturally gifted was but too well predisposed to receive; and he was among the number of those (many of whom are indigenous to our soil even at the present day) who look down from a rank obtained, upon that which has been just quitted, with a contempt, and coldness, and consciousness of elevation, commensurate only with the respect paid to those still above them, and which it belongs only to the little-minded to indulge in.

As a subaltern, M. de Haldimar had ever been considered a pattern of rigid propriety and decorum of conduct.

Not the shadow of military crime had ever been laid to his charge. He was punctual at all parades and drills; kept the company to which he was attached in a perfect hot water of discipline; never missed his distance in marching past, or failed in a military manoeuvre; paid his mess-bill regularly to the hour, nay, minute, of the settling day; and was never, on any one occasion, known to enter the paymaster's office, except on the well-remembered 24th of each month; and, to crown all, he had never asked, consequently never obtained, a day's leave from his regiment, although he had served in it so long, that there was now but one man living who had entered it with him. With all these qualities, Ensign de Haldimar promised to make an excellent soldier; and, as such, was encouraged by the field-officers of the corps, who unhesitatingly pronounced him a lad of discernment and talent, who would one day rival them in all the glorious privileges of martinetism. It was even remarked, as an evidence of his worth, that, when promoted to a lieutenancy, he looked down upon the ensigns with that becoming condescension which befitted his new rank; and up to the captains with the deferential respect he felt to be due to that third step in the five-barred gate of regimental promotion, on which his aspiring but chained foot had not yet succeeded in reposing. What, therefore, he became when he had succeeded in clambering to the top, and looked down from the lordly height he had after many years of plodding service obtained, we must leave it to the imaginations of our readers to determine. We reserve it to a future page, to relate more interesting particulars.

Sufficient has been shown, however, from this outline of his character, as well as from the conversations among his officers, elsewhere transcribed, to account for the governor's conduct in the case of Halloway. That the recommendation of his son, Captain de Haldimar, had not been attended to, arose not from any particular ill-will towards the unhappy man, but simply because he had always been in the habit of making his own selections from the ranks, and that the present recommendation had been warmly urged by one who he fancied pretended to a discrimination superior to his own, in pointing out merits that had escaped his observation. It might be, too, that there was a latent pride about the manner of Halloway that displeased and dissatisfied one who looked upon his subordinates as things that were amendable to the haughtiness of his glance, – not enough of deference in his demeanour, or of supplicating obsequiousness in his speech, to entitle him to the promotion prayed for. Whatever the motive, there was nothing of personality to influence him in the rejection of the appeal made in favour of one who had never injured him; but who, on the contrary, as the whole of the regiment could attest, had saved the life of his son.

Rigid disciplinarian as he was, and holding himself responsible for the safety of the garrison, it was but natural, when the discovery had been made of the unaccountable unfastening of the gate of the fort, suspicion of no ordinary kind should attach to the sentinel posted there; and that he should steadily refuse all credence to a story wearing so much appearance of improbability. Proud, and inflexible, and bigoted to first impressions, his mind was closed against those palliating circumstances, which, adduced by Halloway in his defence, had so mainly contributed to stamp the conviction of his moral innocence on the minds of his judges and the attentive auditory; and could he even have conquered his pride so far as to have admitted the belief of that innocence, still the military crime of which he had been guilty, in infringing a positive order of the garrison, was in itself sufficient to call forth all the unrelenting severity of his nature. Throughout the whole of the proceedings subsequently instituted, he had acted and spoken from a perfect conviction of the treason of the unfortunate soldier, and with the fullest impression of the falsehood of all that had been offered in his defence. The considerations that influenced the minds of his officers, found no entrance into his proud breast, which was closed against every thing but his own dignified sense of superior judgment. Could he, like them, have given credence to the tale of Halloway, or really have believed that Captain de Haldimar, educated under his own military eye, could have been so wanting in subordination, as not merely to have infringed a positive order of the garrison, but to have made a private soldier of that garrison accessary to his delinquency, it is more than probable his stern habits of military discipline would have caused him to overlook the offence of the soldier, in deeper indignation at the conduct of the infinitely more culpable officer; but not one word did he credit of a statement, which he assumed to have been got up by the prisoner with the mere view of shielding himself from punishment: and when to these suspicions of his fidelity was attached the fact of the introduction of his alarming visiter, it must be confessed his motives for indulging in this belief were not without foundation.

The impatience manifested during the trial of Halloway was not a result of any desire of systematic persecution, but of a sense of wounded dignity. It was a thing unheard of, and unpardonable in his eyes, for a private soldier to assert, in his presence, his honour and his respectability in extenuation, even while admitting the justice of a specific charge; and when he remarked the Court listening with that profound attention, which the peculiar history of the prisoner had excited, he could not repress the manifestation of his anger. In justice to him, however, it must be acknowledged that, in causing the charge, to which the unfortunate man pleaded guilty, to be framed, he had only acted from the conviction that, on the two first, there was not sufficient evidence to condemn one whose crime was as clearly established, to his judgment, as if he had been an eye-witness of the treason. It is true, he availed himself of Halloway's voluntary confession, to effect his condemnation; but estimating him as a traitor, he felt little delicacy was necessary to be observed on that score.

Much of the despotic military character of Colonel de Haldimar had been communicated to his private life; so much, indeed that his sons, – both of whom, it has been seen, were of natures that belied their origin from so stern a stock, – were kept at nearly as great a distance from him as any other subordinates of his regiment. But although he seldom indulged in manifestations of parental regard towards those whom he looked upon rather as inferiors in military rank, than as beings connected with him by the ties of blood, Colonel de Haldimar was not without that instinctive love for his children, which every animal in the creation feels for its offspring. He, also, valued and took a pride in, because they reflected a certain degree of lustre upon himself, the talents and accomplishments of his eldest son, who, moreover, was a brave, enterprising officer, and, only wanted, in his father's estimation, that severity of carriage and hauteur of deportment, befitting *his* son, to render him perfect. As for Charles, – the gentle, bland, winning, universally conciliating Charles, – he looked upon him as a mere weak boy, who could never hope to arrive at any post of distinction, if only by reason of the extreme delicacy of his physical organisation; and to have shown any thing like respect for his character, or indulged in any expression of tenderness for one so far below his estimate of what a soldier, a child of his, ought to be, would have been a concession of which his proud nature was incapable. In his daughter Clara, however, the gentleness of sex claimed that warmer affection which was denied to him, who resembled her in almost every attribute of mind and person. Colonel de Haldimar doated on his daughter with a tenderness, for which few, who were familiar with his harsh and unbending nature, ever gave him credit. She was the image of one on whom all of love that he had ever known had been centered; and he had continued in Clara an affection, that seemed in itself to form a portion, distinct and apart, of his existence.

We have already seen, as stated by Charles de Haldimar to the unfortunate wife of Halloway, with what little success he had pleaded in the interview he had requested of his father, for the preserver of his gallant brother's life;

and we have also seen how equally inefficient was the lowly and supplicating anguish of that wretched being, when, on quitting the apartment of his son, Colonel de Haldimar had so unexpectedly found himself clasped in her despairing embrace. There was little to be expected from an intercession on the part of one claiming so little ascendancy over his father's heart, as the universally esteemed young officer; still less from one who, in her shriek of agony, had exposed the haughty chief to the observation both of men and officers, and under circumstances that caused his position to border on the ludicrous. But however these considerations might have failed in effect, there was another which, as a soldier, he could not wholly overlook. Although he had offered no comment on the extraordinary recommendation to mercy annexed to the sentence of the prisoner, it had had a certain weight with him; and he felt, all absolute even as he was, he could not, without exciting strong dissatisfaction among his troops, refuse attention to a document so powerfully worded, and bearing the signature and approval of so old and valued an officer as Captain Blessington. His determination, therefore, had been formed, even before his visit to his son, to act as circumstances might require; and, in the mean while, he commanded every preparation for the execution to be made.

In causing a strong detachment to be marched to the conspicuous point chosen for his purpose, he had acted from a conviction of the necessity of showing the enemy the treason of the soldier had been detected; reserving to himself the determination of carrying the sentence into full effect, or pardoning the condemned, as the event might warrant. Not one moment, meanwhile, did he doubt the guilt of Halloway, whose description of the person of his enemy was, in itself, to him, confirmatory evidence of his treason. It is doubtful whether he would, in any way, have been influenced by the recommendation of the Court, had the first charges been substantiated; but as there was nothing but conjecture to bear out these, and as the prisoner had been convicted only on the ground of suffering Captain de Haldimar to quite the fort contrary to orders, he felt he might possibly go too far in carrying the capital punishment into effect, in decided opposition to the general feeling of the garrison, – both of officers and men.

When the shot was subsequently fired from the hut of the Canadian, and the daring rifleman recognised as the same fearful individual who had gained access to his apartment the preceding night, conviction of the guilt of Halloway came even deeper home to the mind of the governor. It was through François alone that a communication was kept up secretly between the garrison and several of the Canadians without the fort; and the very fact of the mysterious warrior having been there so recently after his daring enterprise, bore evidence that whatever treason was in operation, had been carried on through the instrumentality of mine host of the Fleur de lis. In proof, moreover, there was the hat of Donellan, and the very rope Halloway had stated to be that by which the unfortunate officer had effected his exit. Colonel de Haldimar was not one given to indulge in the mysterious or to believe in the romantic. Every thing was plain matter of fact, as it now appeared before him; and he thought it evident, as though it had been written in words of fire, that if his son and his unfortunate servant had quitted the fort in the manner represented, it was no less certain they had been forced off by a party, at the head of whom was his vindictive enemy, and with the connivance of Halloway. We have seen, that after the discovery of the sex of the supposed drummer-boy when the prisoners were confronted together, Colonel de Haldimar had closely watched the expression of their countenances, but failed in discovering any thing that could be traced into evidence of a guilty recognition. Still he conceived his original impression to have been too forcibly borne out, even by the events of the last half hour, to allow this to have much weight with him; and his determination to carry the thing through all its fearful preliminary stages became more and more confirmed.

In adopting this resolution in the first instance, he was not without a hope that Halloway, standing, as he must feel himself to be, on the verge of the grave, might be induced to make confession of his guilt, and communicate whatever particulars might prove essential not only to the safety of the garrison generally, but to himself individually, as far as his personal enemy was concerned. With this view, he had charged Captain Blessington, in the course of their march from the hut to the fatal bridge, to promise a full pardon, provided he should make such confession of his crime as would lead to a just appreciation of the evils likely to result from the treason that had in part been accomplished. Even in making this provision, however, which was met by the prisoner with solemn yet dignified reiteration of his innocence, Colonel de Haldimar had not made the refusal of pardon altogether conclusive in his own mind: still, in adopting this plan, there was a chance of obtaining a confession; and not until there was no longer a prospect of the unhappy man being led into that confession, did he feel it imperative on him to stay the progress of the tragedy.

What the result would have been, had not Halloway, in the strong excitement of his feelings, sprung to his feet upon the coffin, uttering the exclamation of triumph recorded in the last pages of our first volume, is scarcely doubtful. However much the governor might have contemned and slighted a credulity in which he in no way participated himself, he had too much discrimination not to perceive, that to have persevered in the capital punishment would have been to have rendered himself personally obnoxious to the comrades of the condemned, whose dispirited air and sullen mien, he clearly saw, denounced the punishment as one of unnecessary rigour. The haughty commander was not one to be intimidated by manifestations of discontent; neither was he one to brook a spirit of insubordination, however forcibly supported; but he had too much experience and military judgment, not to determine that this was not a moment, by foregoing an act of compulsory clemency, to instil divisions in the garrison, when the safety of all so much depended on the cheerfulness and unanimity with which they lent themselves to the arduous duties of defence.

However originating in policy, the lenity he might have been induced to have shown, all idea of the kind was chased from his mind by the unfortunate action of the prisoner. At the moment when the distant heights resounded with the fierce yells of the savages, and leaping forms came bounding down the slope, the remarkable warrior of the Fleur de lis – the fearful enemy who had whispered the most demoniac vengeance in his ears the preceding night – was the only one that met and riveted the gaze of the governor. He paused not to observe or to think who the flying man could be of whom the mysterious warrior was in pursuit, – neither did it, indeed, occur to him that it was a pursuit at all. But one idea suggested itself to his mind, and that was an attempt at rescue of the condemned on the part of his accomplice; and when at length Halloway, who had at once, as if by instinct, recognised his captain in the fugitive, shouted forth his gratitude to Heaven that "he at length approached who alone had the power to save him," every shadow of mercy was banished from the mind of the governor, who, labouring under a natural misconception of the causes of his exulting shout, felt that justice imperatively demanded her victim, and no longer hesitated in awarding the doom that became the supposed traitor. It was under this impression that he sternly gave and repeated the fatal order to fire; and by this misjudged and severe, although not absolutely cruel act, not only destroyed one of the noblest beings that ever wore a soldier's uniform, but entailed upon himself and family that terrific curse of his maniac wife, which rang like a prophetic warning in the ears of all, and was often heard in the fitful startings of his own ever-after troubled slumbers.

What his feelings were, when subsequently he discovered, in the wretched fugitive, the son whom he already believed to have been numbered with the dead, and heard from his lips a confirmation of all that had been advanced by the unhappy Halloway, we shall leave it to our readers to imagine. Still, even amid his first regret, the rigid disciplinarian was strong within him; and no sooner had the detachment regained the fort, after performing the last offices of interment over their ill-fated comrade, than Captain de Haldimar received an intimation, through the adjutant, to consider himself under close arrest for disobedience of orders. Finally, however, he succeeded in procuring an interview with his father; in the course of which, disclosing the plot of the Indians, and the short period allotted for its being carried into execution, he painted in the most gloomy colours the alarming dangers which threatened them all, and finished by urgently imploring his father to suffer him to make the attempt to reach their unsuspecting friends at Michillimackinac. Fully impressed with the difficulties attendant on a scheme that offered so few feasible chances of success, Colonel de Haldimar for a period denied his concurrence; but when at length the excited young man dwelt on the horrors that would inevitably await his sister and betrothed cousin, were they to fall into the hands of the savages, these considerations were found to be effective. An after-arrangement included Sir Everard Valletort, who had expressed a strong desire to share his danger in the enterprise; and the services of the Canadian, who had been brought back a prisoner to the fort, and on whom promises and threats were bestowed in an equally lavish manner, were rendered available. In fact, without the assistance of François, there was little chance of their effecting in safety the navigation of the waters through which they were to pass to arrive at the fort. He it was, who, when summoned to attend a conference among the officers, bearing on the means to be adopted, suggested the propriety of their disguising themselves as Canadian duck hunters; in which character they might expect to pass unmolested, even if encountered by any outlying parties of the savages. With the doubts that had previously been entertained of the fidelity of François, there was an air of forlorn hope given to the enterprise; still, as the man expressed sincere earnestness of desire to repay the clemency accorded him, by a faithful exercise of his services, and as the object sought was one that justified the risk, there was, notwithstanding, a latent hope cherished by all parties, that the event would prove successful. We have already seen to what extent their anticipations were realised.

Whether it was that he secretly acknowledged the too excessive sternness of his justice in regard to Halloway (who still, in the true acceptation of facts, had been guilty of a crime that entailed the penalty he had paid), or that the apprehensions that arose to his heart in regard to her on whom he yearned with all a father's fondness governed his conduct, certain it is, that, from the hour of the disclosure made by his son, Colonel de Haldimar became an altered man. Without losing any thing of that dignity of manner, which had hitherto been confounded with the most repellent haughtiness of bearing, his demeanour towards his officers became more courteous; and although, as heretofore, he kept himself entirely aloof, except when occasions of duty brought them together, still, when they did meet, there was more of conciliation in his manner, and less of austerity in his speech. There was, moreover, a dejection in his eye, strongly in contrast with his former imperious glance; and more than one officer remarked, that, if his days were devoted to the customary practical arrangements for defence, his pallid countenance betokened that his nights were nights rather of vigil than of repose.

However natural and deep the alarm entertained for the fate of the sister fort, there could be no apprehension on the mind of Colonel de Haldimar in regard to his own; since, furnished with the means of foiling his enemies with their own weapons of cunning and deceit, a few extraordinary precautions alone were necessary to secure all immunity from danger. Whatever might be the stern peculiarities of his character, – and these had originated chiefly in an education purely military, – Colonel de Haldimar was an officer well calculated to the important trust reposed in him; for, combining experience with judgment in all matters relating to the diplomacy of war, and being fully conversant with the character and habits of the enemy opposed to him, he possessed singular aptitude to seize whatever advantages might present themselves.

The prudence and caution of his policy have already been made manifest in the two several council scenes with the chiefs recorded in our second volume. It may appear singular, that, with the opportunity thus afforded him of retaining the formidable Ponteac, – the strength and sinew of that long protracted and ferocious war, – in his power, he should have waved his advantage; but here Colonel de Haldimar gave evidence of the tact which so eminently distinguished his public conduct throughout. He well knew the noble, fearless character of the chief; and felt, if any hold was to be secured over him, it was by grappling with his generosity, and not by the exercise of intimidation. Even admitting that Ponteac continued his prisoner, and that the troops, pouring their destructive fire upon the mass of enemies so suddenly arrested on the drawbridge, had swept away the whole, still they were but as a mite among the numerous nations that were leagued against the English; and to these nations, it was evident, they must, sooner or later, succumb.

Colonel de Haldimar knew enough of the proud but generous nature of the Ottawa, to deem that the policy he proposed to pursue in the last council scene would not prove altogether without effect on that warrior. It was well known to him, that much pains had been taken to instil into the minds of the Indians the belief that the English were resolved on their final extirpation; and as certain slights, offered to them at various periods, had given a colouring of truth to this assertion, the formidable league which had already accomplished the downfall of so many of the forts had been the consequence of these artful representations. Although well aware that the French had numerous emissaries distributed among the fierce tribes, it was not until after the disclosure made by the haughty Ponteac, at the close of the first council scene, that he became apprised of the alarming influence exercised over the mind of that warrior himself by his own terrible and vindictive enemy. The necessity of counteracting that influence was obvious; and he felt this was only to be done (if at all) by some marked and extraordinary evidence of the peaceful disposition of the English. Hence his determination to suffer the faithless chiefs and their followers to depart unharmed from the fort, even at the moment when the attitude assumed by the prepared garrison fully proved to the assailants their designs had been penetrated and their schemes rendered abortive.

Seven

WITH THE general position of the encampment of the investing Indians, the reader has been made acquainted through the narrative of Captain de Haldimar. It was, as has been shown, situate in a sort of oasis close within the verge of the forest, and (girt by an intervening underwood which Nature, in her caprice, had fashioned after the manner of a defensive barrier) embraced a space sufficient to contain the tents of the fighting men, together with their women and children. This, however, included only the warriors and inferior chiefs. The tents of the leaders were without the belt of underwood, and principally distributed at long intervals on that side of the forest which skirted the open country towards the river; forming, as it were, a chain of external defences, and sweeping in a semicircular direction round the more dense encampment of their followers. At its highest elevation the forest shot out suddenly into a point, naturally enough rendered an object of attraction from whatever part it was commanded.

Darkness was already beginning to spread her mantle over the intervening space, and the night fires of the Indians were kindling into brightness, glimmering occasionally through the wood with that pale and lambent light peculiar to the fire-fly, of which they offered a not inapt representation, when suddenly a lofty tent, the brilliant whiteness of which was thrown into strong relief by the dark field on which it reposed, was seen to rise at a few paces from the abrupt point in the forest just described, and on the extreme summit of a ridge, beyond which lay only the western horizon in golden perspective.

The opening of this tent looked eastward and towards the fort; and on its extreme summit floated a dark flag, which at intervals spread itself before the slight evening breeze, but oftener hung drooping and heavily over the glittering canvass. One solitary pine, whose trunk exceeded not the ordinary thickness of a man's waist, and standing out as a landmark on the ridge, rose at the distance of a few feet from the spot on which the tent had been erected; and to this was bound the tall and elegant figure of one dressed in the coarse garb of a sailor. The arms and legs of this individual were perfectly free; but a strong rope, rendered doubly secure after the manner of what is termed "whipping" among seamen, after having been tightly drawn several times around his waist, and then firmly knotted behind, was again passed round the tree, to which the back of the prisoner was closely lashed; thus enabling, or rather compelling, him to be a spectator of every object within the tent.

Layers of bark, over which were spread the dressed skins of the bear and the buffalo, formed the floor and carpet of the latter; and on these, in various parts, and in characteristic attitudes, reposed the forms of three human beings; – one, the formidable warrior of the Fleur de lis. Attired in the garb in which we first introduced him to our readers, and with the same weapons reposing at his side, the haughty savage lay at his lazy length; his feet reaching beyond the opening of the tent, and his head reposing on a rude pillow formed of a closely compressed pack of skins of wild animals, over which was spread a sort of mantle or blanket. One hand was introduced between the pillow and his head, the other grasped the pipe tomahawk he was smoking; and while the mechanical play of his right foot indicated pre-occupation of thought, his quick and meaning eye glanced frequently and alternately upon the furthest of his companions, the prisoner without, and the distant fort.

Within a few feet of the warrior lay, extended on a buffalo skin, the delicate figure of a female, whose hair, complexion, and hands, denoted her European extraction. Her dress was entirely Indian, however; consisting of a machecoti with leggings, mocassins, and shirt of printed cotton studded with silver brooches, – all of which were of a quality and texture to mark the wearer as the wife of a chief; and her fair hair, done up in a club behind, reposed on a neck of dazzling whiteness. Her eyes were large, blue, but wild and unmeaning; her countenance vacant; and her movements altogether mechanical. A wooden bowl filled with hominy, – a preparation of Indian corn, – was at her side; and from this she was now in the act of feeding herself with a spoon of the same material, but with a negligence and slovenliness that betrayed her almost utter unconsciousness of the action.

At the further side of the tent there was another woman, even more delicate in appearance than the one last mentioned. She, too, was blue-eyed, and of surpassing fairness of skin. Her attitude denoted a mind too powerfully absorbed in grief to be heedful of appearances; for she sat with her knees drawn up to her chin, and rocking her body to and fro with an undulating motion that seemed to have its origin in no effort of volition of her own. Her long fair hair hung negligently over her shoulders; and a blanket drawn over the top of her head like a veil, and extending partly over the person, disclosed here and there portions of an apparel which was strictly European, although rent, and exhibiting in various places stains of blood. A bowl similar to that of her companion, and filled with the same food, was at her side; but this was untasted.

"Why does the girl refuse to eat?" asked the warrior of her next him, as he fiercely rolled a volume of smoke from his lips. "Make her eat, for I would speak to her afterwards."

"Why does the girl refuse to eat?" responded the

woman in the same tone, dropping her spoon as she spoke, and turning to the object of remark with a vacant look. "It is good," she pursued, as she rudely shook the arm of the heedless sufferer. "Come girl, eat."

A shriek burst from the lips of the unhappy girl, as, apparently roused from her abstraction, she suffered the blanket to fall from her head, and staring wildly at her questioner, faintly demanded, –

"Who, in the name of mercy, are you, who address me in this horrid place in my own tongue? Speak; who are you? Surely I should know that voice for that of Ellen, the wife of Frank Halloway!"

A maniac laugh was uttered by the wretched woman. This continued offensively for a moment; and she observed, in an infuriated tone and with a searching eye, – "No, I am not the wife of Halloway. It is false. I am the wife of Wacousta. This is my husband!" and as she spoke she sprang nimbly to her feet, and was in the next instant lying prostrate on the form of the warrior; her arms thrown wildly around him, and her lips imprinting kisses on his cheek.

But Wacousta was in no mood to suffer her endearments. He for the first time seemed alive to the presence of her who lay beyond, and to whose whole appearance a character of animation had been imparted by the temporary excitement of her feelings. He gazed at her a moment, with the air of one endeavouring to recal the memory of days long gone by; and as he continued to do so, his eye dilated, his chest heaved, and his countenance alternately flushed and paled. At length he threw the form that reposed upon his own, violently, and even savagely, from him; sprang eagerly to his feet; and clearing the space that divided him from the object of his attention at a single step, bore her from the earth in his arms with as much ease as if she had been an infant, and then returning to his own rude couch, placed his horror-stricken victim at his side.

"Nay, nay," he urged sarcastically, as she vainly

struggled to free herself; "let the De Haldimar portion of your blood rise up in anger if it will; but that of Clara Beverley, at least —— "

"Gracious Providence! where am I, that I hear the name of my sainted mother thus familiarly pronounced?" interrupted the startled girl; "and who are you," - turning her eyes wildly on the swarthy countenance of the warrior, - "who are you, I ask, who, with the mien and in the garb of a savage of these forests, appear thus acquainted with her name?"

The warrior passed his hand across his brow for a moment, as if some painful and intolerable reflection had been called up by the question; but he speedily recovered his self-possession, and, with an expression of feature that almost petrified his auditor, vehemently observed, -

"You ask who I am! One who knew your mother long before the accursed name of De Haldimar had even been whispered in her ear; and whom love for the one and hatred for the other has rendered the savage you now behold! But," he continued, while a fierce and hideous smile lighted up every feature, "I overlook my past sufferings in my present happiness. The image of Clara Beverley, even such as my soul loved her in its youth, is once more before me in her child; *that* child shall be my wife!"

"Your wife! monster; - never!" shrieked the unhappy girl, again vainly attempting to disengage herself from the encircling arm of the savage. "But," she pursued, in a tone of supplication, while the tears coursed each other down her cheek, "if you ever loved my mother, as you say you have, restore her children to their home; and, if saints may be permitted to look down from heaven in approval of the acts of men, she whom you have loved will bless you for the deed."

A deep groan burst from the vast chest of Wacousta; but, for a moment, he answered not. At length he observed, pointing at the same time with his finger towards the cloudless vault above their heads, - "Do you behold yon blue sky, Clara de Haldimar?"

"I do; – what mean you?" demanded the trembling girl, in whom a momentary hope had been excited by the subdued manner of the savage.

"Nothing," he coolly rejoined; "only that were your mother to appear there at this moment, clad in all the attributes ascribed to angels, her prayer would not alter the destiny that awaits you. Nay, nay; look not thus sorrowfully," he pursued, as, in despite of her efforts to prevent him, he imprinted a burning kiss upon her lips. "Even thus was I once wont to linger on the lips of your mother; but hers ever pouted to be pressed by mine; and not with tears, but with sunniest smiles, did she court them." He paused; bent his head over the face of the shuddering girl; and gazing fixedly for a few minutes on her countenance, while he pressed her struggling form more closely to his own, exultingly pursued, as if to himself, – "Even as her mother was, so is she. Ye powers of hell! who would have ever thought a time would come when both my vengeance and my love would be gratified to the utmost? How strange it never should have occurred to me he had a daughter!"

"What mean you, fierce, unpitying man?" exclaimed the terrified Clara, to whom a full sense of the horror of her position had lent unusual energy of character. "Surely you will not detain a poor defenceless woman in your hands, – the child of her you say you have loved. But it is false! – you never knew her, or you would not now reject my prayer."

"Never knew her!" fiercely repeated Wacousta. Again he paused. "Would I had never known her! and I should not now be the outcast wretch I am," he added, slowly and impressively. Then once more elevating his voice, – "Clara de Haldimar, I have loved your mother as man never loved woman; and I have hated your father" (grinding his teeth with fury as he spoke) "as man never hated man. That love, that hatred are unquenched – unquenchable. Before me I see at once the image of her who, even in death, has lived enshrined in my heart, and the child of him who is my bitterest foe. Clara de Haldimar, do you understand me now?"

"Almighty Providence! is there no one to save me? – can nothing touch your stubborn heart?" exclaimed the affrighted girl; and she turned her swimming eyes on those of the warrior, in appeal; but his glance caused her own to sink in confusion. "Ellen Halloway," she pursued, after a moment's pause, and in the wild accents of despair, "if you are indeed the wife of this man, as you say you are, oh! plead for me with him; and in the name of that kindness, which I once extended to yourself, prevail on him to restore me to my father!"

"Ellen Halloway! – who calls Ellen Halloway?" said the wretched woman, who had again resumed her slovenly meal on the rude couch, apparently without consciousness of the scene enacting at her side. "I am not Ellen Halloway: they said so; but it is not true. My husband was Reginald Morton: but he went for a soldier, and was killed; and I never saw him more."

"Reginald Morton! What mean you, woman? – What know you of Reginald Morton?" demanded Wacousta, with frightful energy, as, leaning over the shrinking form of Clara, he violently grasped and shook the shoulder of the unhappy maniac.

"Stop; do not hurt me, and I will tell you all, sir," she almost screamed. "Oh, sir, Reginald Morton was my husband once; but he was kinder than you are. He did not look so fiercely at me; nor did he pinch me so."

"What of him? – who was he?" furiously repeated Wacousta, as he again impatiently shook the arm of the wretched Ellen. "Where did you know him? – Whence came he?"

"Nay, you must not be jealous of poor Reginald:" and, as she uttered these words in a softening and conciliating tone, her eye was turned upon those of the warrior with a mingled expression of fear and cunning. "But he was very good and very handsome, and generous; and we lived near each other, and we loved each other at first sight. But his

family were very proud, and they quarrelled with him
because he married me; and then we became very poor,
and Reginald went for a soldier, and —— ; but I forget the
rest, it is so long ago." She pressed her hand to her brow,
and sank her head upon her chest.

"Ellen, woman, again I ask you where he came from?
this Reginald Morton that you have named. To what country did he belong?"

"Oh, we were both Cornish," she answered, with a
vivacity singularly in contrast with her recent low and
monotonous tone; "but, as I said before, he was of a great
family, and I only a poor clergyman's daughter."

"Cornish! – Cornish, did you say?" fiercely repeated the
dark Wacousta, while an expression of loathing and disgust seemed for a moment to convulse his features; "then
is it as I had feared. One word more. Was the family seat
called Morton Castle?"

"It was," unhesitatingly returned the poor woman, yet
with the air of one wondering to hear a name repeated,
long forgotten even by herself. "It was a beautiful castle
too, on a lovely ridge of hills; and it commanded such a
nice view of the sea, close to the little port of ——; and the
parsonage stood in such a sweet valley, close under the
castle; and we were all so happy." She paused, again put
her hand to her brow, and pressed it with force, as if
endeavouring to pursue the chain of connection in her
memory, but evidently without success.

"And your father's name was Clayton?" said the warrior enquiringly. "Henry Clayton, if I recollect aright?"

"Ha! who names my father?" shrieked the wretched
woman. "Yes, sir, it was Clayton – Henry Clayton – the
kindest, the noblest of human beings. But the affliction of
his child, and the persecutions of the Morton family, broke
his heart. He is dead, sir, and Reginald is dead too; and I
am a poor lone widow in the world, and have no one to
love me." Here the tears coursed each other rapidly down
her faded cheek, although her eyes were staring and
motionless.

"It is false!" vociferated the warrior, who, now he had gained all that was essential to the elucidation of his doubts, quitted the shoulder he had continued to press with violence in his nervous hand, and once more extended himself at his length; "in me you behold the uncle of your husband. Yes, Ellen Clayton, you have been the wife of two Reginald Mortons. Both," he pursued with unutterable bitterness, while he again started up and shook his tomahawk menacingly in the direction of the fort, – "both have been the victims of yon cold-blooded governor; but the hour of our reckoning is at hand. Ellen," he fiercely added, "do you recollect the curse you pronounced on the family of that haughty man, when he slaughtered your Reginald. By Heaven! it shall be fulfilled; but first shall the love I have so long borne the mother be transferred to the child."

Again he sought to encircle the waist of her whom, in the strong excitement of his rage, he had momentarily quitted; but the unutterable disgust and horror produced in the mind of the unhappy Clara lent an almost supernatural activity to her despair. She dexterously eluded his grasp, gained her feet, and with tottering steps and outstretched arms darted through the opening of the tent, and piteously exclaiming, "Save me! oh, for God's sake, save me!" sank exhausted, and apparently lifeless, on the chest of the prisoner without.

To such of our readers as, deceived by the romantic nature of the attachment stated to have been originally entertained by Sir Everard Valletort for the unseen sister of his friend, have been led to expect a tale abounding in manifestations of its progress when the parties had actually met, we at once announce disappointment. Neither the lover of amorous adventure, nor the admirer of witty dialogue, should dive into these pages. Room for the exercise of the invention might, it is true, be found; but ours is a tale of sad reality, and our heroes and heroines figure under circumstances that would render wit a satire upon the understanding, and love a reflection upon the heart.

Within the bounds of probability have we, therefore, confined ourselves.

What the feelings of the young Baronet must have been, from the first moment when he received from the hands of the unfortunate Captain Baynton (who, although an officer of his own corps, was personally a stranger to him,) that cherished sister of his friend, on whose ideal form his excited imagination had so often latterly loved to linger, up to the present hour, we should vainly attempt to paint. There are emotions of the heart, it would be mockery in the pen to trace. From the instant of his first contributing to preserve her life, on that dreadful day of blood, to that when the schooner fell into the hands of the savages, few words had passed between them, and these had reference merely to the position in which they found themselves, and whenever Sir Everard felt he could, without indelicacy or intrusion, render himself in the slightest way serviceable to her. The very circumstances under which they had met, conduced to the suppression, if not utter extinction, of all of passion attached to the sentiment with which he had been inspired. A new feeling had quickened in his breast; and it was with emotions more assimilated to friendship than to love that he now regarded the beautiful but sorrow-stricken sister of his bosom friend. Still there was a softness, a purity, a delicacy and tenderness in this new feeling, in which the influence of sex secretly though unacknowledgedly predominated; and even while sensible it would have been a profanation of every thing most sacred and delicate in nature to have admitted a thought of love within his breast at such a moment, he also felt he could have entertained a voluptuous joy in making any sacrifice, even to the surrender of life itself, provided the tranquillity of that gentle and suffering being could be by it ensured.

Clara, in her turn, had been in no condition to admit so exclusive a power as that of love within her soul. She had, it is true, even amid the desolation of her shattered spirit, recognised in the young officer the original of a portrait so frequently drawn by her brother, and dwelt on by herself.

She acknowledged, moreover, the fidelity of the painting: but however she might have felt and acted under different circumstances, absorbed as was her heart, and paralysed her imagination, by the harrowing scenes she had gone through, she, too, had room but for one sentiment in her fainting soul, and that was friendship for the friend of her brother; on whom, moreover, she bestowed that woman's gratitude, which could not fail to be awakened by a recollection of the risks he had encountered, conjointly with Frederick, to save her from destruction. During their passage across lake Huron, Sir Everard had usually taken his seat on the deck, at that respectful distance which he conceived the delicacy of the position of the unfortunate cousins demanded; but in such a manner that, while he seemed wholly abstracted from them, his eye had more than once been detected by Clara fixed on hers, with an affectionateness of interest she could not avoid repaying with a glance of recognition and approval. These, however, were the only indications of regard that had passed between them.

If, however, a momentary and irrepressible flashing of that sentiment, which had, at an earlier period, formed a portion of their imaginings, did occasionally steal over their hearts while there was a prospect of reaching their friends in safety, all manifestation of its power was again finally suppressed when the schooner fell into the hands of the savages. Become the immediate prisoners of Wacousta, they had been surrendered to that ferocious chief to be dealt with as he might think proper; and, on disembarking from the canoe in which their transit to the main land had been descried that morning from the fort, had been separated from their equally unfortunate and suffering companions. Captain de Haldimar, Madeline, and the Canadian, were delivered over to the custody of several choice warriors of the tribe in which Wacousta was adopted; and, bound hand and foot, were, at that moment, in the war tent of the fierce savage, which, as Ponteac had once boasted to the governor, was every where hung around with human scalps, both of men, of women, and of children. The object of this mysterious man, in removing Clara to the spot we have described, was one well worthy of his ferocious nature. His vengeance had already devoted her to destruction; and it was within view of the fort, which contained the father whom he loathed, he had resolved his purpose should be accomplished. A refinement of cruelty, such as could scarcely have been supposed to enter the breast even of such a remorseless savage as himself, had caused him to convey to the same spot, him whom he rather suspected than knew to be the lover of the young girl. It was with the view of harrowing up the soul of one whom he had recognised as the officer who had disabled him on the night of the rencontre on the bridge, that he had bound Sir Everard to the tree, whence, as we have already stated, he was a compelled spectator of every thing that passed within the tent; and yet with that free action of limb which only tended to tantalize him the more amid his unavailable efforts to rid himself of his bonds, – a fact that proved not only the dire extent to which the revenge of Wacousta could be carried, but the actual and gratuitous cruelty of his nature.

One must have been similarly circumstanced, to understand all the agony of the young man during this odious scene, and particularly at the fierce and repeated declaration of the savage that Clara should be his bride. More than once had he essayed to remove the ligatures which confined his waist; but his unsuccessful attempts only drew an occasional smile of derision from his enemy, as he glanced his eye rapidly towards him. Conscious at length of the inutility of efforts, which, without benefiting her for whom they were principally prompted, rendered him in some degree ridiculous even in his own eyes, the wretched Valletort desisted altogether, and with his head sunk upon his chest, and his eyes closed, sought at least to shut out a scene which blasted his sight, and harrowed up his very soul.

But when Clara, uttering her wild cry for protection,

and rushing forth from the tent, sank almost unconsciously in his embrace, a thrill of inexplicable joy ran through each awakened fibre of his frame. Bending eagerly forward, he had extended his arms to receive her; and when he felt her light and graceful form pressing upon his own as its last refuge – when he felt her heart beating against his – when he saw her head drooping on his shoulder, in the wild recklessness of despair, – even amid that scene of desolation and grief he could not help enfolding her in tumultuous ecstasy to his breast. Every horrible danger was for an instant forgotten in the soothing consciousness that he at length encircled the form of her, whom in many an hour of solitude he had thus pictured, although under far different circumstances, reposing confidingly on him. There was delight mingled with agony in his sensation of the wild throb of her bosom against his own; and even while his soul fainted within him, as he reflected on the fate that awaited her, he felt as if he could himself now die more happily.

Momentary, however, was the duration of this scene. Furious with anger at the evident disgust of his victim, Wacousta no sooner saw her sink into the arms of her lover, than with that agility for which he was remarkable he was again on his feet, and stood in the next instant at her side. Uniting to the generous strength of his manhood all that was wrung from his mingled love and despair, the officer clasped his hands around the waist of the drooping Clara; and with clenched teeth, and feet firmly set, seemed resolved to defy every effort of the warrior to remove her. Not a word was uttered on either side; but in the fierce smile that curled the lip of the savage, there spoke a language even more terrible than the words that smile implied. Sir Everard could not suppress an involuntary shudder; and when at length Wacousta, after a short but violent struggle, succeeded in again securing and bearing off his prize, the wretchedness of soul of the former was indescribable.

"You see 'tis vain to struggle against your destiny, Clara

de Haldimar," sneered the warrior. "Ours is but a rude nuptial couch, it is true; but the wife of an Indian chief must not expect the luxuries of Europe in the heart of an American wilderness."

"Almighty Heaven! where am I?" exclaimed the wretched girl, again unclosing her eyes to all the horror of her position; for again she lay at the side, and within the encircling arm, of her enemy. "Oh, Sir Everard Valletort, I thought I was with you, and that you had saved me from this monster. Where is my brother? – Where are Frederick and Madeline? – Why have they deserted me? – Ah! my heart will break. I cannot endure this longer, and live."

"Clara, Miss de Haldimar," groaned Sir Everard, in a voice of searching agony; "could I lay down my life for you, I would; but you see these bonds. Oh God! oh God! have pity on the innocent; and for once incline the heart of yon fierce monster to the whisperings of mercy." As he uttered the last sentence, he attempted to sink on his knees in supplication to Him he addressed, but the tension of the cord prevented him; yet were his hands clasped, and his eyes upraised to heaven, while his countenance beamed with an expression of fervent enthusiasm.

"Peace, babbler! or, by Heaven! that prayer shall be your last," vociferated Wacousta. "But no," he pursued to himself, dropping at the same time the point of his upraised tomahawk; "these are but the natural writhings of the crushed worm; and the longer protracted they are, the more complete will be my vengeance." Then turning to the terrified girl, – "You ask, Clara de Haldimar, where you are? In the tent of your mother's lover, I reply, – at the side of him who once pressed her to his heart, even as I now press you, and with a fondness that was only equalled by her own. Come, dear Clara," and his voice assumed a tone of tenderness that was even more revolting than his natural ferocity, "let me woo you to the affection she once possessed. It was a heart of fire in which her image stood enshrined, – it is a heart of fire still, and well worthy of her child."

"Never, never!" shrieked the agonised girl. "Kill me, murder me, if you will; but oh! if you have pity, pollute not my ear with the avowal of your detested love. But again I repeat, it is false that my mother ever knew you. She never could have loved so fierce, so vindictive a being as yourself."

"Ha! do you doubt me still?" sternly demanded the savage. Then drawing the shuddering girl still closer to his vast chest, – "Come hither, Clara, while to convince you I unfold the sad history of my life, and tell you more of your parents than you have ever known. When," he pursued solemnly, "you have learnt the extent of my love for the one, and of my hatred for the other, and the wrongs I have endured from both, you will no longer wonder at the spirit of mingled love and vengeance that dictates my conduct towards yourself. Listen, girl," he continued fiercely, "and judge whether mine are injuries to be tamely pardoned, when a whole life has been devoted to the pursuit of the means of avenging them."

Irresistibly led by a desire to know what possible connection could have existed between her parents and this singular and ferocious man, the wretched girl gave her passive assent. She even hoped that, in the course of his narrative, some softening recollections would pass over his mind, the effect of which might be to predispose him to mercy. Wacousta buried his face for a few moments in his large hand, as if endeavouring to collect and concentrate the remembrances of past years. His countenance, meanwhile, had undergone a change; for there was now a shade of melancholy mixed with the fierceness of expression usually observable there. This, however, was dispelled in the course of his narrative, and as various opposite passions were in turn powerfully and severally developed.

Eight

"IT IS NOW four and twenty years," commenced Wacousta, "since your father and myself first met as subalterns in the regiment he now commands, when, unnatural to say, an intimacy suddenly sprang up between us which, as it was then to our brother officers, has since been a source of utter astonishment to myself. Unnatural, I repeat, for fire and ice are not more opposite than were the elements of which our natures were composed. He, all coldness, prudence, obsequiousness, and forethought. I, all enthusiasm, carelessness, impetuosity, and independence. Whether this incongruous friendship – friendship! no, I will not so far sully the sacred name as thus to term the unnatural union that subsisted between us; – whether this intimacy, then, sprang from the adventitious circumstance of our being more frequently thrown together as officers of the same company, – for we were both attached to the grenadiers, – or that my wild spirit was soothed by the bland amenity of his manners, I know not. The latter, however, is not improbable; for proud, and haughty, and dignified, as the colonel *now* is, such was not *then* the character of the ensign; who seemed thrown out of one of Nature's supplest moulds, to fawn, and cringe, and worm his way to favour by the wily speciousness of his manners. Oh God!" pursued Wacousta, after a momentary pause, and striking his palm against his forehead, "that I ever should have been the dupe of such a cold-blooded hypocrite!

"I have said our intimacy excited surprise among our brother officers. It did; for all understood and read the character of your father, who was as much disliked and distrusted for the speciousness of his false nature, as I was generally esteemed for the frankness and warmth of mine. No one openly censured the evident preference I gave him in my friendship; but we were often sarcastically termed the Pylades and Orestes of the regiment, until my heart was ready to leap into my throat with impatience at the bitterness in which the taunt was conceived; and frequently in my presence was allusion made to the blind folly of him, who should take a cold and slimy serpent to his bosom only to feel its fangs darted into it at the moment when most fostered by its genial heat. All, however, was in vain. On a nature like mine, innuendo was likely to produce an effect directly opposite to that intended; and the more I found them inclined to be severe on him I called my friend, the more marked became my preference. I even fancied that because I was rich, generous, and heir to a title, their observations were prompted by jealousy of the influence he possessed over me, and a desire to supplant him only for their interests' sake. Bitterly have I been punished for the illiberality of such an opinion. Those to whom I principally allude were the subalterns of the regiment, most of whom were nearly of our own age. One or two of the junior captains were also of this number; but, by the elders (as we termed the seniors of that rank) and field officers, Ensign de Haldimar was always regarded as a most prudent and promising young officer.

"What conduced, in a great degree, to the establishment of our intimacy was the assistance I always received from my brother subaltern in whatever related to my military duties. As the lieutenant of the company, the more immediate responsibility attached to myself; but being naturally of a careless habit, or perhaps considering all duty irksome to my impatient nature that was not duty in the field, I was but too often guilty of neglecting it. On these occasions my absence was ever carefully supplied by your father, who, in all the minutiae of regimental economy, was surpassed by no other officer in the corps; so that credit was given to me, when, at the ordinary inspections, the grenadiers were acknowledged to be the company the most perfect in equipment and skilful in manoeuvre. Deeply, deeply," again mused Wacousta, "have these services been repaid.

"As you have just learnt, Cornwall is the country of my birth. I was the eldest of the only two surviving children of a large family; and, as heir to the baronetcy of the proud Mortons, was looked up to by lord and vassal as the future perpetuator of the family name. My brother had been designed for the army; but as this was a profession to which I had attached my inclinations, the point was waved in my favour, and at the age of eighteen I first joined the —— regiment, then quartered in the Highlands of Scotland. During my boyhood I had ever accustomed myself to athletic exercises, and loved to excite myself by encountering danger in its most terrific forms. Often had I passed whole days in climbing the steep and precipitous crags which overhang the sea in the neighbourhood of Morton Castle, ostensibly in the pursuit of the heron or the seagull, but self-acknowledgedly for the mere pleasure of grappling with the difficulties they opposed to me. Often, too, in the most terrific tempests, when sea and sky have met in one black and threatening mass, and when the startled fishermen have in vain attempted to dissuade me from my purpose, have I ventured, in sheer bravado, out of sight of land, and unaccompanied by a human soul. Then, when wind and tide have been against me on my return, have I, with my simple sculls alone, caused my faithful bark to leap through the foaming brine as though a press of canvass had impelled her on. Oh, that this spirit of adventure had never grown with my growth and strengthened with my strength!" sorrowfully added the warrior, again apostrophising himself: "then had I never been the wretch I am.

"The wild daring by which my boyhood had been marked was again powerfully awakened by the bold and romantic scenery of the Scottish Highlands; and as the regiment was at that time quartered in a part of these mountainous districts, where, from the disturbed nature of the times, society was difficult of attainment, many of the officers were driven from necessity, as I was from choice, to indulge in the sports of the chase. On one occasion a party of four of us set out early in the morning in pursuit of deer, numbers of which we knew were to be met with in the mountainous tracts of Bute and Argyleshire. The course we happened to take lay through a succession of dark deep glens, and over frowning rocks; the difficulties of access to which only stirred up my dormant spirit of enterprise the more. We had continued in this course for many hours, overcoming one difficulty only to be encountered by another, and yet without meeting a single deer; when, at length, the faint blast of a horn was heard far above our heads in the distance, and presently a noble stag was seen to ascend a ledge of rocks immediately in front of us. To raise my gun to my shoulder and fire was the work of a moment, after which we all followed in pursuit. On reaching the spot where the deer had first been seen, we observed traces of blood, satisfying us he had been wounded; but the course taken in his flight was one that seemed to defy every human effort to follow in. It was a narrow pointed ledge, ascending boldly towards a huge cliff that projected frowningly from the extreme summit, and on either side lay a dark, deep, and apparently fathomless ravine; to look even on which was sufficient to appal the stoutest heart, and unnerve the steadiest brain. For me, however, long accustomed to dangers of the sort, it had no terror. This was a position in which I had often wished once more to find myself placed, and I felt buoyant and free as the deer itself I intended to pursue. In vain did my companions (and your father was one) implore me to abandon a project so wild and hazardous. I bounded forward, and they turned shuddering away, that their eyes might not witness the destruction that awaited me. Meanwhile, balancing my long gun in my upraised hands, I trod the dangerous path with a buoyancy and elasticity of limb, a lightness of heart, and a fearlessness of consequences, that surprised even myself. Perhaps it was to the latter circumstance I owed my safety, for a single doubt of my security might have impelled a movement that would not have failed to have precipitated me into the yawning gulf below. I had proceeded in this manner about five hundred yards, when I came to the termination of the ledge, from the equally narrow transverse extremity of which branched out three others; the whole contributing to form a figure resembling that of a trident. Pausing here for a moment, I applied the hunting horn, with which I was provided, to my lips. This signal, announcing my safety, was speedily returned by my friends below in a cheering and lively strain, that seemed to express at once surprise and satisfaction; and inspirited by the sound, I prepared to follow up my perilous chase. Along the ledge I had quitted I had remarked occasional traces where the stricken deer had passed; and the same blood-spots now directed me at a point where, but for these, I must have been utterly at fault. The centre of these new ridges, and the narrowest, was that taken by the animal, and on that I once more renewed my pursuit. As I continued to advance I found the ascent became more precipitous, and the difficulties opposed to my progress momentarily more multiplied. Still, nothing daunted, I continued my course towards the main body of rock that now rose within a hundred yards. How this was to be gained I knew not; for it shelved out abruptly from the extreme summit, overhanging the abyss, and presenting an appearance which I cannot more properly render than by comparing it to the sounding-boards placed over the pulpits of our English churches. Still I was resolved to persevere to the close, and I but too unhappily succeeded." Again Wacousta paused. A tear started to his eye, but this he impatiently brushed away with his swarthy hand.

"It was evident to me," he again resumed, "that there must be some opening through which the deer had effected his escape to the precipitous height above; and I felt a wild and fearful triumph in following him to his cover, over passes which it was my pleasure to think none of the hardy mountaineers themselves would have dared to venture upon with impunity. I paused not to consider of the difficulty of bearing away my prize, even if I succeeded in overtaking it. At every step my excitement and determination became stronger, and I felt every fibre of my frame to dilate, as when, in my more boyish days, I used to brave, in my gallant skiff, the mingled fury of the warring elements of sea and storm. Suddenly, while my mind was intent only on the dangers I used then to hold in such light estimation, I found my further progress intercepted by a fissure in the crag. It was not the width of this opening that disconcerted me, for it exceeded not ten feet; but I came upon it so unadvisedly, that, in attempting to check my forward motion, I had nearly lost my equipoise, and fallen into the abyss that now yawned before and on either side of me. To pause upon the danger, would, I felt, be to ensure it. Summoning all my dexterity into a single bound, I cleared the chasm; and with one buskined foot (for my hunting costume was strictly Highland) clung firmly to the ledge, while I secured my balance with the other. At this point the rock became gradually broader, so that I now trod the remainder of the rude path in perfect security, until I at length found myself close to the vast mass of which these ledges were merely ramifications or veins: but still I could discover no outlet by which the wounded deer could have escaped. While I lingered, thoughtfully, for a moment, half in disappointment, half in anger, and with my back leaning against the rock, I fancied I heard a rustling, as of the leaves and branches of underwood, on that part which projected like a canopy, far above the abyss. I bent my eye eagerly and fixedly on the spot whence the sound proceeded, and presently could distinguish the blue sky appearing through an aperture, to which was, the instant afterwards, applied what I conceived to be a human face. No sooner, however, was it seen than withdrawn; and then the rustling of leaves was heard again, and all was still as before.

"Why did my evil genius so will it," resumed Wacousta, after another pause, during which he manifested deep emotion, "that I should have heard those sounds and seen that face? But for these I should have returned to my companions, and my life might have been the life – the plodding life – of the multitude; things that are born merely to crawl through existence and die, knowing not at the moment of death why or how they have lived at all. But who may resist the destiny that presides over him from the cradle to the grave? for, although the mass may be, and are, unworthy of the influencing agency of that Unseen Power, who will presume to deny there are those on whom it stamps its iron seal, even from the moment of their birth to that which sees all that is mortal of them consigned to the tomb? What was it but destiny that whispered to me what I had seen was the face of a woman? I had not traced a feature, nor could I distinctly state that it was a human countenance I had beheld; but mine was ever an imagination into which the wildest improbability was scarce admitted that it did not grow into conviction that instant.

"A new direction was now given to my feelings. I felt a presentiment that my adventure, if prosecuted, would terminate in some extraordinary and characteristic manner; and obeying, as I ever did, the first impulse of my heart, I prepared to grapple once more with the difficulties that yet remained to be surmounted. In order to do this, it was necessary that my feet and hands should be utterly without incumbrance; for it was only by dint of climbing that I could expect to reach that part of the projecting rock to which my attention had been directed. Securing my gun between some twisted roots that grew out of and adhered to the main body of the rock, I commenced the difficult ascent; and, after considerable effort, found myself at length immediately under the aperture. My progress along the lower superficies of this projection was like that of a crawling reptile. My back hung suspended over the chasm, into which one false movement of hand or foot, one yielding of the roots entwined in the rock, must inevitably have precipitated me; and, while my toes wormed themselves into the tortuous fibres of the latter, I passed hand over hand beyond my head, until I had arrived within a foot or two of the point I desired to reach. Here, however, a new difficulty occurred. A slight projection of the rock, close to the aperture, impeded my further progress in the manner hitherto pursued; and, to pass this, I was compelled to drop my whole weight, suspended by one vigorous arm, while, with the other, I separated the bushes that concealed the opening. A violent exertion of every muscle now impelled me upward, until at length I had so far succeeded as to introduce my head and shoulders through the aperture; after which my final success was no longer doubtful. If I have been thus minute in the detail of the dangerous nature of this passage," continued Wacousta, gloomily, "it is not without reason. I would have you to impress the whole of the localities upon your imagination, that you may the better comprehend, from a knowledge of the risks I incurred, how little I have merited the injuries under which I have writhed for years."

Again one of those painful pauses with which his narrative was so often broken, occurred; and, with an energy that terrified her whom he addressed, Wacousta pursued, – "Clara de Haldimar, it was here – in this garden – this paradise – this oasis of the rocks in which I now found myself, that I first saw and loved your mother. Ha! you start: you believe me now. – Loved her!" he continued, after another short pause – "oh, what a feeble word is love to express the concentration of mighty feelings that flowed like burning lava through my veins! Who shall pretend to give a name to the emotion that ran thrillingly – madly through my excited frame, when first I gazed on her, who, in every attribute of womanly beauty, realised all my fondest fancy ever painted? – Listen to me, Clara," he pursued, in a fiercer tone, and with a convulsive pressure of the form he still encircled: – "If, in my younger days, my mind was alive to enterprise, and loved to contemplate danger in its most appalling forms, this was far from being the master passion of my soul; nay, it was the strong necessity I felt of pouring into some devoted bosom the overflowing fulness of my heart, that made me court in solitude those positions of danger with which the image of woman was ever associated. How often, while tossed by the raging elements, now into the blue vault of heaven, now into the lowest gulfs of the sea, have I madly wished to press to my bounding bosom the being of my fancy's creation, who, all enamoured and given to her love, should, even amid the danger that environed her, be alive but to one consciousness, – that of being with him on whom her life's hope alone reposed! How often, too, while bending over some dark and threatening precipice, or standing on the utmost verge of some tall projecting cliff, my aching head (aching with the intenseness of its own conceptions) bared to the angry storm, and my eye fixed unshrinkingly on the boiling ocean far beneath my feet, has my whole soul – my every faculty, been bent on that ideal beauty which controlled every sense! Oh, imagination, how tyrannical is thy sway – how exclusive thy power – how insatiable thy thirst! Surrounded by living beauty, I was insensible to its influence; for, with all the perfection that reality can attain on earth, there was ever to be found some deficiency, either physical or moral, that defaced the symmetry and destroyed the loveliness of the whole; but, no sooner didst thou, with magic wand, conjure up one of thy embodiments, than my heart became a sea of flame, and was consumed in the vastness of its own fires.

"It was in vain that my family sought to awaken me to a sense of the acknowledged loveliness of the daughters of more than one ancient house in the county, with one of whom an alliance was, in many respects, considered desirable. Their beauty, or rather their whole, was insufficient to stir up into madness the dormant passions of my nature; and although my breast was like a glowing furnace, in which fancy cast all the more exciting images of her coinage to secure the last impress of the heart's approval, my outward deportment to some of the fairest and loveliest of earth's realities was that of one on whom the influence of woman's beauty could have no power. From my earliest boyhood I had loved to give the rein to these feelings, until they at length rendered me their slave. Woman was the idol that lay enshrined within my inmost heart; but it was woman such as I had not yet met with, yet felt must somewhere exist in the creation. For her I could have resigned title, fortune, family, every thing that is dear to man, save the life, through which alone the reward of such sacrifice could have been tasted, and to this phantom I had already yielded up all the manlier energies of my nature; but, deeply as I felt the necessity of loving something less unreal, up to the moment of my joining the regiment, my heart had never once throbbed for created woman.

"I have already said that, on gaining the summit of the rock, I found myself in a sort of oasis of the mountains. It was so. Belted on every hand by bold and precipitous crags, that seemed to defy the approach even of the wildest animals, and putting utterly at fault the penetration and curiosity of man, was spread a carpet of verdure, a luxuriance of vegetation, that might have put to shame the fertility of the soft breeze-nourished valleys of Italy and Southern France. Time, however, is not given me to dwell on the mingled beauty and wildness of a scene, so consonant with my ideas of the romantic and the picturesque. Let me rather recur to her (although my heart be lacerated once more in the recollection) who was the presiding deity of the whole, – that being after whom, had I had the fabled power of Prometheus, I should have formed and animated the sharer of that sweet wild solitude, nor once felt that fancy, to whom I was so largely a debtor, had in aught been cheated of what she had, for a series of years, so rigidly claimed.

"At about twenty yards from the aperture, and on a bank, formed of turf, covered with moss, and interspersed with roses and honey-suckles, sat this divinity of the oasis. She, too, was clad in the Highland dress, which gave an air of wildness and elegance to her figure that was in classic harmony with the surrounding scenery. At the moment of my appearance she was in the act of dressing the wounded shoulder of a stag that had recently been shot; and from the broad tartan riband I perceived attached to its neck, added to the fact of the tameness of the animal, I presumed that this stag, evidently a favourite of its mistress, was the same I had fired at and wounded. The rustling I made among the bushes had attracted her attention; she raised her eyes from the deer, and, beholding me, started to her feet, uttering a cry of terror and surprise. Fearing to speak, as if the sound of my own voice were sufficient to dispel the illusion that fascinated both eye and heart into delicious tension on her form, yet, with my soul kindled into all that wild uncontrollable love which had been the accumulation of years of passionate imagining, I stood for some moments as motionless as the rock out of which I appeared to grow. It seemed as though I had not the power to think or act, so fully was every faculty of my being filled with the consciousness that I at length gazed upon her I was destined to love for ever.

"It was this utter immobility on my own part, that ensured me a continuance of the exquisite happiness I then enjoyed. The first movement of the startled girl had been to fly towards her dwelling, which stood at a short distance, half imbedded in the same clustering roses and honey-suckles that adorned her bank of moss; but when she remarked my utter stillness, and apparent absence of purpose, she checked the impulse that would have directed her departure, and stopped, half in curiosity, half in fear, to examine me once more. At that moment all my energies appeared to be restored; I threw myself into an attitude expressive of deep contrition for the intrusion of which I had been unconsciously guilty, and dropping on one knee, and raising my clasped hands, inclined them towards her in token of mingled deprecation of her anger, and respectful homage to herself. At first she hesitated, – then gradually and timidly retrod her way to the seat she had so abruptly quitted in her alarm. Emboldened by this movement, I made a step or two in advance, but no sooner had I done so than she again took to flight. Once more, however, she turned to behold me, and again I had dropped on my knee, and was conjuring her, with the same signs, to remain and bless me with her presence. Again she returned to her seat, and again I advanced. Scarcely less timid, however, than the deer, which followed her every movement, she fled a third time, – a third time looked back, and was again induced, by my supplicating manner, to return. Frequently was this repeated, before I finally found myself at the feet, and pressing the hand – (oh God! what torture in the recollection) – yes, pressing the hand of her for whose smile I would, even at that moment, have sacrificed my soul; and every time she fled, the classic disposition of her graceful limbs, and her whole natural attitude of alarm, could only be compared with those of one of the huntresses of Diana, intruded on in her woodland privacy by the unhallowed presence of some daring mortal. Such was your mother, Clara de Haldimar; yes, even such as I have described her was Clara Beverley."

Again Wacousta paused, and his pause was longer than usual, as, with his large hand again covering his face, he seemed endeavouring to master the feelings which these recollections had called up. Clara scarcely breathed. Unmindful of her own desolate position, her soul was intent only on a history that related so immediately to her beloved mother, of whom all that she had hitherto known was, that she was a native of Scotland, and that her father had married her while quartered in that country. The deep emotion of the terrible being before her, so often manifested in the course of what he had already given of his recital, added to her knowledge of the facts just named, scarcely left a doubt of the truth of his statement on her mind. Her ear was now bent achingly towards him, in expectation of a continuance of his history, but he still remained in the same attitude of absorption. An irresistible impulse caused her to extend her hand, and remove his own from his eyes: they were filled with tears; and even while her mind rapidly embraced the hope that this manifestation of tenderness was but the dawning of mercy towards the children of her he had once loved, her kind nature could not avoid sympathizing with him, whose uncouthness of appearance and savageness of nature was, in some measure, lost sight of in the fact of the powerful love he yet apparently acknowledged.

But no sooner did Wacousta feel the soft pressure of her hand, and meet her eyes turned on his with an expression of interest, than the most rapid transition was effected in his feelings. He drew the form of the weakly resisting girl closer to his heart; again imprinted a kiss upon her lips; and then, while every muscle in his iron frame seemed quivering with emotion, exclaimed, – "By Heaven! that touch, that glance, were Clara Beverley's all over! Oh, let me linger on the recollection, even such as they were, when her arms first opened to receive me in that sweet oasis of the Highlands. Yes, Clara," he proceeded more deliberately, as he scanned her form with an eye that made her shudder, "such as your mother was, so are you; the same delicacy of proportion; the same graceful curvature of limb, only less rounded, less womanly. But you must be younger by about two years than she then was. Your age cannot exceed seventeen; and time will supply what your mere girlhood renders you deficient in."

There was a cool licence of speech – a startling freedom of manner – in the latter part of this address, that disappointed not less than it pained and offended the unhappy Clara. It seemed to her as if the illusion she had just created, were already dispelled by his language, even as her own momentary interest in the fierce man had also been destroyed from the same cause. She shuddered; and sighing bitterly, suffered her tears to force themselves through her closed lids upon her pallid cheek. This change in her appearance seemed to act as a check on the temporary excitement of Wacousta. Again obeying one of these rapid transitions of feeling, for which he was remarkable, he once more assumed an expression of seriousness, and thus continued his narrative.

Nine

"IT BOOTS not now, Clara, to enter upon all that succeeded to my first introduction to your mother. It would
take long to relate, not the gradations of our passion, for
that was like the whirlwind of the desert, sudden and
devastating from the first; but the burning vow, the plighted faith, the reposing confidence, the unchecked abandonment that flew from the lips, and filled the heart of each,
sealed, as they were, with kisses, long, deep, enervating,
even such as I had ever pictured that divine pledge of
human affection should be. Yes, Clara de Haldimar, your
mother was the child of nature *then*. Unspoiled by the
forms, unvitiated by the sophistries of a world with which
she had never mixed, her intelligent innocence made the
most artless avowals to my enraptured ear, – avowals that
the more profligate minded woman of society would have
blushed to whisper even to herself. And for these I loved
her to my own undoing.

"Blind vanity, inconceivable folly!" continued Wacousta, again pressing his forehead with force; "how could
I be so infatuated as not to perceive, that although her
heart was filled with a new and delicious passion, it was
less the individual than the man she loved. And how could
it be otherwise, since I was the first, beside her father, she
had ever seen or recollected to have seen? Still, Clara de
Haldimar," he pursued, with haughty energy, "I was not
always the rugged being I now appear. Of surpassing

strength I had ever been, and fleet of foot, but not then had I attained to my present gigantic stature; neither was my form endowed with the same Herculean rudeness; nor did my complexion wear the swarthy hue of the savage; nor had my features been rendered repulsive, from the perpetual action of those fierce passions which have since assailed my soul. My physical faculties had not yet been developed to their present grossness of maturity, neither had my moral energies acquired that tone of ferocity which often renders me hideous, even in my own eyes. In a word, the milk of my nature (for, with all my impetuosity of character, I *was* generous-hearted and kind) had not yet been turned to gall by villainy and deceit. My form had then all that might attract – my manners all that might win – my enthusiasm of speech all that might persuade – and my heart all that might interest a girl fashioned after nature's manner, and tutored in nature's school. In the regiment, I was called the handsome grenadier; but there was another handsomer than I, – a sly, insidious, wheedling, false, remorseless villain. That villain, Clara de Haldimar, was your father.

"But wherefore," continued Wacousta, chafing with the recollection, "wherefore do I, like a vain and puling schoolboy, enter into this abasing contrast of personal advantages? The proud eagle soars not more above the craven kite, than did my soul, in all that was manly and generous, above that of yon false governor; and who should have prized those qualities, if it were not the woman who, bred in solitude, and taught by fancy to love all that was generous and noble in the heart of man, should have considered mere beauty of feature as dust in the scale, when opposed to sentiments which can invest even deformity with loveliness? In all this I may appear vain; I am only just.

"I have said that your mother had been brought up in solitude, and without having seen the face of another man than her father. Such was the case; – Colonel Beverley, of English name, but Scottish connections, was an old gentleman of considerable eccentricity of character. He had taken a part in the rebellion of 1715; but sick and disgusted with an issue by which his fortunes had been affected, and heart-broken by the loss of a beloved wife, whose death had been accelerated by circumstances connected with the disturbed nature of the times, he had resolved to bury himself and child in some wild, where the face of man, whom he loathed, might no more offend his sight. This oasis of the mountains was the spot selected for his purpose; for he had discovered it some years previously, on an occasion, when, closely pursued by some of the English troops, and separated from his followers, he had only effected his escape by venturing on the ledges of rock I have already described. After minute subsequent search, at the opposite extremity of the oblong belt of rocks that shut it in on every hand, he had discovered an opening, through which the transport of such necessaries as were essential to his object might be effected; and, causing one of his dwelling houses to be pulled down, he had the materials carried across the rocks on the shoulders of the men employed to re-erect them in his chosen solitude. A few months served to complete these arrangements, which included a garden abounding in every fruit and flower that could possibly live in so elevated a region; and this, in time, under his own culture, and that of his daughter, became the Eden it first appeared to me.

"Previous to their entering on this employment, the workmen had been severally sworn to secresy; and when all was declared ready for his reception, the colonel summoned them a second time to his presence; when, after making a handsome present to each, in addition to his hire, he found no difficulty in prevailing on them to renew their oath that they would preserve the most scrupulous silence in regard to the place of his retreat. He then took advantage of a dark and tempestuous night to execute his project; and, attended only by an old woman and her daughter, faithful dependants of the family, set out in quest of his new abode, leaving all his neighbours to discuss and marvel at the singularity of his disappearance. True to his text, however, not even a boy was admitted into his household: and here they had continued to live, unseeing and unseen by man, except when a solitary and distant mountaineer occasionally flitted among the rocks below in pursuit of his game. Fruits and vegetables composed their principal diet; but once a fortnight the old woman was dispatched through the opening already mentioned, which was at other times so secured by her master, that no hand but his own could remove the intricate fastenings. This expedition had for its object the purchase of bread and animal food at the nearest market; and every time she sallied forth an oath was administered to the crone, the purport of which was, not only that she would return, unless prevented by violence or death, but that she would not answer any questions put to her, as to who she was, whence she came, or for whom the fruits of her marketing were intended.

"Meanwhile, wrapped up in his books, which were chiefly classic authors, or writers on abstruse sciences, the misanthropical colonel paid little or no attention to the cultivation of the intellect of his daughter, whom he had merely instructed in the elementary branches of education; in all which, however, she evinced an aptitude and perfectability that indicated quickness of genius and a capability of far higher attainments. Books he principally withheld from her, because they brought the image of man, whom he hated, and wished she should also hate, too often in flattering colours before her; and had any work treating of love been found to have crept accidentally into his own collection, it would instantly and indignantly have been committed to the flames.

"Thus left to the action of her own heart – the guidance of her own feelings – it was but natural your mother should have suffered her imagination to repose on an ideal happiness, which, although in some degree destitute of shape and character, was still powerfully felt. Nature is too

imperious a law-giver to be thwarted in her dictates; and
however we may seek to stifle it, her inextinguishable
voice will make itself heard, whether it be in the lonely
desert or in the crowded capital. Possessed of a glowing
heart and warm sensibilities, Clara Beverley felt the energies of her being had not been given to her to be wasted
on herself. In her dreams by night, and her thoughts by
day, she had pictured a being endowed with those attributes which were the fruit of her own fertility of conception. If she plucked a flower, (and all this she admitted at
our first interview," groaned Wacousta,) "she was sensible
of the absence of one to whom that flower might be given.
If she gazed at the star-studded canopy of heaven, or bent
her head over the frowning precipices by which she was
every where surrounded, she felt the absence of him with
whom she could share the enthusiasm excited by the contemplation of the one, and to whom she could impart the
mingled terror and admiration produced by the dizzying
depths of the other. What dear acknowledgments (alas!
too deceitful,) flowed from her guileless lips, even during
that first interview. With a candour and unreservedness
that spring alone from unsophisticated manners and an
untainted heart, she admitted, that the instant she beheld
me, she felt she had found the being her fancy had been so
long tutored to linger on, and her heart to love. She was
sure I was come to be her husband (for she had understood from her aged attendant that a man who loved a
woman wished to be her husband); and she was glad her
pet stag had been wounded, since it had been the means of
procuring her such happiness. She was not cruel enough
to take pleasure in the sufferings of the poor animal; for
she would nurse it, and it would soon be well again; but
she could not help rejoicing in its disaster, since that circumstance had been the cause of my finding her out, and
loving her even as she loved me. And all this was said with
her head reclining on my chest, and her beautiful countenance irradiated with a glow that had something divine in
the simplicity of purpose it expressed.

"On my demanding to know whether it was not her face I had seen at the opening in the cliff, she replied that it was. Her stag often played the truant, and passed whole hours away from her, rambling beyond the precincts of the solitude that contained its mistress; but no sooner was the small silver bugle, which she wore across her shoulder, applied to her lips, than 'Fidelity' (thus she had named him) was certain to obey the call, and to come bounding up the line of cliff to the main rock, into which it effected its entrance at a point that had escaped my notice. It was her bugle I had heard in the course of my pursuit of the animal; and, from the aperture through which I had effected my entrance, she had looked out to see who was the audacious hunter she had previously observed threading a passage, along which her stag itself never appeared without exciting terror in her bosom. The first glimpse she had caught of my form was at the moment when, after having sounded my own bugle, I cleared the chasm; and this was a leap she had so often trembled to see taken by 'Fidelity,' that she turned away and shuddered when she saw it fearlessly adventured on by a human being. A feeling of curiosity had afterwards induced her to return and see if the bold hunter had cleared the gulf, or perished in his mad attempt; but when she looked outward from the highest pinnacle of her rocky prison, she could discover no traces of him whatever. It then occurred to her, that, if successful in his leap, his progress must have been finally arrested by the impassable rock that terminated the ridge; in which case she might perchance obtain a nearer sight of his person. With this view she had removed the bushes enshrouding the aperture; and, bending low to the earth, thrust her head partially through it. Scarcely had she done so, however, when she beheld me immediately, though far beneath her, with my back reposing against the rock, and my eyes apparently fixed on hers.

"Filled with a variety of opposite sentiments, among which unfeigned alarm was predominant, she had instantaneously removed her head; and, closing the aperture as noiselessly as possible, returned to the moss-covered seat on which I had first surprised her; where, while she applied dressings of herbs to the wound of her favourite, she suffered her mind to ruminate on the singularity of the appearance of a man so immediately in the vicinity of their retreat. The supposed impracticability of the ascent I had accomplished, satisfied, even while (as she admitted) it disappointed her. I must of necessity retrace my way over the dangerous ridge. Great, therefore, was her surprise, when, after having been attracted by the rustling noise of the bushes over the aperture, she presently saw the figure of the same hunter emerge from the abyss it overhung. Terror had winged her flight; but it was terror mingled with a delicious emotion entirely new to her. It was that emotion, momentarily increasing in power, that induced her to pause, look back, hesitate in her course, and finally be won, by my supplicating manner, to return and bless me with her presence.

"Two long and delicious hours," pursued Wacousta, after another painful pause of some moments, "did we pass in this manner; exchanging thought, and speech, and heart, as if the term of our acquaintance had been coëval with the first dawn of our intellectual life; when suddenly a small silver toned bell was heard from the direction of the house, hid from the spot on which we sat by the luxuriant foliage of an intervening laburnum. This sound seemed to dissipate the dreamy calm that had wrapped the soul of your mother into forgetfulness. She started suddenly up, and bade me, if I loved her, begone; as that bell announced her required attendance on her father, who, now awakened from the mid-day slumber in which he ever indulged, was about to take his accustomed walk around the grounds; which was little else, in fact, than a close inspection of the walls of his natural castle. I rose to obey her; our eyes met, and she threw herself into my extended arms. We whispered anew our vows of eternal love. She called me her husband, and I pronounced the endearing name of wife. A burning kiss sealed the compact; and, on her archly observing that the sleep of her father continued about two hours at noon, and that the old woman and her daughter were always occupied within doors, I promised to repeat my visit every second day until she finally quitted her retreat to be my own for life. Again the bell was rung; and this time with a violence that indicated impatience of delay. I tore myself from her arms, darted to the aperture, and kissing my hand in reply to the graceful waving of her scarf as she half turned in her own flight, sunk finally from her view; and at length, after making the same efforts, and mastering the same obstacles that had marked and opposed my advance, once more found myself at the point whence I had set out in pursuit of the wounded deer.

"Many were the congratulations I received from my companions, whom I found waiting my return. They had endured the three hours of my absence with intolerable anxiety and alarm; until, almost despairing of beholding me again, they had resolved on going back without me. They said they had repeatedly sounded their horns; but meeting with no answer from mine, had been compelled to infer either that I had strayed to a point whence return to them was impracticable, or that I must have perished in the abyss. I readily gave in to the former idea; stating I had been led by the traces of the wounded deer to a considerable distance, and over passes which it had proved a work of time and difficulty to surmount, yet without securing my spoil. All this time there was a glow of animation on my cheek, and a buoyancy of spirit in my speech, that accorded ill, the first, with the fatigue one might have been supposed to experience in so perilous a chase; the second, with the disappointment attending its result. Your father, ever cool and quick of penetration, was the first to observe this; and when he significantly remarked, that, to judge from my satisfied countenance, my time had been devoted to the pursuit of more interesting game, I felt for a moment as if he was actually master of my secret, and was sensible my features underwent a change. I, however, parried the attack, by replying indifferently, that if he should have the hardihood to encounter the same dangers, he would, if successful, require no other prompter than the joy of self-preservation to lend the same glow of satisfaction to his own features. Nothing further was said on the subject; but conversing on indifferent topics, we again threaded the mazes of rock and underwood we had passed at an early hour, and finally gained the town in which we were quartered.

"During dinner, as on our way home, although my voice occasionally mixed with the voices of my companions, my heart was far away, and full of the wild but innocent happiness in which it had luxuriated. At length, the more freely to indulge in the recollection, I stole at an early hour from the mess-room, and repaired to my own apartments. In the course of the morning, I had hastily sketched an outline of your mother's features in pencil, with a view to assist me in the design of a miniature I purposed painting from memory. This was an amusement of which I was extremely fond and in which I had attained considerable excellence; being enabled, from memory alone, to give a most correct representation of any object that particularly fixed my attention. She had declared utter ignorance of the art herself, her father having studiously avoided instructing her in it from some unexplained motive; yet as she expressed the most unbounded admiration of those who possessed it, it was my intention to surprise her with a highly finished likeness of herself at my next visit. With this view I now set to work; and made such progress, that before I retired to rest I had completed all but the finishing touches, to which I purposed devoting a leisure hour or two by daylight on the morrow.

"While occupied the second day in its completion, it occurred to me I was in orders for duty on the following, which was that of my promised visit to the oasis; and I despatched my servant with my compliments to your father, and a request that he would be so obliging as to take my guard for me on the morrow, and I would perform his

duty when next his name appeared on the roster. Some
time afterwards I heard the door of the room in which I
sat open, and some one enter. Presuming it to be my
servant, returned from the execution of the message with
which he had just been charged, I paid no attention to the
circumstance; but finding, presently, he did not speak, I
turned round with a view of demanding what answer he
had brought. To my surprise, however, I beheld not my
servant, but your father. He was standing looking over my
shoulder at the work on which I was engaged; and notwithstanding in the instant he resumed the cold, quiet,
smirking look that usually distinguished him, I thought I
could trace the evidence of some deep emotion which my
action had suddenly dispelled. He apologised for his intrusion, although we were on those terms that rendered apol-
ogy unnecessary, but said he had just received my
message, and preferred coming in person to assure me
how happy he should feel to take my duty, or to render me
any other service in his power. I thought he laid unusual
emphasis on the last sentence; yet I thanked him warmly,
stating that the only service I should now exact of him
would be to take my guard, as I was compelled to be
absent nearly the whole of the following morning. He observed, with a smile, he hoped I was not going to venture
my neck on those dangerous precipices a second time,
after the narrow escape I had had on the preceding day.
As he spoke, I thought his eye met mine with a sly yet
scrutinizing glance; and, not wishing to reply immediately
to his question, I asked him what he thought of the work
with which I was endeavouring to beguile an idle hour. He
took it up, and I watched the expression of his handsome
countenance with the anxiety of a lover who wishes that
all should think his mistress beautiful as he does himself.
It betrayed a very indefinite sort of admiration; and yet it
struck me there was an eagerness in his dilating eye that
contrasted strongly with the calm and unconcern of his
other features. At length I asked him, laughingly, what he
thought of my Cornish cousin. He replied, cautiously

enough, that since it was the likeness of a cousin, and he dwelt emphatically on the word, he could not fail to admire it. Candour, however, compelled him to admit, that had I not declared the original to be one so closely connected with me, he should have said the talent of so perfect an artist might have been better employed. Whatever, however, his opinion of the lady might be, there could be no question that the painting was exquisite; yet, he confessed, he could not but be struck with the singularity of the fact of a Cornish girl appearing in the full costume of a female Highlander. This, I replied, was mere matter of fancy and association, arising from my having been so much latterly in the habit of seeing that dress principally worn. He smiled one of his *then* damnable soft smiles of assent, and here the conversation terminated, and he left me.

"The next day saw me again at the side of your mother, who received me with the same artless demonstrations of affection. There was a mellowed softness in her countenance, and a tender languor in her eye, I had not remarked the preceding day. Then there was more of the vivacity and playfulness of the young girl; now, more of the deep fervour and the composed serenity of the thoughtful woman. This change was too consonant to my taste – too flattering to my self-love – not to be rejoiced in; and as I pressed her yielding form in silent rapture to my own, I more than ever felt she was indeed the being for whom my glowing heart had so long yearned. After the first full and unreserved interchange of our souls' best feelings, our conversation turned upon lighter topics; and I took an opportunity to produce the fruit of my application since we had parted. Never shall I forget the surprise and delight that animated her beautiful countenance when first she gazed upon the miniature. The likeness was perfect, even to the minutest shading of her costume; and so forcibly and even childishly did this strike her, that it was with difficulty I could persuade her she was not gazing on some peculiar description of mirror that reflected back her living image. She expressed a strong desire to retain it; and to this I readily assented: stipulating only to retain it until my next visit, in order that I might take an exact copy for myself. With a look of the fondest love, accompanied by a pressure on mine of lips that distilled dewy fragrance where they rested, she thanked me for a gift which she said would remind her, in absence, of the fidelity with which her features had been engraven on my heart. She admitted, moreover, with a sweet blush, that she herself had not been idle. Although her pencil could not call up my image in the same manner, her pen had better repaid her exertions; and, in return for the portrait, she would give me a letter she had written to beguile her loneliness on the preceding day. As she spoke she drew a sealed packet from the bosom of her dress, and placing it in my hand, desired me not to read it until I had returned to my home. But there was an expression of sweet confusion in her lovely countenance, and a trepidation in her manner, that, half disclosing the truth, rendered me utterly impatient of the delay imposed; and eagerly breaking the seal, I devoured rather than read its contents.

"Accursed madness of recollection!" pursued Wacousta, again striking his brow violently with his hand, – "why is it that I ever feel thus unmanned while recurring to those letters? Oh! Clara de Haldimar, never did woman pen to man such declarations of tenderness and attachment as that too dear but faithless letter of your mother contained. Words of fire, emanating from the guilelessness of innocence, glowed in every line; and yet every sentence breathed an utter unconsciousness of the effect those words were likely to produce. Mad, wild, intoxicated, I read the letter but half through; and, as it fell from my trembling hand, my eye turned, beaming with the fires of a thousand emotions, upon that of the worshipped writer. That glance was more than her own could meet. A new consciousness seemed to be stirred up in her soul. Her eye dropped beneath its long and silken fringe – her cheek became crimson – her bosom heaved – and, all confiding-ness, she sank her head upon my chest, which heaved scarcely less wildly than her own.

"Had I been a cold-blooded villain – a selfish and remorseless seducer," continued Wacousta with vehemence – "what was to have prevented my triumph at that moment? But I came not to blight the flower that had long been nurtured, though unseen, with the life-blood of my own being. Whatever I may be *now*, I was *then* the soul of disinterestedness and honour; and had she reposed on the bosom of her own father, that devoted and unresisting girl could not have been pressed there with holier tenderness. But even to this there was too soon a term. The hour of parting at length arrived, announced, as before, by the small bell of her father, and I again tore myself from her arms; not, however, without first securing the treasured letter, and obtaining a promise from your mother that I should receive another at each succeeding visit.

Ten

"NEARLY a month passed away in this manner; and at each interview our affection seemed to increase. The days of our meeting were ever days of pure and unalloyed happiness; while the alternate ones of absence were, on my part, occupied chiefly with reading the glowing letters given me at each parting by your mother. Of all these, however, there was not one so impassioned, so natural, so every way devoted, as the first. Not that she who wrote them felt less, but that the emotion excited in her bosom by the manifestation of mine on that occasion, had imparted a diffidence to her style of expression, plainly indicating the source whence it sprung.

"One day, while preparing to set out on my customary excursion, a report suddenly reached me that the route had arrived for the regiment, who were to march from —— within three days. This intelligence I received with inconceivable delight; for it had been settled between your mother and myself, that this should be the moment chosen for her departure. It was not to be supposed (and I should have been both pained and disappointed had it been otherwise,) that she would consent to abandon her parent without some degree of regret; but, having foreseen this objection from the first, I had gradually prepared her for the sacrifice. This was the less difficult, as he appeared never to have treated her with affection, – seldom with the marked favour that might have been presumed to distinguish the manner of a father towards a lovely and only daughter. Living for himself and the indulgence of his misanthropy alone, he cared little for the immolation of his child's happiness on its unhallowed shrine; and this was an act of injustice I had particularly dwelt upon; upheld in truth, as it was, by the knowledge she herself possessed, that no consideration could induce him to bestow her hand on any one individual of a race he so cordially detested; and this was not without considerable weight in her decision.

"With a glowing cheek, and a countenance radiant with happiness, did your mother receive my proposal to prepare for her departure on the following day. She was sufficiently aware, even through what I had stated myself, that there were certain ceremonies of the Church to be performed, in order to give sanctity to our union, and ensure her own personal respectability in the world; and these, I told her, would be solemnised by the chaplain of the regiment. She implicitly confided in me; and she was right; for I loved her too well to make her my mistress, while no barrier existed to her claim to a dearer title. And had she been the daughter of a peasant, instead of a high-born gentleman, finding her as I had found her, and loving her as I did love her, I should have acted precisely in the same way.

"The only difficulty that now occurred was the manner of her flight. The opening before alluded to as being the point whence the old woman made her weekly sally to the market town, was of so intricate and labyrinthian a character that none but the colonel understood the secret of its fastenings; and the bare thought of my venturing with her on the route by which I had hitherto made my entry into the oasis, was one that curdled my blood with fear. I could absolutely feel my flesh to contract whenever I painted the terrible risk that would be incurred in adopting a plan I had once conceived, – namely, that of lashing your mother to my back, while I again effected my descent to the ledge beneath, in the manner I had hitherto done. I felt that, once on the ridge, I might, without much effort, attain the passage of the fissure already described; for the habit of accomplishing this leap had rendered it so perfectly familiar to me, that I now performed it with the utmost security and ease; but to imagine our united weight suspended over the abyss, as it necessarily must be in the first stage of our flight, when even the dislodgment of a single root or fragment of the rock was sufficient to ensure the horrible destruction of her whom I loved better than my own life, had something too appalling in it to suffer me to dwell on the idea for more than a moment. I had proposed, as the most feasible and rational plan, that the colonel should be compelled to give us egress through the secret passage, when we might command the services of the old woman to guide us through the passes that led to the town; but to this your mother most urgently objected, declaring that she would rather encounter any personal peril that might attend her escape in a different manner, than appear to be a participator in an act of violence against her parent, whose obstinacy of character she moreover knew too well to leave a hope of his being intimidated into the accomplishment of our object, even by a threat of death itself. This plan I was therefore compelled to abandon; and as neither of us were able to discover the passage by which the deer always effected its entrance, I was obliged to fix upon one, which it was agreed should be put in practice on the following day.

"On my return, I occupied myself with preparations for the reception of her who was so speedily to become my wife. Unwilling that she should be seen by any of my companions, until the ceremony was finally performed, I engaged apartments in a small retired cottage, distant about half a mile from the furthest extremity of the town, where I purposed she should remain until the regiment finally quitted the station. This point secured, I hastened to the quarters of the chaplain, to engage his services for the following evening; but he was from home at the time, and I repaired to my own rooms, to prepare the means of escape for your mother. These occupied me until a very late hour; and when at length I retired to rest, it was only to indulge in the fondest imaginings that ever filled the heart of a devoted lover. Alas! (and the dark warrior again sighed heavily) the day-dream of my happiness was already fast drawing to a close.

"At half an hour before noon, I was again in the oasis; your mother was at the wonted spot; and although she received me with her sunniest smiles, there were traces of tears upon her cheek. I kissed them eagerly away, and sought to dissipate the partial gloom that was again clouding her brow. She observed it pained me to see her thus, and she made a greater effort to rally. She implored me to forgive her weakness; but it was the first time she was to be separated from her parent; and conscious as she was that it was to be for ever, she could not repress the feeling that rose, despite of herself, to her heart. She had, however, prepared a letter, at my suggestion, to be left on her favourite moss seat, where it was likely she would first be sought by her father, to assure him of her safety, and of her prospects of future happiness; and the consciousness that he would labour under no harrowing uncertainty in regard to her fate, seemed, at length, to soothe and satisfy her heart.

"I now led her to the aperture, where I had left the apparatus provided for my purpose: this consisted of a close netting, about four feet in depth, with a board for a footstool at the bottom, and furnished at intervals with hoops, so as to keep it full and open. The top of this netting was provided with two handles, to which were attached the ends of a cord many fathoms in length; the whole of such durability, as to have borne weights equal to those of three ordinary sized men, with which I had proved it prior to my setting out. My first care was to bandage the eyes of your mother, (who willingly and fearlessly submitted to all I proposed,) that she might not see, and become faint with seeing, the terrible chasm over which she was about to be suspended. I then placed her within the netting, which, fitting closely to her person, and reaching under her arms, completely secured her; and my next urgent request was, that she would not, on any account, remove the bandage, or make the slightest movement, when she found herself stationary below, until I had joined her. I then dropped her gently through the aperture, lowering fathom after fathom of the rope, the ends of which I had firmly secured round the trunk of a tree, as an additional safeguard, until she finally came on a level with that part of the cliff on which I had reposed when first she beheld me. As she still hung immediately over the abyss, it was necessary to give a gradual impetus to her weight, to enable her to gain the landing-place. I now, therefore, commenced swinging her to and fro, until she at length came so near the point desired, that I clearly saw the principal difficulty was surmounted. The necessary motion having been given to the balance, with one vigorous and final impulsion I dexterously contrived to deposit her several feet from the edge of the lower rock, when, slackening the rope on the instant, I had the inexpressible satisfaction to see that she remained firm and stationary. The waving of her scarf immediately afterwards (a signal previously agreed upon), announced she had sustained no injury in this rather rude collision with the rock, and I in turn commenced my descent.

"Fearing to cast away the ends of the rope, lest their weight should by any chance effect the balance of the footing your mother had obtained, I now secured them around my loins, and accomplishing my descent in the customary manner, speedily found myself once more at the side of my heart's dearest treasure. Here the transport of my joy was too great to be controlled; I felt that *now* my prize was indeed secured to me for ever; and I burst forth into the most passionate exclamations of tenderness, and falling on my knees, raised my hands to Heaven in fervent gratitude for the success with which my enterprise had been crowned. Another would have been discouraged at the difficulties still remaining; but with these I was become too familiar, not to feel the utmost confidence in encountering them, even with the treasure that was equally perilled with myself. For a moment I removed the bandage from the eyes of your mother, that she might behold not only the far distant point whence she had descended, but the frowning precipice I had daily been in the habit of climbing to be blest with her presence. She did so, and her cheek paled, for the first time, with a sense of the danger I had incurred; then turning her soft and beautiful eyes on mine, she smiled a smile that seemed to express how much her love would repay me. Again our lips met, and we were happy even in that lonely spot, beyond all language to describe. Once more, at length, I prepared to execute the remainder of my task; and I again applied the bandage to her eyes, saying that, although the principal danger was over, still there was another I could not bear she should look upon. Again she smiled, and with a touching sweetness of expression that fired my blood, observing at the same time she feared no danger while she was with me, but that if my object was to prevent her from looking at me, the most efficient way certainly was to apply a bandage to her eyes. Oh! woman, woman!" groaned Wacousta, in fierce anguish of spirit, "who shall expound the complex riddle of thy versatile nature?

"Disengaging the rope from the handles of the netting, I now applied to these a broad leathern belt taken from the pouches of two of my men, and stooping with my back to the cherished burden with which I was about to charge myself, passed the centre of the belt across my chest, much in the manner in which, as you are aware, Indian women carry their infant children. As an additional precaution, I had secured the netting round my waist by a strong lacing of cord, and then raising myself to my full height, and satisfying myself of the perfect freedom of action of my limbs, seized a long balancing pole I had left suspended against the rock at my last visit, and commenced my descent of the sloping ridge. On approaching the horrible chasm, a feeling of faintness came over me,

despite of the confidence with which I had previously
armed myself. This, however, was but momentary. Sensible that every thing depended on rapidity of movement, I
paused not in my course; but, quickening my pace as I
gradually drew nearer, gave the necessary impetus to my
motion, and cleared the gap with a facility far exceeding
what had distinguished my first passage, and which was
the fruit of constant practice alone. Here my balance was
sustained by the pole; and at length I had the inexpressible
satisfaction to find myself at the very extremity of the
ridge, and immediately at the point where I had left my
companions in my first memorable pursuit. Alas!" continued the warrior, again interrupting himself with one of
those fierce exclamations of impatient anguish that so
frequently occurred in his narrative, "what subject for
rejoicing was there in this? Better far we had been dashed
to pieces in the abyss, than I should have lived to curse the
hour when first my spirit of adventure led me to traverse
it." Again he resumed: –

"In the deep transport of my joy, I once more threw
myself on my knees in speechless thanksgiving to Providence for the complete success of my undertaking. Your
mother, whom I had previously released from her confinement, did the same; and at that moment the union of our
hearts seemed to be cemented by a divine influence, manifested in the fulness of the gratitude of each. I then raised
her from the earth, imprinting a kiss upon her fair brow,
that was hallowed by the purity of the feeling I had so
recently indulged in; and throwing over her shoulders the
mantle of a youth, which I had secreted near the spot,
enjoined her to follow me closely in the path I was about
to pursue. As she had hitherto encountered no fatigue, and
was, moreover, well provided with strong buskins I had
brought for the purpose, I thought it advisable to discon-
tinue the use of the netting, which must attract notice, and
cause us, perhaps, to be followed, in the event of our being
met by any of the hunters that usually traversed these
parts. To carry her in my arms, as I should have preferred,

might have excited the same curiosity, and I was therefore compelled to decide upon her walking; reserving to myself, however, the sweet task of bearing her in my embrace over the more difficult parts of our course.

"I have not hitherto found it necessary to state," continued Wacousta, his brow lowering with fierce and gloomy thought, "that more than once, latterly, on my return from the oasis, which was usually at a stated hour, I had observed a hunter hovering near the end of the ledge, yet quickly retreating as I advanced. There was something in the figure of this man that recalled to my recollection the form of your father; but ever, on my return to quarters, I found him in uniform, and exhibiting any thing but the appearance of one who had recently been threading his weary way among rocks and fastnesses. Besides, the improbability of this fact was so great, that it occupied not my attention beyond the passing moment. On the present occasion, however, I saw the same hunter, and was more forcibly than ever struck by the resemblance to my friend. Prior to my quitting the point where I had liberated your mother from the netting, I had, in addition to the disguise of the cloak, found it necessary to make some alteration in the arrangement of her hair; the redundancy of which, as it floated gracefully over her polished neck, was in itself sufficient to betray her sex. With this view I had removed her plumed bonnet. It was the first time I had seen her without it; and so deeply impressed was I by the angel-like character of the extreme feminine beauty she, more than ever, then exhibited, that I knelt in silent adoration for some moments at her feet, my eyes and countenance alone expressing the fervent and almost holy emotion of my enraptured soul. Had she been a divinity, I could not have worshipped her with a purer feeling. While I yet knelt, I fancied I heard a sound behind me; and, turning quickly, beheld the head of a man peering above a point of rock at some little distance. He immediately, on witnessing my action, sank again beneath it, but not in sufficient time to prevent my almost assuring myself that it was the face of your father I had beheld. My first impulse was to bound forward, and satisfy myself who it really was who seemed thus ever on the watch to intercept my movements; but a second rapid reflection convinced me, that, having been discovered, it was most likely the intruder had already effected his retreat, and that any attempt at pursuit might not only alarm your mother, but compromise her safety. I determined, however, to tax your father with the fact on my return to quarters; and, from the manner in which he met the charge, to form my own conclusion.

"Meanwhile we pursued our course; and after an hour's rather laborious exertion, at length emerged from the succession of glens and rocks that lay in our way; when, skirting the valley in which the town was situated, we finally reached the cottage where I had secured my lodging. Previous to entering it, I had told your mother, that for the few hours that would intervene before the marriage ceremony could be performed, I should, by way of lulling the curiosity of her hostess, introduce her as a near relative of my own. This I did accordingly; and, having seen that every thing was comfortably arranged for her convenience, and recommending her strongly to the care of the old woman, I set off once more in search of the chaplain of the regiment. Before I could reach his residence, however, I was met by a serjeant of my company, who came running towards me, evidently with some intelligence of moment. He stated, that my presence was required without delay. The grenadiers, with the senior subaltern, were in orders for detachment for an important service; and considerable displeasure had been manifested by the colonel at my absence, especially as of late I had greatly neglected my military duties. He had been looking for me every where, he said, but without success, when Ensign de Haldimar had pointed out to him in what direction it was likely I might be found.

"At a calmer moment, I should have been startled at the last observation; but my mind was too much engrossed with the principal subject of my regret, to pay any atten-

tion to the circumstance. It was said the detachment
would be occupied in this duty a week or ten days, at least;
and how was I to absent myself from her whom I so fondly
loved for this period, without even being permitted first to
see and account to her for my absence? There was torture
in the very thought; and in the height of my impatience, I
told the serjeant he might give my compliments to the
colonel, and say I would see the service d——d rather
than inconvenience myself by going out on this duty at so
short a notice; that I had private business of the highest
importance to myself to transact, and could not absent
myself. As the man, however, prepared coolly to depart, it
suddenly occurred to me, that I might prevail on your
father to take my duty now, as on former occasions he had
willingly done, and I countermanded my message to the
colonel; desiring him, however, to find out Ensign de Haldimar, and say that I requested to see him immediately at
my quarters, whither I was now proceeding to change my
dress.

"With a beating heart did I assume an uniform that
appeared, at that moment, hideous in my eyes; yet I was
not without a hope I might yet get off this ill-timed duty.
Before I had completed my equipment, your father entered; and when I first glanced my eye full upon his, I
thought his countenance exhibited evidences of confusion.
This immediately reminded me of the unknown hunter,
and I asked him if he was not the person I described. His
answer was not a positive denial, but a mixture of raillery
and surprise that lulled my doubts, enfeebled as they were
by the restored calm of his features. I then told him that I
had a particular favour to ask of him, which, in consideration of our friendship, I trusted he would not refuse; and
that was, to take my duty in the expedition about to set
forth. His manner implied concern; and he asked, with a
look that had much deliberate expression in it, 'if I was
aware that it was a duty in which blood was expected to
be shed? He could not suppose that any consideration
would induce me to resign my duty to another officer,

when apprised of this fact.' All this was said with the air of one really interested in my honour; but in my increasing impatience, I told him I wanted none of his cant; I simply asked him a favour, which he would grant or decline as he thought proper. This was a harshness of language I had never indulged in; but my mind was sore under the existing causes of my annoyance, and I could not bear to have my motives reflected on at a moment when my heart was torn with all the agonies attendant on the position in which I found myself placed. His cheek paled and flushed more than once, before he replied, 'that in spite of my unkindness his friendship might induce him to do much for me, even as he had hitherto done, but that on the present occasion it rested not with him. In order to justify himself he would no longer disguise the fact from me, that the colonel had declared, in the presence of the whole regiment, I should take my duty regularly in future, and not be suffered to make a convenience of the service any longer. If, however, he could do any thing for me during my absence, I had but to command him.'

"While I was yet giving vent, in no very measured terms, to the indignation I felt at being made the subject of public censure by the colonel, the same sergeant came into the room, announcing that the company were only waiting for me to march, and that the colonel desired my instant presence. In the agitation of my feelings, I scarcely knew what I did, putting several portions of my regimental equipment on so completely awry, that your father noticed and rectified the errors I had committed; while again, in the presence of the sergeant, I expressed the deepest regret he could not relieve me from a duty that was hateful to the last degree.

"Torn with agony at the thought of the uncertainty in which I was compelled to leave her, whom I so fondly adored, I had now no other alternative than to make a partial confidant of your father. I told him that in the cottage which I pointed out he would find the original of the portrait he had seen me painting on a former occasion, –

the Cornish cousin, whose beauty he professed to hold so cheaply. More he should know of her on my return; but at present I confided her to his honour, and begged he would prove his friendship for me by rendering her whatever attention she might require in her humble abode. With these hurried injunctions he promised to comply; and it has often occurred to me since, although I did not remark it at the time, that while his voice and manner were calm, there was a burning glow upon his handsome cheek, and a suppressed exultation in his eye, that I had never observed on either before. I then quitted the room; and hastening to my company with a gloom on my brow that indicated the wretchedness of my inward spirit, was soon afterwards on the march from ——."

Again the warrior seemed agitated with the most violent emotion; he buried his face in his hands; and the silence that ensued was longer than any he had previously indulged in. At length he made an effort to arouse himself; and again exhibiting his swarthy features, disclosed a brow, not clouded, as before, by grief, but animated with the fiercest and most appalling passions, while he thus impetuously resumed.

Eleven

"IF, HITHERTO, Clara de Haldimar, I have been minute in the detail of all that attended my connection with your mother, it has been with a view to prove to you how deeply I have been injured; but I have now arrived at a part of my history, when to linger on the past would goad me into madness, and render me unfit for the purpose to which I have devoted myself. Brief must be the probing of wounds, that nearly five lustres have been insufficient to heal; brief the tale that reveals the infamy of those who have given you birth, and the utter blighting of the fairest hopes of one whose only fault was that of loving, 'not too wisely, but too well.'

"Will you credit the monstrous truth," he added, in a fierce but composed whisper, while he bent eagerly over the form of the trembling yet attentive girl, "when I tell you that, on my return from that fatal expedition, during my continuance on which her image had never once been absent from my mind, I found Clara Beverley the wife of De Haldimar? Yes," continued Wacousta, his wounded feeling and mortified pride chafing, by the bitter recollection, into increasing fury, while his countenance paled in its swarthiness, "the wife, the wedded wife of yon false and traitorous governor! Well may you look surprised, Clara de Haldimar: such damnable treachery as this may startle his own blood in the veins of another, nor find its justification even in the devotedness of woman's filial piety. To what satanic arts so calculating a villain could have had recourse to effect his object I know not; but it is not the less true, that she, from whom my previous history must have taught you to expect the purity of intention and conduct of an angel, became his wife, – and I a being accursed among men. Even as our common mother is said to have fallen in the garden of Eden, tempted by the wily beauty of the devil, so did your mother fall, seduced by that of the cold, false, traitorous De Haldimar." Here the agitation of Wacousta became terrific. The labouring of his chest was like that of one convulsed with some racking agony; and the swollen veins and arteries of his head seemed to threaten the extinction of life in some fearful paroxysm. At length he burst into a violent fit of tears, more appalling, in one of his iron nature, than the fury which had preceded it, – and it was many minutes before he could so far compose himself as to resume.

"Think not, Clara de Haldimar, I speak without the proof. Her own words confessed, her own lips avowed it, and yet I neither slew her, nor her paramour, nor myself. On my return to the regiment I had flown to the cottage, on the wings of the most impatient and tender love that ever filled the bosom of man for woman. To my enquiries the landlady replied, that my cousin had been married two days previously, by the military chaplain, to a handsome young officer, who had visited her soon after my departure, and was constantly with her from that moment; and that immediately after the ceremony they had left, but she knew not whither. Wild, desperate, almost bereft of reason, and with a heart bounding against my bosom, as if each agonising throb were to be its last, I ran like a maniac back into the town, nor paused till I found myself in the presence of your father. My mind was a volcano, but still I attempted to be calm, even while I charged him, in the most outrageous terms, with his villainy. Deny it he could not; but, far from excusing it, he boldly avowed and justified the step he had taken, intimating, with a smile full of meaning, there was nothing in a connection with the

family of De Haldimar to reflect disgrace on the cousin of
Sir Reginald Morton; and that the highest compliment he
could pay his friend was to attach himself to one whom
that friend had declared to be so near a relative of his
own. There was a coldness of taunt in these remarks, that
implied his sense of the deception I had practised on him,
in regard to the true nature of the relationship; and for a
moment, while my hand firmly grasped the hilt of my
sword, I hesitated whether I should not cut him down at
my feet: I had self-command, however, to abstain from the
outrage, and I have often since regretted I had. My own
blood could have been but spilt in atonement for my just
revenge; and as for the obloquy attached to the memory of
the assassin, it could not have been more bitter than that
which has followed me through life. But what do I say?"
fiercely continued the warrior, an exulting ferocity spark-
ling in his eye, and animating his countenance; "had he
fallen, then my vengeance were but half complete. No; it is
now he shall feel the deadly venom in his heart, that has so
long banqueted on mine.

"Determined to know from her own lips," he pursued,
to the shuddering Clara, whose hopes, hitherto strongly
excited, now began again to fade beneath the new aspect
given to the strange history of this terrible man; – "determined to satisfy myself from her own acknowledgement,
whether all I had heard was not an imposition, I summoned calmness enough to desire that your mother might
confirm in person the alienation of her affection, as nothing short of that could convince me of the truth. He left
the room, and presently re-appeared, conducting her in
from another: I thought she looked more beautiful than
ever, but, alas! I had the inexpressible horror to discover,
before a word was uttered, that all the fondness of her
nature was indeed transferred to your father. How I endured the humiliation of that scene has often been a source
of utter astonishment to myself; but I *did* endure it. To my
wild demand, how she could so soon have forgotten her
vows, and falsified her plighted engagements, she replied,

timidly and confusedly, she had not yet known her own heart; but if she had pained me by her conduct, she was sorry for it, and hoped I would forgive her. She would always be happy to esteem me as a friend, but she loved her Charles far, far better than she had ever loved me. This damning admission, couched in the same language of simplicity that had first touched and won my affection, was like boiling lead upon my brain. In a transport of madness I sprang towards her, caught her in my arms, and swore she should accompany me back to the oasis – when I had taken her there, to be regained by my detested rival, if he could; but that he should not eat the fruit I had plucked at so much peril to myself. She struggled to disengage herself, calling on your father by the most endearing epithets to free her from my embrace. He attempted it, and I struck him senseless to the floor at a single blow with the flat of my sabre, which in my extreme fury I had unsheathed. Instead, however, of profiting by the opportunity thus afforded to execute my threat, a feeling of disgust and contempt came over me, for the woman, whose inconstancy had been the cause of my committing myself in this ungentlemanly manner; and bestowing deep but silent curses on her head, I rushed from the house in a state of frenzy. How often since have I regretted that I had not pursued my first impulse, and borne her to some wild, where, forgetting one by whose beauty of person her eye alone had been seduced, her heart might have returned to its allegiance to him who had first awakened the sympathies of her soul, and would have loved her with a love blending the fiercest fires of the eagle with the gentlest devotedness of the dove. But destiny had differently ordained.

"Did my injuries end here?" pursued the dark warrior, as his eye kindled with rage. "No: for weeks I was insensible to any thing but the dreadful shock my soul had sustained. A heavy stupor weighed me down, and for a period it was supposed my reason was overthrown: no such mercy was reserved for me. The regiment had quitted the Highlands, and were now stationary in ——, whither I had accompanied it in arrest. The restoration of my faculties was the signal for new persecutions. Scarcely had the medical officers reported me fit to sustain the ordeal, when a court-martial was assembled to try me on a variety of charges. Who was my prosecutor? Listen, Clara," and he shook her violently by the arm. "He who had robbed me of all that gave value to life, and incentive to honour, – he who, under the guise of friendship, had stolen into the Eden of my love, and left it barrenless of affection. In a word, yon detested governor, to whose inhuman cruelty even the son of my brother has, by some strange fatality of coincidence, so recently fallen a second sacrifice. Curses, curses on him," he pursued, with frightful vehemence, half rising as he spoke, and holding forth his right arm in a menacing attitude; "but the hour of retribution is at hand, and revenge, the exclusive passion of the gods, shall at length be mine. In no other country in the world – under no other circumstances than the present – could I have so secured it.

"What were the charges preferred against me?" he continued, with a violence that almost petrified the unhappy girl. "Hear them, and judge whether I have not cause for the inextinguishable hate that rankles at my heart. Every trifling disobedience of orders – every partial neglect of duty that could be raked up – was tortured into a specific charge; and, as I have already admitted I had latterly transgressed not a little in this respect, these were numerous enough. Yet they were but preparatory to others of greater magnitude. Next succeeded one that referred to the message I had given, and countermanded, to the sergeant of my company, when in the impatience of my disappointment I had desired him to tell the colonel I would see the service d——d rather than inconvenience myself at that moment for it. This was unsupported by other evidence, however, and therefore failed in the proof. But the web was too closely woven around to admit of my escaping. – Will you, can you believe any thing half so atrocious, as that your father should have called on this same man not only to prove the violent and insubordinate language I had used in reference to the commanding officer in my own rooms, but also to substantiate a charge of cowardice, grounded on the unwillingness I had expressed to accompany the expedition, and the extraordinary trepidation I had evinced, while preparing for the duty, manifested, as it was stated to be, by the various errors he had rectified in my equipment with his own hand? Yes, even this pitiful charge was one of the many preferred; but the severest was that which he had the unblushing effrontery to make the subject of public investigation, rather than of private redress – the blow I had struck him in his own apartments. And who was his witness in this monstrous charge? – your mother, Clara. Yea, I stood as a criminal in her presence; and yet she came forward to tender an evidence that was to consign me to a disgraceful sentence. My vile prosecutor had, moreover, the encouragement, the sanction of his colonel throughout, and by him he was upheld in every contemptible charge his ingenuity could devise. Do you not anticipate the result? – I was found guilty, and dismissed the service.

"How acted my brother officers, when, previously to the trial, I alluded to the damnable treachery of your father? Did they condemn his conduct, or sympathise with me in my misfortune? – No; they shrugged their shoulders, and coldly observed, I ought to have known better than to trust one against whom they had so often cautioned me; but that as I had selected him for my friend, I should have bestowed a whole, and not a half confidence upon him. He had had the hypocrisy to pretend to them he had violated no trust, since he had honourably espoused a lady whom I had introduced to him as a cousin, and in whom I appeared to have no other interest than that of relationship. Not, they said, that they believed he actually did entertain that impression; but still the excuse was too plausible, and had been too well studied by my cunning rival, to be openly refuted. As for the mere fact of his supplanting me, they thought it an excellent thing, – a *ruse d'amour* for which they never would have given him credit; and although they admitted it was provoking enough to be ousted out of one's mistress in that cool sort of way, still I should not so far have forgotten myself, as to have struck him while he was unarmed, when it was so easy to have otherwise fastened an insult on him. Such," bitterly pursued Wacousta, "was the consolation I received from men, who, a few short weeks before, had been sedulous to gain and cultivate my friendship, – but even this was only vouchsafed antecedent to my trial. When the sentence was promulgated, announcing my dismissal from the service, every back was turned upon me, as though I had been found guilty of some dishonourable action, some disgraceful crime; and, on the evening of the same day, when I threw from me for ever an uniform that I now loathed from my inmost soul, there was not one among those who had often banqueted at my expense, who had the humanity to come to me and say, 'Sir Reginald Morton, farewell.'

"What agonies of mind I endured, – what burning tears I nightly shed upon a pillow I was destined to press in freezing loneliness, – what hours of solitude I passed, far from the haunts of my fellow-men, and forming plans of vengeance, – it would take much longer time to relate than I have actually bestowed on my unhappy history. To comprehend their extent and force, you must understand the heart of fire in which the deep sense of injury had taken root; but the night wears away, and briefly told must be the remainder of my tale. The rebellion of forty-five saw me in arms in the Scottish ranks; and, in one instance, opposed to the regiment from which I had been so ignominiously expelled. Never did revenge glow like a living fire in the heart of man as it did in mine; for the effect of my long brooding in solitude had been to inspire me with a detestation, not merely for those who had been most rancorous in their enmity, but for every thing that wore the uniform, from the commanding officer down to the meanest private. Every blow that I dealt, every life that I sacrificed, was an insult washed away from my attainted honour; but him whom I most sought in the mêlée I never could reach. At length the corps to which I had attached myself was repulsed; and I saw, with rage in my heart, that my enemy still lived to triumph in the fruit of his villainy.

"Although I was grown considerably in stature at this period, and was otherwise greatly altered in appearance, I had been recognised in the action by numbers of the regiment; and, indeed, more than once I had, in the intoxication of my rage, accompanied the blow that slew or maimed one of my former associates with a declaration of the name of him who inflicted it. The consequence was, I was denounced as a rebel and an outlaw, and a price was put upon my head. Accustomed, however, as I had ever been, to rocks and fastnesses, I had no difficulty in eluding the vigilance of those who were sent in pursuit of me; and thus compelled to live wholly apart from my species, I at length learned to hate them, and to know that man is the only enemy of man upon earth.

"A change now came over the spirit of my vengeance; for about this period your mother died. I had never ceased to love, even while I despised her; and notwithstanding, had she, after her flagrant inconstancy, thrown herself into my arms, I should have rejected her with scorn, still I was sensible no other woman could ever supply her place in my affection. She was, in truth, the only being I had ever looked upon with fondness; and deeply even as I had been injured by her, I wept her memory with many a scalding tear. This, however, only increased my hatred for him who had rioted in her beauty, and supplanted me in her devotedness. I had the means of learning, occasionally, all that passed in the regiment; and the same account that brought me the news of your mother's death also gave me the intelligence that three children had been the fruit of her union with De Haldimar. How," pursued Wacousta, with bitter energy, "shall I express the deep loathing I felt for those children? It seemed to me as if their existence had stamped a seal of infamy on my own brow; and I hated them, even in their childhood, as the offspring of an abhorred, and, as it appeared to me, an unnatural union. I heard, moreover (and this gave me pleasure), that their father doated on them; and from that moment I resolved to turn his cup of joy into bitterness, even as he had turned mine. I no longer sought his life; for the jealousy that had half impelled that thirst existed no longer: but, deeming his cold nature at least accessible through his parental affection, I was resolved that in his children he should suffer a portion of the agonies he had inflicted on me. I waited, however, until they should be grown up to an age when the heart of the parent would be more likely to mourn their loss; and then I was determined my vengeance should be complete.

"Circumstances singularly favoured my design. Many years afterwards, the regiment formed one of the expedition against Quebec under General Wolfe. They were commanded by your father, who, in the course of promotion, had obtained the lieutenant-colonelcy; and I observed by the army list, that a subaltern of the same name, whom I presumed to be his eldest son, was in the corps. Here was a field for my vengeance beyond any I could have hoped for. I contrived to pass over into Cornwall, the ban of outlawry being still unrepealed; and having procured from my brother a sum sufficient for my necessities, and bade him an eternal farewell, embarked in a fishing-boat for the coast of France, whence I subsequently took a passage to this country. At Montreal I found the French general, who gladly received my allegiance as a subject of France, and gave me a commission in one of the provincial corps that usually served in concert with our Indian allies. With the general I soon became a favourite; and, as a mark of his confidence at the attack on Quebec, he entrusted me with the command of a detached irregular force, consisting partly of Canadians and partly of Indians, intended to harass the flanks of the British army. This gave me an opportunity of being at whatever point of the field I might think most favourable to my design; and I was too familiar with the detested uniform of the regiment not to be able to distinguish it from afar. In a word, Clara, for I am weary of my own tale, in that engagement I had an opportunity of recognising your brother. He struck me by his martial appearance as he encouraged his grenadiers to the attack of the French columns; and, as I turned my eye upon him in admiration, I was stung to the soul by his resemblance to his father. Vengeance thrilled throughout every fibre of my frame at that moment. The opportunity I had long sought was at length arrived; and already, in anticipation, I enjoyed the conquest his fall would occasion to my enemy. I rushed within a few feet of my victim; but the bullet aimed at his heart was received in the breast of a faithful soldier, who had flown to intercept it. How I cursed the meddler for his officiousness!"

"Oh, that soldier was your nephew," eagerly interrupted Clara, pointing towards her companion, who had fallen into a profound slumber, "the husband of this unfortunate woman. Frank Halloway (for by that name was he alone known in the regiment) loved my brother as though he had been of the same blood. He it was who flew to receive the ball that was destined for another. But I nursed him on his couch of suffering, and with my own hands prepared his food and dressed his wound. Oh, if pity can touch your heart (and I will not believe that a heart that once felt as you say yours has felt can be inaccessible to pity), let the recollection of your nephew's devotedness to my mother's child disarm you of vengeance, and induce you to restore us!"

"Never!" thundered Wacousta, – "never! The very circumstance you have now named is an additional incentive to my vengeance. My nephew saved the life of your brother at the hazard of his own; and how has he been rewarded for the generous deed? By an ignominious death, inflicted, perhaps, for some offence not more dishonouring than those which have thrown me an outcast upon these wilds; and that at the command and in the presence of the father of him whose life he was fool enough to preserve. Yet, what but ingratitude of the grossest nature could a Morton expect at the hands of the false family of De Haldimar! They were destined to be our bane, and well have they fulfilled the end for which they were created."

"Almighty Providence!" aspirated the sinking Clara, as she turned her streaming eyes to heaven; "can it be that the human heart can undergo such change? Can this be the being who once loved my mother with a purity and tenderness of affection that angels themselves might hallow with approval; or is all that I have heard but a bewildering dream?"

"No, Clara," calmly and even solemnly returned the warrior; "it is no dream, but a reality – a sad, dreadful, heart-rending reality; yet, if I am that altered being, to whom is the change to be ascribed? Who turned the generous current of my blood into a river of overflowing gall? Who, when my cup was mantling with the only bliss I coveted upon earth, traitorously emptied it, and substituted a heart-corroding poison in its stead? Who blighted my fair name, and cast me forth an alien in the land of my forefathers? Who, in a word, cut me off from every joy that existence can impart to man? Who did all this? Your father! But these are idle words. What I have been, you know; what I now am, and through what agency I have been rendered what I now am, you know also. Not more fixed is fate than my purpose. Your brother dies even on the spot on which my nephew died; and you, Clara, shall be my bride; and the first thing your children shall be taught to lisp shall be the curses on the vile name of De Haldimar!"

"Once more, in the name of my sainted mother, I implore you to have mercy," shrieked the unhappy Clara. "Oh!" she continued, with vehement supplication, "let the days of your early love be brought back to your memory, that your heart may be softened; and cut yourself not wholly off from your God, by the commission of such dreadful outrages. Again I conjure you, restore us to my father."

"Never!" savagely repeated Wacousta. "I have passed years of torture in the hope of such an hour as this; and now that fruition is within my grasp, may I perish if I forego it! Ha, sir!" turning from the almost fainting Clara to Sir Everard, who had listened with deep attention to the history of this extraordinary man; – "for this," and he thrust aside the breast of his hunting coat, exhibiting the scar of a long but superficial wound, – "for this do you owe me a severe reckoning. I would recommend you, however," – and he spoke in mockery, – "when next you drive a weapon into the chest of an unresisting enemy, to be more certain of your aim. Had that been as true as the blow from the butt of your rifle, I should not have lived to triumph in this hour. I little deemed," he pursued, still addressing the nearly heart-broken officer in the same insolent strain, "that my intrigue with that dark-eyed daughter of the old Canadian would have been the means of throwing your companion so speedily into my power, after his first narrow escape. Your disguise was well managed, I confess; and but that there is an instinct about me, enabling me to discover a De Haldimar, as a hound does the deer, by scent, you might have succeeded in passing for what you appeared. But" (and his tone suddenly changed its irony for fierceness) "to the point, sir. That you are the lover of this girl I clearly perceive, and death were preferable to a life embittered by the recollection that she whom we love reposes in the arms of another. No such kindness is meant you, however. To-morrow you shall return to the fort; and, when there, you may tell your colonel, that, in exchange for a certain miniature and letters, which, in the hurry of departure, I dropped in his apartment, some ten days since, Sir Reginald Morton, the outlaw, has taken his daughter Clara to wife, but without the solemnisation of those tedious forms that bound himself in accursed union with her mother. Oh! what would I not give," he continued, bitterly, "to witness the pang inflicted on his false heart, when first the damning truth arrests his ear. Never did I know the triumph of my power until now; for what revenge can be half so sweet as that which attains a loathed enemy through the dishonour of his child? But, hark! what mean those sounds?"

A loud yelling was now heard at some distance in rear of the tent. Presently the bounding of many feet on the turf was distinguishable; and then, at intervals, the peculiar cry that announces the escape of a prisoner. Wacousta started to his feet, and fiercely grasping his tomahawk, advanced to the front of the tent, where he seemed to listen for a moment attentively, as if endeavouring to catch the direction of the pursuit.

"Ha! by Heaven!" he exclaimed, "there must be treachery in this, or yon slippery captain would not so soon be at his flight again, bound as I had bound him." Then uttering a deafening yell, and rushing past Sir Everard, near whom he paused an instant, as if undecided whether he should not first dispose of him, as a precautionary measure, he flew with the speed of an antelope in the direction in which he was guided by the gradually receding sounds.

"The knife, Miss de Haldimar," exclaimed Sir Everard, after a few moments of breathless and intense anxiety. "See, there is one in the belt that Ellen Halloway has girt around her loins. Quick, for Heaven's sake, quick; our only chance of safety is in this."

With an activity arising from her despair, the unhappy Clara sprang from the rude couch on which she had been left by Wacousta, and, stooping over the form of the maniac, extended her hand to remove the weapon from her side; but Ellen, who had been awakened from her long slumber by the yells just uttered, seemed resolute to prevent it. A struggle for its possession now ensued between these frail and delicate beings; in which Clara, however, had the advantage, not only from the recumbent position of her opponent, but from the greater security of her grasp. At length, with a violent effort, she contrived to disengage it from the sheath, around which Ellen had closely clasped both her hands; but, with the quickness of thought, the latter were again clenched round the naked blade, and without any other evident motive than what originated in the obstinacy of her madness, the unfortunate woman fiercely attempted to wrest it away. In the act of doing so, her hands were dreadfully cut; and Clara, shocked at the sight of the blood she had been the means of shedding, lost all the energy she had summoned, and sunk senseless at the feet of the maniac, who now began to utter the most piteous cries.

"Oh, God! we are lost," exclaimed Sir Everard; "the voice of that wretched woman has alarmed our enemy, and even now I hear him approaching. Quick, Clara, give me the knife. But no, it is now too late; he is here."

At that instant, the dark form of a warrior rushed noiselessly to the spot on which he stood. The officer turned his eyes in desperation on his enemy, but a single glance was sufficient to assure him it was not Wacousta. The Indian paused not in his course, but passing close round the tree to which the baronet was attached, made a circular movement, that brought him in a line with the direction that had been taken by his enemy; and again they were left alone.

A new fear now oppressed the heart of the unfortunate Valletort, even to agony: Clara still lay senseless, speechless, before him; and his impression was, that, in the struggle, Ellen Halloway had murdered her. The latter yet continued her cries; and, as she held up her hands, he could see by the fire-light they were covered with blood. An instinctive impulse caused him to bound forward to the assistance of the motionless Clara; when, to his infinite surprise and joy, he discovered the cord, which had bound him to the tree, to be severed. The Indian who had just passed had evidently been his deliverer; and a sudden flash of recollection recalled the figure of the young warrior that had escaped from the schooner and was supposed to have leaped into the canoe of Oucanasta at the moment when Madeline de Haldimar was removed into that of the Canadian.

In a transport of conflicting feelings, Sir Everard now raised the insensible Clara from the ground; and, having satisfied himself she had sustained no serious injury, prepared for a flight which he felt to be desperate, if not altogether hopeless. There was not a moment to be lost, for the cries of the wretched Ellen increased in violence, as she seemed sensible she was about to be left utterly alone; and ever and anon, although afar off, yet evidently drawing nearer, was to be heard the fierce denouncing yell of Wacousta. The spot on which the officer stood, was not far from that whence his unfortunate friend had commenced his flight on the first memorable occasion; and as the moon shone brightly in the cloudless heavens, there could be no mistake in the course he was to pursue. Dashing down the steep, therefore, with all the speed his beloved burden would enable him to attain, he made immediately for the bridge, over which his only chance of safety lay.

It unfortunately happened, however, that, induced either by the malice of her insanity, or really terrified at the loneliness of her position, the wretched Ellen Halloway had likewise quitted the tent, and now followed close in the rear of the fugitives, still uttering the same piercing cries of anguish. The voice of Wacousta was also again heard in the distance; and Sir Everard had the inexpressible horror to find that, guided by the shrieks of the maniac woman, he was now shaping his course, not to the tent where he had left his prisoners, but in an oblique direction towards the bridge, where he evidently hoped to intercept them. Aware of the extreme disadvantages under which he laboured in a competition of speed with his active enemy, the unhappy officer would have here terminated the struggle, had he not been partially sustained by the hope that the detachment prayed for by De Haldimar, through the friendly young chief, to whom he owed his own liberation, might be about this time on its way to attempt their rescue. This thought supported his faltering resolution, although nearly exhausted with his efforts – compelled, as he was, to sustain the motionless form of the slowly reviving Clara; and he again braced himself to the unequal flight. The moon still shone beautifully bright, and he could now distinctly see the bridge over which he was to pass; but notwithstanding he strained his eyes as he advanced, no vestige of a British uniform was to be seen in the open space that lay beyond. Once he turned to regard his pursuers. Ellen was a few yards only in his rear; and considerably beyond her rose, in tall relief against the heavens, the gigantic form of the warrior. The pursuit of the latter was now conducted with a silence that terrified even more than the yells he had previously uttered; and he gained so rapidly on his victims, that the tread of his large feet was now distinctly audible. Again the officer, with despair in his heart, made the most incredible exertions to reach the bridge, without seeming to reflect that, even when there, no security was offered him against his enemy. Once, as he drew nearer, he fancied he saw the dark heads of human beings peering from under that part of the arch which had afforded cover to De Haldimar and himself on the memorable occasion of their departure with the Canadian; and, convinced that the warriors of Wacousta had been sent there to lie in ambuscade and intercept his retreat, his hopes were utterly paralysed; and although he stopped not, his flight was rather mechanical than the fruit of any systematic plan of escape.

He had now gained the extremity of the bridge, with Ellen Halloway and Wacousta close in his rear, when suddenly the heads of many men were once more distinguishable, even in the shadow of the arch that overhung the sands of the river. Three individuals detached themselves from the group, and leaping upon the further extremity of the bridge, moved rapidly to meet him. Meanwhile the baronet had stopped suddenly, as if in doubt whether to advance or to recede. His suspense was but momentary. Although the persons of these men were disguised as Indian warriors, the broad moonlight that beamed full on their countenances, disclosed the well-remembered features of Blessington, Erskine, and Charles de Haldimar. The latter sprang before his companions, and, uttering a cry of joy, sank in speechless agony on the neck of his still unconscious sister.

"For God's sake, free me, De Haldimar!" exclaimed the excited baronet, disengaging his charge from the embrace of his friend. "This is no moment for gratulation. Erskine, Blessington, see you not who is behind me? Be upon your guard; defend your lives!" And as he spoke, he rushed forward with faint and tottering steps to place his companions between the unhappy girl and the danger that threatened her.

The swords of the officers were drawn; but instead of advancing upon the formidable being, who stood as if paralysed at this unexpected rencontre, the two seniors contented themselves with assuming a defensive attitude, – retiring slowly and gradually towards the other extremity of the bridge.

Overcome by his emotion, Charles de Haldimar had not noticed this action of his companions, and stood apparently riveted to the spot. The voice of Blessington calling on him by name to retire, seemed to arouse the dormant consciousness of the unhappy maniac. She uttered a piercing shriek, and, springing forward, sank on her knees at his feet, exclaiming, as she forcibly detained him by his dress, –

"Almighty Heaven! where am I? surely that was Captain Blessington's kind voice I heard; and you – you are Charles de Haldimar. Oh! save my husband; plead for him with your father! – but no," she continued wildly, – "he is dead – he is murdered! Behold these hands all covered with his blood! Oh! – "

"Ha! another De Haldimar!" exclaimed Wacousta, recovering his slumbering energies, "this spot seems indeed fated for our meeting. More than thrice have I been baulked of my just revenge, but now will I secure it. Thus, Ellen, do I avenge your husband's and my nephew's death.

My own wrongs demand another sacrifice. But, ha! where is she? where is Clara? where is my bride?"

Bounding over the ill-fated De Haldimar, who lay, even in death, firmly clasped in the embrace of the wretched Ellen, the fierce man dashed furiously forward to renew his pursuit of the fugitives. But suddenly the extremity of the bridge was filled with a column of armed men, that kept issuing from the arch beneath. Sensible of his danger, he sought to make good his retreat; but when he turned for the purpose, the same formidable array met his view at the opposite extremity; and both parties now rapidly advanced in double quick time, evidently with a view of closing upon and taking him prisoner. In this dilemma, his only hope was in the assistance that might be rendered him by his warriors. A yell, so terrific as to be distinctly heard in the fort itself, burst from his vast chest, and rolled in prolonged echoes through the forest. It was faintly answered from the encampment, and met by deep but noiseless curses from the exasperated soldiery, whom the sight of their murdered officer was momentarily working into frenzy.

"Kill him not, for your lives! – I command you, men, kill him not!" muttered Captain Blessington with suppressed passion, as his troops were preparing to immolate him on their clustering bayonets. "Such a death were, indeed, mercy to such a villain."

"Ha! ha!" laughed Wacousta in bitter scorn; "who is there of all your accursed regiment who will dare to take him alive?" Then brandishing his tomahawk around him, to prevent their finally closing, he dealt his blows with such astonishing velocity, that no unguarded point was left about his person; and more than one soldier was brought to the earth in the course of the unequal struggle.

"By G——d!" said Captain Erskine, "are the two best companies of the regiment to be kept at bay by a single desperado? Shame on ye, fellows! If his hands are too many for you, lay him by the heels."

This ruse was practised with success. In attempting to

defend himself from the attack of those who sought to throw him down, the warrior necessarily left his upper person exposed; when advantage was taken to close with him and deprive him of the play of his arms. It was not, however, without considerable difficulty, that they succeeded in disarming and binding his hands; after which a strong cord being fastened round his waist, he was tightly lashed to a gun, which, contrary to the original intention of the governor, had been sent out with the expedition. The retreat of the detachment then commenced rapidly; but it was not without being hotly pursued by the band of warriors the yell of Wacousta had summoned in pursuit, that they finally gained the fort: under what feelings of sorrow for the fate of an officer so beloved, we leave it to our readers to imagine.

Twelve

T HE MORNING of the next day dawned on few who had pressed their customary couches – on none, whose feverish pulse and bloodshot eye failed to attest the utter sleeplessness in which the night had been passed. Numerous groups of men were to be seen assembling after the reveillé, in various parts of the barrack square – those who had borne a part in the recent expedition commingling with those who had not, and recounting to the latter, with mournful look and voice, the circumstances connected with the bereavement of their universally lamented officer. As none, however, had seen the blow struck that deprived him of life, although each had heard the frantic explanations of a voice that had been recognised for Ellen Halloway's, much of the marvellous was necessarily mixed up with truth in their narrative, – some positively affirming Mr. de Haldimar had not once quitted his party, and declaring that nothing short of a supernatural agency could have transported him unnoticed to the fatal spot, where, in their advance, they had beheld him murdered. The singular appearance of Ellen Halloway also, at that moment, on the very bridge on which she had pronounced her curse on the family of De Haldimar, and in company with the terrible and mysterious being who had borne her off in triumph on that occasion to the forest, and under circumstances calculated to excite the most superstitious impressions, was not without its weight in determining their rude speculations; and all concurred in opinion, that the death of the unfortunate young officer was a judgment on their colonel for the little mercy he had extended to the noble-hearted Halloway.

Then followed allusion to their captive, whose gigantic stature and efforts at escape, tremendous even as the latter were, were duly exaggerated by each, with the very laudable view of claiming a proportionate share of credit for his own individual exertions; and many and various were the opinions expressed as to the manner of death he should be made to suffer. Among the most conspicuous of the orators were those with whom our readers have already made slight acquaintance in our account of the sortie by Captain Erskine's company for the recovery of the supposed body of Frederick de Haldimar. One was for impaling him alive, and setting him up to rot on the platform above the gate. Another for blowing him from the muzzle of a twenty-four pounder, into the centre of the first band of Indians that approached the fort, that thus perceiving they had lost the strength and sinew of their cunning war, they might be the more easily induced to propose terms of peace. A third was of opinion he ought to be chained to the top of the flag-staff, as a target, to be shot at with arrows only, contriving never to touch a mortal part. A fourth would have had him tied naked over the sharp spikes that constituted the chevaux-de-frise garnishing the sides of the drawbridge. Each devised some new death – proposed some new torture; but all were of opinion, that simply to be shot, or even to be hanged, was too merciful a punishment for the wretch who had so wantonly and inhumanly butchered the kind-hearted, gentle-mannered officer, whom they had almost all known and loved from his very boyhood; and they looked forward, with mingled anxiety and vengeance, to the moment when, summoned as it was expected he shortly would be, before the assembled garrison, he would be made to expiate the atrocity with his blood.

While the men thus gave indulgence to their indignation

and their grief, their officers were even more painfully
affected. The body of the ill-fated Charles had been borne
to his apartment, where, divested of its disguise, it had
again been inducted in such apparel as was deemed suited
to the purpose. Extended on the very bed on which he lay
at the moment when she, whose maniac raving, and forcible detention, had been the immediate cause of his destruction, had preferred her wild but fruitless supplication
for mercy, he exhibited, even in death, the same delicate
beauty that had characterised him on that occasion; yet,
with a mildness and serenity of expression on his still, pale
features, strongly in contrast with the agitation and glow
of excitement that then distinguished him. Never was
human loveliness in death so marked as in Charles de
Haldimar; and but for the deep wound that, dividing his
clustering locks, had entered from the very crown of the
head to the opening of his marble brow, one ignorant of his
fate might have believed he but profoundly slept. Several
women of the regiment were occupied in those offices
about the corpse, which women alone are capable of performing at such moments, and as they did so, suffered
their tears to flow silently yet abundantly over him, who
was no longer sensible either of human grief or of human
joy. Close at the head of the bed stood an old man, with his
face buried in his hands; the latter reposing against the
wainscoting of the room. He, too, wept, but his weeping
was more audible, more painful, and accompanied by suffocating sobs. It was the humble, yet almost paternally
attached servant of the defunct – the veteran Morrison.

Around the bed were grouped nearly all the officers,
standing in attitudes indicative of anxiety and interest, and
gazing mournfully on the placid features of their ill-fated
friend. All, on entering, moved noiselessly over the rude
floor, as though fearful of disturbing the repose of one
who merely slumbered; and the same precaution was extended to the brief but heartfelt expressions of sorrow that
passed from one to the other, as they gazed on all that
remained of the gentle De Haldimar. At length the prepa-

rations of the women having been completed, they retired from the room, leaving one of their number only, rather out of respect than necessity, to remain by the corpse. When they were departed, this woman, the wife of one of Blessington's sergeants, and the same who had been present at the scene between Ellen Halloway and the deceased, cut off a large lock of his beautiful hair, and separating it into small tresses, handed one to each of the officers. This considerate action, although unsolicited on the part of the latter, deeply touched them, as indicating a sense of the high estimation in which the youth had been held. It was a tribute to the memory of him they mourned, of the purest kind; and each, as he received his portion, acknowledged with a mournful but approving look, or nod, or word, the motive that had prompted the offering. Nor was it a source of less satisfaction, melancholy even as that satisfaction was, to perceive that, after having set aside another lock, probably for the sister of the deceased, she selected and consigned to the bosom of her dress a third, evidently intended for herself. The whole scene was in striking contrast with the almost utter absence of all preparation or concern that had preceded the interment of Murphy, on a former occasion. In one, the rude soldier was mourned, – in the other, the gentle friend was lamented; nor the latter alone by the companions to whom intimacy had endeared him, but by those humbler dependents, who knew him only through those amiable attributes of character, which were ever equally extended to all. Gradually the officers now moved away in the same noiseless manner in which they had approached, either in pursuance of their several duties, or to make their toilet of the morning. Two only of their number remained near the couch of death.

"Poor unfortunate De Haldimar!" observed one of these, in a low tone, as if speaking to himself; "too fatally, indeed, have your forebodings been realised; and what I considered as the mere despondency of a mind crushed into feebleness by an accumulation of suffering, was, after all, but the first presentiment of a death no human power might avert. By Heaven! I would give up half my own being to be able to reanimate that form once more, – but the wish is vain."

"Who shall announce the intelligence to his sister?" sighed his companion. "Never will that already nearly heart-broken girl be able to survive the shock of her brother's death. Blessington, you alone are fitted to such a task; and, painful as it is, you must undertake it. Is the colonel apprised of the dreadful truth, do you know?"

"He is. It was told him at the moment of our arrival last night; but from the little outward emotion displayed by him, I should be tempted to infer he had almost anticipated some such catastrophe."

"Poor, poor Charles!" bitterly exclaimed Sir Everard Valletort – for it was he. "What would I not give to recal the rude manner in which I spurned you from me last night. But, alas! what could I do, laden with such a trust, and pursued, without the power of defence, by such an enemy? Little, indeed, did I imagine what was so speedily to be your doom! Blessington," he pursued, with increased emotion, "it grieves me to wretchedness to think that he, whom I loved as though he had been my twin brother, should have perished with his last thoughts, perhaps, lingering on the seeming unkindness with which I had greeted him after so anxious an absence."

"Nay, if there be blame, it must attach to me," sorrowfully observed Captain Blessington. "Had Erskine and myself not retired before the savage, as we did, our unfortunate friend would in all probability have been alive at this very hour. But in our anxiety to draw the former into the ambuscade we had prepared for him, we utterly overlooked that Charles was not retreating with us."

"How happened it," demanded Sir Everard, his attention naturally directed to the subject by the preceding remarks, "that you lay thus in ambuscade, when the object of the expedition, as solicited by Frederick de Haldimar, was an attempt to reach us in the encampment of the Indians?"

"It certainly was under that impression we left the fort; but, on coming to the spot where the friendly Indian lay waiting to conduct us, he proposed the plan we subsequently adopted as the most likely, not only to secure the escape of the prisoners, whom he pledged himself to liberate, but to defend ourselves with advantage against Wacousta and the immediate guard set over them, should they follow in pursuit. Erskine approving, as well as myself, of the plan, we halted at the bridge, and disposed of our men under each extremity; so that, if attacked by the Indians in front, we might be enabled to throw them into confusion by taking them in rear, as they flung themselves upon the bridge. The event seemed to answer our expectations. The alarm raised in the encampment satisfied us the young Indian had contrived to fulfil his promise; and we momentarily looked for the appearance of those whose flight we naturally supposed would be directed towards the bridge. To our great surprise, however, we remarked that the sounds of pursuit, instead of approaching us, seemed to take an opposite direction, apparently towards the point whence we had seen the prisoners disembarked in the morning. At length, when almost tempted to regret we had not pushed boldly on, in conformity with our first intention, we heard the shrill cries of a woman; and, not long afterwards, the sounds of human feet rushing down the slope. What our sensations were, you may imagine; for we all believed it to be either Clara or Madeline de Haldimar fleeing alone, and pursued by our ferocious enemies. To show ourselves would, we were sensible, be to ensure the death of the pursued, before we could possibly come up; and, although it was with difficulty we repressed the desire to rush forward to the rescue, our better judgment prevailed. Finally we saw you approach, followed closely by what appeared to be a mere boy of an Indian, and, at a considerable distance, by the tall warrior of the Fleur de lis. We imagined there was time enough for you to gain the bridge; and finding your more formidable pursuer was only accompanied by the youth already alluded to, conceived at that moment the design of making him our prisoner. Still there were half a dozen muskets ready to be levelled on him should he approach too near to his fugitives, or manifest any other design than that of simply recapturing them. How well our plan succeeded you are aware; but, alas!" and he glanced sorrowfully at the corpse, "why was our success to be embittered by so great a sacrifice?"

"Ah, would to Heaven that he at least had been spared," sighed Sir Everard, as he took the wan white hand of his friend in his own; "and yet I know not: he looks so calm, so happy in death, it is almost selfish to repine he has escaped the horrors that still await us in this dreadful warfare. But what of Frederick and Madeline de Haldimar? From the statement you have given, they must have been liberated by the young Ottawa before he came to me; yet, what could have induced them to have taken a course of flight so opposite to that which promised their only chance of safety?"

"Heaven only knows," returned Captain Blessington. "I fear they have again been recaptured by the savages; in which case their doom is scarcely doubtful; unless, indeed, our prisoner of last night be given up in exchange for them."

"Then will their liberty be purchased at a terrible price," remarked the baronet. "Will you believe, Blessington, that that man, whose enmity to our colonel seems almost devilish, was once an officer in this very regiment?"

"You astonish me, Valletort. – Impossible! and yet it has always been apparent to me they were once associates."

"I heard him relate his history only last night to Clara, whom he had the audacity to sully with proposals to become his bride," pursued the baronet. "His tale was a most extraordinary one. He narrated it, however, only up to the period when the life of De Haldimar was attempted by him at Quebec. But with his subsequent history we are all acquainted, through the fame of his bloody atrocities in all the posts that have fallen into the hands of Ponteac.

That man, savage and even fiendish as he now is, was once possessed of the noblest qualities. I am sorry to say it; but Colonel de Haldimar has brought this present affliction upon himself. At some future period I will tell you all."

"Alas!" said Captain Blessington, "poor Charles, then, has been made to pay the penalty of his father's errors; and, certainly, the greatest of these was his dooming the unfortunate Halloway to death in the manner he did."

"What think you of the fact of Halloway being the nephew of this extraordinary man, and both of high family?" demanded Sir Everard.

"Indeed! and was the latter, then, aware of the connection?"

"Not until last night," replied Sir Everard. "Some observations made by the wretched wife of Halloway, in the course of which she named his true name, (which was that of the warrior also,) first indicated the fact to the latter. But, what became of that unfortunate creature? – was she brought in?"

"I understand not," said Captain Blessington. "In the confusion and hurry of securing our prisoner, and the apprehension of immediate attack from his warriors, Ellen was entirely overlooked. Some of my men say they left her lying, insensible, on the spot whence they had raised the body of our unfortunate friend, which they had some difficulty in releasing from her convulsive embrace. But, hark! there is the first drum for parade, and I have not yet exchanged my Indian garb."

Captain Blessington now quitted the room, and Sir Everard, relieved from the restraining presence of his companions, gave free vent to his emotion, throwing himself upon the body of his friend, and giving utterance to the feelings of anguish that oppressed his heart.

He had continued some minutes in this position, when he fancied he felt the warm tears of a human being bedewing a hand that reposed on the neck of his unfortunate friend. He looked up, and, to his infinite surprise, beheld

Clara de Haldimar standing before him at the opposite side of the bed. Her likeness to her brother, at that moment, was so striking, that, for a second or two, the irrepressible thought passed through the mind of the officer, it was not a living being he gazed upon, but the immaterial spirit of his friend. The whole attitude and appearance of the wretched girl, independently of the fact of her noiseless entrance, tended to favour the delusion. Her features, of an ashy paleness, seemed fixed, even as those of the corpse beneath him; and, but for the tears that coursed silently down her cheek, there was scarcely an outward evidence of emotion. Her dress was a simple white robe, fastened round her waist with a pale blue riband; and over her shoulders hung her redundant hair, resembling in colour, and disposed much in the manner of that of her brother, which had been drawn negligently down to conceal the wound on his brow. For some moments the baronet gazed at her in speechless agony. Her tranquil exterior was torture to him; for he feared it betokened some alienation of reason. He would have preferred to witness the most hysteric convulsion of grief, rather than that traitorous calm; and yet he had not the power to seek to remove it.

"You are surprised to see me here, mingling my grief with yours, Sir Everard," she at length observed, with the same calm mien, and in tones of touching sweetness. "I came, with my father's permission, to take a last farewell of him whose death has broken my heart. I expected to be alone; but – Nay, do not go," she added, perceiving that the officer was about to depart. "Had you not been here, I should have sent for you; for we have both a sacred duty to perform. May I not ask your hand?"

More and more dismayed at her collected manner, the young officer gazed at her with the deepest sorrow depicted in every line of his own countenance. He extended his hand, and Clara, to his surprise, grasped and pressed it firmly.

"It was the wish of this poor boy that his Clara should be the wife of his friend, Sir Everard. Did he ever express such to you?"

"It was the fondest desire of his heart," returned the baronet, unable to restrain the emotion of joy that mingled, despite of himself, with his worst apprehensions.

"I need not ask how you received his proposal," continued Clara, with the same calmness of manner. "Last night," she pursued solemnly, "I was the bride of the murderer of my brother, of the lover of my mother, – tomorrow night I may be the bride of death; but to-night I am the bride of my brother's friend. Yes, here am I come to pledge myself to the fulfilment of his wish. If you deem a heart-broken girl not unworthy of you, I am your wife, Sir Everard; and, recollect, it is a solemn pledge, that which a sister gives over the lifeless body of a brother, beloved as this has been."

"Oh, Clara – dearest Clara," passionately exclaimed the excited young man, "if a life devoted to your happiness can repay you for this, count upon it as you would upon your eternal salvation. In you will I love both my friend and the sister he has bequeathed to me. Clara, my betrothed wife, summon all the energies of your nature to sustain this cruel shock; and exert yourself for him who will be to you both a brother and a husband."

As he spoke he drew the unresisting girl towards him, and, locking her in his embrace, pressed, for the first time, the lips, which it had maddened him the preceding night to see polluted by the forcible kisses of Wacousta. But Clara shared not, but merely suffered his momentary happiness. Her cheek wore not the crimson of excitement, neither were her tears discontinued. She seemed as one who mechanically submitted to what she had no power of resistance to oppose; and even in the embrace of her affianced husband, she exhibited the same deathlike calm that had startled him at her first appearance. Religion could not hallow a purer feeling than that which had impelled the action of the young officer. The very consciousness of the sacred pledge having been exchanged over the corpse of his friend, imparted a holiness of fervour to his mind; and even while he pressed her, whom he secretly swore to love with all the affection of a fond brother and a husband united, he felt that if the spirit of him, who slept unconscious of the scene, were suffered to linger near, it would be to hallow it with approval.

"And now," said Clara at length, yet without attempting to disengage herself, – "now that we are united, I would be alone with my brother. My husband, leave me."

Deeply touched at the name of husband, Sir Everard could not refrain from imprinting another kiss on the lips that uttered it. He then gently disengaged himself from his lovely but suffering charge, whom he deposited with her head resting on the bed; and making a significant motion of his hand to the woman, who, as well as old Morrison, had been spectators of the whole scene, stole gently from the apartment, under what mingled emotions of joy and grief it would be difficult to describe.

Thirteen

IT WAS the eighth hour of morning, and both officers and men, quitting their ill-relished meal, were to be seen issuing to the parade, where the monotonous roll of the *assemblée* now summoned them. Presently the garrison was formed in the order we have described in our first volume; that is to say, presenting three equal sides of a square. The vacant space fronted the guard-house, near one extremity of which was to be seen a flight of steps communicating with the rampart, where the flag-staff was erected. Several men were employed at this staff, passing strong ropes through iron pulleys that were suspended from the extreme top, while in the basement of the staff itself, to a height of about twenty feet, were stuck at intervals strong wooden pegs, serving as steps to the artillerymen for greater facility in clearing, when foul, the lines to which the colours were attached. The latter had been removed; and, from the substitution of a cord considerably stronger than that which usually appeared there, it seemed as if some far heavier weight was about to be appended to it. Gradually the men, having completed their unusual preparations, quitted the rampart, and the flag-staff, which was of tapering pine, was left totally unguarded.

The "Attention!" of Major Blackwater to the troops, who had been hitherto standing in attitudes of expectancy that rendered the injunction almost superfluous, announced the approach of the governor. Soon afterwards that officer entered the area, wearing his characteristic dignity of manner, yet exhibiting every evidence of one who had suffered deeply. Preparation for a drum-head court-martial, as in the first case of Halloway, had already been made within the square, and the only actor wanting in the drama was he who was to be tried.

Once Colonel de Haldimar made an effort to command his appearance, but the huskiness of his voice choked his utterance, and he was compelled to pause. After the lapse of a few moments, he again ordered, but in a voice that was remarked to falter, -

"Mr. Lawson, let the prisoner be brought forth."

The feeling of suspense that ensued between the delivery and execution of this command was painful throughout the ranks. All were penetrated with curiosity to behold a man who had several times appeared to them under the most appalling circumstances, and against whom the strongest feeling of indignation had been excited for his barbarous murder of Charles de Haldimar. It was with mingled awe and anger they now awaited his approach. At length the captive was seen advancing from the cell in which he had been confined, his gigantic form towering far above those of the guard of grenadiers by whom he was surrounded; and with a haughtiness in his air, and insolence in his manner, that told he came to confront his enemy with a spirit unsubdued by the fate that too probably awaited him.

Many an eye was turned upon the governor at that moment. He was evidently struggling for composure to meet the scene he felt it to be impossible to avoid; and he turned pale and paler as his enemy drew near.

At length the prisoner stood nearly in the same spot where his unfortunate nephew had lingered on a former occasion. He was unchained; but his hands were firmly secured behind his back. He threw himself into an attitude of carelessness, resting on one foot, and tapping the earth with the other; riveting his eye, at the same time, with an expression of the most daring insolence, on the governor, while his swarthy cheek was moreover lighted up with a smile of the deepest scorn.

"You are Reginald Morton the outlaw, I believe," at length observed the governor in an uncertain tone, that, however, acquired greater firmness as he proceeded, – "one whose life has already been forfeited through his treasonable practices in Europe, and who has, moreover, incurred the penalty of an ignominious death, by acting in this country as a spy of the enemies of England. What say you, Reginald Morton, that you should not be convicted in the death that awaits the traitor?"

"Ha! ha! by Heaven, such cold, pompous insolence amuses me," vociferated Wacousta. "It reminds me of Ensign de Haldimar of nearly five and twenty years back, who was then as cunning a dissembler as he is now." Suddenly changing his ribald tone to one of scorn and rage: – "You *believe* me, you say, to be Reginald Morton the outlaw. Well do you know it. I am that Sir Reginald Morton, who became an outlaw, not through his own crimes, but through your villainy. Ay, frown as you may, I heed it not. You may award me death, but shall not chain my tongue. To your whole regiment do I proclaim you for a false, remorseless villain." Then turning his flashing eye along the ranks: – "I was once an officer in this corps, and long before any of you wore the accursed uniform. That man, that fiend, affected to be my friend; and under the guise of friendship, stole into the heart I loved better than my own life. Yes," fervently pursued the excited prisoner, stamping violently with his foot upon the earth, "he robbed me of my affianced wife; and for that I resented an outrage that should have banished him to some lone region, where he might never again pollute human nature with his presence – he caused me to be tried by a court-martial, and dismissed the service. Then, indeed, I became the outlaw he has described, but not until then. Now, Colonel de Haldimar, that I have proclaimed your infamy, poor and inefficient as the triumph be, do your worst – I ask no mercy. Yesterday I thought that years of toilsome pursuit of the means of vengeance were about to be crowned with success; but fate has turned the tables on me, and I yield."

To all but the baronet and Captain Blessington this declaration was productive of the utmost surprise. Every eye was turned upon the colonel. He grew impatient under the scrutiny, and demanded if the court, who meanwhile had been deliberating, satisfied of the guilt of the prisoner, had come to a decision in regard to his punishment. An affirmative answer was given, and Colonel de Haldimar proceeded.

"Reginald Morton, with the private misfortunes of your former life we have nothing to do. It is the decision of this court, who are merely met out of form, that you suffer immediate death by hanging, as a just recompense for your double treason to your country. There," and he pointed to the flag-staff, "will you be exhibited to the misguided people whom your wicked artifices have stirred up into hostility against us. When they behold your fate, they will take warning from your example; and, finding we have heads and arms not to suffer offence with impunity, be more readily brought to obedience."

"I understand your allusion," coolly rejoined Wacousta, glancing earnestly at, and apparently measuring with his eye, the dimensions of the conspicuous scaffold on which he was to suffer. "You had ever a calculating head, De Haldimar, where any secret villainy, any thing to promote your own selfish ends, was to be gained by it; but your calculation seems now, methinks, at fault."

Colonel de Haldimar looked at him enquiringly.

"You have *still* a son left," pursued the prisoner with the same recklessness of manner, and in a tone denoting allusion to him who was no more, that caused an universal shudder throughout the ranks. "He is in the hands of the Ottawa Indians, and I am the friend of their great chief, inferior only in power among the tribe to himself. Think you that he will see me hanged up like a dog, and fail to avenge my disgraceful death?"

"Ha! presumptuous renegade, is this the deep game you have in view? Hope you then to stipulate for the preservation of a life every way forfeited to the offended justice of your country? Dare you to cherish the belief, that, after the horrible threats so often denounced by you, you will again be let loose upon a career of crime and blood?"

"None of your cant, De Haldimar, as I once observed to you before," coolly retorted Wacousta, with bitter sarcasm. "Consult your own heart, and ask if its catalogue of crime be not far greater than my own: yet I ask not my life. I would but have the manner of my fate altered, and fain would die the death of the soldier I *was* before you rendered me the wretch I *am*. Methinks the boon is not so great, if the restoration of your son be the price."

"Do you mean, then," eagerly returned the governor, "that if the mere mode of your death be changed, my son shall be restored?"

"I do," was the calm reply.

"What pledge have we of the fact? What faith can we repose in the word of a fiend, whose brutal vengeance has already sacrificed the gentlest life that ever animated human clay?" Here the emotion of the governor almost choked his utterance, and considerable agitation and murmuring were manifested in the ranks.

"Gentle, said you?" replied the prisoner, musingly; "then did he resemble his mother, whom I loved, even as his brother resembles you whom I have so much reason to hate. Had I known the boy to be what you describe, I might have felt some touch of pity even while I delayed not to strike his death blow; but the false moonlight deceived me, and the detested name of De Haldimar, pronounced by the lips of my nephew's wife – that wife whom your cold-blooded severity had widowed and driven mad – was in itself sufficient to ensure his doom."

"Inhuman ruffian!" exclaimed the governor, with increasing indignation; "to the point. What pledge have you to offer that my son will be restored?"

"Nay, the pledge is easily given, and without much risk.

You have only to defer my death until your messenger return from his interview with Ponteac. If Captain de Haldimar accompany him back, shoot me as I have requested; if he come not, then it is but to hang me after all."

"Ha! I understand you; this is but a pretext to gain time, a device to enable your subtle brain to plan some mode of escape."

"As you will, Colonel de Haldimar," calmly retorted Wacousta; and again he sank into silence, with the air of one utterly indifferent to results.

"Do you mean," resumed the colonel, "that a request from yourself to the Ottawa chief will obtain the liberation of my son?"

"Unless the Indian be false as yourself, I do."

"And of the lady who is with him?" continued the colonel, colouring with anger.

"Of both."

"How is the message to be conveyed?"

"Ha, sir!" returned the prisoner, drawing himself up to his full height, "now are you arrived at a point that is pertinent. My wampum belt will be the passport, and the safeguard of him you send; then for the communication. There are certain figures, as you are aware, that, traced on bark, answer the same purpose among the Indians with the European language of letters. Let my hands be cast loose," he pursued, but in a tone in which agitation and excitement might be detected, "and if bark be brought me, and a burnt stick or coal, I will give you not only a sample of Indian ingenuity, but a specimen of my own progress in Indian acquirements."

"What, free your hands, and thus afford you a chance of escape?" observed the governor, doubtingly.

Wacousta bent his stedfast gaze on him for a few moments, as if he questioned he had heard aright. Then bursting into a wild and scornful laugh, – "By Heaven!" he exclaimed, "this is, indeed, a high compliment you pay me at the expense of these fine fellows. What, Colonel de Haldimar afraid to liberate an unarmed prisoner, hemmed

in by a forest of bayonets? This is good; gentlemen," and
he bent himself in sarcastic reverence to the astonished
troops, "I beg to offer you my very best congratulations
on the high estimation in which you are held by your
colonel."

"Peace, sirrah!" exclaimed the governor, enraged
beyond measure at the insolence of him who thus held
him up to contempt before his men, "or, by Heaven, I will
have your tongue cut out! – Mr. Lawson, let what this
fellow requires be procured immediately." Then addressing Lieutenant Boyce, who commanded the immediate
guard over the prisoner, – "Let his hands be liberated, sir,
and enjoin your men to be watchful of the movements of
this supple traitor. His activity I know of old to be great,
and he seems to have doubled it since he assumed that
garb."

The command was executed, and the prisoner stood,
once more, free and unfettered in every muscular limb. A
deep and unbroken silence ensued; and the return of the
adjutant was momentarily expected. Suddenly a loud
scream was heard, and the slight figure of a female, clad
in white, came rushing from the piazza in which the
apartment of the deceased De Haldimar was situated. It
was Clara. The guard of Wacousta formed the fourth
front of the square; but they were drawn up somewhat in
the distance, so as to leave an open space of several feet at
the angles. Through one of these the excited girl now
passed into the area, with a wildness in her air and appearance that riveted every eye in painful interest upon
her. She paused not until she had gained the side of the
captive, at whose feet she now sank in an attitude expressive of the most profound despair.

"Tiger! – monster!" she raved, "restore my brother! –
give me back the gentle life you have taken, or destroy my
own! See, I am a weak defenceless girl: can you not
strike? – you who have no pity for the innocent. But
come," she pursued, mournfully, regaining her feet and
grasping his iron hand, – "come and see the sweet calm

face of him you have slain: – come with me, and behold the image of Clara Beverley; and, if you ever loved her as you say you did, let your soul be touched with remorse for your crime."

The excitement and confusion produced by this unexpected interruption was great. Murmurs of compassion for the unhappy Clara, and of indignation against the prisoner, were no longer sought to be repressed by the men; while the officers, quitting their places in the ranks, grouped themselves indiscriminately in the foreground. One, more impatient than his companions, sprang forward, and forcibly drew away the delicate hand that still grasped that of the captive. It was Sir Everard Valletort.

"Clara, my beloved wife!" he exclaimed, to the astonishment of all who heard him, "pollute not your lips by further communion with such a wretch; his heart is as inaccessible to pity as the rugged rocks on which his spring-life was passed. For Heaven's sake, – for my sake, – linger not within his reach. There is death in his very presence."

"Your wife, sir!" haughtily observed the governor, with irrepressible astonishment and indignation in his voice; "what mean you? – Gentlemen, resume your places in the ranks. – Clara – Miss de Haldimar, I command you to retire instantly to your apartment. – We will discourse of this later, Sir Everard Valletort. I trust you have not dared to offer an indignity to my child."

While he was yet turned to that officer, who had taken his post, as commanded, in the inner angle of the square, and with a countenance that denoted the conflicting emotions of his soul, he was suddenly startled by the confused shout and rushing forward of the whole body, both of officers and men. Before he had time to turn, a loud and well-remembered yell burst upon his ear. The next moment, to his infinite surprise and horror, he beheld the bold warrior rapidly ascending the very staff that had been destined for his scaffold, and with Clara in his arms.

Great was the confusion that ensued. To rush forward

and surround the flag-staff, was the immediate action of the troops. Many of the men raised their muskets, and in the excitement of the moment, would have fired, had they not been restrained by their officers, who pointed out the certain destruction it would entail on the unfortunate Clara. With the rapidity of thought, Wacousta had snatched up his victim, while the attention of the troops was directed to the singular conversation passing between the governor and Sir Everard Valletort, and darting through one of the open angles already alluded to, had gained the rampart before they had recovered from the stupor produced by his daring action. Stepping lightly upon the pegs, he had rapidly ascended to the utmost height of these, before any one thought of following him; and then grasping in his teeth the cord which was to have served for his execution, and holding Clara firmly against his chest, while he embraced the smooth staff with knees and feet closely compressed around it, accomplished the difficult ascent with an ease that astonished all who beheld him. Gradually, as he approached the top, the tapering pine waved to and fro; and at each moment it was expected, that, yielding to their united weight, it would snap asunder, and precipitate both Clara and himself, either upon the rampart, or into the ditch beyond.

More than one officer now attempted to follow the fugitive in his adventurous course; but even Lieutenant Johnstone, the most active and experienced in climbing of the party, was unable to rise more than a few yards above the pegs that afforded a footing, and the enterprise was abandoned as an impossibility. At length Wacousta was seen to gain the extreme summit. For a moment he turned his gaze anxiously beyond the town, in the direction of the bridge; and, after pealing forth one of his terrific yells, exclaimed, exultingly, as he turned his eye upon his enemy: –

"Well, colonel, what think you of this sample of Indian ingenuity? Did I not tell you," he continued, in mockery, "that, if my hands were but free, I would give you a specimen of my progress in Indian acquirements?"

"If you would avoid a death even more terrible than that of hanging," shouted the governor, in a voice of mingled rage and terror, "restore my daughter."

"Ha! ha! ha! - excellent!" vociferated the savage. "You threaten largely, my good governor; but your threats are harmless as those of a weak besieging army before an impregnable fortress. It is for the strongest, however, to propose his terms. - If I restore this girl to life, will you pledge yourself to mine?"

"Never!" thundered Colonel de Haldimar, with unusual energy. - "Men, procure axes; cut the flag-staff down, since this is the only means left of securing yon insolent traitor! Quick to your work: and mark, who first seizes him shall have promotion on the spot."

Axes were instantly procured, and two of the men now lent themselves vigorously to the task. Wacousta seemed to watch these preparations with evident anxiety; and to all it appeared as if his courage had been paralysed by this unexpected action. No sooner, however, had the axemen reached the heart of the staff, than, holding Clara forth over the edge of the rampart, he shouted, -

"One stroke more, and she perishes!"

Instantaneously the work was discontinued. A silence of a few moments ensued. Every eye was turned upward, - every heart beat with terror to see the delicate girl, held by a single arm, and apparently about to be precipitated from that dizzying height. Again Wacousta shouted, -

"Life for life, De Haldimar! If I yield her shall I live?"

"No terms shall be dictated to me by a rebel, in the heart of my own fort," returned the governor. "Restore my child, and we will then consider what mercy may be extended to you."

"Well do I know what mercy dwells in such a heart as yours," gloomily remarked the prisoner; "but I come."

"Surround the staff, men," ordered the governor, in a

low tone. "The instant he descends, secure him: lash him in every limb, nor suffer even his insolent tongue to be longer at liberty."

"Boyce, for God's sake open the gate, and place men in readiness to lower the drawbridge," implored Sir Everard of the officer of the guard, and in a tone of deep emotion that was not meant to be overheard by the governor. "I fear the boldness of this vengeful man may lead him to some desperate means of escape."

While the officer whom he addressed issued a command, the responsibility of which he fancied he might, under the peculiar circumstances of the moment, take upon himself, Wacousta began his descent, not as before, by adhering to the staff, but by the rope which he held in his left hand, while he still supported the apparently senseless Clara against his right chest with the other.

"Now, Colonel de Haldimar, I hope your heart is at rest," he shouted, as he rapidly glided by the cord; "enjoy your triumph as best may suit your pleasure."

Every eye followed his movement with interest; every heart beat lighter at the certainty of Clara being again restored, and without other injury than the terror she must have experienced in such a scene. Each congratulated himself on the favourable termination of the terrible adventure, yet were all ready to spring upon and secure the desperate author of the wrong. Wacousta had now reached the centre of the flag-staff. Pausing for a moment, he grappled it with his strong and nervous feet, on which he apparently rested, to give a momentary relief to the muscles of his left arm. He then abruptly abandoned his hold, swinging himself out a few yards from the staff, and returning again, dashed his feet against it with a force that caused the weakened mass to vibrate to its very foundation. Impelled by his weight, and the violence of his action, the creaking pine gave way; its lofty top gradually bending over the exterior rampart until it finally snapped asunder, and fell with a loud crash across the ditch.

"Open the gate, down with the drawbridge!" exclaimed the excited governor.

"Down with the drawbridge," repeated Sir Everard to the men already stationed there ready to let loose at the first order. The heavy chains rattled sullenly through the rusty pulleys, and to each the bridge seemed an hour descending. Before it had reached its level, it was covered with the weight of many armed men rushing confusedly to the front; and the foremost of these leaped to the earth before it had sunk into its customary bed. Sir Everard Valletort and Lieutenant Johnstone were in the front, both armed with their rifles, which had been brought them before Wacousta commenced his descent. Without order or combination, Erskine, Blessington, and nearly half of their respective companies, followed as they could; and dispersing as they advanced, sought only which could out-step his fellows in the pursuit.

Meanwhile the fugitive, assisted in his fall by the gradual rending asunder of the staff, had obeyed the impulsion first given to his active form, until, suddenly checking himself by the rope, he dropped with his feet downward into the centre of the ditch. For a moment he disappeared, then came again uninjured to the surface; and in the face of more than fifty men, who, lining the rampart with their muskets levelled to take him at advantage the instant he should reappear, seemed to laugh their efforts to scorn. Holding Clara before him as a shield, through which the bullets of his enemies must pass before they could attain him, he impelled his gigantic form with a backward movement towards the opposite bank, which he rapidly ascended; and, still fronting his enemies, commenced his flight in that manner with a speed which (considering the additional weight of the drenched garments of both) was inconceivable. The course taken by him was not through the town, but circuitously across the common until he arrived on that immediate line whence, as we have before stated, the bridge was distinctly visible from the rampart;

on which, nearly the whole of the remaining troops, in defiance of the presence of their austere chief, were now eagerly assembled, watching, with unspeakable interest, the progress of the chase.

Desperate as were the exertions of Wacousta, who evidently continued this mode of flight from a conviction that the instant his person was left exposed the fire-arms of his pursuers would be brought to bear upon him, the two officers in front, animated by the most extraordinary exertions, were rapidly gaining upon him. Already was one within fifty yards of him, when a loud yell was heard from the bridge. This was fiercely answered by the fleeing man, and in a manner that implied his glad sense of coming rescue. In the wild exultation of the moment, he raised Clara high above his head, to show her in triumph to the governor, whose person his keen eye could easily distinguish among those crowded upon the rampart. In the gratified vengeance of that hour, he seemed utterly to overlook the actions of those who were so near him. During this brief scene, Sir Everard had dropped upon one knee, and supporting his elbow on the other, aimed his rifle at the heart of the ravisher of his wife. An exulting shout burst from the pursuing troops. Wacousta bounded a few feet in air, and placing his hand to his side, uttered another yell, more appalling than any that had hitherto escaped him. His flight was now uncertain and wavering. He staggered as one who had received a mortal wound; and discontinuing his unequal mode of retreat, turned his back upon his pursuers, and threw all his remaining energies into a final effort at escape.

Inspirited by the success of his shot, and expecting momentarily to see him fall weakened with the loss of blood, the excited Valletort re-doubled his exertions. To his infinite joy, he found that the efforts of the fugitive became feebler at each moment. Johnstone was about twenty paces behind him, and the pursuing party at about the same distance from Johnstone. The baronet had now reached his enemy, and already was the butt of his rifle raised with both hands with murderous intent, when suddenly Wacousta, every feature distorted with rage and pain, turned like a wounded lion at bay, and eluding the blow, deposited the unconscious form of his victim upon the sward. Springing upon his infinitely weaker pursuer, he grappled him furiously by the throat, exclaiming through his clenched teeth: –

"Nay then, since you will provoke your fate – be it so. Die like a dog, and be d——d, for having balked me of my just revenge!"

As he spoke, he hurled the gasping officer to the earth with a violence that betrayed the dreadful excitement of his soul, and again hastened to assure himself of his prize.

Meanwhile, Lieutenant Johnstone had come up, and, seeing his companion struggling as he presumed, with advantage, with his severely wounded enemy, made it his first care to secure the unhappy girl; for whose recovery the pursuit had been principally instituted. Quitting his rifle, he now essayed to raise her in his arms. She was without life or consciousness, and the impression on his mind was that she was dead.

While in the act of raising her, the terrible Wacousta stood at his side, his vast chest heaving forth a laugh of mingled rage and contempt. Before the officer could extricate, with a view of defending himself, his arms were pinioned as though in a vice; and ere he could recover from his surprise, he felt himself lifted up and thrown to a considerable distance. When he opened his eyes a moment afterwards, he was lying amid the moving feet of his own men.

From the instant of the closing of the unfortunate Valletort with his enemy, the Indians, hastening to the assistance of their chief, had come up, and a desultory fire had already commenced, diverting, in a great degree, the attention of the troops from the pursued. Emboldened by this new aspect of things, Wacousta now deliberately grasped the rifle that had been abandoned by Johnstone; and raising it to his shoulder, fired among the group col-

lected on the ramparts. For a moment he watched the
result of his shot, and then, pealing forth another fierce
yell, he hurled the now useless weapon into the very heart
of his pursuers; and again raising Clara in his arms, once
more commenced his retreat, which, under cover of the
fire of his party, was easily effected.

"Who has fallen?" demanded the governor of his adjutant, perceiving that some one had been hit at his side, yet
without taking his eyes off the terrible enemy.

"Mr. Delme, sir," was the reply. "He has been shot
through the heart, and his men are bearing him from the
rampart."

"This must not be," resumed the governor with energy.
"Private feelings must no longer be studied at the expense
of the public good. That pursuit is hopeless; and already
too many of my officers have fallen. Desire the retreat to
be sounded, Mr. Lawson. Captain Wentworth, let one or
two covering guns be brought to bear upon the savages.
They are gradually increasing in numbers; and if we delay,
the party will be wholly cut off."

In issuing these orders, Colonel de Haldimar evinced a
composedness that astonished all who heard him. But although his voice was calm, despair was upon his brow.
Still he continued to gaze fixedly on the retreating form of
his enemy, until he finally disappeared behind the orchard
of the Canadian of the Fleur de lis.

Obeying the summons from the fort, the troops without
now commenced their retreat, bearing off the bodies of
their fallen officers and several of their comrades who had
fallen by the Indian fire. There was a show of harassing
them on their return; but they were too near the fort to
apprehend much danger. Two or three well-directed dis-
charges of artillery effectually checked the onward progress of the savages; and, in the course of a minute, they
had again wholly disappeared.

In gloomy silence, and with anger and disappointment
in their hearts, the detachment now re-entered the fort.
Johnstone was only severely bruised; Sir Everard Valletort

not dead. Both were conveyed to the same room, where they were instantly attended by the surgeon, who pronounced the situation of the latter hopeless.

Major Blackwater, Captains Blessington and Erskine, Lieutenants Leslie and Boyce, and the Ensigns Fortescue and Sumners, were now the only regimental officers that remained of thirteen originally comprising the strength of the garrison. The whole of these stood grouped around the colonel, who seemed transfixed to the spot he had first occupied on the rampart, with his arms folded, and his gaze bent in the direction in which he had lost sight of Wacousta and his child.

Hitherto the morning had been cold and cheerless, and objects in the far distance were but indistinctly seen through a humid atmosphere. At about half an hour before mid-day the air became more rarified, and, the murky clouds gradually disappearing, left the blue autumnal sky without spot or blemish. Presently, as the bells of the fort struck twelve, a yell as of a legion of devils rent the air; and, riveting their gaze in that direction, all beheld the bridge, hitherto deserted, suddenly covered with a multitude of savages, among whom were several individuals attired in the European garb, and evidently prisoners. Each officer had a telescope raised to his eye, and each prepared himself, shudderingly, for some horrid consummation. Presently the bridge was cleared of all but a double line of what appeared to be women, armed with war-clubs and tomahawks. Along the line were now seen to pass, in slow succession, the prisoners that had previously been observed. At each step they took (and it was evident they had been compelled to run the gauntlet), a blow was inflicted by some one or other of the line, until the wretched victims were successively despatched. A loud yell from the warriors, who, although hidden from view by the intervening orchards, were evidently merely spectators in the bloody drama, announced each death. These yells were repeated, at intervals, to about the number of thirty, when, suddenly, the bridge was again deserted as before.

After the lapse of a minute, the tall figure of a warrior was seen to advance, holding a female in his arms. No one could mistake, even at that distance, the gigantic proportions of Wacousta, as he stood in the extreme centre of the bridge, in imposing relief against the flood that glittered like a sea of glass beyond. From his chest there now burst a single yell; but, although audible, it was fainter than any remembered ever to have been heard from him by the garrison. He then advanced to the extreme edge of the bridge; and, raising the form of the female far above his head with his left hand, seemed to wave her in vengeful triumph. A second warrior was seen upon the bridge, and stealing cautiously to the same point. The right hand of the first warrior was now raised and brandished in air; in the next instant it descended upon the breast of the female, who fell from his arms into the ravine beneath. Yells of triumph from the Indians, and shouts of execration from the soldiers, mingled faintly together. At that moment the arm of the second warrior was raised, and a blade was seen to glitter in the sunshine. His arm descended, and Wacousta was observed to stagger forward and fall heavily into the abyss into which his victim had the instant before been precipitated. Another loud yell, but of disappointment and anger, was heard drowning that of exultation pealed by the triumphant warrior, who, darting to the open extremity of the bridge, directed his flight along the margin of the river, where a light canoe was ready to receive him. Into this he sprang, and, seizing the paddle, sent the waters foaming from its sides; and, pursuing his way across the river, had nearly gained the shores of Canada before a bark was to be seen following in pursuit.

How felt – how acted Colonel de Haldimar throughout this brief but terrible scene? He uttered not a word. With his arms still folded across his breast, he gazed upon the murder of his child; but he heaved not a groan, he shed not a tear. A momentary triumph seemed to irradiate his pallid features, when he saw the blow struck that annihilated his enemy; but it was again instantly shaded by an expression of the most profound despair.

"It is done, gentlemen," he at length remarked. "The tragedy is closed, the curse of Ellen Halloway is fulfilled, and I am - childless! - Blackwater," he pursued, endeavouring to stifle the emotion produced by the last reflection, "pay every attention to the security of the garrison, see that the drawbridge is again properly chained up, and direct that the duties of the troops be prosecuted in every way as heretofore."

Leaving his officers to wonder at and pity that apathy of mind that could mingle the mere forms of duty with the most heart-rending associations, Colonel de Haldimar now quitted the rampart; and, with a head that was remarked for the first time to droop over his chest, paced his way musingly to his apartments.

Fourteen

NIGHT HAD long since drawn her circling mantle over the western hemisphere; and deeper, far deeper than the gloom of that night was the despair which filled every bosom of the devoted garrison, whose fortunes it has fallen to our lot to record. A silence, profound as that of death, pervaded the ramparts and exterior defences of the fortress, interrupted only, at long intervals, by the customary "All's well!" of the several sentinels; which, after the awful events of the day, seemed to many who now heard it as if uttered in mockery of their hopelessness of sorrow. The lights within the barracks of the men had been long since extinguished; and, consigned to a mere repose of limb, in which the eye and heart shared not, the inferior soldiery pressed their rude couches with spirits worn out by a succession of painful excitements, and frames debilitated by much abstinence and watching. It was an hour at which sleep was wont to afford them the blessing of a temporary forgetfulness of endurances that weighed the more heavily as they were believed to be endless and without fruit; but sleep had now apparently been banished from all; for the low and confused murmur that met the ear from the several block-houses was continuous and general, betraying at times, and in a louder key, words that bore reference to the tragic occurrences of the day.

The only lights visible in the fort proceeded from the guard-house and a room adjoining that of the ill-fated

Charles de Haldimar. Within the latter were collected, with the exception of the governor, and grouped around a bed on which lay one of their companions in a nearly expiring state, the officers of the garrison, reduced nearly one third in number since we first offered them to the notice of our readers. The dying man was Sir Everard Valletort, who, supported by pillows, was concluding a narrative that had chained the earnest attention of his auditory, even amid the deep and heartfelt sympathy perceptible in each for the forlorn and hopeless condition of the narrator. At the side of the unhappy baronet, and enveloped in a dressing gown, as if recently out of bed, sat, reclining in a rude elbow chair, one whose pallid countenance denoted, that, although far less seriously injured, he, too, had suffered severely: – it was Lieutenant Johnstone.

The narrative was at length closed; and the officer, exhausted by the effort he had made in his anxiety to communicate every particular to his attentive and surprised companions, had sunk back upon his pillow, when, suddenly, the loud and unusual "Who comes there?" of the sentinel stationed on the rampart above the gateway, arrested every ear. A moment of pause succeeded, when again was heard the "Stand, friend!" evidently given in reply to the familiar answer to the original challenge. Then were audible rapid movements in the guard-house, as of men aroused from temporary slumber, and hastening to the point whence the voice proceeded.

Silently yet hurriedly the officers now quitted the bedside of the dying man, leaving only the surgeon and the invalid Johnstone behind them; and, flying to the rampart, stood in the next minute confounded with the guard, who were already grouped round the challenging sentinel, bending their gaze eagerly in the direction of the road.

"What now, man? – whom have you challenged?" asked Major Blackwater.

"It is I – De Haldimar," hoarsely exclaimed one of four dark figures that, hitherto, unnoticed by the officers, stood immediately beyond the ditch, with a burden deposited at their feet. "Quick, Blackwater, let us in for God's sake! Each succeeding minute may bring a scouting party on our track. Lower the drawbridge!"

"Impossible!" exclaimed the major: "after all that has passed, it is more than my commission is worth to lower the bridge without permission. Mr. Lawson, quick to the governor, and report that Captain de Haldimar is here: with whom shall he say?" again addressing the impatient and almost indignant officer.

"With Miss de Haldimar, François the Canadian, and one to whom we all owe our lives," hurriedly returned the officer; "and you may add," he continued gloomily, "the corpse of my sister. But while we stand in parley here, we are lost: Lawson, fly to my father, and tell him we wait for entrance."

With nearly the speed enjoined the adjutant departed. Scarcely a minute elapsed when he again stood upon the rampart, and advancing closely to the major, whispered a few words in his ear.

"Good God! can it be possible? When? How came this? but we will enquire later. Open the gate; down with the bridge, Leslie," addressing the officer of the guard.

The command was instantly obeyed. The officers flew to receive the fugitives; and as the latter crossed the draw-bridge, the light of a lantern, that had been brought from the guard-room, flashed full upon the harassed counte-nances of Captain and Miss de Haldimar, François the Canadian, and the devoted Oucanasta.

Silent and melancholy was the greeting that took place between the parties: the voice spoke not; the hand alone was eloquent; but it was in the eloquence of sorrow only that it indulged. Pleasure, even in this almost despaired of re-union, could not be expressed; and even the eye shrank from mutual encounter, as if its very glance at such a moment were sacrilege. Recalled to a sense of her situa-tion by the preparation of the men to raise the bridge, the Indian woman was the first to break the silence.

"The Saganaw is safe within his fort, and the girl of the pale faces will lay her head upon his bosom," she remarked solemnly. "Oucanasta will go to her solitary wigwam among the red skins."

The heart of Madeline de Haldimar was oppressed by the weight of many griefs; yet she could not see the generous preserver of her life, and the rescuer of the body of her ill-fated cousin, depart without emotion. Drawing a ring, of some value and great beauty, from her finger, which she had more than once observed the Indian to admire, she placed it on her hand; and then, throwing herself on the bosom of the faithful creature, embraced her with deep manifestations of affection, but without uttering a word.

Oucanasta was sensibly gratified: she raised her large eyes to heaven as if in thankfulness; and by the light of the lantern, which fell upon her dark but expressive countenance, tears were to be seen starting unbidden from their source.

Released from the embrace of her, whose life she had twice preserved at imminent peril to her own, the Indian again prepared to depart; but there was another, who, like Madeline, although stricken by many sorrows, could not forego the testimony of his heart's gratitude. Captain de Haldimar, who, during this short scene, had despatched a messenger to his room for the purpose, now advanced to the poor girl, bearing a short but elegantly mounted dagger, which he begged her to deliver as a token of his friendship to the young chief her brother. He then dropped on one knee at her feet, and raising her hand, pressed it fervently against his heart; an action which, even to the untutored mind of the Indian, bore evidence only of the feeling that prompted it. A heavy sigh escaped her labouring chest; and as the officer now rose and quitted her hand, she turned slowly and with dignity from him, and crossing the drawbridge, was in a few minutes lost in the surrounding gloom.

Our readers have, doubtless, anticipated the communication made to Major Blackwater by the Adjutant Lawson. Bowed down to the dust by the accomplishment of the curse of Ellen Halloway, the inflexibility of Colonel de Haldimar's pride was not proof against the utter annihilation wrought to his hopes as a father by the unrelenting hatred of the enemy his early falsehood and treachery had raised up to him. When the adjutant entered his apartment, the stony coldness of his cheek attested he had been dead some hours.

We pass over the few days of bitter trial that succeeded to the restoration of Captain de Haldimar and his bride to their friends; days, during which were consigned to the same grave the bodies of the governor, his lamented children, and the scarcely less regretted Sir Everard Valletort. The funeral service was attempted by Captain Blessington; but the strong affection of that excellent officer, for three of the defunct parties at least, was not armed against the trial. He had undertaken a task far beyond his strength; and scarcely had commenced, ere he was compelled to relinquish the performance of the ritual to the adjutant. A large grave had been dug close under the rampart, and near the fatal flag-staff, to receive the bodies of their deceased friends; and, as they were lowered successively into their last earthly resting place, tears fell unrestrainedly over the bronzed cheeks of the oldest soldiers, while many a female sob blended with and gave touching solemnity to the scene.

On the morning of the third day from this quadruple interment, notice was given by one of the sentinels that an Indian was approaching the fort, making signs as if in demand for a parley. The officers, headed by Major Blackwater, now become the commandant of the place, immediately ascended the rampart, when the stranger was at once recognised by Captain de Haldimar for the young Ottawa, the preserver of his life, and the avenger of the deaths of those they mourned, in whose girdle was thrust, in seeming pride, the richly mounted dagger that officer had caused to be conveyed to him through his no less generous sister. A long conference ensued, in the language of the Ottawas, between the parties just named, the purport of which was of high moment to the garrison, now nearly reduced to the last extremity. The young chief had come to apprise them, that, won by the noble conduct of the English, on a late occasion, when his warriors were wholly in their power, Ponteac had expressed a generous determination to conclude a peace with the garrison, and henceforth to consider them as his friends. This he had publicly declared in a large council of the chiefs, held the preceding night; and the motive of the Ottawa's coming was, to assure the English, that, on this occasion, their great leader was perfectly sincere in a resolution, at which he had the more readily arrived, now that his terrible coadjutor and vindictive adviser was no more. He prepared them for the coming of Ponteac and the principal chiefs of the league to demand a council on the morrow; and, with this final communication, again withdrew.

The Ottawa was right. Within a week from that period the English were to be seen once more issuing from their fort; and, although many months elapsed before the wounds of their suffering hearts were healed, still were they grateful to Providence for their final preservation from a doom that had fallen, without exception, on every fortress on the line of frontier in which they lay.

Time rolled on; and, in the course of years, Oucanasta might be seen associating with and bearing curious presents, the fruits of Indian ingenuity, to the daughters of De Haldimar, now become the colonel of the —— regiment; while her brother, the chief, instructed his sons in the athletic and active exercises peculiar to his race. As for poor Ellen Halloway, search had been made for her, but she never was heard of afterwards.

Introduction to the 1851 Edition

It is well known to every man conversant with the earlier history of this country that, shortly subsequent to the cession of the Canadas to England by France, Pontiac, the great head of the Indian race of that period, had formed a federation of the various tribes, threatening extermination to the British posts established along the Western frontier. These were nine in number, and the following stratagem was resorted to by the artful chief to effect their reduction. Investing one fort with his warriors, so as to cut off all communication with the others, and to leave no hope of succor, his practice was to offer terms of surrender, which never were kept in the honorable spirit in which the far more noble and generous Tecumseh always acted with his enemies, and thus, in turn, seven of these outposts fell victims to their confidence in his truth.

Detroit and Michilimackinac, or Mackinaw as it is now called, remained, and all the ingenuity of the chieftain was directed to the possession of these strongholds. The following plan, well worthy of his invention, was at length determined upon. During a temporary truce, and while Pontiac was holding forth proposals for an ultimate and durable peace, a game of lacrosse was arranged by him to take place simultaneously on the common or clearing on which rested the forts of Michilimackinac and Detroit. The better to accomplish their object, the guns of the warriors had been cut short and given to their women, who were instructed to conceal them under their blankets, and during the game, and seemingly without design, to approach the drawbridge of the fort. This precaution taken, the players were to approach and throw over their ball, permission to regain which they presumed would not be denied. On approaching the drawbridge they were with fierce yells to make a general rush, and, securing the arms concealed by the women, to massacre the unprepared garrison.

The day was fixed; the game commenced, and was proceeded with in the manner previously arranged. The ball was dexterously hurled into the fort, and permission asked to recover it. It was granted. The drawbridge was lowered, and the Indians dashed forward for the accomplishment of their work of blood. How different the results in the two garrisons! At Detroit, Pontiac and his warriors had scarcely crossed the drawbridge when, to their astonishment and disappointment, they beheld the guns of the ramparts depressed – the artillerymen with lighted matches at their posts and covering the little garrison, composed of a few companies of the 42nd Highlanders, who were also under arms, and so distributed as to take the enemy most at an advantage. Suddenly they withdrew and without other indication of their purpose than what had been expressed in their manner, and carried off the missing ball. Their design had been discovered and made known by means of significant warnings to the Governor by an Indian woman who owed a debt of gratitude to his family, and was resolved, at all hazards, to save them.

On the same day the same artifice was resorted to at Michilimackinac, and with the most complete success. There was no guardian angel there to warn them of danger, and all fell beneath the rifle, the tomahawk, the warclub, and the knife, one or two of the traders – a Mr. Henry among the rest – alone excepted.

It was not long after this event when the head of the military authorities in the Colony, apprised of the fate of these captured posts, and made acquainted with the perilous condition of Fort Detroit, which was then reduced to the last extremity, sought an officer who would volunteer the charge of supplies from Albany to Buffalo, and thence across the lake to Detroit, which, if possible, he was to relieve. That volunteer was promptly found in my maternal grandfather, Mr. Erskine, from Strabane, in the North of Ireland, then an officer in the Commissariat Department. The difficulty of the undertaking will be obvious to those who understand the danger attending a journey through the Western wilderness, beset as it was by the warriors of Pontiac, ever on the lookout to prevent succor to the garrison, and yet the duty was successfully accomplished. He left Albany with provisions and ammunition sufficient to fill several Schenectady boats – I think seven – and yet conducted his charge with such prudence and foresight, that notwithstanding the vigilance of Pontiac, he finally and after long watching succeeded, under cover of a dark and stormy night, in throwing into the fort the supplies of which the remnant of the gallant "Black Watch," as the 42nd was originally named, and a company of whom, while out reconnoitering, had been massacred at a spot in the vicinity of the town, thereafter called the Bloody Run, stood so greatly in need. This important service rendered, Mr. Erskine, in compliance with the instructions he had received, returned to Albany, where he reported the success of the expedition.

The colonial authorities were not regardless of his interests. When the Pontiac confederacy had been dissolved, and quiet and security restored in that remote region, large tracts of land were granted to Mr. Erskine, and other privileges accorded which eventually gave him the command of nearly a hundred thousand dollars [an] enormous sum to have been realized at that early period of the country. But it was not destined that he should retain this. The great bulk of his capital was expended on almost the first commercial shipping that ever skimmed the surface of Lakes Huron and Erie. Shortly prior to the Revolution, he was possessed of seven vessels of different tonnage, and the trade in which he had embarked, and of which he was the head, was rapidly increasing his already large fortune, when one of those autumnal hurricanes, which even to this day continue to desolate the waters of the treacherous lake last named, suddenly arose and buried beneath its engulfing waves not less than six of the schooners laden with such riches, chiefly furs, of the West as then were most an object of barter.

Mr. Erskine, who had married the daughter of one of the earliest settlers from France, and of a family well known in history, a lady who had been in Detroit during the siege of the British garrison by Pontiac, now abandoned speculation, and contenting himself with the remnant of his fortune, established himself near the banks of the river, within a short distance of the Bloody Run. Here he continued throughout the Revolution. Early, however, in the present century, he quitted Detroit and repaired to the Canadian shore, where on a property nearly opposite, which he obtained in exchange, and which in honor of his native country he named Strabane – known as such to this day – he passed the autumn of his days. The last time I beheld him was a day or two subsequent to the affair of the Thames, when General Harrison and Colonel Johnson were temporary inmates of his dwelling.

My father, of a younger branch of the Annandale family, the head of which was attainted in the Scottish rebellion of 1745, was an officer of Simcoe's well-known Rangers, in which regiment, and about the same period, the present Lord Hardinge commenced his services in this country. Being quartered at Fort Erie, he met and married at the house of one of the earliest Canadian merchants a daughter of Mr. Erskine, then on a visit to her sister, and by her had eight children, of whom I am the oldest and only survivor. Having a few years after his marriage been ordered to St. Joseph's, near Michilimackinac, my father thought it expedient to leave me with Mr. Erskine at Detroit, where I received the first rudiments of my education. But here I did not remain long, for it was during the period of the stay of the detachment of Simcoe's Rangers at St. Joseph that Mr. Erskine repaired with his family to the Canadian shore, where on the more elevated and conspicuous part of his grounds, which are situated nearly opposite the foot of Hog Island, so repeatedly alluded to in "Wacousta," he had caused a flag-staff to be erected, from which each Sabbath day proudly floated the colors under which he had served, and which he never could bring himself to disown.

It was at Strabane that the old lady, with whom I was a great favorite, used to enchain my young interest by detailing various facts connected with the siege she so well remembered, and infused into me a longing to grow up to manhood that I might write a book about it. The details of the Pontiac plan for the capture of the two forts were what she most enlarged upon, and although a long lapse of years of absence from the scene, and ten thousand incidents of a higher and more immediate importance might have been supposed to weaken the recollections of so early a period of life, the impression has ever vividly remained. Hence the first appearance of "Wacousta" in London in 1832, more than a quarter of a century later. The story is founded solely on the artifice of Pontiac to possess himself of those two last British forts. All else is imaginary.

It is not a little curious that I, only a few years subsequent to the narration by old Mrs. Erskine of the daring and cunning feats of Pontiac, and his vain attempt to secure the fort of Detroit, should myself have entered it in arms. But it was so. I had ever hated school with a most bitter hatred, and I gladly availed myself of an offer from General Brock to obtain for me a commission in the King's service. Meanwhile I did duty as a cadet with the gallant 41st regiment, to which the English edition of "Wacousta" was inscribed, and was one of the guard of honor who took possession of the fort. The duty of a sentinel over the British colors, which had just been hoisted was assigned to me, and I certainly felt not a little proud of the distinction.

Five times within half a century had the flag of that fortress been changed. First the lily of France, then the red cross of England, and next the stars and stripes of America had floated over its ramparts; and then again the red cross, and lastly the stars. On my return to this country a few years since, I visited those scenes of stirring excitement in which my boyhood had been passed, but I looked in vain for the ancient fortifications which had given a classical interest to that region. The unsparing hand of utilitarianism had passed over them, destroying almost every vestige of the past. Where had risen the only fortress in America at all worthy to give antiquity to the scene, streets had been laid out and made, and houses had been built, leaving not a trace of its existence save the well that formerly supplied the closely besieged garrison with water; and this, half imbedded in the herbage of an enclosure of a dwelling house of mean appearance, was rather to be guessed at than seen; while at the opposite extremity of the city, where had been conspicuous for years the Bloody Run, cultivation and improvement had nearly obliterated every trace of the past.

Two objections have been urged against "Wacousta" as a consistent tale – the one as involving an improbability, the other a geographical error. It has been assumed that the startling feat accomplished by that man of deep revenge, who is not alone in his bitter hatred and contempt for the base among those who, like spaniels, crawl and kiss the dust at the instigation of their superiors, and yet arrogate to themselves a claim to be considered gentlemen and men of honor and independence – it has, I repeat, been assumed that the feat attributed to him in connection with the flagstaff of the fort was impossible. No one who has ever seen these erections on the small forts of that day would pronounce the same criticism. Never very lofty, they were ascended at least one-third of their height by means of small projections nailed to them for footholds for the artillerymen, frequently compelled to clear the flag lines entangled at the truck; therefore a strong and active man, such as Wacousta is described to have been, might very well have been supposed, in his strong anxiety for revenge and escape with his victim, to have doubled his strength and activity on so important an occasion, rendering that easy of attainment by himself which an ordinary and unexcited man might deem impossible. I myself have knocked down a gate, almost without feeling the resistance, in order to escape the stilettos of assassins.

The second objection is to the narrowness attributed in the tale to the river St. Clair. This was done in the license usually accorded to a writer of fiction, in order to give greater effect to the scene represented as having occurred there, and, of course, in no way intended as a geographical description of the river, nor was it necessary. In the same spirit and for the same purpose it has been continued.

It will be seen that at the termination of the tragedy enacted at the bridge, by which the Bloody Run was in those days crossed, that the wretched wife of the condemned soldier pronounced a curse that could not, of course, well be fulfilled in the course of the tale. Some few years ago I published in Canada – I might as well have done so in Kamschatka – the continuation, which was to have been dedicated to the last King of England, but which, after the death of that monarch, was inscribed to Sir John Harvey, whose letter, as making honorable mention of a gallant and beloved brother, I feel it a duty to the memory of the latter to* subjoin.

*"GOVERNMENT HOUSE, FREDERICTON, N.B.,
November 26th, 1839.

"Dear Sir, – I am favored with your very interesting communication of the 2nd instant, by which I learn that you are the brother of two youths whose gallantry and merits – and with regard to one of them, his sufferings – during the late war, excited my warmest admiration and sympathy. I beg you to believe that I am far from insensible to the affecting proofs which you have made known to me of this grateful recollection of any little service I may have had it in my power to render them; and I will add that the desire which I felt to serve the father will be found to extend itself to the son, if your nephew should ever find himself under circum-

The "Prophecy Fulfilled," which, however, has never been seen out of the small country in which it appeared – Detroit, perhaps, alone excepted – embraces and indeed is intimately connected with the Beauchamp tragedy, which took place at or near Weisiger's Hotel, in Frankfort, Kentucky, where I had been many years before confined as a prisoner of war. While connecting it with the "Prophecy Fulfilled," and making it subservient to the end I had in view, I had not read or even heard of the existence of a work of the same character, which had already appeared from the pen of an American author. Indeed, I have reason to believe that the "Prophecy Fulfilled," although not published until after a lapse of years, was the first written. No similarity of treatment of the subject exists between the two versions, and this, be it remembered, I remark without in the slightest degree impugning the merit of the production of my fellow-laborer in the same field.

THE AUTHOR.

New York City, January 1st, 1851.

---

stances to require from me any service which it may be within my power to render him.

"With regard to your very flattering proposition to inscribe your present work to me, I can only say that, independent of the respect to which the author of so very charming a production as 'Wacousta' is entitled, the interesting facts and circumstances so unexpectedly brought to my knowledge and recollection would ensure a ready acquiescence on my part.

"I remain, dear Sir, your very faithful servant,

"(Signed)   J. HARVEY.

"Major Richardson, Montreal."

Afterword

BY JAMES REANEY

The ideal afterword for *Wacousta* would be its sequel, *The Canadian Brothers; or, The Prophecy Fulfilled*, in which, a generation and some years later, the story picks up descendants of both De Haldimar and Wacousta, and eventually kills them all off in the War of 1812, a last duo of representatives locked together in mortal combat falling headlong into the Niagara abyss.

Would it not seem that Major John Richardson took a rather dark nihilistic view of life? Sure, but there is no need to get too high-minded about this, for such a conclusion to this Gothic romance epic is also a good, rousing, operatic way to end a long, intricate, and violent story. Always remember that Richardson is *par excellence* a storyteller. Brought up by Scottish and Canadian parents and grandparents with a large library (at the latter's Detroit house, Strabane), he also had a large repertory of true stories of the old Northwest in which Grandmother and Grandfather Askin had experienced the Pontiac Conspiracy (1763) at first hand, the latter as local fur trader and as secret supplier to the besieged fort. All this authentic tradition is why, when James Fenimore Cooper's *The Last of the Mohicans* came out in 1826, Richardson vowed that, since he knew Indians much better than Cooper did, he would someday give him a run for his money. *Wacousta* is Canada's answer to an American bestseller, a literary battle of which, alas, our southern cousins now seem hardly aware. In its day, however, *Wacousta* - along with Richardson's other works - had a large readership in New York and Philadelphia.

Richardson also has a metaphysical side to him, beloved by university teachers, but first and foremost, it seems that if he believes in anything at all, it is *raconter pour raconter*; like his mentors - Sir Walter Scott, Bulwer Lytton, Ann Radcliffe, and, I strongly suspect, Ariosto - Richardson might often justify characters' motivations with "I'm here because I'm here!" In short, he is an exuberant practitioner of Gothic romance and melodrama, of what Northrop Frye has called *The Secular Scripture*, or the People's Logos. His book is welcome here, and welcome too, after more than a century and a half of mutilated American editions. At last, you can pick up *Wacousta* and sail through it as easily as you do a Buchan - *Prester John*? Or even a Zane Grey? But, as I shall keep pointing out, there is more to *Wacousta* than just another adventure romance. It is more exact to call the book a New World Sir Walter Scott Gothic with a generous helping of sadism and eroticism, which Sir Walter generally muzzles.

This delightful lowbrow trait aside, there are several other reasons why I have fallen in love with any and all of Richardson's stories: a) I had always been searching for a father figure to reverence as the progenitor of our tradition here in what Richardson calls "the land of the Canadas"; b) I was once connected with a theatre company (1976-1981) called NDWT (Ne'er Do Well Thespians), which specialized in stories about Southwestern Ontario that would give audiences there a much needed sense of their past, particularly the deep, primitive, heroic, archaic, aboriginal past; both *Wacousta* and *The Canadian Brothers* make effective theatre, and would be even more effective as films.

Wacousta is the noble outlaw, an innocent degraded and enraged by a corrupt society. Let us work along these lines and take a glance at Wordsworth's *The Prelude*, in which the growth of a poet's mind from very early childhood is seen as a series of unifying opposites – harsh, rugged, fearsome cliffs with gentle meadows, terror with beauty, dark with light until a mountain-top epiphany proves a psychic graduation ceremony. Richardson seems to have a similar scenario in mind for his hero. Starting out as an athletic Cornish nobleman, Sir Reginald Morton not only climbs cliffs, swims in rough seas, boats there too – dreaming of love somehow being the result – but he is also a painter of great skill and refinement. What seems to be afoot when he climbs a high mountain in Argyleshire and, after negotiating deep abysses, finds a beautiful girl hidden away in a secret oasis by her Jacobite father is some sort of final marriage between sublime and beautiful.

When this metamorphosis is aborted – he should never have let his "best friend," De Haldimar, see the miniature he painted of Clara Beverley – he rapidly turns into a monster, physically larger, ferocious, evil, a backwoods Hamlet filled with dangerous cliffs and rough seas, no pretty girls to bring all that energy home.

Supporting this theme of aborted arrival at a complete self is an almost pornographic obsession on Richardson's part with what everybody is wearing. The reason one of *The Canadian Brothers* kills his brother is that the latter dares to appear at the battle of Queenston Heights dressed as a Kentuckian huntsman. Automatically his brother shoots him – since that is the game being played – then goes mad when he discovers that it is his *Canadian* brother, who has just escaped from prison camp in Kentucky and walked all the way up to rejoin his family in Canada – dressed as an enemy! So the fictional gloating over clothing and coiffure probably takes its source from Richardson's long experience with army etiquette where one could, if not dressed correctly, be court martialled or in certain cases be shot as a spy.

After he is betrayed, Sir Reginald Morton not only changes his name to Wacousta, but he too falls into costume fetishism. Not only does he dress like a museum

Ottawa huntsman, complete with feathered felt hat straight out of von Weber's *Der Freischütz*, but when he acquires Ellen Halloway in *mariage du pays*, he makes sure that she wears an accurate machecoti and a "shirt of printed cotton studded with silver brooches," a picture book chieftain's wife. And after Sir Reginald turns into Frankenstein's monster, his revenge techniques are always *artistically* managed – a painter gone beserk with human vermilion!

Some of the dress obsession seems to be part of a love-hate relationship with the long years (he was commissioned at the age of sixteen) Richardson spent in the British army. He had ample opportunity to observe in action the pecking order of regiments filled with Iago-like ensigns eager to see their superiors killed in action so they could change their insignia for something symbolic of more pay, more power, and higher up "the six-barred gate of promotion." You may now recall the early episode where Frederick's corpse is apparently discovered lying outside the fort. Mourned over at first, it is then dropped like a hot potato when its hair is discovered to be "coarse." Why, it is only Frederick's valet dressed up in his master's elegant officer's costume: "How comes it that an officer of the English garrison appears here in the garb of a servant?" thunders Wacousta in faultless upper-class English at the hapless Frederick who, you remember, has recently exchanged clothes with his now dead valet, Donellan.

Perhaps the whole trajectory of this old story whose background scans the very beginnings of our own history as a separate entity, just beginning to tear away from the thirteen colonies to the south (see the Quebec Act, 1763) ... the whole thrust of Richardson's meaning is contained in this question by his wild hero. We remember that once upon a time there was a young artist-officer of sensibility and feeling named Sir Reginald Morton who cared nothing for uniforms, neither their inspection with regard to his men, nor the correctness of his own garb. What happened to this idealistic youngster has also, it could be implied, happened to a whole world of imperializing killers obsessed with the minutiae of power. In the case of the evil Colonel de Haldimar, there is a former ensign quite willing to gain love and power in exchange for the complete degradation of his best friend.

But I could go on and on about the various kinds of spells that *Wacousta* can work on readers whose minds are not completely riddled with scientific materialism. As Sir Everard remarks to a fellow officer who has not read his Coleridge on the necessity for suspending disbelief, "Depend upon it, there is more in all this than is dreamt of in our philosophy." This is a conscious authorial tribute to that very first Gothic "novel" about a Danish fort named Elsinore in which a not dissimilar armed ghost gets into the castle at midnight and raises up subsequent great harrowing guilt and slaughter. And so, a *Hamlet* of the Canadas?

BY JOHN RICHARDSON

AUTOBIOGRAPHY
Journal of the Movements of the British Legion (1836)
Personal Memoirs of Major Richardson (1838)
Eight Years in Canada (1847)
The Guards in Canada; or, The Point of Honour (1848)
*Tecumseh and Richardson; The Story of a Trip to Walpole
Island and Port Sarnia* [ed. A.H.U. Colquhoun] (1924)

FICTION
Escarté; or, The Salons of Paris (1829)
Frascati's; or, Scenes in Paris (1830)
Wacousta; or, The Prophecy (1832)
The Canadian Brothers; or, The Prophecy Fulfilled (1840)
The Monk Knight of St. John (1850)
Handscrabble; or, The Fall of Chicago (1851)
Wau-nan-gee; or, The Massacre at Chicago (1852)
Westbrook, The Outlaw! or, The Avenging Wolf (1853)
Major John Richardson's Short Stories
[ed. David Beasley] (1985)

HISTORY
War of 1812 (1842)

POETRY
Tecumseh; or, The Warrior of the West (1828)
Kensington Gardens in 1830 (1830)

New Canadian Library
The Best of Canadian Writing

NCL – A Series Worth Collecting

NCL – A Series Worth Collecting

New Canadian Library
The Best of Canadian Writing

M&S

NCL – A Series Worth Collecting

New Canadian Library
The Best of Canadian Writing

M&S NCL